ENGINEERING FATE

OUTER LIMITS QUADRANT BOOK 1

ALEXIS B. OSBORNE

Dark Moon
PUBLISHING

Copyright © 2021 by Alexis B. Osborne

All rights reserved. No part of this book may be reproduced, stored, or transmitted in any form or by any electronic or mechanical means, including information storage and retrieval systems, without express written permission from the author, except for the use of brief quotations in a book review. Purchase only authorized electronic editions via Amazon and do not participate in or encourage electronic piracy of copyrighted materials. Thank you for supporting artists.

ISBN: 978-1-957341-13-2 (eBook)

ISBN: 978-1-957341-14-9 (Paperback)

The characters and events portrayed in this book are fictitious. Names, characters, places, and incidents are the product of the author's imagination.

Second Printing 2022

Cover by Sam Griffin

Editing by Lindsay York of LY Publishing

Published by Dark Moon Publishing

Printed in the United States of America

To request permissions, contact the author at alexisosborneromance@gmail.com

CONTENT WARNINGS

I<small>F YOU DO NOT HAVE TRIGGERS AND YOU DON'T WANT TO READ</small> potential spoilers then skip this page. The trigger warnings listed below are accurate to this novel but this list may not be complete.

Spoiler Zone - Spoiler Zone - Spoiler Zone

Engineering Fate is an action packed sci-fi alien romance that contains mature themes of: ableism, adult language, animal death, birth control, blood, BDSM, childhood neglect and abandonment (discussion of), classism, criminal activity, death, food deprivation, gambling, gore, guns, kidnapping, killing, needles, slavery, sex (consensual), sex slavery, sex work, sexual assault (attempted on-page and discussion of), torture, trafficking of sentients, war (discussion of). Pregnancy and (discussion of) abortion are found in the bonus epilogue.

THE MILKY WAY GALAXY AND THE FOUR COLONY SHIPS OF HUMANITY

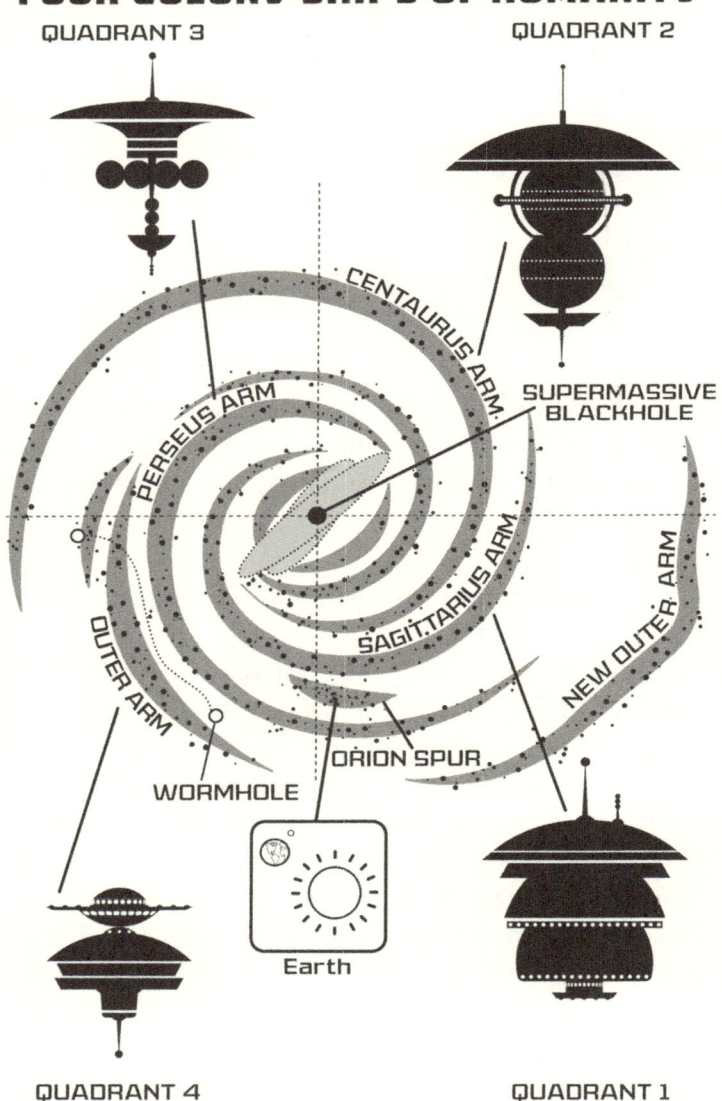

QUADRANT 3

QUADRANT 2

CENTAURUS ARM

PERSEUS ARM

SUPERMASSIVE BLACKHOLE

SAGITTARIUS ARM

OUTER ARM

NEW OUTER ARM

ORION SPUR

WORMHOLE

Earth

QUADRANT 4

QUADRANT 1

ALIEN RACES OF THE 4 QUADRANTS

Quadrant 1: Sagittarius
    Bera - ursidae shifter race (Ice Planet Prison)
    Ma'arat - capra race
    Rounaii - nonbinary ichthyo race (Mate for the Alien P*rn Star)
    Tou'de'nan - elvish race

Quadrant 2: Centaurus

Quadrant 3: Perseus

Quadrant 4: Outer Limits
    Diggi - avian race
    Kursh - feline race (Engineering Fate)
    Raxion - reptilian race (Doctoring Fate)

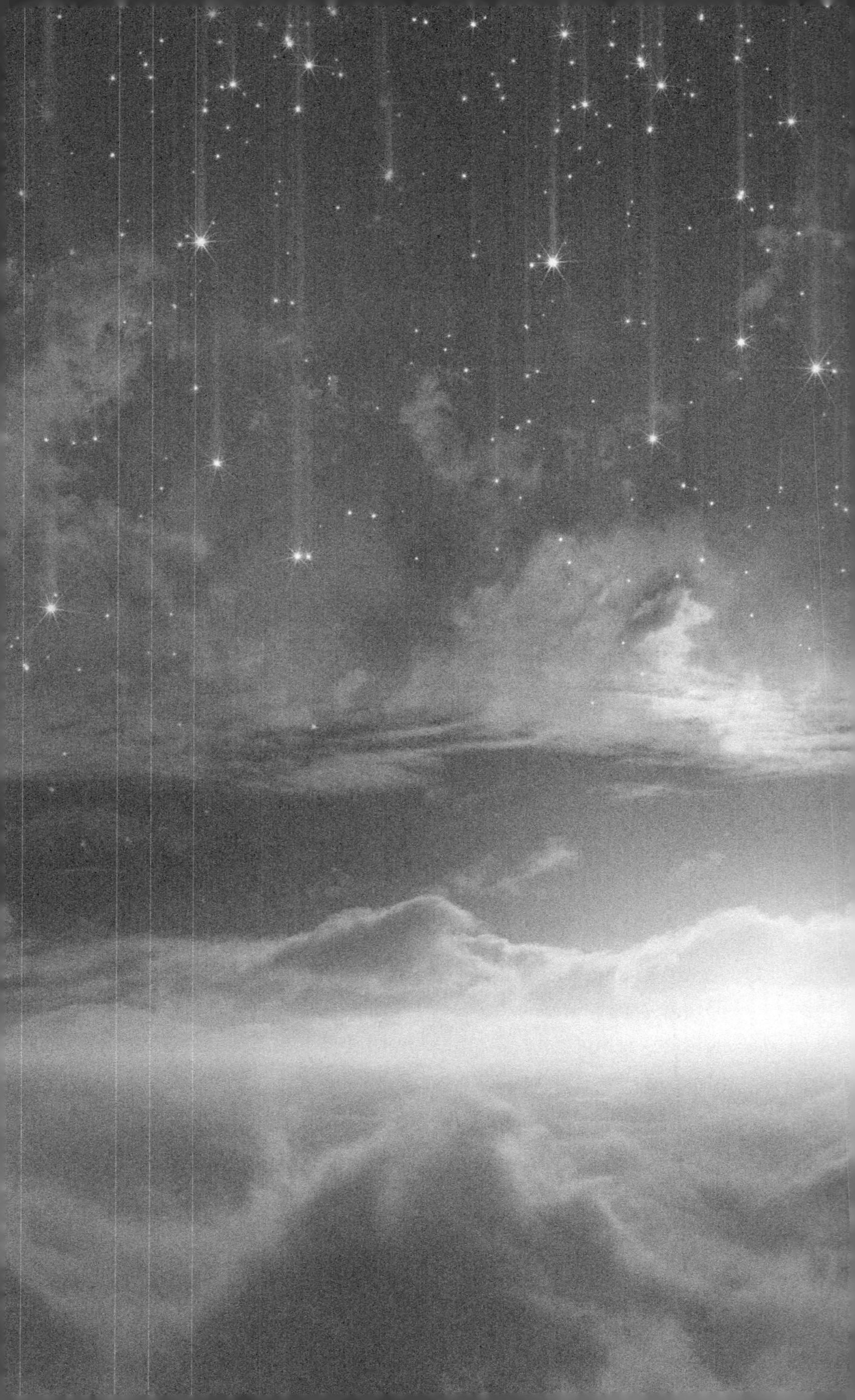

AN OUTER LIMITS BOOK
ENGINEERING -FATE-

ALEXIS B. OSBORNE

CHAPTER ONE

SASHA

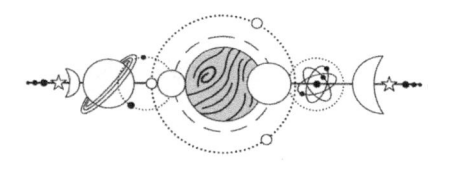

4th Quadrant, Orbiting Colony Ship *Outer Limits*, Year 2,336 AD

STRUGGLING TO GET THE RUSTED BOLT OFF THE THING THAT looked more like space junk than the satellite it was supposed to be, Sasha spat out a stream of curses under her breath as she worked at her miserable job.

Explore the mysteries of space! Have adventures and see new planets!

It was all a bunch of lies, a marketing ploy to convince desperate third-level nobodies to sign their lives away for a little bit of hazard pay. Money they'd probably never have the opportunity to spend before dying a miserable death alone out in the cold recesses of space.

"If the pirates don't kill you first, then the boredom will," she muttered to herself.

There wasn't any takeout, or shopping, and there definitely weren't any new holofilms half a lightyear deep into space. It was just you and your thoughts hurtling through the big, deep black.

"At least I don't have to pretend to like my coworkers," she joked, glancing over toward the console with its slowly blinking lights.

Since I don't have any.

Joana, her plasticine clock that was shaped like a flower, wiggled back and forth in perfect timing, saying nothing. Not that Sasha expected her to. Joana was just an inanimate object, and even though she'd been alone in deep space for three standard months and twelve days, she wasn't that crazy.

Not yet, anyway.

The wrench slipped, smacking into her other hand hard enough to bruise. It clanged against the rusty, greased up bit of machinery that she was trying, and probably failing, to fix.

"Aww, shit," she sighed as she finagled the wrench back into place and kept working on the stupid bolt that was sorely testing her patience. The cold vacuum of space had frozen the joint as it decayed. The satellite was a total piece of crap, and it probably should have been junked a while ago.

Why the frack they want me to come all the way out here to fix it is just absolutely beyond me. They should just forget it even exists.

Static crackled, and a vaguely female monotone voice filled the repair pod. "Proximity alert. Evasive maneuvers will initiate in ten seconds," the disembodied voice warned.

Her wrench slipped again and fell down into a crevice deep within the broken piece of satellite.

Crap. That's the best wrench I have.

"Override!" she yelled up to her ship's white ceiling in frustration as she wiped the sweat off her brow and sat back on her heels.

Stupid glitchy navigation software. I'd just pilot the damn thing myself if the ship's console wasn't also a total piece of space junk. I hate relying on AI systems. Now how am I going to get that wrench out of there?

"Override denied. Evasive maneuvers beginning in five... four... three... " the software chirped.

Surging to her feet and rushing to the solitary porthole window, Sasha peered outside her tiny viewing pane. Deep black space with just a few twinkling stars spread out before her. She could see the bulk of the busted satellite that she'd been sent out to repair off to her right.

Everything was just as she left it when she'd hauled the smaller, more delicate broken pieces inside for the more complicated repairs.

The bits she wouldn't have been able to fit her space suit gloved hand through to repair the corroded, broken down bits.

There wasn't any hazardous space debris in sight. Glancing at the console, she saw it looked fine. There weren't any flashing warning lights on the radar to indicate wherever this nonexistent space debris was supposedly coming from.

"Disengage evasive maneuvers. Override code is Mercury in Retrograde," Sasha ordered.

"Override denied," the AI responded in its monotone voice.

Her ship jostled and shook, nearly throwing her to the floor.

Frack, that's not good.

"Evasive maneuvers initiating," the navigation system announced.

Sasha had just enough time to throw herself into the pilot's chair and strap in before her deep space explorer took a hard left and all the loose bits of machinery that she'd been working on slid, scraping gouges in the floor.

Double frack.

"Detailed report of the threat!" she barked as she started mashing buttons on the console.

Side-eyeing the navigation, she frowned as her ship moved

of its own accord. Balling up her fist, she hit the proximity indicator warning screen hard, ignoring the dull throb in her hand.

The dim display lit up with a brilliant green glow as dozens of dots appeared all around the white center dot that indicated her ship. As the display came to life, it showed that she was surrounded with lots of bright green dots that were moving fast.

Of course I've been sent into deep space with faulty tech. Cheap bastards.

Something struck the pod full force on one side, and her teeth gnashed, her hair slapping her in the face, as everything went ricocheting in the opposite direction.

"Multiple moving objects noted with forty percent in a direct path toward impact. Object size ranges from approximately one to twenty meters in size."

Looking down at the indicator screen, she studied it.

It's not a ship. That would be red. So it's got to be either space debris or a meteor shower.

Except that this part of the quadrant didn't have any active meteor showers. They'd passed this way some time ago, damaging the satellite that she'd been sent out to repair. The dots were moving fast, but as she studied them, she began to pick out a pattern.

They're not moving randomly.

The pod lurched again as the AI system tried to avoid getting hit, mostly succeeding.

She was jerked in every direction as the navigation system tried to maneuver the ship out of the path of danger. There didn't seem to be a clear path in sight.

Sasha watched as more and more green dots lit up the navigation screen. Dozens soon became hundreds.

"Divert all nonessential power to shields," she commanded as she reached up and grabbed a spare life support helmet disc from the rack, slipping it into a pocket on the breast of her space suit.

"Diverting all nonessential resources. Shield power restored to seventy-eight percent. Fuel cell at sixty percent capacity," it answered.

The ship rumbled as the artificial gravity system turned off, the engine diverting that power away. Sasha swatted strands of floating hair out of her eyes as she tightened her harness.

Looking up at the small viewing pane, she was able to just barely see a little of what was happening out there.

I'm not going crazy. Everything is moving in one direction. But it's not like any meteor field that I've ever seen. It's too... directional. Intentional.

"Kill the interior lights and turn on the exterior flood lights," she said through gritted teeth.

"Exterior flood lights will reduce the fuel cell by eight percent. Please confirm," it argued back.

"Just do it," she snapped. Sasha glanced down at her little plasticine bobbing flower clock. "It's not looking good, kid," she told her clock. Joana was silent, as always.

The lights went out one by one, and by the time she looked back up toward the porthole, the exterior lights were on and she could finally see what was assaulting her ship. Space junk. Broken pieces of machinery from satellites or spaceships, rocks, and trash. Deep space was full of that sort of stuff.

Things broke down or got expelled and there was hardly anyone to care if it ever got cleaned up again.

Her eyes strained to make out what was ahead of her, but it was still too dark to make it out.

That's... strange. The flood lights should be doing a pretty bang-up job of lighting up my little corner of space.

"Report on the exterior conditions!" Sasha ordered.

The flood lights dimmed as the AI moved power around to

do a quick scan and survey. "Shields at forty-two percent. Fuel cell at thirty-nine percent capacity. Size of moving objects ranges from one to one hundred meters."

Bile rose in her throat, her head spinning as the ship careened left and right as it alternated between dodging blows and taking hits it couldn't avoid. She swallowed her sickness down, taking a deep breath through her nostrils and blowing it out through her mouth to calm her nerves. Her heart was racing in her chest.

This is so not good that I'm officially calling it royally fracked.

"Extinguish the exterior lights. Report on the large object located at three degrees starboard," she said.

The flood lights dimmed and then extinguished, yet there wasn't any answer from the AI system.

The ship jerked forward like a dog on a leash as it collided with larger chunks of space debris. Her heart sank into the pit of her stomach as she realized that this might be it for her.

If she was in an actual ship and not just the small explorer, she might have had a real chance, but her tiny single-occupant craft couldn't stand up to this minefield.

In this ship, her flying skills were nearly useless, and it just drove home how much she hated autopilot. If she was gonna go down, she'd rather go down by her own instead of being at the mercy of some computer code made up of a bunch of ones and zeros.

"Report on the large unidentified object at three degrees starboard," she repeated the command, her voice bordering on a scream.

If the unidentified object was even in that direction, now. Who could tell after all of that jostling? There wasn't any up or down in space, and with most of the lights out, except for the faint glow of the ship's amber emergency lights, it was almost impossible to see anything at all.

"Apologies for the delay, Captain. My processes are slowed by the drain of resources. The anomaly at three degrees has been identified as an Einstein Rosen bridge," the computer answered.

Her eyes widened as she sucked in a breath. "Are you *kidding* me?" she yelled. "When were you planning to tell me that we're headed straight into a damn wormhole?"

The ship rumbled, an ominous sound, as debris continued to crash into it. Sasha, sitting in her little tin can, felt like just another bit of space junk that was about to get sucked into almost certain death.

"Ship, turn on interior lights. Record this message," she said.

The viewing screen clouded over as the captain's log camera turned on. "This is Engineering Private Sasha Robinson of the Outer Limits quadrant, Alpha Centauri colony, Identification number R01M3279. I was sent to sector seventy-six to repair satellite number 1,382. While making repairs, I encountered unexpected space debris, which damaged the ship, and I have just been informed that I am caught in the path of a wormhole. I am sending the coordinates now. I believe that I have been sucked into its path and my ship no longer has enough power to escape its pull. Please tell my brother that he was right... and that I love him. I leave everything I own to him."

Raising her hand in the air, she swiped it to the side to cut the recording.

"Would you like me to delete or send that message, Captain?" the AI asked.

The ship rumbled, the sound of metal groaning as its framing flexed and shifted, feeling like it was about to be shaken apart at any moment if just one more rock jostled it the wrong way.

"Send the message," she croaked out past the lump in her

throat. Unshed tears burned her eyes, and she had to bite her lip to stop its wobbling.

"Message sent. Your video will be delivered in approximately six point two standard hours," it confirmed.

Six hours. I'll probably be long dead by the time they get it. Stop crying, dammit. There's no use in crying. What's done is done, and tears never solve anything.

"Computer, turn off all lights and nonessentials. Divert engine power to shields, override code mayday. We're going along for the ride," she told it.

The lights of the console blinked out along with all interior and exterior lights, and then she was alone in a dark tin can hurtling through a sea of rocks toward a vacuum of death.

My brother was right. I am an idiot for signing up for a deep space solo mission. The hazard pay really wasn't worth it.

"Computer, report on the ship's function," she whispered into the dark, afraid of the answer but still needing to know.

The navigation system glitched for a few harrowing seconds before it answered, "Shields are at sixty-one percent. Fuel is at thirty percent."

Letting out a shaky breath, Sasha tried her best to stay calm, to focus on her breathing and slow it down, ignoring the hammering of her heart in her chest.

Her mouth ran dry, her next words taking extra focus to bite out. "Reduce life support by half and divert the energy to shields. Override code mayday."

"Affirmative. My analysis shows that ship oxygen levels are at thirty percent and should support life for approximately four standard hours at the current rate of consumption."

The jostling slowed as the shields gained energy, buffering the hits from the space debris that was getting sucked in with her.

She didn't know if it would matter in the end, but it was the only thing that she could think to do. They hadn't exactly taught them about wormhole survival at the academy, not even when she'd been on the military side of things.

She didn't know if there was an end to this thing, or what might be on the other side of it, but on the slim chance that she survived this, she wanted to end up in one piece instead of cut out of her dinky little ship, floating in the frozen vacuum of space.

Besides, there's always more oxygen in the cabin than the computer says.

Closing her eyes against the dark, a shiver ran through her as the cabin slowly grew colder. Minutes passed, or maybe hours. There was no way to know how much time had passed when the lights began to flicker on and off.

"Computer, explain," she ordered.

Static and white noise filled the room as the navigation system failed to answer her. As unsettling as the AI system's canned responses were, its absence was even eerier.

Her stomach rose into her chest, and it felt like she was falling, even though there was no such thing as falling in space. You needed an atmosphere, artificial or real, for gravity.

The pressure in the cabin increased, her body pressing uncomfortably hard against the seat.

Her head felt like it was being squashed by giant, invisible hands. Her body felt heavy and dense, her head too heavy for her neck despite the zero-g inside the ship.

Unaware of passing out at some point, Sasha awoke, her neck sore and her mouth tasting like copper and salt. Tonguing her lip, she found small indentations where she'd bitten through until it bled. It was already beginning to heal, the small crescent marks filling in as she explored them to see how deep they were, grimacing at the taste.

Streaks of light exploded around her, lighting up the inside of the ship with a gentle golden glow.

Her hair settled around her shoulders as gravity came back into play. Glancing around, she took stock of herself and her ship.

I'm alive. Holy shit.

There were pinging sounds as floating things dropped out of the air and hit the floor. Sasha had just enough time to look up in surprise as her wrench fell right toward her head.

Frack me.

GETTING KNOCKED UNCONSCIOUS WAS NOTHING LIKE THEY portrayed in the holofilms.

There wasn't any fade to black, vision tunneling, or dreams. It wasn't like sleeping at all. She was conscious from one moment to the next with zero lapse in time. It was as if she'd blinked and found herself in different circumstances with no accounting for the time in between.

One moment she'd been sitting strapped into the chair of her ship as she hurtled uncontrollably through a wormhole, and the next she was staring up at an unfamiliar ceiling.

Sasha had a giant splitting headache that was wrecking her joy at discovering that she wasn't dead yet. She tried to sit up to look around, but the movement made her head swim until she felt like she was going to throw up.

Pressing a shaking hand to her abdomen, she explored her body, but she couldn't feel anything wrong. Her joints were protesting from lying in an awkward position for what felt like hours, and her head was pounding, but her body felt fine when she touched it.

Nothing was broken or malformed. Or, if it had been, her body had already been healed.

It stinks in here.

Gagging on the stench that permeated all around her, saliva flooded her mouth, and all she could focus on was breathing through the nausea until it passed.

I probably have a pretty bad concussion. Shit. Ugh, it smells like a farm in here.

Her eyes were half closed of their own volition before she jolted back awake, unaware that her consciousness had dipped. She summoned up her last dregs of willpower to force them back open.

The ceiling looked like it had been white at some point in its miserable existence before it was covered with a thick layer of grime. More importantly, that ceiling wasn't hers. She didn't recognize it at all.

I'm not on my ship, and this place smells like the exact opposite of a medical bay. Where the frack am I?

Musk and excrement stung her eyes until they watered. She closed them hard for a count of five, then opened them and inched her pounding head to the side to look around. Black spots danced in her vision, but she tried to look past it to survey her surroundings.

Metal. That was all she could see as her eyes adjusted to the low, ambient lighting. But it wasn't sheets of metal that she was looking at, it was bars.

Cautious, so she didn't get dizzy and make herself throw up, she turned her head to the other side and saw more of the same. Beyond the confines of the metal bars her eyes adjusted to the dark and took in the rest of the room.

Cages.

Rows and rows of them lined up side by side and stacked one on top of the other.

The room was filled, and each cage was crowded with animals and filth inside. Dark shapes huddled in the shadows of their prisons, filth-covered bedding spilling out onto the floor through their bars.

I'm in a cage.

Animals shifted, the sounds of them rustling around in their cages filling the room. As her eyes adjusted to the dark she studied her surroundings, her gaze skipping from cage to cage as she took in the strange shapes that her mind didn't want to process.

They were beyond different or unusual; they were alien.

Great. This is just great. I'm probably the first person to ever travel through a wormhole, survive, and make an encounter with extraterrestrials from another dimension... universe... whatever... and I end up in a cage.

Focusing on her breathing, the dizziness passed just enough that she was able to sit up against the bars. There was only about an inch or two of room between the top of her head and the cage.

It wasn't designed for humans or anything much larger than her, and she couldn't do much more than crouch, sit with her legs extended, or lie down in the fetal position.

The black spots in her vision passed as she drew her legs up under her and took a better look around the cramped room. Cages lined every wall except for what she assumed was the door. Across the way, she saw fanged beasts that paced and stared at her with hungry golden eyes.

There was one animal in particular that appeared very interested in her.

It looked vaguely like a spotted dog with its big, boxy head and ears, but it had a stripe of coarse, tufted fur that ran down the length of its back to a long, thin, tail that looked more cat-like along with its feline face.

Its oversized fangs poking out of its lips were horrifying, like some paleolithic nightmare creature.

The animal paced, scanning the room until its eyes landed on her more often than she was comfortable with as it surveyed the other cages and their inhabitants. Sasha stared it down until it lost interest in her, settling down into a corner of its large cage.

Rule number two of academy training: don't back down from enemies who are sizing you up.

Smaller cages lined her area of the room, most of which had multiple animals inside of them. The cage that was right next to hers had little furry things with long thin tails and big eyes. Their hands and feet were shaped for grasping in a way that made them look like they lived in trees, but they looked more like a cross between a squirrel and a fox than a monkey. Huddled together in a corner of their cage, they stared at her with wary golden eyes.

Some sort of bird squawked, ruffling its inky black feathers as it readjusted its grip on its perch. Brilliant yellow eyes swiveled and trained on her as she shifted. There was a cunning intelligence behind them.

From what she could see, she'd been placed on the prey side of the room if her nearby companions were anything like the animals she was used to.

With a glance back over at the predator side of the room, she was grateful that she hadn't been placed next to that hungry-looking prehistoric cat-dog thing.

A reptilian creature with four eyes blinked at her, its long red tongue flicking through the air. Scenting her. The sight of it made her shudder.

The whole experience felt surreal, and she would have thought it was all a dream if her head didn't hurt so badly and her mouth didn't feel like it was filled with fuzzy scum and the rusty tang of blood. Her jaw was sore, and her cheek felt raw as if she'd bitten it at some point.

It must be a deep wound to be taking so long to heal.

Shifting her attention to what looked like the door of the cage, she reached a hand through the bars. If there was a door, then there had to be a latch and hinges. Her fingers explored the cool metal until she found something smooth that felt like a keypad. Its texture was rougher than the metal of the bars, but there wasn't any keyhole opening that she could find.

With a beep, a door opened in the wall in front of her. Sasha withdrew her hand back into her cage while she looked.

Holding her breath with anticipation, she watched as two aliens walked into the room.

They were so strange-looking that she didn't even know where to start. The first one carried a clipboard and was wearing brightly colored clothing, but that was as humanoid as he was. Covered in a fine down of feathers tapering to larger feathers that decorated its arms and legs, its mouth was protruding and beaklike with eyes placed on the sides of its head.

The alien was writing something down as it scanned the room and Sasha saw that the hand that held the pen only had three talon-like fingers on it.

Her eyes skimmed down past the clipboard and she noticed that it wasn't wearing shoes. Instead, the alien had bare bird-like feet with wicked claws that clicked as it walked around the room scanning the cages, jotting down notes.

Looking past the bird alien to the other one behind him, she saw that this one was staring straight at her.

The second alien had to be a different species altogether, because this one couldn't be anymore different than the first. It was taller, for starters, with a body that was long and lean and covered in a short layer of tawny-colored fur instead of feathers. Its nose was wide and blunt, and its eyes were a startling, brilliant shade of gold that were slitted with oval pupils.

Small cat-like ears poked through its hair, the sight of them filling her with the immediate urge to play with them. Her fingers itched to touch them, to run down their rim and watch them twitch.

Long brown hair that had been rolled and matted into locks, decorated with little silver beads came down to its shoulders. This alien, at least, was wearing boots. Although its hands were hidden from view, tucked away inside of pant pockets. As her eyes traveled down his body, she got more than an eyeful.

Okay, he's a guy for sure... Those are some really tight leather pants, and holy hell, that's a really impressive bulge.

His tunic was leather too giving him a vaguely renaissance looking appearance. More surprising was the lack of a gun strapped to his belt. He looked like the cross between a pirate and a bandit.

"Ehve seeyea?" cat guy said, looking at the bird guy.

Her translator chip was unable to make out a single word. There was a growl to his voice that slurred the words together in a strange cadence. The bird alien's feathers ruffled in every direction as it dragged its pen along the clipboard, its writing intensifying into an angry scrawl.

"Yek ji karsaziya wee nay," it chirped back at the cat alien.

Sasha wanted to shout, *"Hello! I think you've made a huge mistake because I'm a person, not an animal, and can you kindly let me out of this cage now, please?"* but she wasn't sure if that would make a difference.

They pulled me out of my ship and stuck me in a cage.

They had to know she was a person, not an animal. Mouth gone dry, she forgot how to speak for a moment as the weight of everything that happened settled on her. Running a hand down herself, she found that everything was still in place.

They must have seen my ship if they extracted me from it somehow. There's no way they found me floating in space, still alive. They can definitely see that I'm wearing manufactured clothing.

Choking down the urge to panic, she thought.

Okay. First things first, I have to make them acknowledge that I am a person, not an exotic pet.

"My name is Sasha," she said.

It was always polite to lead an introduction with your name.

I mean, they never trained us on first encounters with new alien species at the Academy, but that's probably what they would have suggested if they did.

The aliens both turned to look at her like she was a dog that had just solved a math problem. Cat guy's eyes sharpened as he gave her a piercing look while the bird alien looked hopping mad with fluffed-up neck feathers.

"My name is Sasha, Sasha Robinson," she repeated.

Meandering over to her cage, cat guy pressed his face right up to my bars like a little kid who wanted a better look at the puppy in the pet store. She cringed away from him until her back hit the opposite side of the bars.

Their eyes met, and she held his gaze. It was part curiosity and part instinct on her end.

You weren't supposed to take your eyes off a predator that was looking at you. While Sasha didn't see any weapons on this guy, that didn't mean that he didn't have any on him or that he wasn't dangerous without one. He was an alien. She didn't know anything about him, or his kind.

He could melt me with his mind, for all I know.

"Dipeyivin," he said in his rumbly speech as he continued to stare her down.

"Sasha," she replied, pressing a hand to her chest, not knowing how else to communicate with this alien except in this stunted type of speech.

"Neheq be," bird guy squawked as he stepped forward,

looking even more irritable, although it was difficult to tell because its face wasn't very expressive. The bird alien reached a three-fingered hand out, rattling the bars of her cage. "Ew tenea heywanek e."

The jostling movement made her concussed head pound even harder. Wincing, she shot the bird a dirty glare.

"My name is Sasha, and I am a person, you fracking asshole," she seethed through gritted teeth.

Bird guy pulled away from the cage with a squeak as if he was surprised at her anger.

I've been sucked through a wormhole, and my ship has probably been destroyed beyond repair. I have no way home, I've been concussed with my own damn wrench, and now I'm stuck in a cage like a dog.

It had been a really shitty day.

"Ez nizanim ew ew te hez dikim," the cat guy smirked at his companion as the bird guy scribbled furiously on his clipboard.

"Ez li vir ceebuu," bird guy chirps back in a shrill voice as he headed to the doorway in a huff.

Cat guy lingered behind for a moment, continuing to look at her. Sasha held his gaze and stared him down while she pretended that she wasn't huddled in the corner of a cage on an alien spaceship.

Eventually, cat guy turned and left as nonchalantly as he'd arrived and the door shut behind them, leaving her alone with the other poor caged animals.

Tears started to prick at her eyes again, and she gnashed her teeth to stop the tears from falling. It was no use, however, and holding them back proved impossible. With an uncontrollable whimper, the floodgates opened, and Sasha collapsed into a heap on the floor of her cage and sobbed.

CHAPTER TWO

ARDALON

"Ardalon, this is a surprise. I didn't expect to hear from you so soon. Have you accomplished your objective already?" the chancellor said over his neural implant. Before Ardalon could get a word in, the chancellor continued, "I know that you are hungry for a promotion, but there's no need to rush and make too much haste."

Ardalon paced his bunk, trying to control his racing thoughts. "I have run into a complication."

It took days for him to find this one moment of privacy to make the call. Asa had been watching him even closer since he'd dared to question and tease the self-important Diggi in the holding room.

I will never get used to this implant.

"What sort of complication?" the chancellor asked.

Resisting the urge to run his claws through his hair, he considered what to say. "The poachers I've infiltrated have captured a rather unique species that I've never seen before. I can't find it in any species index either."

The chancellor sighed, the sound traveling straight into Ardalon's brain even though the male was clear on the other side of inhabited space.

"Unsavory business, but that is what poachers do. The Diggi tribe will lead us to their buyers, and those at the top of command believe that's the key for catching our primary objective in a criminal act. Sometimes we must overlook a small evil in order to right an even bigger one," the chancellor hedged.

Pacing in his cramped room, Ardalon expended some of his restless energy. It was hard for him to be still when he also felt pressured to act. To do something. Intervene.

"Yes, and I do not mean to disagree with you, Chancellor, however, I have reason to believe that this situation is a bit more complicated than that. I suspect that this creature is both sentient and sapient," Ardalon insisted.

The connection went silent, and for a moment he wondered if his call had been intercepted or dropped.

"Chancellor?"

"Unfortunate, but illegal trade of sentient species does happen among the less savory circles. Your objective is your only concern. If you can tag the creature without being seen, then we can attempt to intervene on its behalf once the mission is completed," the chancellor answered.

Ardalon raked his hands through his hair, a nail snagging on one of the beads in his locks. He ripped the strands free, careful not to cut them on the sharp edge of his nail. "Of course, sir, but I've tried to match it to every database I have access to and it can't be found. It's completely unlisted. It... it looked at me like it was a person, sir, but not a race I've ever seen before."

"What are you saying?" the chancellor asked.

"I'm not a xenobiologist, sir, but I think it's a new alien species," Ardalon admitted, saying the words that had been rattling around in his head since he saw it... saw *her*.

"An unidentified, new race... interesting. If you can prove that the poachers are aware of its sentience and intend to sell it anyways, then we can add slaving to their list of crimes. Proving it may be difficult, and we cannot let it undermine the mission. I will have to run this up above my head. They may not agree to intervene if it risks our objective. You understand, of course. There is a lot at stake here," the chancellor debated.

He nodded, even though he knew that the chancellor couldn't see him unless Ardalon was looking in a mirror. The visual transfer with his optical implant only went one way.

"I am sending you photos of it... of *her* now. I will gather more information while I await your orders," Ardalon assured him while he uploaded pieces of his recorded memories to the link.

"Good," the chancellor said. "Continue the mission and gather more intel. I will have the photos looked at by experts in the meantime while we wait for directions from above. Capture some video footage if possible, but do not jeopardize the primary objective. We can't afford to have your cover blown at this tenuous stage," he cautioned.

The call ended without a goodbye.

After a few minutes of waiting to ensure that everything was quiet, Ardalon left his tiny bunk and headed up to the second deck to find Rodo.

There was always someone gambling in the second deck supply closet, and wherever a game of chance was, you could bet that Rodo would be there. He was as lazy as he was unlucky, but that didn't stop him from gambling whenever the Diggi got a chance.

It shouldn't be too difficult to lose my cushy watch duty to him.

Mopping the ship was a thankless, endless job, and the under deck, where the animals were kept, was the worst part of it. That was why it went to Rodo, who couldn't be trusted to do anything more complicated than mindless janitorial duties in the filthiest part of the ship.

An hour and three purposely thrown games of dice later, Ardalon had Rodo's mop and was making his way to the holding room as he dodged curious looks from the other crew members.

The room was dark and quiet as he entered and turned on the lights. Some of the animals stirred, but the ones that had been there the longest no longer roused from their corners except to eat their food and eliminate their waste before going back to sleep.

His eyes zeroed in on the strange creature in the too small cage.

She tilted her head to meet his gaze and he saw that she was lying down on her side. Huddled into a ball with her arms wrapped around her legs, she looked so small and delicate. Fragile with the way her hair fell on her cheek.

Mop in hand, Ardalon started on one end of the room as he made his way toward her, cleaning as he shuffled closer. When he got close to her cage, he craned his head to check that the hallway was empty.

Activating the recording feature of his implant with a double blink, he turned back to face her.

Her eyes were open, and her gaze was fixed on him with keen interest.

"Nat sepozed to be hir, huh, kat boi?" she said in her lilting, musical voice.

"Sha sha," he replied, trying to remember the pronunciation of what he thought might be her name. She'd patted her hand to her chest as she'd repeated it over and over again yesterday.

Her eyes went wide as she sat up in her cage. "Saw shuh,"

she repeated, slowing it down for him as, once again, she pressed a small, clawless hand to her breast and tapped herself at her center.

He nodded to tell her that he understood. "Sa-shuh."

"Klose enuff," she sighed with a nod and a face twitch, but then she bared her teeth at him and scooted forward to the front of her cage.

Ardalon stiffened at the aggressive movement, getting a firmer grasp on his mop until he noticed that her teeth were blunted and her eyes still looked gentle.

She didn't look like a warrior who was about to attack. His tension softened.

Miscommunications were bound to happen with two very different species. There was no reason to believe that she knew the cultural norms of his people or the Diggis. The thought that she operated with her own alien sense of social cues and norms was enough to give him a headache.

This is far beyond my training... but I'm all she has... I have to try.

Putting a hand to his chest, he tried his best to mimic her. "Ardalon," he told her, dragging the syllables apart as he made sure to pronounce it slowly and clearly.

Her brow scrunched up with wrinkles showing on her furless skin. "Arr duh lon," she tried, but it came out all sing-song just like the rest of her words. There was no gruff to the d sound and no roll to the lon at the end.

"Close enough," he encouraged her with smiling eyes as she tried saying it again.

"Ardalon halp Sa-shuh," she said with a hurried tone as she gripped the bars to her cage and rattled them.

There was no doubt left in his mind now that this was a sentient, sapient creature.

Her words weren't animal mimicking. She was learning,

working to understand them and communicate. He could guess at what this word "halp" meant.

She wants out of her captivity.

"Ardalon halp Sasha," he agreed, with a slow blink.

She bared her teeth again, then started to chatter, but he couldn't catch any of her words' meaning. There were far too many of them, and she said them way too fast.

"O thangk gawd becuz I kant tayke much mor uf this ofel kage," she rushed out.

Approaching her cage, he held a hand palm side up and within reach of her. He didn't want to stick his hand into her small space and startle her. He also didn't want to accidentally offend her and lose a hand. Just because you didn't see claws didn't mean some species couldn't grow them when needed.

I'm not a complete fool, no matter what my littermates say.

She stuck her hand out of her cage and pressed her palm against his. Ardalon looked at their joined hands and saw that they weren't shaped so differently after all. While she was mostly furless, her skin covered with a nearly invisible blanket of fine down, and she had a relatively flat face, she still had five digits on her hands and the shape of them were similar enough to his.

Her fingers were longer, and the pad of her hand appeared smaller in comparison, like a cub who hadn't grown to adulthood yet. Perhaps this was normal for the females of her species, or maybe she was stunted.

He glanced down at the rest of her and noticed the swells of breasts and the flare of her hips. There wasn't much about her that looked childlike to him, even if she was small enough to maybe pass for one on the cusp of adulthood.

Letting go of her, he touched the material of her sleeve before she could withdraw completely away from him.

It was a fine-knit garment, and the seams were nearly invisible. The stitching was evenly spaced and too perfect to have been done by hand unless it was made by some master craftsman.

The clothing looked machine-made, and the material was unlike anything he'd ever seen before.

Her people have industry. They're advanced. And she is here. She got here... somehow.

The poachers hadn't made a planetside stop since refueling on Xithis's moon, and he had been on guard duty in the cargo bay at the time. He was certain that he'd have seen her if she'd been picked up there.

Where did she come from?

Ardalon's eyes found hers again, and he saw that she had some other emotion expressed on her face that he couldn't quite understand. She moved so much and with tiny nuances that confused him. Her face was nearly as expressive as her lilting, birdlike voice.

"Klothz," she said as she touched her strange garment with her free hand.

He repeated the word, sounding it out as best he could, and she nodded. She went through a flurry of naming things, barely giving him time to catch up and process each new word, let alone commit them to memory.

He repeated each one, her eyes shining brighter and brighter with each iteration as she continued.

"Haer," she explained as she touched her soft looking brown mane. "Uyes," as she indicated her blue eyes. "Noz," as she touched her snout, and "mowth" as she touched her flat, pink muzzle.

Tilting his head, he repeated each word dutifully before pointing down to her swollen teats.

Has she had a cub recently? If so, where is it?

A mother with teats as swollen as that should never be

weaned from her cub. It was far too soon and they will likely die without her and her milk. Perhaps that's why she's so eager to get out of her captivity.

Maybe she had a family somewhere with cubs to return to.

She paused for a long while before answering him. "Brests."

Her face color deepened, turning red, and he was shocked at this abrupt change in color. He flinched back a bit in case it was a signal of attack. Her eyes found his again, and she must have seen the surprise in them because she let out a short barking sound that was just as surprising as her abrupt color change.

The sound echoed, her eyes softening with it, as she raised a hand to cover her exposed teeth.

I have a feeling she's laughing at me.

A rumble built up in his chest, and then it was her turn to look surprised. Her expression-filled face maneuvered into some new look, the whites of her eyes showing all around as the strips of hair above them rose up.

He laughed harder, making her bark more, but this time it was a dry chuffing sound that started in her throat instead of her chest.

"Uf kors yur a bewb giy. Whet els did I ikspect?" she mumbled, her eyes rolling around in their sockets. She bared her teeth again, but her eyes were still soft.

He wasn't sure what she meant, but her tone sounded different, and he had a sneaking suspicion that she was mocking him.

Footsteps in the hallway outside alerted him to the passing patrol. He'd lost track of time, something that never happened to him. This was exactly how undercover operatives got caught.

No one could afford for him to make such a sloppy mistake. Stepping away from her cage, Ardalon went about the rest of his chores.

As he mopped, he uploaded the video clip onto his drive via his neural link. A Diggi walked past but didn't do more than quickly glance inside as the bird made his way down the hallway. It wasn't Asa, and for that he was thankful.

Asa had gotten wary of him lately. Listening to the Diggi's passing footsteps, he turned to glance back at her only to find her watching him. She was quiet and still, appearing contemplative as she tilted her head while giving him a wry look.

"Yu dont wont berd boi to no yoor hir," she whispered as she glanced between him and the empty doorway as if she understood.

Clever of her to have figured out that I don't want the others to know that we're talking.

He made a mental warning to not underestimate her intelligence just because she couldn't speak Common. Ignorance was not the same thing as stupidity.

She must be from a far-off place if she doesn't speak or understand the nearly universal trader's language.

"Ardalon halp Sa-shuh," he stumbled to explain, but he didn't have the words. "Diggi… " he trailed off, shaking his head.

The Diggi wouldn't help her. They'd sell her to some rich backwater merchant who had a taste for exotic slaves. And that's if she was lucky. If she wasn't lucky, she'd go to some high end, exotic brothel where she'd be worked until she died.

And with her being so strange and new and soft-looking, that end will likely be sooner rather than later.

His stomach twisted at that thought. Such places were cesspits, but the Peacekeepers already had their hands full trying to maintain basic law and order without also trying to shut down the brothels that ran all along the fringes of the galaxy. When one was struck down, two more rose up to take its place.

It was an endless game of frustration that they didn't have the resources to play.

Finishing his mopping, he turned to face her one last time.

"Good night, Sa-shuh," he told her as he turned the lights down and left.

The longer he stayed, the more danger he put both of them in. Him and his mission, and her and her life.

If the Diggi caught wind that the authorities were onto them and that they'd been caught trading in sentients, then they'd kill the both of them and space the evidence out of the nearest airlock.

CHAPTER THREE

SASHA

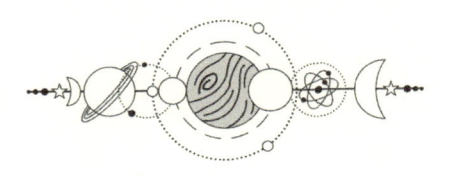

It had been days since Ardalon last visited her. He was the only one who had seemed to really understand that she was a person. He'd promised to help her...

At least I think that's what he was trying to say.

She'd chattered at a few of the bird guys, but they ignored her no matter what she did to get their attention. Sometimes they looked at her with their nearly expressionless faces before they went back to their mopping and tidying.

It was like she was some parrot who just made noises that sounded like words and phrases, but no one really knew if the animal understood that the words had meaning.

Sasha was listening and beginning to learn their language.

Her translator implant was working overtime, making short work of something that would otherwise take her weeks to do on her own. The headaches were worth it to be able to understand what was being said around her.

She was also learning the patterns to their movements. It was hard to tell the time of day since there weren't any clocks or windows in the room where they were holding her. She didn't know if she'd be able to read one of their alien clocks even if there was one. They probably didn't use the same number system. Their days likely weren't divided the same as hers, either.

While she was used to not having a sunset or sunrise to manage her day due to how much time she spent in space, the lack of a way to keep track of the passage of time was slowly driving her insane.

To get around it, she'd come up with her own timekeeping system. She knew that they were fed and given water twice a day, and the floors were swept and mopped every fourth shift.

The waste hole tube system in the corner of the cage was humiliating, but at least the cage stayed fairly clean. She'd had to get creative with the leafy bedding that they threw in every morning.

Still, she was starting to smell pretty rank. A self-cleaning suit could only do so much before it needed a good soaking and scrubbing with cleaning enzymes.

In the meantime, to maintain her sanity she was practicing talking in their language. She couldn't quite manage to get the tone right, and there were a lot of sounds that her throat couldn't make, but that was probably because the birds were rather nasal.

It must have been their dialect because it was different than Ardalon's gruff, rumbly speech.

The end result was most likely a disaster, and she was probably speaking with a bizarre accent, but at least she was learning.

Her translator implant picked up words here and there once she'd heard it repeated enough times, but the rest of it was just time and determination and paying careful attention to every single word they spoke around her.

There was no greater motivator than being locked up in a cage in a room full of animals.

Ardalon was what they called a Kursh, but she didn't know if that was the name of his species or his job title or... hell, maybe it was just a rude nickname they called him behind his back. The birds didn't seem to like him, which made her wonder why he was there.

Stretching her legs as much as the cramped cage would let her, Sasha shifted positions. Her cage didn't let her move around too much, but it was better than doing nothing.

Rolling onto her stomach, she saw the little fuzzy tree animals all staring at her. They were rather cute, even if their too-big eyes had freaked her out at first. Grabbing a lock of hair, she dangled it into their cage.

They scattered at the intrusion into their space before one brave little fox-squirrel-monkey edged forward to sniff at the lock of her hair.

Flicking it at the creature, she giggled as it ran back into the corner, huddling up with its brethren. It took a few more moments of holding still before another one dared to creep forward and brave a sniff. It wandered over, but this one didn't run away when she twitched her lock of hair at him.

The hair plopped onto its head, and Sasha watched him sniff at it from underneath.

The door dissolved open, and she saw from the corner of her eye as one of the bird aliens, one who she'd never seen before, entered carrying a bucket of breakfast chow. The fox-eared monkey squirrels scattered, and she withdrew her arm back into her cage.

Her stomach dropped at the sight of those ghastly brown pellets. They were as horrendous tasting as they looked and smelled, like cardboard with a bitter aftertaste of minerals.

Since she was on the prey side of the room, she got the prey food, but that had turned out to be a blessing since the predators got a pinkish gray-colored goop that smelled fishy.

I'll take the dust pellets, thanks, even if it means having to choke them down with stale water.

That's not what really caught her eye, though. What grabbed her attention was the key card clipped to his shirt. Most of the bird guards seemed to wear them on a lanyard around their neck that they tucked into their tunics. The card controlled the doors and lights, and she had a feeling that it controlled the cages too.

Everything appeared to run on radio frequency chips here, which wasn't all that different from old Earth technology.

She tracked him and his progress as he walked around the room, her eyes never leaving his swaying key card.

The bird made his way from left to right, talking to each animal for a moment as he moved around the room distributing the food pellets. The fox-squirrel-monkeys in the cage next to hers dug into their breakfast while she sat up against the back of her cage and stretched out her legs.

She watched him turn toward her cage, waiting for his eyes to find her through the bars.

"I'd like a word with your chef about the quality of this shit food," she snarked in a sweet-sounding, high-pitched voice as she inched forward to the front bars.

The last thing she wanted was to spook the bird, so she kept her teeth hidden. They seemed to view smiling as aggression, like a dog baring its teeth before it attacked. Probably because, as far as she could tell, the birds didn't seem to have teeth. Just little serrated nubs that lined the inside of their beak.

He stepped closer and angled his head to get a better look at her. It had to be annoying to have your eyes on the side of your head.

"You creaturestrange are," he trilled to himself as he reached into his bucket for his scoop.

Her translator chip managed a rough interpretation of his strange words, but it hadn't mastered their grammar yet. It didn't matter though, not when she had half a plan brewing.

This might be my chance.

Her heart started pounding wildly in her chest, and her mouth ran dry, her tongue sticking to the roof of it as she focused on keeping her face neutral and her body language soft and passive.

Frack waiting for Ardalon to live up to his promise and help me. I'm getting out of this cage today.

She felt the pressure for escape mounting until it clawed at her from the pit of anxiety that had nestled in the base of her hindbrain. She'd been listening to every word of conversation she overheard, and she was 99% positive that if she stuck around much longer then shit was going to get bad for her, fast.

Just that morning, she'd overheard that they were parked outside of some planet, waiting for permission to dock. If she didn't do something quickly, then her narrow window of opportunity would close. Likely forever.

I have a bad feeling that once we're docked, I'll be out of choices.

Slowly, so as not to spook him, she stuck her hands through the cage bars and wiggled her fingers while she gave him a closed lipped smile.

"You look new. I'm guessing that's how you got stuck with this shit assignment. What, did you piss off your boss or something?" Sasha asked him in a soft voice as she tried to lure him closer.

He inched toward the cage and she hoped that he couldn't hear her heart beating like a drum in her chest. An opportunity this good might not come around again before it was too late. The bird guy cocked his head as he looked at her with one eye.

Closer... closer...

She lured him with slow, careful movements. Hunched her shoulders to make herself look smaller and less intimidating as she kept talking to him in her baby talk voice.

"Come on, bird brain, just a little bit more," she chattered.

He stepped within range, and Sasha thrust her hand through the cage, grabbing a fistful of his gaudy, frilly tunic, as she yanked him forward, face-first into the bars. His beak cracked against the cage, and he looked dazed, squawking in surprise and pain.

It took all of her waning strength to keep him pulled up against the bars as she slid her other hand through and grabbed his badge. It came free from his shirt on the second tug, and then it was in her hand. Her breath rushed out in a muffled yell of triumph as she worked the badge free and palmed it.

Brushing it against the keypad, it chimed and the cage door made a mechanical sound as the bolt unlatched.

Bird boy's eye swiveled in its socket, his pupil expanding, and she could see him starting to panic the moment he realized she'd just freed herself. He began to make a lot of noise as he struggled against her.

Pressing both feet against the cage door and bracing against the back of it, she let go of his tunic just as she kicked the door open with all of her strength.

It's a good thing I've been stretching and exercising as much as this cage allows.

He flew back from the force of her kick, sprawling out onto the ground while she clambered out of the cage. Standing was difficult, her back protesting the abuse her body had been put through, but then the adrenaline kicked in and she was able to ignore her discomfort long enough to cross the room to where the bird was trying to crawl away from her.

His beak opened and closed and she saw his gray tongue moving, but he wasn't making any sound.

She grabbed him, pulling him into a chokehold. It only took a minute or so before his half-hearted struggling stopped and he became dead weight as he passed out. Letting him drop to the ground, she glanced around the room.

An idea popped into her head. She was out of the cage, and she had an access pass, but she had no idea how far this badge would get her.

She was going to need all the help she could get if she wanted to escape these aliens.

A distraction would help. She eyed the rows of cages stacked on top of one another in the filthy, smelly room.

With resolve, she made her way back over to the row of cages containing the prey animals. The card reader beeped, the lock mechanism disengaging as she opened a cage. The fox-squirrel-monkeys chirped at her as their door sprang open, but the little guys were too scared to make a break for it. Leaving their door unlocked and cracked, she moved around the room opening one cage after another as she went.

A feather-covered pig creature made a dash from the room, and that was all the other animals needed to see for their courage to swell. They began to make a dash for freedom as she unlocked their prisons, one by one.

The black bird with red eyes and wicked-looking claws flew over her head, dropping a feather in the process as it found the door and made its escape. A tall and slender beast that was a bizarre amalgamation of hoofed legs and a tentacle-covered head occupied the larger cage in the back.

Wary, she unlocked it, her stomach turning as she watched it skitter across the metal floor in its escape.

Turning to the predator side of the room, she suppressed a shiver as the fanged cat-dog stared her down while she opened up the cages to the smaller, less deadly-looking creatures around it. Scaled things slithered out, and small green striped tufted cats loped from the room as they joined the stampede of escaping animals.

Roars and snarls filled the small room, echoing. The four-eyed reptile that was as large as a dog flicked its long forked tongue in the air as if it was tasting the chaos in the room. It shuffled out faster than she thought it could reasonably move.

Definitely don't want to run into one of those things in the wild. Yuck.

The large prehistoric cat-dog was the only thing left. It was huge, reaching almost to her waist, and when it yawned and its mouth gaped open she saw the deadly, sharp-curved teeth of a natural-born predator.

An alarm began to ring overhead, its deafening claxon sounding and echoing, coming through hidden speakers, and then the sound of heavy footsteps began to resound from somewhere down the hallway.

Frack! I waited too long to escape and now my window is closing.

The sounds of footsteps and shouting were getting louder as she looked at the giant beast once more. Its eyes bored into hers, promising death. She stared it down in return, meeting its lethal gaze without flinching.

"I really, really hope I don't regret this," she whispered as she slid herself into a narrow crevice between two cages.

She held the badge to the locking mechanism of the cat-dog's cage. She was as barricaded as she could get. Her arm just barely made the stretch as she waved her pilfered badge near the card reader.

The door beeped, the lock disengaging, and the beast nudged it open with its fanged muzzle as it crossed the threshold on four silent paws. She pulled the cat-dog's cage door all the way open until it was blocking off her hiding place, giving her a little more protection from the thing as it slunk out of its confinement.

Its golden eyes found her through the bars of her hiding spot, and its shoulders tensed before relaxing as it flexed its disused muscles.

Before it could crouch down and spring at her, the first bird alien finally made it into the room, a gun clenched in its feather-covered three-taloned hand.

Huh. So they do have weapons after all.

The beast's attention switched to the new interloper, and the animal attacked him quicker than her eye could even process the movement. It sprang across the room in an amazing leap, sinking its enormous fangs into the bird's neck and ripping.

Blood and feathers sprayed across the room. The alien screamed, his hand tightening and his gun firing a blinding green laser in an arc that missed its intended target by a wide margin. The creature bit harder until bones crunched under its jaws.

Growls and screams filled the room until the bird was either dead or dying.

The beast licked blood from its dripping muzzle, rising from its crouch. It seemed that she'd been forgotten for tastier prey as the beast darted from the room in search of more feathered friends to hunt.

The hallway was in utter chaos as animals roared and screeched and bird guys shouted out their panicked commands and screamed with terror.

Moving from her hiding place, she grabbed the gun from his limp grip, prying it from his leathery claws. It looked simple enough. There was a trigger and a dial. She aimed it at the wall and gave it a whirl, pulling on the trigger until it tightened under her pointer finger.

A green laser shot out, hitting the wall, leaving a faint mark on the riveted metal as she let the trigger go. A grin split her face for the first time since her capture.

Sure feels nice to be armed again.

The dial had five settings if she was interpreting the dots correctly. It looked like the row of dots was the indicator for the power setting. Grinning, she cranked the dial up from one dot to three.

These frackers locked me in a cage for days and wanted to sell me. I'm not feeling nice.

Knees soft in a slight crouch to stay agile, she made her way to the doorway and scanned the hallway. The chaos had moved elsewhere. There was blood and bits of fabric and feathers strewn everywhere. Sounds of carnage echoed down the hallway, coming from both directions.

The siren continued to blare overhead, adding to the confusion.

No time like the present. Time to find a ride and get the heck outta dodge.

Springing up from a crouch, she worked her way down the hallway, stepping over the torn bodies of dead and dying animals and aliens as she kept her newly acquired gun at the ready and picked a direction at random.

Ardalon

The ship alarm interrupted his call to the chancellor.

"What's happening?" the chancellor asked.

"I'm not certain," he answered, moving closer to his door to listen. "But it sounds like the ship is under attack. I can hear fighting and screaming through my door."

The chancellor let out an irritated sound. "Well, go and find out, then report back. If your cover has been blown then you must abort the mission by any means necessary. We cannot afford your capture, do you understand?" the chancellor ordered.

Ardalon bent down to tighten the laces on his boots. "Understood."

He moved away from the door and headed over to his trunk,

popping open the lid and grabbing his pulse pistol. Flicking the safety off, he walked back to the door and crouched as he cracked it open, surveying the hallway.

A tintrilli scampered by while the emergency lights flickered overhead.

What?

He blinked, dumbstruck, until understanding hit him.

Oh no... the alien.

An out-of-breath Diggi made a haphazard dash through the hallway, and it took Ardalon a second to see that it was Asa.

"What's happening?" Ardalon asked him, shutting the door at his back, then following alongside him.

The hallway was abandoned. Asa's head swiveled on his neck as the first mate looked back, glaring at him. It wasn't the first time that Ardalon had been on the receiving end of a dark look from Asa.

If he's suspicious of me, then it's best to learn about it here and now where I can quietly dispose of him in the chaos.

"That awful creature! That's what happened! It's out—and all the other animals too!" Asa grumbled.

Ardalon followed behind Asa as they ran down the hall toward the main control tower. He'd never been allowed in there before. This was a prime opportunity that he couldn't let go to waste.

Screams and the sound of gunfire echoed in a confusing jumble of discordant sounds down the hallway. This merchant turned poaching vessel hadn't been designed for battle. The hallways were a twisting, convoluted maze with no reinforcement.

Up ahead, he saw a Diggi running for his life, clawed feet scratching gouges into the metal floor as he ran. A moment later, Ardalon saw a scaled hydrox lumbering after the running Diggi.

Poor bastard.

The poisonous bite of a hydrox was a nasty, slow, and exceedingly painful way to die.

"The animals have all escaped their cages?" Ardalon clarified, suppressing the glee that threatened to emerge in his voice.

He pushed the feeling back down as he raised his gun and aimed it at the hydrox in case the animal changed courses and ran toward them. The Diggi and its pursuer disappeared out of sight, but he still didn't lower his gun.

Who knew what else they might encounter in the hallway?

"Keep up, you moron! She let them out! I don't know how she did it, but I know it was her," Asa seethed, huffing and puffing while they ran down the hallway to the control center.

Ardalon followed him, surveying from side to side as they moved, watching for any predators that might be hunting them. They approached a junction that was splattered with blood and bloody footprints stamped onto the metal floor in a trail of destruction.

Skirting the shredded remains of a dead Diggi, he glanced at the identification tag and saw that it was poor dumb Rodo.

"The strange new creature... are you certain?" Ardalon asked.

Asa laughed, a sharp and derisive sound that held no pleasure in it. "It had to be her! Who else? I knew we should have just left her where we'd found her. I knew she'd be big trouble, but does anyone listen to me? No, of course not. Greedy bastards. This is exactly why I don't deal with sentients. They're way too much trouble."

A wave of victory swallowed him up, the urge to flash a fang nearly impossible to fight off. He maintained his composure as he kept his grip on his pulse pistol light, scanning the hallway for enemies as they neared their goal.

Asa had no idea how deeply he'd just dug his own grave with that careless remark. The poacher was facing a lifetime in prison for admitting to such a heinous crime... if he even survived this.

They made it to the control tower without further incidence and Asa sighed in relief as the heavy door sealed shut behind them.

The control tower was the safest part of the ship. It was also where they kept the mainframe and the central monitoring system, as well as the ship's logs and records.

I've just hit a goldmine of information.

Metal clanked as Ardalon slid the emergency override lock into place, then turned and raised his pistol, aiming it at Asa.

"Regrettable," Ardalon smirked, letting his facade slip after weeks of being so cautious.

His heart was racing, beating a rapid rhythm in his chest. A fang dug into his lower lip as he gave into the feeling, leveling his gaze on the ship's first mate. All of the emotions that he'd kept out of his eyes, he finally allowed them to show.

Asa glanced at him over a shoulder, scowling and chirping unhappily.

"Put your gun away before you shoot me by accident, you stupid mercenary. That door is a meter thick. Nothing is getting through it," he sniped.

If Asa saw the truth in Ardalon's eyes, the Diggi didn't show it.

Ardalon dropped the muzzle of his pulse pistol a fraction. Just enough to make Asa comfortable, but not so far that it couldn't be where he needed it in just a moment.

Asa turned back to the monitors, and Ardalon turned to look at them too. The monitors beeped, their bank of alarms flashing emergent signals as the ship reported back on its condition.

There were dozens of screens that showed the carnage from every angle. Animals were running amuck as poorly trained guards tried—and failed—to deal with them. It was a bloody disaster. His eyes flicked through screen after screen until he finally found her.

So much for the plan. It's all gone to shit at this point. Now I just have to figure out how to turn this to my advantage.

He watched her on the screens as she moved about the ship. If there was any doubt in his mind of what she was, then that was completely gone now.

The fluid way that she moved down the hallway in a half-crouch, a stolen pulse pistol leading her way, showed that not only was she highly evolved, but she was trained for warfare too.

With practiced skill, Sa-shuh cleared hallways and ducked through doorways as beasts and aliens alike passed her by in the chaos.

He wasn't certain what her goal was, but he knew in his bones that he had to help her. No one else would, if he didn't. Not helping her had never really been an option.

An idea flitted through his mind and he mulled it over, looking at it from multiple angles while he tried to decide if it was a viable course of action. After a moment's contemplation, he was ready and committed to this change.

With plan B solidified, he turned and trained his gun on Asa, who was too busy flipping through an emergency response binder to notice being trapped inside a cage with the biggest threat on the entire ship.

Ardalon's fanged grin was wide and malevolent when Asa finally noticed the gun pointed directly at him. The Diggi's eyes widened in response, his beak dropping open.

"What! What do you think you're doing?" Asa chirped nervously.

"Taking control. I'd think that would be obvious," Ardalon smirked. "Now take a step to your right and place your arms behind your back," he ordered as he used his free hand to pull a hidden pair of cuffs from the secret compartment hidden inside the sole of his right boot.

Asa sputtered in outrage, his feathers ruffling as he stepped back.

Ardalon took great pleasure in seeing the slimy poacher's fear. "Under the authority of the United Council, I am placing you under arrest for the trafficking of stolen exotic animals, distribution of endangered species, violation of the Sentient Species Protection Act, and whatever else I can get to stick to your sorry excuse of a carcass."

Holstering his pistol, Ardalon stalked forward and yanked Asa'a arm behind his back. He maneuvered him across the room, restraining his arms together and manhandling him into a corner as he cuffed him.

Asa scratched at the ground and squawked in protest. "You can't do this!" he shouted.

"Watch me," Ardalon answered, turning his attention to the monitors again, calling up the chancellor over his neural implant.

He scanned the screens until he found Sa-shuh. She'd made it all the way to the far side of the ship from the cages, but she was headed in the wrong direction.

"Report, agent," the chancellor barked inside Ardalon's mind.

Ardalon tightened Asa's restraints until the Diggi groaned. "The operation needs adjustment, sir. The ship is in turmoil. The animals have been released and are running rampant, killing poachers and hired mercs. I have arrested the first mate who has confessed on audiovisual record to the illegal kidnapping and transporting of sentients, and I've assumed control of the ship. I need backup in tactical to subdue both the cargo and the crew," he reported.

The chancellor sighed. "I will report that the mission is to be aborted. Your backup and an extraction team are on the way."

"Negative on the extraction, sir. The mission may continue with slight alterations," Ardalon contradicted him. "I'll need the girl, though."

"Backup is en route and coming in cloaked. What girl? Explain your intentions, Ardalon," the chancellor grumbled.

Ardalon's eyes cut to his prisoner. Asa was looking over a shoulder at him as if he'd grown a second head or sprouted a second set of eyes. The Diggi's eyes widened, then narrowed in anger.

Ardalon smirked. "The alien, sir. I have an idea... if we can get her to cooperate. I'll find a way to bring her to safety from the animals. If we replace the ship's staff with our own, then we can continue with the mission as planned with just a few adjustments. I believe the first mate will agree to cooperate in return for lighter sentencing, won't you, Asa?"

Asa nodded. "O-Of course! Anything for the good of the Council!"

The Chancellor sighed again, a weary, drawn-out sound. "All right, but your ass is on the line for this, Bavara. Do what you must, for now, and brief me in full when the ship is under our control," the chancellor added before the connection dropped and Ardalon's stealth implant went back into standby mode.

Shoving the cuffed Diggi away from him, Ardalon glanced down at the screen where he last saw Sa-shuh.

She was shooting at a stray Diggi before she ducked for cover from the poacher's return blast. It looked like she was heading in the opposite way of the control tower, and he wanted to groan out loud.

He needed to figure out a way to get her to come to him, because he couldn't leave.

The control tower was safe. If he could just get her there. He needed a way to communicate with her. To instruct her on which route to take. The only hitch was they couldn't talk to one another because she didn't speak Common.

If I leave Asa alone, the idiot might manage to free himself and warn others... but if I don't find a way to help her then she could get eaten or killed, and then I blew my cover for nothing. Think. Think, think, think.

And then he realized that he was an idiot, because he was standing in a control tower, and the control tower did a lot more than just steer the ship. It controlled everything on and about the ship, including the cameras and lights.

Scanning the bank of controls, he found the kill switch for the emergency alarm and flicked it. The deafening noise stopped abruptly. Next was the button for the intercom. He pressed it and leaned into the intercom's microphone.

"Sa-shuh!" he called out to get her attention. She stumbled, and he could have cursed himself for being a fool and distracting her without looking first to see if she was safe. Thankfully, the hallway she was in was clear, and he hadn't done more than startle her.

"It's Ardalon. I'm going to help you. Ardalon halp Sa-shuh," he said, hoping that she would understand him. That she would trust him.

A Diggi turned a corner and appeared in front of her, taking a quick blast to the shoulder from the business end of Sa-shuh's pulse pistol. The poacher turned and ran.

Ardalon watched as she cleared the hall, then looked around, scanning the room from floor to ceiling. He could tell when she spied the camera in the ceiling because she looked straight at it and from his position in the control tower it felt like she was staring straight at him even though they were separated by half a ship's length.

His spine tingled as their eyes locked through the security feed.

He palmed the control panel, his fingers finding the right buttons as he pulled up the control for the lights. A diagram of the ship came onto the screen, and bright dots appeared. Glancing at the monitor, he saw what sector she was in and quickly matched it to the display.

Toggling the control, flickering her light on and off and on again, he did the same to the lights in the next room, showing her where he wanted her to go.

Ardalon held his breath as he watched her and waited to see if she understood his silent message. If she trusted him enough to follow his path of lights as he led her through the ship.

Follow the blinking lights.

A moment later, he had his answer.

She cleared her path and glanced behind her, checking her six, before she headed toward the flickering light. Ardalon began to lead her toward the safety of the control tower where he waited for her.

He tracked her movements on the camera as he scanned the upcoming rooms for enemies and threats as he altered and adjusted her route, beginning to lead her around the worst of the action.

The grin that split his face was wide and full of teeth.

This is the most fun I've had in ages.

CHAPTER FOUR

SASHA

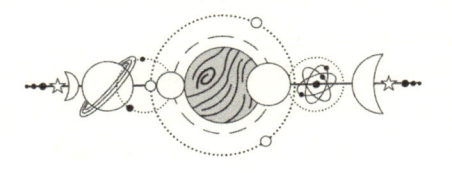

Sasha fired, hitting another bird directly in the middle of his torso, which sent him running. She wasn't sure exactly who these guys were, but they weren't trained fighters, that was for certain.

She'd cleared the room, taking a moment to glance around to get her bearings just before the hall light to her left flickered.

Gun drawn and leading the way, she was halfway down it when her first predator encounter happened. It was one of the smaller cats, a fierce little thing that only came up to her knee, and while it might have been a true predator in the wild where it had optimal hunting conditions, it appeared frazzled and disoriented in this chaotic mess.

Tightening her finger on the trigger, she hesitated because she didn't want to shoot the little guy if she didn't have to.

It started to stalk toward her with slinky movements as she turned her gun down to just one dot. Reaching up and spreading her arms up and out, she stood tall to become more imposing, making threatening gestures. The cat stilled and stared at her in confusion, its tail flicking back and forth behind it uncertainly as its ears flattened on its skull.

"Sorry, kitty cat, but I don't feel like playing mouse today. Go find a big juicy bird instead," she ordered, bringing her gun in front of her and letting off a warning shot just a hair's breadth away from the cat's frontmost paw.

The animal must have taken the hint that it was facing down a larger, meaner predator, because it backed up until it found a side hallway, then disappeared from view one smooth lope as it ran away.

Letting out a relieved sigh, she turned around, continuing her escape. She was going to get free, or she was going to die trying. She was never going into a cage again.

Lights blinked on and off up ahead, then stopped abruptly which was strange because when Ardalon blinked them like that they didn't usually stop until she was nearly there. Scoping the room, she found the almost invisible camera in the ceiling and stared at it for a few moments until finally a smaller side hallway to her right started blinking.

He'd changed his mind on which way to send her.

Turning, she headed that way, hoping she wasn't headed directly into a trap. She didn't have much choice, though. The alien ship was confusing, and nothing made sense to her. She'd been running blind before.

I either trust that Ardalon meant it when he said he'd help me or I might as well lock myself back up in that cage. If I'm being honest, my escape plan was kind of shit, since I can't read their stupid alien language.

Her translator chip wasn't capable of deciphering their bizarre writing, and she couldn't tell one wavy squiggle with dots from another. She didn't even know if they read left-to-right or right-to-left. For all she knew, they might read from the center moving outward.

They were aliens, after all.

Leading with her pilfered gun, she headed down yet another

empty hallway into what appeared to be another purposeless room.

This was the strangest space ship that she'd ever seen. It was just endless hallways and empty rooms and walls covered with gibberish squiggles. Left, right, it all looked the same to her, like a labyrinth designed to confuse and disorient.

Ardalon led her through the hallways and rooms with his blinking lights.

She cleared each room, scaring off whatever birds and beasts were in them. A few had shot at her until she encouraged them to leave with return blasts of her own. Word of her escape must have been spreading because she didn't even have to shoot at the bird aliens anymore; they just ran from her on sight.

Her lips quirked up in a satisfied smile. That felt pretty nice, actually. After spending a few days—maybe a week—in a cage, it was awesome to feel in control again.

It had been a while since training, so she thanked her lucky stars for her muscle memory.

The lights started flickering on and off all around her in a confusing mess. She couldn't tell what he wanted her to see. There were five hallways at this large intersection, but they all looked the same to her. If she was doubling back, then she'd never realize it.

The ship was built like an insect tunnel.

The hairs on the back of her neck stood up and a chill ran down her spine. Spinning around, she saw the enormous cat-dog staring at her from the other end of the long hallway.

"Shit," she cursed as she aimed her gun at it.

Now this one, she had absolutely no qualms about killing. She didn't think that she could make herself look big and mean enough to scare it off, and if she had to choose between her or it, then you could bet a hundred credits that she was going to pick herself.

I didn't survive a wormhole and these asshole giant finch-looking aliens to get fracking eaten alive during my grand escape.

Without taking her eyes off it, she reached down and thumbed the power control, dialing the gun all the way up to its highest setting. Three dots had left scorch marks in the ship's metal walls. She was excited to see what five dots could do.

The big snarling cat-dog broke into a run. She aimed her stolen gun and pulled the trigger. The gun let out a pathetic little *pew pew* sound, its tiny green lights fading, before going dim.

Shit, shit, shit. Outta juice.

Dropping the useless gun to the floor, she turned and ran. It was her only option left.

She pushed thoughts of razor-sharp claws and huge, sharp teeth from her mind as she shoved all of her nearly depleted energy into running blindly through the ship.

There was no time for help from Ardalon, now.

She'd been reduced to pure animalistic instinct as she weaved a zigzag path through the ship. Adrenaline pumped through her system, and she could feel the nanos that floated in her blood repairing her fatigued muscles as she pushed her tired, weakened body to its limit.

The creature wasn't as fast as her, its bulky frame more suited for jumping down on prey from above, but it looked like it had been built to overpower its prey. She couldn't let it catch her.

Her small lead was just enough to put some distance between them until a bird alien darted out from a cross hallway, his feathered arms spread wide as it tried to grab her.

Smashing an elbow in his face and kicking to sweep his legs out from under him, she dodged. He sprawled out on the floor, but she didn't have time to savor his surprised squawks. Instead, she kept running, hoping that the giant ass sabertooth cat-dog would eat the bird instead.

Her breath came out in rapid pants as she took a second to get her bearings.

Squawking grumbles turned to shrill screaming that stopped as abruptly as it started.

So it found the bird after all.

A twinge of remorse filled her for a moment before she shoved that useless emotion away. There were no sentiments allowed in survival. Sometimes, it was kill or be killed. Or eat or be eaten, in this case.

And I'm not dying today.

She glanced up and down the never-ending hallway, but it all looked the same to her.

How the frack am I supposed to make heads or tails of this ass-backward ship when it's just endless hallways that all look the same?

Blowing out a frustrated breath through her nose, she turned and punched one of the confusing squiggles painted on the wall.

A door opened, the wall dissolving right in front of her. Jaw dropping open in utter surprise, her body reacted on instinct. She was through the threshold before she could second guess the decision. Once she was on the other side she slapped the illegible lettering again.

The door closed again, disappearing like it wasn't there at all.

Oh. My. Stars. There have been doors to other rooms in the hall this entire fracking time?

Unable to stop herself from laughing, she took a moment to breathe and let the nanos repair the damage of her flight from the cat-dog beast. Her hands were shaking from the adrenaline rush as her fight-or-flight hormones settled in her system.

The room was dark and she was a little hesitant to go flailing around or mashing on random wall writing in the hopes of turning on a light. The last thing she wanted to do was accidentally open a door and have to face her furry little friend again, sans weapon.

Hands out in front of her, she blindly walked further into the room. She'd only taken a few steps when the lights turned on, blinding her.

Maybe there's a sensor? Or he found me?

Blinking a few times, she took a good look around.

Her jaw dropped when she realized she'd just stumbled into what appeared to be their ship storage bay. The giant flight deck was packed wall to wall with small spaceships and large metal crates. Sasha walked from one side of the room to another, looking at each ship as she passed them.

There were small ships that reminded her of her own, and then there were larger ships that were equipped with artillery.

A bank of what looked like escape pods lined an entire wall. Large, somewhat transparent sections of the ship showed her a view of space.

Is that how they fly in and out?

Wandering over to the nearest crate, she hooked her fingers under the lid and pried it off, finding that it was full of bolts of brightly colored cloth.

Merchants... or pirates?

Considering the poacher's zoo they'd kept her in, she was putting her money on pirates. It made her feel less guilty now after so many birds were eaten or injured by the animals they'd captured.

Serves the frackers right.

Moving to the next crate, she pried its lid off and was absolutely delighted to find that this one was full of more of the laser guns that the birds carried with them. There had to be at least two dozen of them packed in some sort of dense foam-like material.

Yup. Definitely pirates.

She pried a gun from the foam and dropped the lid back down on top.

Finders keepers. Besides, it's going to take a lot more than a gun or two to feel even after they kidnapped me and locked me in a cage and fed me sawdust for a week.

She'd just settled on a medium-sized ship with two large mounted guns when the door to the deck opened and five birds ran in, their own guns raised and pointed vaguely in her direction.

Ducking behind a crate, she took cover. Her heart was pounding, adrenaline flooding her system once more. She dialed the gun to three dots, leaned out and aimed, firing off a shot before they could spot her. One took a hit in the torso and another on the shoulder.

They squawked and flailed, taking cover. A return blast hit the crate to her left, missing her by a wide margin.

Wow, their aim is total shit.

Once their firing slowed she took her chance, leaning around her cover as she lured one out and hit him right between the eyes. He slumped to the floor, either dead or unconscious. She was past the point of caring.

The return volley forced her back into hiding as they sprayed the wall of crates that were sheltering her with a stream of laser blasts. Fragments of metal flew apart as the crate shielding her was punched through with holes.

A piece of debris caught her on the cheek, and she closed her eyes tight against the rain of shrapnel as she crouched down lower, using an arm to shield what she could of her face.

When she heard the little *pew pew* noises of their depleted guns she dashed for new cover, firing three shots at them as she ran. Her aim was wild and rushed, and all she managed was a few maiming shots that would only slow them down, not stop them.

A growl at the door made all of their heads whip up.

Oh, frack me.

They'd left the door open and the sabretooth cat-dog had come to join the party.

The birds squawked, and one tried to make a run for it. It was a bad idea. The beast leapt, quicker and further than its bulky frame looked like it should be able to move, and it snapped those terrifyingly overgrown teeth down onto the alien.

Ducking back against her crate, she scanned the room to see what she had to work with.

Squawks turned to panicked screams interspersed with the crunching of bones and the rending of flesh. She tuned out the noise as she dialed her gun all the way up to five dots while she kicked herself for not grabbing a second gun from the crate when she'd had her chance.

The ship she'd picked out wasn't too far away, but the haphazard maze of crates and pallets of goods in the hanger made a winding path that was going to slow her down. She slanted her gaze to the left and saw a big red button on the wall with a transparent cover over it.

Huh.

Taking a moment to look about, she saw it was the only one like it in the room. She blinked, her thoughts racing as she pieced it all together.

The ships and crates and shit had to get loaded in and out. You wouldn't want a button that opens up those doorways to outer space to be easily pushed by accident. They'd have made it very noticeable and impossible to accidentally hit.

Like covering it with a hard cover and making it an eye-catching color, then placing it up high on a wall.

Improvised plan in place, she tucked her legs under her and sprang up, sprinting toward the red button. She pushed every ounce of strength into her legs, knowing that if she was wrong then it might be over for her.

She pushed her legs to pump faster, her thighs straining with the exertion after her week of forced immobility. Her nanos flooded her body, rushing through her with the release of adrenaline.

A growl and a skittering of claws on metal behind her raised the hairs on her arms.

She ignored the urge to look over her shoulder.

Snarling, deep and primal, sounded behind her. Pushing her body harder and faster, she closed the distance between herself and the wall.

Her body slammed into it, knocking the air from her lungs, as she reached up. Double clicking her heels together, she felt the magnets in her spacewalk boots lock onto the metal floors, and she breathed in a sigh of relief, thankful it wasn't made of the alien version of aluminum.

Keeping her gun up, she fired off a stream of green beams directly into the beast's path as her other hand fumbled at the zipper on her shoulder. The beast faltered, adjusting its weaving path as it dodged her constant stream of attack.

She plucked the portable life support helmet from the tiny pocket in her suit, ripping the foil cover open with her teeth and slapping it onto her nose and mouth.

The cold, gelatinous shield tasted disgusting, but she couldn't have been more grateful. She only had about thirty minutes of aerated gel to work with.

Should be plenty long enough to get this cargo bay cleared of enemies and steal a ship.

A grinding warning noise and a high-pitched nasal shriek from some hidden overhead speaker sounded throughout the room. The snarling grew louder, the cat-dog closing in. A wall shimmered, turning transparent.

The inky black of space and stars and the far off curve of a planet came into view as a large opening in the wall shimmered into existence. She turned, gun raised, and sprayed a wide line of green energy at the lunging beast.

Still, the creature came for her, her death reflected back at her in its hateful, golden eyes. The sabretooth cat-dog beast was clawing long furrows into the metal floor as it closed in on her.

Grabbing onto a handhold built into the wall, she flipped the protective cover up and hit the big, red button.

A sucking wind formed in the hangar as her hair whipped around her face. The glowing wall dissolved, and then the room exploded into the vacuum of space. Anything not bolted or magnetized down was blown out.

Her body swayed forward, held in place by her magnetic spacewalk boots and the grip she held onto with all her might.

Ice crusted on her eyelashes, every inch of her bare skin chilling from exposure as her flight suit attempted to withstand the harsh exposure to space. It was made to withstand a wide variety of elements, but it wasn't intended for actual space walks. Anything longer than a few minutes was going to get dangerous.

Bye bye, pirates and devil cat-dog.

Eyes shut to protect them from the cold, she counted to ten and hit the button again. Her hair settled, and the pull on her body slackened until she only felt the faintest tug. Opening her eyes, she saw that the birds and the creature were gone.

The wall was lit with a golden glow, the view of space beyond it slightly visible through the sheerness of whatever alien force field covered it. A faint pull was still there, her body leaning toward it at an angle as she let go of her hand hold and tested it.

Whatever barrier existed there between the cargo bay and outer space was dampening the decompression.

She took a step and stumbled, her body not fully under her control. Palms slapping against the floor as she kneeled, she blinked droplets of melting ice off her eyelashes. Magnetizing her boots again, she stood.

Now what?

She had to make a choice. There was a wall of what looked like escape pods right there for the taking. Or she could open that door back up and keep going toward Ardalon. To wherever it was he was leading her.

He left you in a cage. He never even came back after that last time.

Blinking the melting ice off her eyelashes, she hesitated. She glanced at the pods again. It was strange how everything was alien, yet so achingly familiar.

Could she live with herself knowing she had freedom within her grasp but she didn't jump to take it?

Before she hesitated too long, risking being caught by another wave of armed pirates, Sasha decided. Doing a heel to toe walk that released and then re-attached as she stepped with the magnets in her boots, she made slow progress toward the escape pod she'd chosen.

Hoping that she wasn't about to shoot herself in the butt, she slid the pistol into the belt on her suit. Thanks to a week of rabbit food and water, she had a little extra wiggle room in her belt notches to accommodate its bulk.

Climbing the metal ladder up to the pod's hatch was harder than she thought it should have been. There were a bunch of squiggles and dots on the paint. She tapped it while hoping that it was the door button.

The seams in the metal widened, a narrow entryway sliding

open, and she breathed a sigh of relief as she hauled herself into it and disengaged the magnets on her boots.

The door shut itself behind her. Automatic lights flickered on and bathed the pod in an artificial glow. There were two bucket chairs with harnesses in front of what she assumed was the navigation equipment.

Instead of the typical bank of switches and buttons with a steering wheel or joystick, there was a glowing white sphere that hovered between the two seats.

Huh. I've never seen a ship that's piloted by spinning a sphere before.

Still, a ship was a ship. She would figure it out.

She settled into the leftmost chair, placing the large floating ball under her right hand. As she tapped it, the electronic elements in front of her lit up.

Smiling, she studied them, looking for anything that seemed to make sense to her. The ship had an atmosphere according to the diagnostic sleeve of her suit, so she peeled the emergency life support gel from her face and slapped it up on the ceiling.

The writing on the panels did nothing for her. But there probably was, at the very least, some sort of autopilot feature for emergencies. She just had to find and activate it.

Trailing fingers over the smooth metal and plasticine buttons, she found a cubby hole with a dusty, yellowing paper booklet shoved all the way in the back. It looked like a manual. She flipped through it, skimming each line of text that looked like it was written in multiple languages and, better yet, there were diagrams below that.

Following its instructions, she started the ignition sequence.

The engines purred to life with a gentle thrum that she felt with her body, the vibrations moving through her feet. She flipped the page and adjusted the row of switches before her so that it looked just like the pictures. Sasha turned the page and studied the next few diagrams.

The clear viewing window in front of her turned opaque, and she flinched, startled as a video feed was patched in.

"Sa-shuh!" Ardalon shouted. He looked worried, although it was difficult for her to tell. His projected muzzle made different expressions than what she was used to. His eyes looked at her, a ring of white around his iris showing surprise, or maybe worry.

Ardalon said something in rapid-fire alien speak that her translator couldn't pick up or even begin to sort through. His speech was too fast and the pitch too rough and growly.

The mean old bird, the one she'd seen with the clipboard, was standing next to him, feathers ruffled and spitting mad. Birdie squawked something. Her translator roughly picked it up, working to decipher it.

"Will never... too dumb... of course... stupid girl."

Leveling the bird with a withering glare, she flicked the next button on the autopilot launching sequence.

Ardalon and the bird's eyes both widened.

Surprised? Idiots. How do they think I got here? Obviously I know how spaceships work. I mean, yeah, it would be easier if I could read their language, but that's just a detail.

Raising her eyebrows and giving the bird guy a nasty look, she finished the activation sequence and enjoyed the way that the thrusters' vibrations felt underneath the seat. She could feel the thrum of the engines as they powered up. An indicator light began to fill up at the bottom of the screen.

Ardalon ceased his rapid alien speech, putting his hands up in a placating gesture that said, *"Stay there, stop,"* as he flicked them downward.

It was both familiar and different, and she found it strange which things translated and which didn't.

Did she trust him? That's what it came down to. He'd led her through the ship, but he'd also left her in that cage for days. And there he was standing next to the alien who, from what she could tell, seemed to be in charge.

She huffed and shook her head.

"I don't think so. I waited a week for help that wasn't coming. I'm sure as shit not gonna stop now that I have freedom within my grasp," she told him.

The indicator bar filled three quarters of the way up, the engine's thrum changing as it finished powering up.

A sigil glowed to life on the armrest of her seat. She tapped it, flinching when a harness shot out, securing her into the seat.

"Ardalon halp Sa-shuh," he insisted, his voice tense.

She shook her head to tell him that no, he didn't really help her like he'd promised. "Sasha helps Sasha," she answered.

She'd been on her own for a long time. Trusting people, depending on them, had only ever gotten her hurt. At least if she fracked something up, she only had herself to blame.

The escape pod started to detach from the wall, and she glanced at the camera feeds on the corners of the screen. Suited-up birds were advancing on her with guns.

She turned back to the feed of Ardalon and the bird boss beside him, and she leveled him with a look full of hate and hurt.

Was he just the distraction while reinforcements were sent? What had been the point of trying to gain her trust?

Something inside of her twinged. She didn't have time for hurt feelings. Not with enemy fire coming her way and a cage waiting for her, or worse, if she got caught again. Assuming that they didn't just kill her this time.

Yeah, flying in alien tech is scary as hell, but I'd rather die by my own two stupid hands than get caught up again by slavers.

Ardalon's eyes were full of some emotion that she simply didn't have the time to decipher, but the vindictive gleam of delight in the bird boss's face was easy to read.

She gave the bird a great big smile full of teeth, and flipped him the middle finger while she punched the last button that started the auto-landing.

The escape pod took off, and, for better or worse, she was flying once more.

The hangar disappeared, and then she was in the big black. Distant stars, unfamiliar to her, twinkled.

The planet she'd just barely caught a glimpse of before looked so much like the pictures she'd seen of Earth that, for a moment, her heart stuttered and a heavy weight crushed her chest. It was grief and longing. Homesickness for a planet she'd never even stepped foot on.

This planet was a swirl of blue ocean and the white clouds interspersed with the green and brown or multicolored landmasses. Blue water and green plants meant it was life sustaining and clouds meant it had an atmosphere she could probably breathe.

She hoped that the air wasn't ninety percent methane or something equally as lethal to her lungs.

She'd never felt lightheaded or sick on the ship. Sasha assumed that if she could breathe the ship's air just fine and they were headed for this planet, then it stood to reason that its atmosphere was probably safe for her as well.

Even if it wasn't a perfect match, her nanos would smooth out any minor irregularities.

Only one way to find out.

As the planet grew closer, she could see the clustering of a sprawling city. Artificial lights and the dark gray of buildings and roads loomed before her. She angled the ship away from it and pointed herself to a denser patch of green. She'd had enough of aliens. It was probably best to land somewhere more rural until she figured out her next steps.

As she flipped to the back of the instruction manual to take a look at the pod's auto-landing procedures, the view screen turned opaque again.

A brown reptilian alien with tan ridges around his eyes and forehead barked something at her in alien speak.

"Rawestan! Ev hewayek sînorkirî ye!" the angry-looking reptile yelled at her.

She looked at him and blinked before shrugging her shoulders and throwing her hands up in frustration, instruction manual flapping. "Sorry, I don't speak alien."

His brows furrowed, the ridges on his forehead rippling with the movement, and he glanced off screen for a moment before looking back at her and giving her a good long look, up and down.

They stared at one another in mutual curiosity. She blinked at him and let him look his fill.

"Tevgera agirbestê!" he ordered.

"Sorry, but I *still* don't speak alien," she told him flippantly as she started flicking switches on the dashboard, activating the ship's landing mechanism.

The planet loomed closer, a new part of the display flickering to life as some sort of proximity and altitude alert appeared at the top of the screen but she didn't know which characters were numbers and which were letters.

The crenelations on his brow stood up on end and she could see now that they were actually fleshy covered spines.

The alien on her screen went into what she guessed was full-on alarm mode, because he stood up from his seat and started shouting something to someone else offscreen.

Ignoring the irritated alien, she tried to see around the frosted glass of his projected video feed. She'd have really appreciated having the full view of her windshield while she was trying to make sure she didn't end up in the ocean or something.

Red flashed on her screen, and a little video popped up showing a missile that had been launched her way.

"What the actual frack?" she yelled at the startled alien as she waved a hand toward the video feed he probably couldn't see. "You're shooting at me?"

She shouldn't be surprised, and yet she was.

Stolen, caged, almost eaten, betrayed, and now shot at by a planet full of lizardmen. Ugh!

"Aliens suck!"

The escape pod seemed to notice the missile because it did a barrel roll. Gorge rose into her throat from the topsy turvy maneuver as her stomach flipped up into her heart. The missile sailed past her. A glance at her feeds showed that it merely course corrected, looping around.

It looked as if it had some sort of target locking mechanism built into it.

Teeth gritted, she suffered through another dodge. It took the pod a lot of loops and rolls to ditch the missile, and the angle of descent was completely off, now.

She was coming in too steep and way too fast. Sensors and alarms blared. At around thirty thousand feet, the missiles peeled off her ass and disappeared.

Either they'd changed their minds about shooting her down, or they didn't want to hit her when she was flying this low. That was a big city she was passing.

Saved by civilians.

If they blasted her apart now, this low in the sky, her debris would do a lot of damage because it wouldn't burn up in the atmosphere.

She wasn't high enough to celebrate, though. They'd left her escape pod no time to course correct or change its angle.

She was coming down hot and quick, and it wasn't going to be pretty. Mentally, she said her peace.

Dying in a crash landing on my harrowing escape to freedom is probably a thousand times better than whatever fresh hell those birds had planned for me.

It had only taken her translator about five days to work out the nuances of the word pleasure house.

"No fracking way. I'm no one's slave or pet."

The pod shuddered, and something popped. Flames licked up the sides of the pod's viewport as it burned through the sky.

Closing her eyes and saying a quick prayer, she forced her body to go limp as she waited for impact.

CHAPTER FIVE

ARDALON

The Raxion officer on Ardalon's screen was pissed, his corona fully frilled with dangerous fluorescent yellow spots that bloomed along the thin membrane of the skin between the spines. He must have been truly enraged to have summoned up that much venom into his system.

If looks could kill, then I'd be dead on the spot. Good thing I'm not within spitting distance.

The man's eyes bore into his with a seething, righteous fury.

"Let me get this straight," the Raxion General hissed at him over the audiovisual link, "a weaponized ship comes into *my* air space and lands on *my* territory without *my* permission and you want me to do what exactly?"

"Nothing," Ardalon repeated.

"Yes that's what I thought you said. Care to explain this situation to me? Because my border control agents here are at a complete loss, and they're raving about an unidentified species who doesn't understand Common. Meanwhile, I have reports pouring in from all across the capital. Our audio lines are jammed solid with complaints, and your little ship crash landed in a protected part of the jungle and started a fire. So let me get this straight. The direct order from the United Council on this matter of national security is for the Raxian military force on El'bazahara to do... nothing."

Ardalon bit back the sigh that threatened to escape and adjusted his posture to something that he hoped hinted at him being cool, calm, and collected, even though he felt the exact opposite.

His mission and career were on the line, as well as Sa-shuh's life and safety.

He downloaded the recording of her trying to land a fighter ship onto a Raxion-controlled planet while evading their heat seeking missiles. His stomach was in knots, and his tongue felt thick and stupid.

If she's dead...

Shaking his head, he put those thoughts aside. Until he had confirmation of a fatality he had to keep working under the assumption that she'd survived.

He settled for clearing his throat, instead. "The United Council has placed jurisdiction of this delicate matter into my hands. I will take a small landing shuttle to the surface and assess the damage at the crash site. The fire will be mitigated and the ecosystem will be repaired with terraforming equipment. The Council will provide the equipment and manpower, of course."

The general's frills flattened to his head, and he looked marginally less pissed. It was as much of an improvement as Ardalon was going to get.

"How kind of the Council," the general condescended with narrow, slitted eyes.

Ardalon was quiet for a moment as they stared at one another over the visual link. Neither of them wanted to be the first to budge.

"And my border agent's report and recordings of this alien

creature, I suppose everyone would be relieved if this information was to somehow… get lost?" the General asked.

Ardalon fought to keep his eyes from tightening, struggling to retain his ambivalent expression.

"Apologies, General, however I am unable to either confirm or deny the existence of a new unidentified species at this time. Council business, I am sure you understand. The ship debris will be collected and the ecosystem repaired back to its pre-existing condition. If you happen to have a paperwork issue… well, those things do happen. I am certain that a male of your esteemed position has far more important things to concern yourself with than a stolen ship that crashed due to an autopilot malfunction into a remote, uninhabited area outside of your capital. Seeing as how no civilians were harmed and no property was damaged, I mean."

The general blinked nictitating membranes at him, the Raxion version of a cutting glare.

Sighing, the general leaned one elbow against his paperwork-strewn desk and cocked his head. "The Council has full permission to retrieve its detritus and play housekeeping at their expense. I would suggest you hurry, though, Agent Bavara, because your little ship crashed just two clicks from Lowdera territory, and it's nesting season. That fire is bound to stir some things up… if the crash didn't piss them off already."

Ardalon gave the General a small nod and a proper, military salute. "The Council thanks you for your full cooperation."

The General shook his head and muttered something unintelligible but derisive about politics as the link to the feed cut out.

Ardalon exited the command tower and made his way to the loading bay where the UC Peacekeepers were taking inventory and seeing what was salvageable.

Approaching his best officer, Ardalon addressed the male he trusted the most. "Davi, I want you to oversee this mess in my absence. Keep the Diggi crew locked up tight and get this ship back to normal. You've rounded up all of the animals?"

Davi glanced down at his clipboard, skimming a finger over the papers. "The only missing animal so far is the comoros, but we lost a few of the smaller ones. Their bodies were tagged and bagged as evidence and put into cold storage. I've got a few more hours of inventorying to do here. The guns weren't on the ship's manifest, nor is there any record of this alien of yours, and we've got some stolen medical equipment. Serial numbers popped right up when we ran them."

Ardalon nodded, glancing around the cargo bay, watching his team working. "Right. Looks like the Diggi were doing a lot more than just hustling exotics. Good work. Let me know when the terraforming equipment and the team arrives. Until then, I'm going planetside. Keep the first mate in seclusion in his rooms. The captain stays in interrogation. Keep on him. I want two armed officers on them both at all times. If either one tries anything, stun them. The rest of the crew can stay holed up in either the brig or the infirmary. If they're not dying, then they can wait for medical."

Davi scribbled notes in the margins of his copy of the ship's manifest. "Can do, boss. Oh, hey, before I forget, the captain's been hollering something fierce. Says he has rights and he's demanding to speak to a legal team. What do you want me to tell him?"

That made Ardalon grin. His teeth flashed in a fanged smile as he glanced back up at Davi. "Let him stew. He voided his legal rights when he got caught enslaving a sentient. I'll be back in a few hours. Hold this down until I get back, and then I'll debrief everyone and we'll go from there."

Davi nodded, going back to his notetaking as he slid the lid off another crate to finish inventorying the pirates' stolen cargo and contraband.

Heading over to a small, armed exploration pod, Ardalon climbed up the loading stairs two at a time. His heart beat wildly in his chest, adrenaline surging as he climbed in and strapped into the chair, going through the launching sequence.

His sense of smell was heightened as his body slipped into hunting mode. The engines thrummed to life and revved beneath his feet.

The officers in the cargo bay tapped the sides of their helmets. Once they were all ensconced in their space suits, someone opened up his bay's door and he eased the Starcraft forward, taking off toward El'bazahara and the blinking red light that indicated the location of the crash site on his map.

Ardalon navigated his ship away from the capital, marveling at it even as he steered away. The city was breathtaking from a distance, a hazardous mishmash of towering buildings that tried to dwarf one another in some twisted competition for height.

Some of the buildings had been added onto so much that each succeeding floor was wider than the one before it until eventually the buildings crowded the streets, nearly touching at the top, creating a network of dark streets lit by bioluminescent tubes that cast an eerie glow, day and night.

All of the horrors that come with an overcrowded city—the poverty and crime and disease—were still better than the alternative.

That jungle was filled with danger.

Flying low, the heat from the engines rustling the tops of the trees, he found the crash site much quicker than he'd first anticipated. All he had to do was fly down to the coordinates and trace the smoldering path of wreckage that Sa-shuh's pod had made as it crashed and burned through the dense jungle of the planet's outer regions.

She'd landed far beyond the walled-off city limits.

Dense foliage and vine wrapped trees withered and burned

and there were great, long scratch marks in the soft ground below.

A few swipes through the navigational tool sent a copy of the map and the pin points of interest to his wrist com. He tagged the trail that the escape pod had carved through the earth in its rocky descent. The clean up crew could use it afterward to assist them in their repairs to the planet's native flora.

Setting his borrowed starcraft down in a small clearing where the fire had already burned itself out, he landed.

Ardalon unclicked his harness and stood. Rooting through a netted off emergency supply bin granted him a bag filled with water, nonperishable ration bars, a portable light, and a wicked-looking utility knife.

One side of the blade was smooth and sharp, the other side serrated and notched. It looked like it could cut down vines and branches with ease.

He slipped the knife and its holster onto his blaster belt and slung the pack onto his back.

It was overkill, probably, but on a dangerous planet like El'bazahara, it paid to be over prepared and cautious. There was a reason why the planet's citizens resided in their far too small walled-off metropolis.

It was easier to simply continue building upward and add taller skyscrapers than it was to try to reclaim more of the surrounding jungle from the beasts that called it home. If Lowdera were the biggest threat that they faced today, then he would consider himself a lucky male and thank the fates.

His stomach twisted at the thought of Sa-shuh out there, alone and injured in the jungle somewhere with predators chasing down her scent.

Worrying wasn't going to help, though. It would just serve to distract him.

Regardless of the fact that she seemed to be a fierce and

capable warrior, one person all alone would never survive even a single night out in these wilds. He needed her alive and well for the next stage of his mission.

Poaching and the buying and selling of exotic, endangered species was bad enough, but slavery of sentients was a capital offense.

For once, they'd finally found an iron clad way to root out the corruption within the Kursh government. The public outrage alone would ensure that Senator Brodyn never stepped foot inside a hallowed hall again, even if he managed to wiggle and bribe his way out of the emperor's prison.

Armed, outfitted, and as ready as he could be, he opened up the ship's hatch and climbed out, closing it tight behind him.

Eyes sweeping the smoldering clearing, he took silent steps through the path of the wreckage and made his way toward Sa-shuh's stolen ship.

Long gouges had been carved into the soft, loam-covered jungle floor.

Tall trees that were older than him had been cracked in half and ripped to shreds. Small plants that had never seen unfiltered sunlight before withered and died, their edges browned and curling under from the direct sunlight and heat.

The animals in the area seemed to have abandoned this small portion of the jungle for less dangerous territory, but it was only a matter of time before the larger, fiercer, and more curious ones returned.

The jungle was silent and eerie, but the lack of sound only exacerbated his sense of unease. There should have been the trilling of birds and howling of tree climbers, or at least the dull thrum of buzzing insects. Instead, the jungle held her breath as she waited to see what had changed.

His team was probably right, it was foolish to insist on coming into such dangerous territory alone, but he found himself unable to resist the urge to hunt her down, roll her distinctive scent through his sinuses, and track her through the wild.

It was a throwback to old urges from when his people lived in huts and moved with the herds. The urge to slink through tall grass, patient and watchful, until the right moment to pounce presented itself, was too strong, still buried deep beneath the veneer of society and refinement that covered up such base instincts.

His fangs pricked against his bottom lip, and again, his self control slipped. He blamed it on watching her run through the halls while being chased by the comoros.

On being helpless to intervene while she was shot at and assaulted. In the stark terror that gripped him when she managed to not only steal a ship and work it, but then succeeded in flying it, only to watch her get shot down and crash.

There was no doubt within him that her ship would not have crashed if the Raxion's hadn't sought to bring her down for violating their airspace. A fierce warrior, intelligent, brave, and strong.

Wonderful traits for a mate and mother to your cubs to possess, his subconscious teased him.

He shoved those intrusive thoughts down deep and tried to focus.

Using his wrist com, he dropped coordinate pins on his hologram projected map, marking the locations of various bits of ship debris that would need to be collected. His nostrils flared, eager to sift through the layers of scents as he tracked his prey, but there was only the acrid stench of fire and burning. It smothered everything with an oppressive cloud of pollution.

The path of debris grew easier to spot, and the stench of burning metal and plasticine thickened as he stumbled, finally, upon the wreckage of her stolen ship.

The pod itself teeter-tottered halfway over a gorge. Just a little bit further and it would have dropped below into a chasm.

He picked his way over to the edge and peered down. It was a long drop with a rushing river below, one that would drown whatever had managed to survive the fall and the outcroppings of sharp rocks that bordered the water's edge.

Sa-shuh's scent teased him. She'd been here, although her scent trail was faded, old, and patchy. It made him furious that the Raxion's had delayed him for hours while they barked their complaints up their chain of command.

Did she stumble over the edge, concussed and injured while I waited to speak to the general? Did she survive the crash just to tumble off this gorge and drown in the tumultuous waters below?

If so, then there was little he could do at this point. His stomach felt heavy as he considered it. He turned back toward the pod, eager to be proven wrong.

Her scent trail was thicker here where it was less exposed to the elements. The smell of salt and metal pulled at his attention. Crouching down, he eyed a few drops of something red that splattered in a line along the landing stairs.

The door to the ship had been left open, but he couldn't see any gouges in the metal that would hint that clawed animals had pried it open.

She was alive, or she had been when she'd exited the pod, and she was injured, because he suspected that those red drops were her blood. It appeared that she left the pod of her own accord, a discovery that eased the tension in his gut.

Leaning down, he pulled the scent of her blood into his nostrils.

He wasn't the only thing that was going to be hunting her if she was injured and leaving such an obvious scent trail through this jungle.

Swiping a handkerchief through the drying dots, he picked up as much of her blood and scent as he could and pressed it to his nose for just a moment before he folded it and tucked it away inside a pocket.

The urge to hurry was there, but he managed to wrangle his emotions and make careful, silent progress forward instead. He followed her scent through the foliage, his com marking his path as he moved. A glance at the map confirmed that he was headed down the ridge toward the outlet for the river.

He was proud of her survival instincts, but at the same time he cursed her naive foolishness.

Water was necessary, and learning how to find it was an essential survival skill, but watering holes weren't safe places at night and the sun was already beginning its descent past its zenith.

The jungle may have been shocked into silence, for now, but it was unlikely to stay that way for long. And if she was headed toward the river, then her chance of encountering predators just rose steeply. Ardalon increased the speed of his steps and abandoned his pursuit of silence as he followed her scent trail and picked his way down to the tributary.

Blaster raised and ready, he paused at the edge of the trees and surveyed the stretch of land around him.

The lake was deceptively pretty. Large rocks, which had probably cracked off of the canyon above, littered the shore in between giant, green ferns. Banya trees with their dense, green leaves grew tall and strong, shading the edges of the water. Sunlight filtered through the breaks in the foliage and sparkled on the gently rippling blue-green water. The crashing sound of the waterfall that cascaded down from the cliff above filled the area with a noise that echoed.

His eyes and blaster swept across the space, but the absence of any obvious threats didn't alleviate the prickling on the back of his neck. He wouldn't feel safe until he had her back on his ship.

He knew better than to assume that there wasn't any danger here just because his eyes couldn't see it. The universe was vast, and nature had created many lethal marvels across its several inhabitable planets and moons.

Her scent trail led him to a large rock at the water's edge where he found her curious clothing and boots. Her stolen blaster was here too.

The unitard she'd worn had been washed, he suspected. It was wet, the smell that clung to it faint, and it was clear that it had been laid out in a patch of sunny rock to dry. Her bizarre-looking footwear sat next to it. They were far heavier than he thought they probably should be.

Is this how she stood in the opened cargo bay when everything else that wasn't bolted down got sucked out into space?

He'd seen the strange contraption that she'd affixed to her lower face. A sort of breathing apparatus, he'd assumed at the time. It was foolish to assume that her people were less advanced than his own just because she was different.

She may not speak our language or read our writing, but clearly her own society is just as advanced as ours if they have achieved space exploration.

Yet she didn't appear to know any better than to wash the masking scent of filth from her clothing while deep in unfamiliar, dangerous territory. She would be easier to track without the stink of filth or dirt to mask her unique scent.

It was a juxtaposition of strange, conflicting facts.

Advanced enough to explore the stars, but clearly not used to being anything less than the most apex of predators if she didn't know how to avoid them.

The memory of her blunted teeth and nails disturbed him. He looked down, staring at her blaster which she'd left out of reach.

His stomach clenched in fear for her and he wanted nothing more than to shake and shout at her that she needed to be more careful.

What if I hadn't found her?

Instead, he settled for picking the suit up and pressing it to his face. He got just a faint whiff of faded blood and sweat. The garment was cleaner after its washing.

Once she began to perspire, her scent would radiate. She would unknowingly broadcast her presence to every predator with a keen nose and a thirst for blood for the next klick in every direction.

A disturbance in the sounds around him made him whip his head up from where he was bent over Sa-shuh's clothing. He scanned his surroundings, his blaster raised, as he cleared his back and swept from left to right, and then he saw her.

Long brown hair, made darker from the water, clinging to creamy, furless skin. Her wet mane was plastered to her body from the force of the crashing waterfall. It clung in wet tendrils to her neck, shoulders, and face.

Full, heavy breasts tipped with dusky pink nipples pebbled from the cold water. He was entranced by their swinging movement as she raised her arms above her head and slicked her wet mane away from her face. Her bulky suit had masked her true shape.

There was no question of her adulthood now. Her nipped-in waist flared out to wide hips, and a triangular tuft of brown fur covered the details of her sex.

As she turned, he saw the rounded globes of her ass, her lack of a tail impossible to miss.

The moment that she spotted him perched on the rock near her clothing and blaster, she gasped and ducked her naked body back under the water. He'd offended her sense of modesty by watching her bathe and glancing at her naked form.

His ears twitched in amusement. Her safety meant more to him than her comfort. The urge to haul her over his lap and spank sense into her crossed his mind for a moment. There was a defiant streak in her that his baser urges longed to dominate.

Those thoughts are wildly inappropriate.

He shoved them back down and settled for perching on the rock with her garments. If she wished to conceal her nudity, then she would need to approach him first. He schooled his face into an impassive mask and eyed her calmly as if he saw naked, vulnerable alien females all day long.

The strips of fur that shaded her eyes furrowed, a line creasing between her eyes. Her jaw clenched, grinding. She was clearly mad at him.

He brought her suit back up to his nose and made a show of sniffing it as he stared her down from the corners of his eyes, a blankness over his face. Her cheeks pinkened, the blush of redness spreading down her neck and collarbone.

How deep does that color go?

He wanted to lick her all over and find out what other parts of her body changed color.

"Ardalon," she threatened in a gravelly voice. "Givmee bak mahy klohthz," she growled as she covered her chest with one arm and waded forward through the water to him.

Angry, embarrassed, unarmed, and exceedingly vulnerable right now, and yet she still strode forward toward him, confident and sure of herself in this situation.

He admired that spark of defiance within her. As if she knew on some instinctual level that he would not harm her.

His pride swelled at that, even though he was angry with her too.

He was a male with a well-formed sense of duty and honor and the knowledge of what was right, but others would find it easy to ignore her pitiful protests. To hurt her. The thought of that made him angry.

She seemed to have no natural defenses. Stripped of her weapon, she would be an easy conquest. With his teeth at her throat and his claws digging into her arms, he knew that he could wrestle her to the ground and slide into her moist, warm core with very little struggle.

The thought of doing such a thing to her disgusted and excited him all at once.

Whether it was the idea that he was capable of such depraved thoughts, or that he was lusting after a stranger, he wasn't certain.

Something in him wanted her. He'd never had such thoughts about a female before. Passing fancies and childhood crushes, yes. Short flings that fizzled out and ended mutually, of course. And he'd seen the inside of the brothel district more than once in his days as a young trainee at the academy, but this felt... different.

He liked that she was vulnerable, but feisty all at the same time. It made him want to pin her down and rut her into the dirt, then feed her buttered seed cakes and stroke his claws through her shiny, luscious mane while he told her the stories of his youth.

Viruk, she's going to be the death of me.

Tipping his head at her, he feigned ignorance as he crouched on the rock and pressed the bit of fabric that had once covered that junction between her thighs to his nose.

Hints of her musk and scent were still there. He teased it up through the fabric and rolled it over his tongue, dragging it deep into the recesses of his sinuses.

His dick started to swell and pressed, hard and uncomfortable, inside the confines of his pants. He'd have moaned at the torture of it, except that she was wading through the water and had stopped within arm's reach of him.

Her pink face was red now and he found it utterly delightful.

How deep can I make the shade go?

He wondered if he pressed his mouth between her thighs and licked, would she turn red as she came and shuddered on his face? They were both bipedal, and she wasn't too much smaller than him.

I think we would fit together.

One of her hands darted out, grabbing the sleeve of her garment. She tugged on it but he was enjoying teasing her, so he tightened his grip, careful to keep his claws from puncturing the fabric. He didn't wish to harm her or the garment, just annoy her. He had no desire to make her truly angry.

A thought crossed his mind that she had no qualms about shooting a couple of diggi's. A smarter male wouldn't taunt the angry female in front of him.

Too bad for her that my littermates never accused me of being terribly bright.

"Oh, I'm sorry, do you want this?" he teased her as he tightened his grip and pulled it back.

It didn't take too much effort on his part to win back the small ground that she'd gained. Her footing slipped against the slick algae-covered rocks of the lake floor, and he tugged her closer to him. If he lunged, then he could catch her up before she could fight him off.

His baser instincts screamed at him to do just that, to haul her forward and press his teeth to her throat and bite her, marking her as his. The thought was disconcerting, and he almost loosened his grip on her unitard.

She abandoned modesty, adding another hand to the mix, her breasts swaying with her struggle to pry the garment from his fingers while her eyes flashed at him with fire. It excited him instead of scaring him, which would probably have pissed her off further if she knew.

"Let goh, yoo big duhm jurk!" she hissed at him as she tugged with renewed vigor.

The words were an insult, he was certain. His ears flicked with delight.

He let his eyes drop down to her enticingly pink nipples before dropping them lower. Her stomach was flat and toned, and there were no marks of pregnancy on her skin to suggest she'd ever borne young before.

Unless her kind lay eggs? No, not with such prominent mammary glands. She's a mammal.

Although it was true that he wasn't a xenobiologist, he'd still stake money on it. *Brests*, she'd called them. It was his new favorite word. A thought struck him, sending a jolt of fire up his spine. If this was how large her mammaries were before her milk came in then...

His dick hardened further at the thought, his grip on her garment slackening. The idea of her lying naked, pink, and flushed on his bed with her belly swollen with his child slithered through his mind, haunting him.

She needed to get dressed before he lost all sense of self-control and dignity. Once he'd stopped actively fighting her, she wrestled the clothing away from him.

He stood from his crouch and extended a hand down to help her climb up onto the smooth rock. She glanced between him and the suit nervously. It was clear that she wished to dress, but she needed to clamber out of the water to do so.

I should be a gentleman and walk away, turn my back, and give her a moment of privacy.

Her face made a wide variety of movements that were unfamiliar to him before finally she sighed, rolling her eyes so he could see the whites go all around. *She's frustrated*, he thought, although she made no move to attack him, which didn't make him think that she was truly distressed by his voyeurism.

His movements were slow as he reached down and grabbed her by one arm, hauling her up onto the rock. She gasped, but only blinked at him. He let her go once her feet had found their purchase and he was certain she wouldn't tumble back in. He didn't want to see her get hurt.

The memory of the trail of blood that he'd followed hit him. He dug the blood-splattered handkerchief from his pocket and showed it to her.

"Where are you injured?" he asked as he pointed to the smears of red on the scrap of white fabric.

Her face bunched, and her nose scrunched up in disapproval. "Ooo, iz thut mahy bluhd?"

Taking advantage of her distraction, he skimmed his eyes over her naked figure. He couldn't see any mark of violence on her, and her bathing had showered away any evidence of an injury, but the blood was too mingled with her scent to be some other creature's.

How quickly does she heal? Fast. Perhaps that's why she has no natural defenses. Her evolution took a different path.

Shoving the handkerchief back into his pocket, he rubbed his hands up and down her limbs in a clinical manner, checking for injuries that weren't visible to his eye.

"Hey! Hands awf, miss-tur!" she shouted at him as he spun her around and lifted her wet mane off her shoulders.

Their inability to communicate in any meaningful way was infuriating.

He wanted to ask her why there was blood in the pod, ask her where she was hurt, and tell her that she could trust him because he planned to help her. But he couldn't do anything except pantomime and manhandle her. She hated it, he could tell, but her safety was more important to him than her comfort or dignity.

Sa-shuh's backside was plump and round, but free of wounds. He ran his hands all the way up her legs and ass and back, looking for broken bones, and then he speared his fingers through her hair while checking for any lacerations or contusions along her scalp.

Head wounds bled a lot more than others, and blows to the head could be more dangerous than they appeared at first.

She didn't seem overly confused or different than before, but he also didn't know her well enough to say that with any degree of absolute certainty. Her customs were strange, and her language made no sense to him.

How do I know that she's not spouting gibberish?

There wasn't anything hiding there in her mane, no gaping, bleeding wound. And for that, he was grateful, even when she turned in his arms and socked him right in the shoulder. Ardalon grunted at the force of the blow, smiling at her with his eyes.

He liked her fire. Her little sparks of temper that made him want to tame her even more. He grinned at her, not caring if it made him appear like a fool.

She looked at him, wary, as she edged away from him as much as the small rock would allow. He turned his gaze away from her naked, shapely legs as she slipped them into her clothing while he scanned their surroundings.

He'd let her naked body distract him from ensuring their safety.

It was enough of a jolt to pull him out of this playfulness, submerging him back into his training.

He shoved away his relief at finding her alive and unharmed. If he forgot where they were, then they were dead already. A breeze rustled through the leaves on the bushes and trees, and he scanned each one, looking for stalking predators, before moving on to the next.

It was a miracle that they hadn't been accosted yet.

The pod's crash landing, and then the subsequent fire, must have really scattered all the animals. He wasn't foolish enough to believe that this quiet would last much longer, however.

How much time has passed since she crashed? Since I landed? Too much.

The sunlight had grown more golden and dimmer as he hiked down to the lake and night was coming upon them sooner than he'd have liked.

He wondered if there was even enough time to make it back to where he'd landed. They could probably make it back to his ship if they ran for small portions and they didn't run into any predators, but he had a sneaking suspicion that while Sa-shuh was toned and fit, she wasn't going to be able to run as fast as him.

If the trek wasn't uphill, he'd just carry her, but they would likely make too much noise going up the hill if he had to carry her weight too. Especially in the dark. A portable light was only going to attract attention they didn't want. Mission parameters adjusted and decision made, he pulled up the holographic map on his com and scanned their surroundings.

There was a cave system here somewhere if he could just recall where he'd seen it before.

Sa-shuh made a high-pitched coo in his ear, a sound he'd never heard come from her before.

"Aww! Heez soh kyoot!"

Glancing up, he followed her line of sight. A small furry creature darted out of the brush and inched toward the water's edge. A yinooki, a harmless prey animal that lived in fallen, decaying trees and liked to eat plants.

But if prey animals were feeling safe enough to return to

their favored spots, then that meant that the predators weren't too far behind them if they weren't already there.

"Time to go," he said, nodding toward the animal and gesturing to her clunky boots.

Her brow scrunched at him, but then she leaned over and hopped in place on their flat-topped rock as she shoved one of her feet into a shoe. He grabbed her shoulder to steady her when she lost her balance and almost toppled back into the lake.

The yinooki edged toward the water, leaning down to sniff it while eying it warily, taking a long drink. The water exploded around the small creature as a baroon surged up onto the shore and snapped the creature up in its terrifying, reptilian teeth.

"Oh mahy gawd, wuht the frahk iz thut?" Sa-shuh yelled as she shoved her other foot in her boot and latched them closed. "Thet thing wuz enther withme?"

Once her hands were done with her boots, Ardalon scooped her blaster up and shoved it into her limp grip, then grabbed her under the armpit, hauling her over the large, flat rocks that jutted out of the water. He tugged her unprotesting form behind him as he landed them both on the shore, heading deeper into the jungle.

"I dohnt thingk wee shood goh in thair," she whispered at him in protest as they enter the dense foliage.

Turning to press one finger to her lips, he shushed her.

Her eyes were wide and startled, but he didn't have any words to calm her or put her at ease. They didn't speak the same language, and he didn't know how to pantomime that the local watering hole was actually more dangerous for them than the dense jungle.

At least in the jungle there were spots to hide in and trees to climb. Flat open spaces wouldn't help them outrun and dodge a pissed off lowdera mother protecting her clutch.

The herbivores weren't usually dangerous, but they were

enormous, and getting between a mother and her offspring could be lethal.

Her hand trembled in his as he led them through the dense, untraveled foliage. Her footsteps were clumsy. She didn't know how to walk silently or stalk, but picking her up and carrying her would only slow them down. The cave was about a klick and a half away and the sun was setting rapidly. Already, the warm, muggy air was cooling down.

Once the sun completely set and the moon rose, it would be cold, and he had no idea how resilient she was to temperature changes. She didn't have any fur to keep her warm, and the thin stretch material of her garment seemed flimsy.

He could only hope he hadn't doomed them both to failure with his insistent, instinctual need to be the only male around her until he'd claimed her.

If I'd brought an extraction team with me...

He shoved those thoughts aside. They would only be a distraction.

What's done is done. We just have to survive the night.

CHAPTER SIX

SASHA

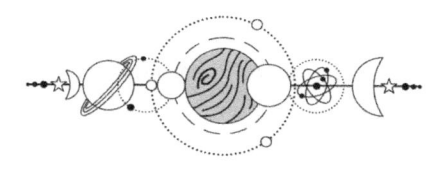

Sasha was still reeling from watching the adorable little rabbit-mouse get eaten.

Dinosaurs.

This crazy alien planet was inhabited by fracking dinosaurs.

The image of the creature's snapping jaws and the pained squeals of the poor little rabbit mouse still rang in her ears. She'd just gotten her own upfront and personal nature documentary as she'd watched that... that *thing* lunge out of the water, snapping up its dinner in one fell bite.

The thought that she'd just been in that water, that the dinosaur thing had been in there with her, made her brain thick, dumb, and stupid with fear.

Ardalon's tight grip pulling her through the maze of jungle foliage was a lifeline. The press of his warm, lightly furred forearm and the rough calluses of his fingers with the sharp little pricks of his claws as they dug into her while he pulled her sorry ass forward was the grounding force that brought her back to reality.

They were running for their lives, she realized.

If there was one dinosaur she could see, then there were

probably more that she couldn't. Snapping out of her fog, she put a little pep into her step and ran. He glanced back at her, and his expression looked... relieved? It was so hard to tell. The bridge of his nose was thick, the tip of it blunt and wide like a cat's. It made deciphering his expressions a real challenge.

Eager to prove that she wasn't dead weight, she pushed what little energy she had left into running, using her fear to let the adrenaline surge help her leap forward on steadier legs.

Ardalon jumped over a fallen, decaying tree, and she jumped too. The gentle burn in her thighs signaled that her nanos were working overtime to repair the damage of her run. There wouldn't be any lactic acid build up to make her stiff, and she wouldn't fatigue as easily as she would have without them.

The cuts and bumps and scrapes and broken arm she'd endured earlier from the crash had healed hours ago.

Ardalon made sharp left and right turns after glancing at his wrist and its floating holographic map a couple of times. She trusted that he knew where he was going. After seeing that dinosaur thing, she sure wasn't going to object to being hauled around.

Aiming for a rural space had seemed like a really good idea at the time. She'd wanted to avoid aliens, but now she understood why the citizens all seemed to live in a tiny walled-off city.

Animals were just so scarce on Alpha Centauri that it hadn't occurred to her there might be things more dangerous than alien people out there. It was incredibly dumb. This was a different world, with completely different species, ecosystems, languages, and cultures. She needed to stop thinking like she was still at home.

It was weird how seeing that dinosaur was what really hit it home for her.

She glanced up at Ardalon's back, watching the play of muscles in his shoulders as he ran.

You'd think that the big, hulking cat man dragging me through an alien jungle or the giant fracking bird men who stuck me in a cage would have sunk that reality home for me, but nope, it was the dinosaur that really did it. I am never going home again.

The weight of this revelation brought tears into her eyes, making running even harder as her vision blurred.

I'm never going home again.

Her foot hit a jutting root and she tripped, going down hard with their momentum.

Claws raked deep furrows into her arm as she slipped through his tight grip. Her jaw snapped shut and her teeth tore into her cheek, cutting it open.

Blood filled her mouth with its coppery metallic taste from where she'd bitten herself, and she fought the rising urge to hurl up bile from her empty stomach.

Ardalon doubled back at her shriek, hauling her up off the mossy, leaf-strewn jungle floor. He threw her over his shoulder and started running again.

The world being upside-down as she was jostled about with a shoulder in her stomach made her queasiness worse, but it was the glittering green eyes and spittle-covered teeth of a two legged dinosaur silently chasing them down through the brush that made her gasp and swallow the gorge back down.

She was thankful that she'd kept the gun in her numb grip. Ardalon's arm clasped her thighs tight against his chest. She dropped the fistful of his shirt that she had in her hand and dialed up the charge on her gun.

Five dots all the way, baby. No way I'm getting eaten by dinosaurs tonight. I did not survive two crash landings and a fracking cage just to get eaten by motherfracking dinosaurs.

Aiming while slung over a shoulder was difficult, so she levered herself up as best as she could, pointing the gun at the dinosaur. Her laser hit it right in the dead center of its gaping mouth just as it roared at them, leaping forward.

Ardalon cut to the right, and she scanned the trees and brush behind them, looking for more threats. The jungle was quiet, and all she could hear was their heavy breathing as he ran with her over his shoulder. The laser guns were fairly quiet, at least, and she hoped that the sound of their shooting didn't drive more predators toward them.

Ardalon's steps were less noisy than anything his size had any right to be as he carried her through the jungle.

He weaved left, jumping them across a small, rock-strewn stream. A rustle in a nearby tree pulled her eyes up. A giant coiled snake-like creature with two heads writhed on a low hanging branch. She aimed and fired off two shots at it in rapid succession. The creature's left head exploded, and it hung limp, dangling from its branch.

Not today!

Hysteria bubbled up inside of her. The academy had never trained them for alien dinosaurs and anaconda-sized snakes that hung out in trees.

If I ever manage to find my way back home, I'll be sure to give them a piece of my mind and let them know we're woefully unprepared for interdimensional travel.

The foliage thinned around them, and then they we're out of the treeline completely. She twisted on his shoulder, trying to see why they'd slowed down. His hands grabbed her hips and butt, his touch all business as he pulled her off his shoulder and set her on her feet. He pointed her at the jungle and raised her arm with the gun.

Cover his ass with suppressive fire, got it.

She nodded, to let him know that she understood. "Yeah, cool, roger that."

Sasha watched him from the corner of her eye as he clambered up the side of the rocky cliff and disappeared from sight. Sweat dripped down the back of her neck and beaded up on her forehead. It cooled quickly in the rapidly dropping temperatures.

She stunk again already. A bath had helped immensely to wash the dirt and grime of the last week off of her, but their mad dash through the jungle had wrecked her again. Her thoughts drifted back to the lurking threat she hadn't been aware of during her soak and frolic in the river-fed lake.

You won't catch me dipping a toe into any large body of water here ever again.

Leaves rustled up ahead, and she trained her gun on it. She was concentrating so hard that Ardalon's grip on her shoulder startled her until she nearly pulled the trigger on her gun in reflex like a rookie.

"Vî alî," he told her in that guttural, growly alien language of his. "Min xanî me dît."

She didn't know what he was saying, but the tugs on her elbow meant that whatever he'd been looking for, he'd found, and he wanted her to follow him. They climbed up the rocky path together and she was careful of her footing while also constantly checking their six, making sure that nothing was creeping up behind them.

Ardalon led her to a cave and practically shoved her inside.

She turned to glance at him when she didn't hear him following. There was grunting and scraping and the sound of rock sliding over rock, and then she saw that he was shouldering an enormous stone into the mouth of the cave.

Her eyes widened as she watched him. That rock must have weighed a ton, and he moved it like it was little more than an inconvenience. Once it was nearly in place at the opening, he slipped inside the crevice and maneuvered it to block the entrance.

It wasn't a perfect fit, but it did cover up the vast majority of the opening in the hill. The light dimmed until she could barely see anything at all as he blocked them in. It made her wonder just how strong he was, exactly. He'd hauled her up out of the water like she was a ragdoll, and then he'd picked her up and thrown her over his shoulder like a sack of potatoes.

Now he was shoving boulders around.

Damn, that's hot.

Suddenly she realized that she'd been alone in space for a long, long time. Too long. Her interest was piqued, for an alien, and it disturbed her that she wasn't bothered by how different and strange he looked.

We're more alike than not.

The heat that wrapped around her wrist meant that her nanos were repairing her scratches. She glanced down at the mark, her eyes tracing over the lacerations in her forearm.

Blood dripped down her arm, beading up on the bony protuberance of her wrist before dropping off, splattering on the dirt floor of the cave. It was warm as it dripped down her chilled arm, staining the sleeve of her suit as it spread. The bleeding slowed, and then stopped.

Boy, his nails are sharp. Okay, not nails. Face it, girl, those are claws. He has claws. He really is like a cat. How did I not see that he has claws before? Maybe they're retractable. It would get annoying to have sharp claws getting constantly in your way all the time. Like when trying to put on pants or wipe your butt or write your grocery list or while you're shooting a gun. So yeah, retractable claws...

It made sense.

Ardalon stopped fussing with the makeshift door and walked over to her. She could hear his footsteps on the uneven ground as he scattered pebbles, leaves, and various biological detritus with each step.

The cave stunk, like something used to live in it, but it was a musty and vague scent, as if whatever had dwelled there was long gone. She didn't think that Ardalon would have stuck them in a cave with a prehistoric, alien version of a cave bear, or something equally as frightening, hiding in the back. There was rustling, then a thump, and a moment later a beam of light shone, lighting up the cave.

"Oh, thank God, you have a flashlight," she sighed. She knew that he didn't understand her, but it still felt nice to talk to him.

The light was dim and small, and the beam hurt her eyes when he flashed it at her. She winced and closed them. When the light shifted away, she opened them again to find him assessing her.

He was shining the light up and down her body. It stopped when he got to her left arm. She looked down and groaned when she saw the state of her shredded sleeve.

Aww, shit. My suit isn't easy to cut or rip. How sharp are those things?

The fibers were reinforced, and its inner layer was insulated. Blood stained the torn cloth. His hands were gentle as he rolled her sleeve up to expose the already healed skin. His claws must not have gotten her too deep when she tripped and ripped her arm out of his grasp if it had healed already.

"It's okay. You didn't hurt me. Not really. I'm fine, I mean," she reassured him.

Ardalon rubbed at the crusted blood until it flaked off, showing the pristine skin underneath. The pads of his fingers were rough and thick against her skin. Her breathing slowed, evening out from its heavy pants as she recovered from their dash through the jungle.

As the adrenaline rush faded and the nanos in her blood and tissue went back into stasis, she felt herself start to tremble.

The soft circles he was rubbing along her wrist stopped, and his hand withdrew from her. She glanced up at him, but there wasn't enough light to see him with. He was the one with the light and currently it was trained on her. She got the feeling that he thought she was scared of him, though. Licking her lips, she struggled to explain it with their limited ways of communication.

He couldn't understand her and they hadn't had nearly enough time together to learn how to talk to one another. This Tarzan meets Jane-type speech was getting old, fast.

Body language is universal, though right? Even though he's an alien?

Stepping into Ardalon's personal space, she threw her arms around him in an enveloping hug. He tensed for just a moment before finally relaxing, and then his arms were around her too as he pulled her in tighter into his chest.

She buried her face in the warm, soft velvet that covered his chest. His shirt had slipped, and he smelled warm, musky, and male. Something tense inside of her relaxed. After so much solitude she was more touch starved than she'd thought.

She took a deep, shuddering breath and was surprised at the hot prick of tears in her eyes again. She wasn't a crier, but it had been a really shitty week. The thought made her laugh just a little.

His hands dipped to the small of her waist as he held her tight. It felt good after living completely alone for over three months, being stuck in a tiny ship, and then shoved into a cage before being chased by monsters that wanted to kill and eat her.

The hug was kind and comforting. His heart beat a steady thump against her ear as she pressed the side of her face into his chest. She forgave him for not busting her out of that zoo earlier since he'd just saved her life.

"Ardalon help Sasha," she told him. It was the only way she knew how to tell him that she understood that he didn't mean to hurt her, that she was fine, that she'd healed. She was alive and thankful.

"Ardalon halp Sa-shuh," he repeated in his growly, staccato voice.

His breath tickled the fine hairs along her forehead, and the moment stretched a little too long, becoming awkward. Her grip was the first to slacken, but then he dropped his arms from around her as she stepped back to put a little distance between them. She didn't know what sort of societal rules these aliens had.

It didn't seem like he minded it, though, so she guessed that hugging after a near-death experience was okay.

There was a rustling and then he pressed something solid but springy into her hands. She glanced down at it, not that she could really see what it was since he still had the light.

"Uh... thanks?" she hazarded as she tried to figure out what it was by feel alone.

He growled at her, that deep rumbly noise that he'd made before.

She thought it was his version of a chuckle. It sounded menacing, especially in the dark, where she couldn't see him. The hairs on the back of her neck stood up on end, warning her that she was near a predator, even though she knew that it was stupid. He wouldn't have risked his hide to come and save her sorry ass if he was just going to murder her in a cave.

The memory of sharp claws sliding through her skin made her shiver.

It's just cold in here. Don't be dumb.

Squashing the instinctual fear back down, she moved away, forcing herself to go slowly until she found a part of the cave that wasn't littered with crunchy leaves—or worse—and sat.

She squished the thing in her hand, feeling it, but she had no idea what it was. It felt sort of like a water balloon, except it was slightly firmer and there was an odd bump in one spot.

"Okay..." she muttered as she turned it over with her hands and stared up at him in confusion.

Ardalon propped the flashlight up on a rock and sat down next to her, and she could see a little now that the light was shining between them.

He took the object back from her and bit off the little nub with his teeth, palming the bitten-off top, before carefully placing it back into her hands. He pantomimed raising it to his face. She looked at him with a skeptical expression, but raised it to her face. A bit of water splashed over the now exposed rim, wetting her fingers.

Oh, man, it's the alien version of a water bottle, and he must think I'm an utter moron.

She put the opening of the water globe in her mouth and drank. It shrank in her hand as she tipped it back and swallowed. After drinking half of it down, she handed it back to him. He drank the rest of it until the orb was as small as her palm. He put the shrunken container back into the backpack.

A foil-wrapped packet was next. He pulled two from the bag, unwrapped one and handed it to her, then opened the other and took a large bite. She stared down at the nondescript brown bar.

It looked and smelled vaguely like a protein bar, although the aroma of its particular blend of metallic vitamins and minerals was foreign to her. Her stomach growled at the sight of it, even though it looked as bland as it probably tasted.

Still, after a week of alien rabbit food she wasn't going to be picky.

Taking a bite of it, she chewed, surprised that it was softer than she'd expected, and the flavor wasn't terrible. It was a bit chalky and minerally, but there was a sweet and salty edge to it that made it tolerable. Before her stomach was truly satisfied, the protein bar was gone.

The silver foil wrapper crinkled in her hand as she turned it over, studying it. Their writing was so bizarre to her, but then again, human languages varied too. If you'd handed her a text written in arabic she wouldn't have been able to read that either.

It didn't escape her notice that the protein bar had clearly been mass produced by a machine.

While she hadn't gotten to see very much of the alien city that she'd flown over while she was a little busy dodging warheads, she did notice that their buildings were quite tall.

It was a little reminiscent of old world New York City photos she'd seen in her ancient cities and ruins class. It was a radioactive wasteland now, but at one point it had been one of the most populated cities in the United States. It was all vastly different from her subterranean life on Alpha Centauri.

Handing the crinkled wrapper back to Ardalon, he shoved the garbage back into his bag. It was ecologically sensitive of him to pick up his trash and carry it back out, leaving nothing behind but footsteps.

She realized that she was feeling a bit delirious now from the constant ups and downs of the past few hours.

"Got any playing cards in there?" she asked him with a lopsided grin and a quirked brow, even though she knew the answer was a no.

Not like she'd have been able to read them or understand the rules of any game he might know. They could scratch in the dirt and play tic-tac-toe, she supposed.

Except that the sun must have been rapidly setting because the cracks of light that managed to sneak around the slivers of empty space between their boulder door and the cave opening had grown dim, and the little flashlight barely illuminated the immediate area around it.

A high pitched screeching outside made her inhale sharply, her back going ramrod stiff as some primordial fear response drove all higher thought from her mind.

Run, hide, fight.

Ardalon's arm reached out, wrapping around her and tugging her firmly into his side as he pulled her down with him until they were lying flat on the leaf covered dirt floor.

He clicked the flashlight off and let the darkness wrap around them. He was warm and real under her as she fisted one grasping hand into his shirt, curling up tight into the hollow of his larger body. Tucking her head into his neck, she leaned into him as his hand slid down her side to settle loosely on her hip. She blinked against the dark, even though she knew that it wouldn't do any good to strain to see.

Still, she was too frightened to close her eyes.

His chest rumbled, and her entire body twitched against him in surprise.

Oh. My. God. He's purring.

It rattled her teeth a little, but she decided that it wasn't all that strange. Nuzzling her cheek against his chest, she changed her mind and decided that it was actually quite nice. Her eyes drifted shut of their own volition. After everything that had happened, she was physically tired as well as emotionally drained.

Nanos were the pinnacle of human technology, but even they could only do so much without proper food and rest, and she'd had very little of either lately.

Two sprints to safety in one day is my limit.

He was as warm as a heated blanket as she snuggled into him. Eager to sap some more of his body heat, she stretched her entire body against him and draped an arm across his belly. Her fingers trailed across his stomach. His abdomen was firm and well defined.

Dude's got muscles for days. You wouldn't think so, with all the stupid frilly shirts he wears.

Her hand traced the line of his obliques, his purr stuttering before it continued. The thought that he was ticklish was funnier than it should have been to her sleep-deprived mind.

Big, strong lion alien being brought down to a writhing mass on the floor by tickling.

It was tempting, but she did have a little bit of self-preservation, and she thought that tickling him until he roared probably fell firmly under the header of "very bad plans." Making noise and attracting dinosaurs to their hidey hole wasn't a good idea, so she didn't tickle him, even though it would have been hilarious.

Feeling warmer, fuller, and safer than she had in a week was all it took for her to drift off to sleep.

A SCREECHING NOISE STARTLED HER AWAKE, AND ONCE SHE WAS pulled up to consciousness she was aware that her teeth were chattering. There still wasn't any light in their hiding place. Ardalon's grip on her hip altered, signaling that he'd awakened too.

He growled something that her sleep drunk, tired mind was too sluggish to really hear, let alone attempt to process. She wasn't sure when the temperature had dropped so dramatically. Her suit should have kept her warm even if the temperature dipped below freezing temperatures, but it was ripped and still a bit damp from its washing.

Stupid. I should have known better.

The waterfall had been just too damn beautiful and tempting to resist.

Her fingers moved to the zipper, eager to work it down and

wiggle out of her damp, half-frozen suit, but they wouldn't work properly. She was too stiff to maneuver it down. Letting out a frustrated sound, she gave up, too tired and sleepy to try a second time.

Ardalon moved, and then hands were fumbling at her zipper as his fingers brushed over her chest and torso. He worked the metal pull tab down the track of teeth until it got caught on her belt. Her skin broke out into goosebumps as it was exposed to the chilled air of the cave.

She felt useless from the cold and fatigue as he fumbled with her belt, unzipping her suit down the rest of the way.

He peeled her out of the sleeves, the slashed part ripping even more as he slid it down her trembling arm. His hands rubbed heat back into her skin until she was warmed up enough that she managed to help him peel the cold, soggy layer off of the rest of her. She was naked again.

Her panties and sports bra had been sacrificed to her toileting needs days ago before she'd run out of fabric and started using the weird leaves that the birds tossed into her cage.

There was more movement and rustling as he undressed, and then he wrapped himself around her. Wherever the soft down of his fur covered her skin, the bite of cold dissipated with time.

It took a little while for her teeth to stop chattering, but eventually they did. She burrowed into his warm embrace and tried to ignore the fact that they were probably both naked now. A small part of her wished there was light so she could see him.

He got a good look at me earlier. Fair is fair.

Did the fur go all the way down? Did he have feet or paws? She'd only ever seen him in boots. What did he look like *down there*?

Idle curiosity, she told herself. He was the first alien that she'd ever cuddled with, so it was only natural that she wanted to see how they were similar and how they were different. She tried to lie to herself and pretend that it had nothing at all to do with the way he smelled or how good it felt when he held her.

I'm just touch starved, that's all.

Over one hundred days alone in space would do that to anyone, not to mention all the trauma that she'd just been through.

Of course I'm going to latch onto the first person who's kind of nice to me. It's just survival instinct.

"Ardalon halp Sa-shuh," he whispered into her hair as his arms stroked gently up and down her back.

Her heart skipped a beat and melted.

His large, rough hands rubbed up and down her goose-bumped skin as he worked on bringing circulation back into her chilled skin, but he didn't take advantage of their forced proximity and her nudity. He didn't slide those hands lower to grab her ass, or hook a leg up and slide himself into her. She was distinctly aware of the fact that he could if he wanted to.

His stiffening cock pressed against her stomach where it was trapped between them. She could feel every inch of him where he was pressed against her.

Now that she'd eaten and rehydrated and her brain had figured out that she wasn't about to get chomped to death by dinosaurs, her lizard brain had moved onto other basic urges.

They were safe, and her body wanted to celebrate the fact that they weren't dead. As her core clenched, she was reminded that she hadn't had a good lay in about four months.

That shipping-out bang with her ex had been more disappointing than gratifying, and there was no way in hell that she was going to fill out the request forms to ask for special permission to bring her vibrator with her into deep space.

Every single item that went on or off that ship was standard issue and provided by Starfleet. Special exceptions were made only after extensive amounts of paperwork were filled out.

She was angry again that the guys she worked with always seemed to get it easier. Jerking off probably wasn't so bad, but trying to rub one out with just fingers got old after a while. Sometimes a girl needed a little motor assisted help.

Her nipples were painfully erect and rubbing against the fur of his well defined chest.

The hairs that covered him were scratchy and soft all at once, the sensation a bizarre mix of stimulation that was surprisingly pleasant as well as arousing. Her breasts pressed up against him, and his semi-erect penis twitched against her lower stomach.

He's not even human! You can't feel like this for an alien!

He rubbed the cold from her until she felt warm and comfortable, her muscles loose. Moisture gathered between her thighs as she shifted on the cold, hard ground. It was difficult to lay there with her face tucked under his chin and his breath tickling her forehead.

She shifted again, and he released her enough that she could roll over onto her other hip so that they were spooning back to front.

This is better, right? Less awkward? I mean, the cave is so dark that it's not like we were staring at one another, but surely facing away from him makes it easier for the both of us. This is just about survival.

Erections happened. That was just biology. Guys got morning wood all the time, and it probably didn't mean anything. But she remembered the way he'd stared at her breasts with interest. Maybe that was just a normal, automatic, male reaction to boobies, though.

Tit appreciation is universal even among aliens?

When morning comes and we get out of here, this is just going to be something that gets laughed about later. We're not even the same species. There's no way he wants to screw me, just like I don't actually want to screw him. I'm just happy to be alive and horny from job-induced orgasm denial.

It's just normal biological functioning. Nothing at all to be embarrassed about or ashamed of... like getting hungry, or thirsty, or having to pee.

Ardalon's arms wrapped around her, tugging her against his body. He pulled her back, pressing her to him from hip to hollow against the warmth of his body.

The change in angles means that he covered her from her toes to her head, but it also meant that his stiffening dick was now firmly lodged between her buttcheeks. Her body thrummed, needy and wanting.

She opened her eyes and stared into the darkness.

How the hell am I supposed to fall back asleep like this?

She must have fallen back asleep because she woke up again after having the most erotic dream of her life.

My subconscious is a masochist.

Dim, filtered light brightened up the cave as the sun rose outside. She'd have celebrated the fact that they'd survived the night, except that all of her awareness was zeroed in on the dick digging into her ass.

And here I thought that he had a semi last night.

Her eyes widened in surprise. He was hard, swollen, and large. It felt bigger than a penis had any right to be. Something pricked at her nipple, and she glanced down to see that he'd grabbed one of her boobs in his sleep.

His face nuzzled into the crook of her shoulder and his mouth was warm where it pressed against his skin.

He better not be drooling on me.

Conflicting thoughts about if he was awake or not flitted through her sleep addled, horny brain.

Her heart was pounding in her chest and her mouth felt dry, but whether that was from dehydration or panic or happy anticipation, she wasn't certain. He was one good twist and push away from sliding right into her if he just went for it.

Her thighs were wet.

It was a very good sex dream, I guess.

Morning sex in the spooning position had always been her favorite way to wake up. His breath was warm and even against her throat, and the prick of his claws on her breast made her want to wiggle and squirm against him. A mix of pain with her pleasure had always brought her the best orgasms.

She held herself very still, her breath coming in shallow pants as she struggled to even out her breathing. Morning light filtered in through the cracks in their blocked up entrance.

She realized that if he lifted her leg and pressed that cock against her, then she'd just decided that she wasn't going to stop him.

Apparently I'm a hundred percent a-okay with alien sex.

Ardalon did nothing of the sort, however. He stirred and woke, rolling himself and his impressive erection away from her before rising. Ignoring the keen sense of loss, she shut her eyes, too embarrassed to look at him as he shuffled about the cavern with his massive erection.

He deserved a little respect and privacy, considering he'd saved her life yesterday, so she pretended to still be asleep as he went about his morning routine.

It wasn't his fault that she'd gotten cold and she hadn't gotten laid in forever.

Okay... so I'm attracted to an alien. Go figure. Learn something new about yourself everyday I suppose.

He wandered toward the back of the cave, and she heard a

stream of fluid hitting some leaves. The notion that they had a designated pee corner in their cave made her want to laugh.

Biting back the noise before it could escape, she took advantage of his moment of distraction to sit up and wiggle back into her stiff, cold suit. The seam at the crotch rubbed against her, but the wicking, self-cleaning fabric helped with her little damp down-there situation.

Feeling marginally more human, she watched as he stumbled back into the main portion of the cavern with his tight leather pants stretched across his hips. He was shirtless, and his bulge was just as impressive as always.

Looking away from it, she hid her blush with her hair as she ignored him and made her way back around the corner into the little designated nook where they answered the call of nature.

CHAPTER SEVEN

ARDALON

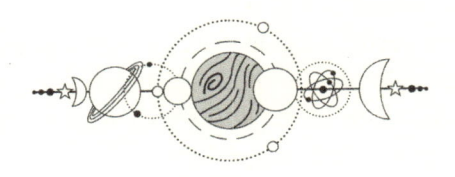

She was going to be the death of him. He'd had an inkling that her arrival meant change was coming into his life when he'd first met her, but he thought that it meant she'd help further his career, not completely upheave his entire life.

He would discover her, pass her off to those smarter and better equipped than him, and then he'd close out his mission and accept his long overdue promotion with all its perks and bonuses.

He hadn't expected her to dredge up these long-buried thoughts and feelings.

He'd never counted on liking her so much. Couldn't have foreseen enjoying the sight of her naked, furless skin so much, or the feel of her, all soft and fragile in his arms... the flashes of temper and wit... the way that she godsdamned moaned in her sleep, rubbing her plump rear against him.

Such sounds should have been a crime coming out of something so sweet and harmless-looking. Each grind of her ass against him had undone his conviction to not take advantage of the situation.

It would be reprehensible.

She was fragile, alone, scared, and she'd just survived several harrowing, life and death situations. Of course she just wanted some sense of comfort and normalcy. And that was fine. He could give her comfort. Help her remember that she wasn't dead. Celebrate being alive together in the best way possible.

That idea rang hollow inside of him, and he knew that for the lie it was. Her arousal, that sweet, inviting scent that wafted from her sex as she slept, wasn't an invitation, it was a bodily function.

He didn't want a quick viruck and to just walk away after, leaving her in the care of doctors, scientists, and politicians. That thought riled him almost to the point of growling.

His teeth were so close to her throat. It would have been so easy to set them into her soft flesh and bite his mark into her skin. Bite her so damned deep the scar would never fade and everyone would always know she was his.

She wouldn't even know the significance of it until it was too late.

She was just so damned soft and smooth, her smell tantalizing. The scent of her made him want to lick her all over, burying his nose in her sweet little center until he saw what it took to make more of those ragged little whines that she'd been making in her sleep.

I need to get a grip.

Shoving his base thoughts and primitive instincts back down into the muck they crawled out of, he took a shuddering breath and peeled himself away from her, standing up and stretching out tense muscles.

This isn't me. This is not who I am.

Standing, he went to the back of the cave to relieve himself as he busied himself with ignoring her and the temptation she represented. Pointedly not looking at her, he heard her shuffling movements as she got dressed and moved about their temporary shelter.

Tucking himself away into his pants, he moved back to their sleeping spot to gather up their things.

Sa-shuh finished relieving herself in the back of the cave and he caught her staring at him from the corner of her eye as he made a show of pulling his shirt on over his head. Her eyes skittered over his physique. He flexed a little more than was necessary as he tugged it down his back.

He remembered the way her probing fingers had caught on every ripple of his muscles last night.

Even though she was clothed now, he could still smell her arousal between her thighs. The scent was faint, but present. It had invaded his receptors so deeply that he thought she'd been permanently etched into his brain.

Time will tell if that's a good or bad thing.

It only took a moment to pack everything back into his carryall bag. They split another hydration orb and the last ration bar. He hoped they'd be back on his borrowed starcraft before midday. He caught her gaze and noticed that she seemed more timid and unsure this morning.

Swallowing the last bite, he moved to the rock that he'd jammed into the entrance of the cave, listening for the sound of predators outside.

Whether she regretted their forced intimacy last night or not, he wasn't certain. Her face was carefully blank, devoid of any of the extreme expressions she normally wore.

Deciding that he much preferred her feisty and yelling at him, he teased her, making a show of tucking his shirt into his pants and adjusting himself. She pinkened again, her skin changing color as she pretended she wasn't looking at him.

Sa-shuh, standing meek and timid next to him, made him nervous that he'd offended her irreparably.

She was modest about her nudity. A product of her hairlessness, he guessed. Not having a fine layer of fur would certainly make someone feel vulnerable while naked. Perhaps her people were more conservative than his own, and he'd gravely offended her by keeping her warm the only way that he knew how. Her clothing had been damp and ill-suited to the cold.

It was just for her survival, that's all. No female would ever choose me.

Looking away, he leaned his shoulder into the boulder. Pausing often to listen for any hint that they were about to be ambushed or attacked, he pushed all thoughts other than survival from his mind. They weren't out of danger yet, although the larger predators would be less active during this hour of the day.

The rock shifted, scratching furrows into the dirt as he moved it out of the way until more light filtered into the cave.

Once he was certain that the path from the cave was clear, he motioned for her to follow, pressing a finger to his muzzle to tell her they must be quiet.

She nodded her understanding and followed behind him. Her footsteps echoed around them, making him want to cringe with each loud step.

If I can hear her, then so can everything else out here. Our best chance is to head straight back.

A glance at the map in his com showed that they were about two klicks away from their goal. The detour from his ship to her pod, and then the waterfall, was a longer distance than the return trip would be. It bolstered his hopes for their survival.

Motioning for her to follow, he picked his way down the rocks and they set off into the jungle. His eyes scanned the brush left and right, his ears swiveling toward her when she shifted her weight. She was sweeping her gaze and blaster behind them, covering their backs. He felt grateful that they could divide their attention this way because it would make the climb up the steep hill easier.

She wasn't a graceful predator, but she was well trained and that—

Her next step landed wrong, snapping a dried branch in half. He spun around to look at her. She hunched her shoulders, her face twisted in a new expression that looked tense as if she knew she'd just endangered them.

Stopping their progress, they swept the environment together for threats, listening to the sounds of the jungle around them.

The ambient noises continued as normal. Insects buzzed, and small creatures scurried about through the dense foliage. Raising two fingers in the air and swiping them, he motioned for them to continue, listening to her too-heavy footsteps behind him as she followed.

Halfway up the hill, they had their first run in. It was a diplocus, which was bad for them, because while the two legged beast was small to be too much of a threat alone, it also hunted in packs. If you could see one of them, then you needed to keep looking because there were at least three or four more hiding in the bush, circling.

He tightened the space between them so that they were back to back.

Holding up four digits, he made a circle around them, trying to tell her to stay on guard and watch for others. Risking a glance at her over his shoulder, he saw that she looked uncertain, and he frowned, not sure how to get her to understand the danger they were in with these small but vicious knee-high creatures.

The diplocus stalked forward, angling its head and chirping, but he ignored it and kept scanning their surroundings, looking for the rest of them. This one was the bait, and it was unlikely to attack them directly before the rest of its pack was in place.

A flash of sunlight glinting off a leaf snapped his attention to the left. He raised his blaster and fired off short bursts of light. One must have hit, because there was screeching as something fell to the ground, writhing in pain among the jungle floor.

The brush around them exploded, and Sa-shuh yelled something at him, her blaster going off until there was more screeching as the rest of the pack descended upon them. Hitting two more with direct shots to their torsos, he turned to see that she had taken down the one that had acted as bait.

The jungle fell silent around them as nature took a breath, and sighed.

No more predators came slinking out. He counted the bodies that he could see and came up with five. If there was a straggler hiding in the bushes, then it was unlikely to attack them without its sisters at its back.

They still needed to move, though. The sounds of the diplocus pack dying and the smell of their spilled blood would attract larger things. Hungry things.

He tugged on Sa-shuh's ripped sleeve, urging her forward in silence. They couldn't stop now. Her eyes were wild with fear, but her face was set with something that looked both stubborn and determined, and his heart swelled with pride.

She hoisted her gun back up to waist level, her head swiveling as she scanned the brush.

Fierce little thing. She'll take her foes down with her if that's what it takes.

He bit back the bloodthirsty grin that wanted to split his face. She was scared enough without him adding anything else to her list of things to be frightened of today. A Kursh grin with its sharp, pointed teeth would probably frighten her. Her own teeth were mostly flat, save for four pointlessly angled petite canines.

Sa-shuh stomped through the jungle behind him, and they'd gone another half a klick before he noticed that the ambient sounds of the jungle had all but stopped. The dull hum of winged insects went still, and small things scattered, hiding.

Focusing, he noticed that the ground vibrated beneath their feet as he glanced at the map projection that hovered above his wrist.

Gods be damned. We must have stumbled too close to a nest... It's still too far to run.

He clamped a hand over her mouth and shoved her down into the foliage, covering her with his body. The mood between them grew tense as she went ramrod still underneath him.

Her back was plastered against his front, her breath hot against his hand. It felt like an eternity while they waited.

The lowdera lumbered nearby as they hid in the bushes. Small pebbles rattled against the ground with each of the monstrous beast's steps as it moved through its domain. Its eyesight was poor, especially during the day. If they were still and quiet, then there was a good chance that it would walk right past them. It wouldn't want to be far from its nest for too long, lest a rival destroy her whole clutch or a smaller predator stole one of her precious eggs.

As long as they didn't mark themselves as easy prey or a threat, the female would probably keep going.

The jolting steps of the beast grew closer. Sa-shuh's breathing was fast and hard against his hand. Ardalon pressed his face tight against hers as he willed her to be silent with his mind. If she whimpered now, they were dead.

Tall trees cracked and swayed as the queen of this jungle forged her path through them, leaving a trail of broken plants and deep impressions in the dirt behind her.

What felt like an eternity finally passed, and the lowdera's steps faded into the distance. The ground stopped shaking, and the insects began their dull hum again.

"We need to move now," he whispered as he stood and pulled her up. "The other animals will be restless."

Sa-shuh must have heard the urgency in his voice. Her face was pale and pinched, and she didn't protest when he hauled her trembling frame up onto his shoulder and ran. He could make the last half a klick while carrying her, especially if he didn't have to check behind them.

Sasha wiggled on his shoulder, and from the corner of his eye he saw her blaster come up as she positioned herself to protect his back just like she had before.

Good girl.

He wanted to nip her thigh to let her know how happy he was. She had good instincts. Deciding to be good, he restrained himself against his baser urges. If he started biting her, he wouldn't stop.

Politics, careers, and scientific marvels be damned.

If he got his teeth on her sweet, smooth skin, he wasn't going to stop until he'd claimed her.

Better keep my teeth to myself.

The map led them the rest of the way to his ship, and luckily they made the rest of their journey unmolested.

Slapping a palm to the opening mechanism of his starcraft, he set Sa-shuh down on her feet, and hit the door closed behind them, the ship brightening up to life. Sa-shuh sank to the floor in a puddle of exhausted limbs. She'd traded in her pallor for bright pink cheeks.

Her eyes were wide and a little frenzied as she glanced up at him, but she chuffed out what he thought was a laugh as she pulled herself up off the floor and sat in one of the chairs.

Doing a double-take, he noticed that she'd sat in the captain's seat. It made him smile, even as he reached down and grabbed her wrist, pulling her up out of it.

It's cute that she thinks she gets the captain's chair.

When she moved to settle into the other chair, he hauled her back and sat her on his lap instead. It was wildly inappropriate, he knew, but his blood was singing and he needed to feel her body pressed against his.

They'd survived.

He wrapped an arm around her waist and held her to him as he flicked switches, moving through the starting sequence. The dashboard came to life, the display brightening.

She wiggled on her perch, then settled with one leg straddling either side of one of his thighs. It kept their centers from touching, but it didn't stop him from smelling the spike in her arousal as her legs parted.

She likes being bossed around a little.

The thought tempted him, made him want to test the limits of the new compulsions that he had. He focused on the lift off preparations, instead, pinging the local command center to let them know he'd be in their airspace.

Would she run from me? Maybe if I asked her to?

The shuttle vibrated as it broke through the planet's atmosphere. The memory of her frantic run through the ship replayed in his mind. He imagined trading places with the comoros. Stalking her through halls, tracking her scent, chasing her down until she was exhausted, then pinning her to the ground and...

His teeth ached to sink into flesh and bite until he tasted blood.

It was wrong. He was one of the ashima. Taking a mate wasn't an option for him, and besides, she was an alien, and a female dependent on him for her safety and care.

This budding attraction for her was wrong on every level.

The viewport clouded over as someone from the ship pinged them with an incoming call. Sa-shuh startled, stiffening in his arms. He splayed his fingers across her stomach, holding her in place as he accepted the incoming call as audio only. Davi's voice broadcasted over the speakers.

"Sir, I repeat, can you hear me?" Davi asked, the connection full of interference.

"I hear you, Davi. Status update!" Ardalon ordered.

"Thank the gods! Remulus said you were dead for sure. I told him that command would have alerted us immediately if your link went down, but then we couldn't get through to you via your implant. The chancellor even tried a couple of times. Everyone was concerned when you didn't return last night. Hey, why is your visual link down? Did your ship take damage? Do you need us to come in and get you? Because I can—" Davi said in rapid fire succession.

"I'm fine," Ardalon interrupted before Davi could steamroll him anymore than he already had. "There's no ship damage. I just didn't want your ugly mug scaring the poor female. She's had enough of a fright already. The satellite links probably just didn't work through the dense jungle is all. We're headed back now. Be there in fifteen. And Davi, have medical there on standby."

Sa-shuh shifted in the perch on his leg, her face thoughtful as she stared at him out of the corner of her eye. He flipped through the rest of the takeoff sequence, the hum of the engines coming on.

"Medical?" Davi repeated the order.

He cut the feed before Davi could argue the point further or think up any more banal questions to ask. The engines accelerated, and once they were up to full speed, he took them up.

The flight back up to the poacher's ship was uncomplicated. The Raxions, true to their word, stayed out of his business. They were going to need an informal thank you gift, he supposed. Davi could handle that. The Raxions liked… fruit? Maybe. Davi would probably know.

Sa-shuh stiffened in his arms as he maneuvered the explorer pod into the dock on the larger ship. They slid through the port and waited for the gate to close and for the cargo bay to reatmospherize.

She looked at him with a cagey expression, betrayal in her eyes, like she wasn't sure that he hadn't just saved her ass only to lock her back up into a cage.

Never.

"Gotta get you to medical, little one, so they can put a translator in you so that we can finally talk," he said, aware that she couldn't understand him but enjoying speaking to her nonetheless.

Her eyes met his like she wanted to trust him, but there was just a little too much doubt and fear.

Well, that won't do.

"If yoo lok mee uhp ugheyn, ahy am gohing to kil yoo," she told him in a low, even voice that sounded sweet despite the fire in her eyes that threatened him with retribution should he dare to double cross her.

His muzzle twitched with amusement. He shouldn't have been enjoying this, yet he did. He pressed his nose to her shoulder, keeping their gazes locked. Hand still wrapped around her stomach, she was pressed against him, her sweet little center still perched on top of his thigh, her pheromones and scent soaking down into the fabric of his pants.

Her eyes narrowed at him, her lips twisted down and the hair above her eyes pinched together. He bounced her on his knee, enjoying the way that her eyes sharpened with unspoken threats.

Yep. Definitely prefer her feisty.

Tongue flicking out, he licked up a bead of sweat and scent off of her skin, rolling it back into his throat and pushing it up into his sinuses.

She gasped, wiggling on his lap, the smell of her musk intensifying. He could drown in it and die a happy male. He jostled her again, wanting to smell more of it, pleased when her pussy twitched on his thigh and she groaned a frustrated sound in the back of her throat.

It reminded him of the play growling that young cubs made when they mock-battled with their littermates.

"Oh mahy gawd, yoor tuhng feels lahyk sandpeyper!" she gasped.

He licked a trail all the way up her arm and neck, right up to the fine hairs of her glorious mane. She squirmed again when he grazed his teeth just lightly along her nape. A fang brushed against the shell of her rounded ear, making her moan, her face turning such a dark shade of pink again that even the tops of her ears darkened.

The sound of it made him stiffen in his pants, and he cursed himself as a fool ten ways to sunset.

I just had to go and tease her, and she teased me right back. I deserved that.

The urge to bite her now and bind them together beat at him from the dark recesses of his mind as she straddled his leg, her arousal growing and thickening in the air between them.

She can't stop us without claws and fangs, some dark part of his mind whispered, urging him to do it.

To bite her.

Claim her.

Make her his. How this female, a stranger and an alien, had broken down his carefully erected defenses, he wasn't certain.

Mine.

Gathering every last bit of self control, Ardalon reeled back in the urge to nuzzle lower down her neck and bite. It was fearful how she unhinged him. He wasn't a male who got so undone by a little flash of ass and cuddling, and he'd never once been tempted to take a bed companion before.

He wondered what it was about her that drove him to feel so primal.

Like an animal. A stupid, rutting beast. He hadn't been this hormone crazed since puberty when his fangs had come in.

"Gotta get you to medical, kitten," he murmured against her neck as he nuzzled his way back up to her earlobe.

How does she smell this good?

He felt drunk on the scent of her, his head muddled with her very essence.

Resigned that at some point he had to let her go, he tugged her more firmly onto his lap. He slid his teeth away from her soft, white throat, rubbing his cheek and its scent glands up and down her neck and shoulder instead.

It was wrong to mark her with his scent like this. She probably didn't even understand what he was doing. But if he couldn't have his bite decorating her throat, he was damn well going to make her smell like him.

He rubbed his scent up and down her shoulder and the hollow of her throat, his purr rumbling against her skin until she made that chortling laugh of hers again as she tucked her face against his throat. He took advantage of the change in angle, rubbing more of his scent along the top of her head for good measure.

"Gud kitee," she said, laughing as she patted his shoulder. She was teasing him, he guessed by the strange, singsong inflection in her voice.

She can say whatever she wants as long as she smells this sweet and feels this good. So viruking soft.

Someone pinged the ship again, and he scowled up at the screen as the audio link turned active.

"What?" he barked out, pissed to be interrupted and glad at the same time that Davi had waited as long as he did.

"Sir! I have medical here. Do you require assistance getting out of the starcraft? They've brought a stretcher in case you're injured," Davi inquired.

Nudging Sa-shuh off his lap, he stood and cupped her elbow, placing his palm on the hatch and opening the door without a reply. Her face lost its hint of softness. It filled him with regret, but this was necessary. It had to be done.

She can berate me later once we can finally speak to one another.

CHAPTER EIGHT

SASHA

Ardalon's grip wasn't forceful, but he did pull her out of the ship and down the ramp that he extended as if she didn't know how to walk, but she was grateful for his assistance even though she didn't want him to know that either. The whiplash from being nuzzled to being pulled down off a ship was severe and her body was still flushing the arousal from her system.

Did he have to nibble on my neck and ear like that?

She was uncomfortably damp between her legs, tired from sleeping on a stone floor, dirty from her trek through the jungle, and unbelievably hungry. She needed a shower, a meal, and a twenty-hour-long nap, and she wasn't picky about the order of it.

Looking around, she saw that the cargo bay had been tidied up in their absence. She could still see the charred marks on the metal walls and floor from her laser fire fight with the birds and the sabertooth cat-dog creature.

Wonder where all the birds went.

There wasn't a single one in sight. Instead, a slender cat guy stood at the bottom of the ramp, his back ramrod straight, as he waited for them to descend. His fur was a lighter shade of tawny, his hair more golden, shorter and tidier than

Ardalon's. This new cat guy stared at her with rich, warm brown eyes, his expression curious as he pretended not to stare at her.

He looked every bit like a lion would look if he were a man, except that there was something overly tidy about his appearance.

His clothes had been pressed with neat creases down the middle of his slacks, and he definitely wasn't wearing a ruffled shirt. The top he wore looked like the sort of military-issue dress shirt that she wore sometimes to functions. A few bits of colored metal decorated his shoulders.

It was jarring to see someone who looked just like Ardalon without looking like Ardalon at all.

Ardalon looked… fierce, even in his ridiculous, old-timey pirate outfit. Between the tight leather pants and the gun belt slung low on his hips, his whole look was just plain doing it for her. Even his locked hair was big and boisterous. The silver charms that had been woven into the strands clinked together as he walked them down the ship's stairs. He moved down the ramp with a swagger, his hair decorations clicking with each step.

It was amazing how in the jungle he'd moved as silent as a panther, and now he jingled with every movement.

She glanced between the two aliens, studying their similarities and differences in depth as they got closer.

"Sir?" the male asked in a wary tone as he glanced nervously between Ardalon and her. This one growled less, so her translator was able to pick his words apart.

Ardalon grumbled something long and alien back. She only caught a few words of what he said. Something about her and yes and everything was fine. It was always hard to decipher Ardalon's words. Her translator had a harder time with his gruff voice and the way he rolled his tongue. The birds' nasally words were a lot easier to pick up because there was a lot more consistency between them all whenever they spoke.

The new guy leaned forward, sniffing the air as they passed, his flat nostrils flaring, making her face burn in embarrassment. Ardalon growled, a rumbling sound of warning that came from deep within his chest.

Oh, stars. He can't, like, smell me... right?

It clicked, and she stumbled on her last step off the ramp.

If this one can smell my arousal now, then that means... Ardalon knew when I was horny back in the cave.

Her face felt like it was on fire, and she wanted the ground to swallow her whole. Ardalon tugged her elbow closer so that she was plastered against his side as they walked. His hand came around her shoulder in a possessive, guarding gesture, his unsheathed claws catching in the threads of her suit.

"Is it rengek that color be?" the unfamiliar cat guy asked with what sounded like an amusing lilt to their normally gruff speech.

She risked a glance over her shoulder to confirm that yes, the male looked amused as he stared at her. It had taken her quite a lot of careful watching and a whole lot of deciphering to determine the subtleties of their facial expressions.

They seemed to do most of their nonverbal communication with their eyes. It sort of made sense because of their faces having a blunt muzzle and an almost nonexistent, flat upper lip.

Kind of hard to frown when you don't have much to speak of in the way of lips and your mouth juts out from your face like that.

"Derxistin," Ardalon growled, leaving little room for arguing.

Ooh... is that a curse word? It definitely sounds like one.

Ardalon's hand on her shoulder kept her flush against his side, his growl fading back into an inaudible purr that she felt through their physical connection. He stared straight ahead, looking focused and determined. She glanced up at him, then looked back over her shoulder at the other amused lion.

Leveling her best icy glare at him, she repeated the phrase as best she could, knowing that she was probably butchering it with her terrible accent or bad pronunciation. "Der xis tin."

The lion erupted into those dry chuffing sounds, which she assumed was their version of uncontrollable laughter, but she was too distracted by the brown reptile-skinned alien in the military uniform who approached them to really care.

For a moment, she thought that maybe it was the same one who'd come up on her screen and fired missiles at her during her botched escape attempt. On second glance, however, she saw that this one looked older.

His face was lined with age, and his coloring was blotchy and a bit uneven. He stood at parade rest, looking them over with a calm air that said that he was used to being in charge and others listened whenever he spoke.

The lizard man and Ardalon talked for a moment, and she tried to listen in on their conversation, but many of the words were too advanced for her. All she understood was that the lizard wanted to take her somewhere.

From the cut of his coat and the stiffness of his posture, she gathered that this was a guy who wasn't used to having to repeat himself. She glanced between them while the lizard alien looked her up and down before turning, leading them out of the loading bay and down the hallway.

They passed through the empty and deserted ship, and it felt weird to her to be walking through it now that it was like this. The last time she was in these hallways she was fighting and running for her life.

Was that really just yesterday?

It felt like it had been longer than that.

It's been a strange week.

The lizard waved his hand over the marking that decorated a hidden door and she watched as the wall slid open, revealing a brightly lit room behind him.

Silver tables, counters, and sharp-tipped instruments lined the gleaming pristine white room. An examination table was front and center, and above it was a robotic mechanism that hung suspended from the ceiling.

The room looked like a nightmare, like the start of every horror vid she'd ever streamed and then regretted afterward when it was time to sleep.

Sasha balked, crashing into Ardalon, who caught her by both of her elbows and propelled her forward.

Nuh-uh. No way. I'm not getting probed today.

Irrational panic took hold, clamping down on her in fear. The hairs on the nape of her neck stood up, and she broke out into a cold sweat. Her eyes scanned the room, skimming over glass jars of silver instruments and trays of needles and knives.

Should have taken my chances with the dinosaurs.

Ardalon urged her forward toward the table.

"Nope! Sorry. No can do," she protested as she flailed, trying to shove her way past a hundred and eighty pounds of six-foot-plus lion man.

His arms wrapped around her in a bear hug that trapped them to her sides, lifting her straight up off the ground and carrying her forward toward the table like she weighed nothing and he did this sort of thing daily. Her arms were trapped at her sides, but her legs were free.

She kicked him, trying to catch him in either the balls or one of his knees.

He dodged her attacks, grunting when she connected with his thigh. She half expected him to retaliate, or squeeze the air out of her, but he didn't. He carried her over toward the table in the center of the room like she was a sack of flour.

For a moment, she considered leaning forward and biting him. His neck was right there, the cords of his veins pulsing within reach of her teeth.

Her butt hit the table, and then he was leaning over her, his arms wrapped around her and his legs caging her body between them.

This was infinitely worse than the cage. She would gladly go back in the cage if they just took her off this damn table. She could already feel the phantom slicing of a laser right down her abdomen.

"Don't do this, don't do this, don't, d-don't," she pleaded.

"Ew wergêrr e," Ardalon answered. "Ew ê tenê hinekî bieşe. Soree, Sa-shuh, soree," he said, the words coming through as her translator worked to interpret his growl-slurred words.

Tears rolled down her face from unrealized rage as her body thrummed with untapped adrenaline while she sat there, restrained, and disgusted by her helplessness. His arms tightened, leaving her no room to get away from him or lever up against him. She scraped her nails against him as she clawed at him, but he was impervious to any small amount of pain she caused.

His fur might have been short, but it was still too thick for her to do any real damage with her blunt, broken nails.

The lizard alien said something terse and long from somewhere behind her, causing her body to tense up with fear. She didn't like having that one at her back where she couldn't see him. She caught the pathetic sob that wanted to leave her throat, channeling it into rage instead. She was more comfortable with anger than fear.

From the corner of her eye, she caught the glint of a needle. The lizard man was walking toward her with the largest needle she'd ever seen in his hand. It gleamed in the bright overhead light, a drop of fluid gathered on its beveled tip.

The lizard man asked something again. "Piştrastin?" he said in a dispassionate, clinical voice.

"Yess," Ardalon insisted, "doo et."

He's betrayed me. Can't trust any of them, the aliens. They want to experiment on me. Cut me open...

She snapped, the fear and anger too much to bear as hysteria overwhelmed her and dragged her under their all-consuming waves. Leaning forward, she zeroed in on the juncture between his neck and shoulder, saw the corded pulse there, and bit.

If she had to feel pain, then he did too.

Her blunt teeth did more squeezing than cutting, but it still felt satisfying to hear his grunt of pain. She broke skin, just a little, as his hands tightened on her back, his claws pricking her through her suit. His blood tasted metallic just like hers.

Something cold pressed into the base of her neck, sliding deep.

There was a pinch, and then her spine was on fire and—*oh, God*—she could feel something crawling and it was inside of her. Cold tendrils moved up her neck, unfurling inside of her body. Invading her mind. The sensation moved upward, her brain tingling from the shock of it. Something pinched, burrowed, and expanded.

Unable to get away from Ardalon's firm hold or the lizard man's hands on her neck and head, she scissored her teeth, gnawing his skin open, determined to do what little harm she was capable of before whatever they'd just done finished its job on her.

He grunted again, barely flinching from the little pain she caused him.

No longer in control of her body, she went completely still, her jaws locked on him, and then she was dimly aware of going slack, pitching forward, her vision and hearing going in and out like someone had their thumb on the change channel button of her body's control panel.

Awareness of her surroundings flickered as her nanos surged, racing to repair whatever damage the aliens had just caused. It was a pale sort of reassurance. Not all wounds were physical, and not everything could be healed with fancy tech.

Her jaw's grip on him eased, her body no longer under her control as she slumped against him, head lolling like a ragdoll.

Heat bloomed at the base of her neck as the puncture closed, her flesh knitting back together. As her spine stopped leaking fluid, the resulting headache dissipated as cold tendrils wrapped themselves inside of her, burying themselves deeper into her mind. It was horrible.

Ardalon cupped her chin and tipped her head back as her vision flickered in and out, and she was vaguely aware of being laid out on the cold metal table.

She felt stupid for ever trusting him in the first place.

He probably just chased me down because I'm valuable. All that nonsense about trusting him... stupid. And then I... ugh. Is he laughing about it? At me? With those awful birds who ripped me out of my ship and stuck me in a cage so they could sell me?

Consciousness flickered in and out, returning slowly as the world faded back into existence, an aperture expanding.

Shouting filled the room when she thoroughly came back to.

"They said you were the best! So then explain to me, doctor, why she's unconscious from a simple translator implant!" Ardalon roared.

Turning her head to look at the speaker took an extreme amount of energy, leaving her exhausted. The doctor didn't look threatened at all. He gestured up to a holographic rendering of a human figure that hovered in the air before them. She squinted at it, trying to make sense of what she was seeing, as the fog in her head lifted.

The shapes in the room solidified as her double vision knitted back together and the two wavering, glowing shapes merged together into the in-air projection of a naked human woman.

Is that... me?

The crescent-shaped scar on the palm of her left hand, a kitchen injury she'd received before she'd gotten her nano shot from the military for enlisting, was distinct enough.

Is that really what my butt looks like?

The room stopped spinning, but she was still too sore and tired to get off the metal table. Everything still felt a million miles away and fuzzy, and her eyelids felt heavy. The urge to go back to sleep was difficult to ignore.

"You failed to notify me that she already had one. It's dangerous to load two implants into the same region of the brain. Best case scenario, they merge and work in tandem," the lizard countered.

"And the worst case scenario?" Ardalon demanded in a cold voice that promised pain if he didn't like the answer.

The doctor frowned, the frills on his forehead fluttering. "Inconsequential. We will know soon enough which way it will go. In the meantime, I don't like to borrow trouble. She will recover, or not. Worrying about it now will not affect the outcome," the lizard doctor said.

Ardalon paced the room, growling under his breath.

Sasha let her eyes drift closed, too tired to keep them open for more than a second or two at a time.

That lizard better keep the rest of his needles to himself or he's gonna find one stuck somewhere he doesn't like.

The doctor typed something at the computer terminal he was operating, the keys clicking. "The scans found another one in her arm too. I found it once I knew what to look for. Foreign tech. Strange material. Nothing I've ever seen before. That one seems to be secreting chemicals. It explains why the implanter didn't refuse to inject. It couldn't sense the chip."

"I wonder what it's made of… and there's something in her blood too," the doctor added. "That one concerns me more. It's everywhere. A parasite or a bacteria, maybe. Perhaps a virus. All I know for certain right now is that she's not radioactive. I'll need a larger blood sample to confirm anything more concrete."

"In the meantime, I'd recommend a full decontamination for the both of you to be safe. A course of broad spectrum antibiotics and antivirals would probably be warranted too if you want to cover all of your bases. I'll need to discuss a vaccination schedule with an immunologist since I don't know how robust her species is or if she'll react poorly to any of our medications."

The shuffling sound stopped. "What do you mean there's something in her blood?" Ardalon asked. "Is she sick?"

She cracked her eyes open, glancing at them through her lashes. The doctor waved him off, bending his head back down to his glowing screen as he clicked something on the computer terminal, the hologram enlarging and zeroing in on some internal organ.

"I have work to do," the doctor deflected. "Also, she's awake."

Ardalon rushed over to her, his worried gaze finding hers as his long legs ate up the distance between them.

"Sa-shuh," he whispered, his eyes wary as he approached the table.

She was still too woozy to do much more than lie there quietly on the surgical table.

"It's Sash-ah, actually," she over pronounced her name for him.

His eyes lit up, the sharp worried lines under his eyes easing into something softer. "Sasha," he corrected. "It's good to hear your voice and finally understand the meanings of your words."

She eyed him for a moment, letting go of her anger and wariness. It didn't seem like the Doctor was about to start probing anything, and Ardalon looked like he'd punished himself better than she could have.

"Oh, I don't know. You understood the meaning of the word "'breast'" well enough. If you'd just been patient, my translator would have worked it all out in another two or three weeks. It's your fault, you know. I actually understood the birds pretty well toward the end, but you growl a lot. I can't pick out the nuances of your speech and parse it out when you don't pronounce your vowels," Sasha argued.

The doctor snorted from his corner of the room as he fiddled with the computer, the layers of the projected rendering of her body peeling apart one by one as he worked his way down her skin to her organs. "Her assessment of you is valid."

The heat produced by her nanos faded, the damage from the alien translator's implanting healing as it finished worming in.

The alien doctor looked happy to play with the digital rendering of her body instead of slicing into her to look inside. She heaved out a relieved sigh. The doctor glanced between her and the hologram projection, looking thoughtful.

"Sorry for all of the... uh, biting," Sasha said, her gaze flicking to the saliva-spiked fur on Ardalon's neck.

She shifted on the table, testing out sitting. Her head spun. Sitting was not a great idea, her head felt dizzy and her body was weak, so she settled for leaning up on one elbow on the exam table instead until that faded.

"About that," the doctor said, "I'd like to examine that marking, see if it initiated the b—"

"I'm fine," Ardalon interrupted, his ears laying flat against his head.

The doctor looked up at them from his computer station, then shrugged and returned back to his work. "If you insist."

Glancing between them, she frowned. "Yeah... it just hurt like a son of a bitch, ya know? The nanos are great and all, but they make anesthetics a real problem. I don't need antibiotics, by the way. I can't get an infection. But I'm certainly not going to turn down a long, hot shower with actual soap. And shampoo. I'd kill for some shampoo and conditioner."

The doctor's typing paused as he glanced up at her over his glowing terminal screen. His forehead frills ruffled, the edges turning a bright yellow color. "You're feeling homicidal tendencies right now?"

Ardalon growled deep in his chest, his attention turning from her to the doctor as he shifted, stepping between them and breaking her line of sight.

"What? Oh, no, it's just a figure of speech," she explained, sitting up a little higher.

The doctor's frill settled back down as he went back to working on his computer, muttering something about aggression. "I'd still like to get a blood sample so I can run more tests."

Her stomach twisted, unease moving through her. "Can I say no?" she asked, glancing at Ardalon.

His eyes widened a bit, his ears popping back up through his hair. "Of course you can say no. The translator was... necessary. Similar to a life saving procedure. Nothing else will be done to you without your consent."

Ardalon's hand brushed against hers, and the rough calluses of his palm on her shoulder calmed her. He was still the same male that he'd been a few hours ago, just with a lot more to say now that they could finally understand one another.

The loss of adrenaline and the emotional rollercoaster she'd been on in the last two days had made her a bit jumpy and on edge.

"I see no evidence of organ damage," the doctor murmured from his corner of the room. "But I do see remodeling in a few bones. Some are old. This one in your left arm is newer, I think."

With the dizziness abating, she managed to sit up and swing her legs over the side of the table so that they were dangling. Ardalon's hand came up to her elbow, as if to prevent her from toppling off should she get dizzy again. She flashed smile eyes at him until his wary expression loosened.

It felt better to not be lying down on the table. Knowing that she could jump off of it at any moment made it easier to sit there calmly instead of freaking out.

She glanced back over at the lizard doctor. "You probably wouldn't see much scarring in my soft tissue. I heal quickly. Bone is harder to fix, though. It never really knits back quite the same before it was broken, you know?" she explained. "Nanos. They help me heal rapidly, fight off infection and illnesses, and help me adjust to strenuous environments and situations like space and other planets' atmospheres and gravities."

She could see the doctor pondering the uses of such technology as he mulled her words over. He had the same glint in his eye and faraway look on his face that she'd seen on the military research doctors who'd injected her with them. It set her on edge.

"They're attuned to my DNA. Even if you extracted it they wouldn't do much of anything but swim around in your petri dish," she warned him before he could get too many ideas.

She didn't want him drawing any of her blood. It was true that the nanos were attuned to her, but it was also possible that someone very skilled could potentially reverse engineer them.

In the right hands, they were a useful tool for soldiers, scientists and colonizers who needed to survive extreme conditions.

In the wrong hands, they could be weaponized like they had been in the early days of their invention.

The lions and this doctor seemed mostly okay, but she hadn't forgotten that another one of the lizards had shot her out of the sky, and those birds had locked her in a cage with plans to sell her. She didn't think that people were all good or all bad based on the representation of a few, and there was evil in every culture, or species, but she wasn't naive enough to blindly hand over such a weapon.

"If you change your mind about that sample," the doctor tried again.

His voice was even, but she could sense his eagerness from across the room. He was probably thinking about all of the diseases and illnesses that he could cure with her tech. Others would think about injecting them into their soldiers, then invading and gassing cities until everyone without the nanos dropped dead wherever they stood in the streets. A genocide accomplished in a day without dropping a single dirty bomb.

What's that old Earth saying? The road to hell is paved with good intentions.

"I won't change my mind," she answered.

"Enough," Ardalon ordered. "She's made her wishes clear. If there's nothing more for you to do, here, doctor?" Ardalon butted in as he prompted her to get off the table.

The jump down made her dizzy and she swayed into him, her cheek hitting his chest. His arm curved around her in a protective gesture as she leaned her weight against him and he led her toward the door. The squiggles were still—disappointingly—just squiggles. Her alien translator didn't seem to convert their writing.

"I have more than enough to entertain myself," the doctor said as he lost interest in them, going back to his scans of her body. It was weird to see all of your organs projected up in a glowing, suspended hologram in the middle of the room. She wasn't certain that she appreciated the gleam in the doctor's eyes as he looked at her kidneys.

She glanced up at Ardalon as he dipped his head down toward her as they headed toward the door, as if they were co-conspirators or he was hanging on her every word.

Who exactly is he? How does a janitor dressed like a pirate order people about?

He led her out of the medical bay, the door sliding shut behind them, and then they were alone again in the hallway.

It was obvious that he wasn't what he'd seemed at first. The birds had barely tolerated his presence. These guys deferred to him, and he looked comfortable with giving orders. It meant that he had a certain level of authority and rank. More worrying was her concern about where all of the birds had gone. She didn't see a single one as he walked her down the hallway. It was time for some answers to her questions.

They owe me that much.

"I was serious about that shower," she deadpanned, staring up at Ardalon.

She needed a shower, and her flight suit needed to meet some soap and water in the worst way. Its quick rinse in the waterfall had helped, but it wasn't enough. Their little trek through the jungle had dirtied her right back up. She may as well have not bathed at all.

Ardalon opened his mouth to say something, but her stomach rumbled loudly, reminding them both that she hadn't eaten much in at least a week. He laughed instead of answering her, that dry chuffing sound that made her lips twitch up in a smile.

"Of course," he answered. "This way."

His fingertips on her elbow guided her forward, and she wondered if his species was just very tactile. She tried to recall if she'd even seen him act so touchy feely with anyone else.

It was a challenge to not read into it after she'd woken up

with his morning erection pressing into her butt, and then the way he'd pulled her onto his lap on the flight back to the ship...

She would have been completely embarrassed about it—except she was wrung dry of emotions and she had nothing left to give. The constant ups and downs and highs and lows had left her feeling numb.

The blood and feathers and gore had all been cleaned up, but the occasional charred mark still showed on the walls, ceiling, or floor providing proof that she hadn't hallucinated everything.

"Where are we going?" she asked, glancing around as they walked. The ship was still foreign to her, and she had no idea where they were headed. It wasn't like she'd had the time to sightsee and take it all in when she was running for her life, trying to escape. "And where did all the birds go?"

What's going to happen to me now?

That was the real question that she wanted to ask him. The question that made her palms sweat, whose answer she feared because she was a stranger in a strange land and one misstep might land her right back in a cage or back on a cutting table.

"The pirates have been confined below deck. You no longer need to worry about them. My name is Ardalon Bavara, and I work as a Peacekeeper for the United Council. I was working in secret as a hired mercenary on this ship. Captain Rulondulph was suspected of being the head of a smuggling operation, and I was sent to infiltrate his crew and gather evidence as part of my mission," he explained.

Her thoughts drifted back to the makeshift zoo where they'd kept her locked up with all of those animals. "Poachers? And you're... what, an undercover cop?"

"Exactly," he said as he placed his hand on the small of her back, opening a door and ushering her inside.

The room wasn't at all what she'd expected. The questions

that she had on the tip of her tongue died as she glanced around. The bedchamber was small, but loudly decorated.

There was color, and fabric and pillows were everywhere. The center of the room was a sunken circle, and it was heavily padded and decorated with brightly patterned pillows that lined the entire rim. The rest of the room's furnishings were sparse. There was little to speak of in the way of furniture, but there was more writing on the walls here and there, suggesting that there was more to explore and it was just hidden from plain sight.

She hoped there was a bathroom behind at least one of those markings and that the toilet wasn't too strange.

I really need to learn how to read alien.

"It's a nest," she decided, tilting her head as she studied the bizarre little room. The thought was so sudden and hilarious to her trauma-addled mind that she barely wrangled down the hysterical laughter that bubbled up inside of her. The mental image of a fluffed-up Diggi bird preening in this pillow-strewn nest made her want to laugh until she cried.

Whoever had used this room before her liked the color red. She was reminded of the animal documentaries that her brother had always forced her to watch with him when they were children.

A refined, accented narrator's voice popped into her head. *And see the nest, here. The Diggi gathers decorations from far and wide and arranges these pleasing odds and ends in a manner that makes sense only to him. The goal of such behavior is to create an eye-catching display. When mating season comes around, the Diggi male will build his nest in the hopes that a female finds it tempting enough to mate with him.*

Ardalon stood in the doorway and cleared his throat, snapping her from her delirious inner monologue. From the expression in his eyes and his posture, it was clear that he didn't intend to follow her in.

"Shower, eat, and rest. I have some business to attend to in the meantime. When I return, I will explain things in greater detail," he instructed.

Swallowing down her protests, she stamped down her irrational feelings, aware that mentally she was all over the place. She'd latched onto the first person who showed her any sort of decency, and now she didn't want him to leave her all alone.

Scared for her future, and afraid that she'd never get back home or see her brother and his new wife again, she needed companionship. Wanting to ask him to stay, to beg Ardalon not to leave, she bit her lip.

What am I supposed to say? Don't go. Please don't leave me. I don't want to be alone right now. What's going to happen to me? Am I ever going to see my home again?

His eyes look gentle as if he knows her thoughts. She considered, briefly, that he was an alien and that she really didn't know much about him or his species. It wasn't entirely out of the realm of possibility for him to be able to read her mind or smell her emotions or something.

She stared at him in silence, waiting to see if he reacted to her irrational thoughts. Warm golden eyes stared back at her in answer, and she noticed, for the first time, that his colored irises took up nearly his entire eye.

So alien, yet not. It's weird.

She was already getting used to looking at these people shaped like lions and lizards and birds.

Shaking her head a little to clear away the distracting thoughts, she dismissed the idea that he could read her mind.

If he was a mind reader, then he'd have screwed me this morning.

Ardalon's wide, flat nasal bridge wrinkled. "Sasha? Are you well enough for me to leave you for a short time?"

She blushed, feeling awkward and embarrassed at the intrusive thought that had come out of nowhere. Hesitation tied her tongue in knots as she tried to start the conversation that they needed to have twenty different ways, but she couldn't force herself to say a single one of them out loud. Everything sounded stupid in her head.

Awkwardness stretched between them, twisting up her discomfort.

He reached forward, the back of his hand pressing against her forehead, brushing a few strands of loose hair aside. "Are you certain you are well? Perhaps I should escort you back to the doctor," he said.

"No! I mean, no, erm, thanks. I'm fine. Well, not fine, but… yeah," she said, feeling self-conscious. "It's just… everything's been… a lot."

His eyes softened, his fingers brushing her loose strands of hair behind her ear as he dropped his touch from her and took a step back, nodding.

"Rest, and I will return for you," he told her, palming the door open with a hand against the writing on the wall.

She studied the markings, committing them to memory so she'd never get stuck in a room and not know how to get out of it again. When the door opened, Ardalon stepped through and turned to glance back at her. He nodded, and they stared at one another as the door closed itself, and then she was alone.

Sasha might have dismissed waking up to his erection pressing firm and hard against her ass, chalking it up to morning wood just being a normal male, biological function or maybe a cultural misunderstanding due to a difference in views on things like nudity and personal space, but then he'd tugged her onto his lap and licked her.

He wants me too.

The thought was as exhilarating as it was confusing and

alarming. She'd been in deep space for a looooong time, and a girl had needs.

But... an alien?

She felt like she should have been weirded out, not interested.

He has fur!

Her exhausted body thrummed instead of settling, a pulse beating between her legs.

Oh my God, I want to frack him.

Staring at the door with her hands fisted in her jumpsuit, her mouth dropped open and closed several times as she worked through her conflicted emotions. Now that they could finally speak to one another, she felt shy. Freed from her cage, she felt directionless.

Given her independence back, she found that she didn't know what to do with it.

Me, shy and speechless? Ethain would be rolling on the floor laughing at me right now.

Despite the twelve or so hours between waking up bloodied and broken in the second crash and Ardalon finding her at the lake, this was the most alone she'd felt since she'd stepped on board her small engineering ship and set out on her satellite repair job almost four months ago.

There had always been some end goal just ahead to keep her going. Finish the satellite repair job, escape the cage, find a ship, run from dinosaurs. Now she was standing in an elegant bedroom on an alien spaceship. There was no goal, no objective, and no plan. She'd just learned that the universe was larger than anyone could have ever imagined, and she had no idea what to do with that information.

She felt small and insignificant.

There was no brother waiting for her to return home, because she was most likely never going to see her home again.

She didn't have a Starfleet captain to report to after another job well done, because there was no Starfleet in this star system. Her apartment, small and shabby as it was, would gather dust until her bank account ran out and her rent went unpaid and her landlord gave it to someone else, throwing her things in the garbage pit. She had nothing in the world but the soiled clothes on her back.

There was no ex-boyfriend to avoid, or academy friends to further lose touch with over the years as they grew up and apart. Here, she didn't know anyone except for Ardalon, and h*e had things to do.* A mission to salvage, a job, a boss to report to... a family?

She couldn't help but wonder just how she was going to manage now.

A dark, insidious thought crawled up to the surface of her mind and it wouldn't leave her alone. It wondered if she'd traded one cage for another. Glancing up at the writing on the wall, she pursed her lips.

Did he lock me in?

It made her wonder how much she could actually trust him.

She thought back to that horrible cage she'd been kept in, and then the curious and almost manic gleam in the reptile doctor's eyes as she'd explained the nanos in her blood to him. It frightened her. A week ago, she'd been a person. Now, she was a commodity.

Shuddering, she thought about how humans would react if they happened upon a stranded, helpless alien. They'd probably get locked up in some military bunker while their ship was dissected down to each single nut and bolt, and the alien probably wouldn't fare any better than their ship.

Do we have stolen and repurposed alien tech in our hands? Were they cut open, studied, and locked away out of public view?

That thought brought her no comfort. Staring at her hands,

she wondered if their nano and warp drive technology had come from some nonhuman source. She studied the glowing sigil that marked the door.

Is the door locked?

Stomach sinking with dread, she steeled her nerves and tapped her fingers against the writing on the wall, waiting.

The door opened, revealing the empty hallway. A breath she hadn't realized she was holding escaped her lips. Grateful that it had opened and she wasn't being kept under armed guard either, she let the door shutter closed and retreated back into the room, intent on finding the shower and a bar of soap.

CHAPTER NINE

ARDALON

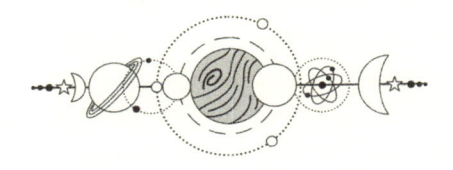

"Be reasonable," he said to Asa, staring down the ship's first mate from across the impromptu interrogation table of what used to be the officer's dining room just two days ago.

"I still have rights, you know! I know my rights, and I'm entitled to legal counsel!" Asa chirped, his expression smug.

Blinking slowly at Asa and letting the Diggi stew in his own silence, Ardalon focused on looking bored.

Oh, look, was that a bit of something lodged in a split in one of his claws? Extending one finger, the razor sharp claw slid out of its sheath. Why, yes, that was a bit of cloth wedged in a split in the left middle claw. Pretending that time didn't matter, he picked the fibers free, discarding them on the table.

It was a little bit of Sasha's strange suit, he assumed, lodged in his claw from when she'd tripped and fallen, cutting her arm to ribbons on his nails. Her furless skin was so delicate, and he said a quick prayer to thank the gods that she healed rapidly with her people's strange blood technology.

Asa swallowed, looking nervous. "I have nothing to say to you, you uncivilized beast," Asa spat, his crown feathers ruffling with his ire. "You can threaten me all you like, but I know my rights."

With the bits of threads pulled free from his claw, Ardalon sheathed them and schooled his expression into boredom as he stared at the ship's first mate with half-lidded eyes. "Hey, Davi," he called over his shoulder.

Davi shifted on his feet from where he stood guard at the door. "Yeah, boss?"

"The comoros' cage hasn't been cleaned out yet, right?" he asked even though he already knew the answer. The poacher's cages had been refilled with their missing animals, then photographed for the report. Cleaned and restocked with food and water and fresh substrate on the floor was the best they were going to get for a little while.

Davi scratched his chin with one claw like he had to think about it before he finally nodded. "Don't think it has, boss."

Leveling his gaze on Asa, he gave the filthy pirate a predatory smile full of teeth. "Good. Show our prisoner to his cell. Maybe his answer will be different after he's had a few hours alone to think about his willingness to cooperate as a good citizen of the United Forces."

Asa's crown feathers flattened to his head. "Y-You wouldn't dare," he sputtered.

Ardalon's evil grin widened, his eyes narrowing in challenge.

Davi and another officer yanked the Diggi pirate up from his chair, leading him out of the room to show him to his new accommodations.

Ardalon's com blinked, and he looked down at it to see that he'd received a message from the chancellor. He held the com up to his eye for the retinal scan before the encrypted file would play. The holographic recording materialized above his wrist.

The chancellor's face was grim, yet composed. "Reports of the retrieval of an unknown sentient being have been confirmed, and an emergency council meeting has been called to determine how best to handle this new development. A representative from each parent planet will be in attendance to ensure transparency and cooperation. The meeting will begin in three hours. Bring the female."

The message completed and then deleted itself, and he looked at the clock on his com, grimacing. Three hours wasn't a lot of time to prepare Sasha for what lay ahead for her. Not that he even really knew what that was. The council could potentially declare her dangerous and aggressive, stripping her of her rights as a sentient. How many laws had she broken? How many Diggi were wounded or dead?

His stomach clenched with unease.

Sasha

IT TOOK A MOMENT FOR HER SLEEP-FOGGED BRAIN TO understand that someone was playing a chime through her door. She lifted her head up from the mountain of pillows, blinking sand-dry grit from her eyes.

"Come in," she called out even though what she really wanted to do was roll back over and pretend she'd never heard the noise at all.

The door opened, and Ardalon stepped inside carrying a tray of something that steamed the air above it. The sight and smell of it was enough to make her sit up.

The shower and nap and change of clothing had been great, but food—actual, real food that smelled like spices and fat and salt—was amazing.

Her mouth watered the moment she smelled it, and her stomach cramped with hunger, reminding her that she'd barely eaten for about a week.

Ardalon crossed the threshold, the door swirling shut behind him. He sat down on the edge of the depressed sleeping area in one languid, graceful movement. If she'd tried to pull that maneuver off, she'd have probably fallen flat on her face, but he made it look effortless as he sat with his legs tucked up under him, the tray balanced on the edge of the bed depression.

"I thought that you may like to try something that does not come prepackaged for long-term voyages," he explained.

Gracelessly digging her way out of pillow mountain, she crawled toward him on her knees. She'd discovered after her shower that walking on the bed was a bad idea. She didn't have the grace or balance for it. The Diggi's idea of comfort translated to mattresses stuffed with tiny pellets. Great for sleeping on, not so great for walking across with human shaped feet.

His ears twitched and she could tell that he was amused. She ignored it because she was too focused on the food to care about anything else. Ardalon lifted the cover off one dish, and she stared at everything.

There was brown soupy stuff with blobs in it that looked like your basic stew made up of some sort of vegetable mix and small chunks of meat. Next to that was a bread roll, except it was a deep shade of purple that was so dark it was very nearly black. In a smaller bowl there was something that vaguely resembled raspberries if raspberries were blue and furry like a kiwi.

"The doctor said that you were most likely omnivorous based on your scans so I brought you a variety of things to try. There's Oxpi stew with yara roots and ceradon, a bannock, and these are yuvei fruit. It grows on vines on my home planet, and they're a personal favorite of the females in my house," he explained.

She picked up one of the little fuzzy blue berries and popped the whole thing into her mouth. It was tart instead of sweet, her mouth puckering in response, but the juice was crisp and refreshing and she didn't mind the furry skin as much as she'd thought she would as she chewed it and swallowed.

The aftertaste was mellow with a hint of sweetness and citrus.

"How the hell did you manage to get fresh fruit on a spaceship?" she asked him as she tried a second one. This one was a tad bit sweeter on the first bite, and she found the flavor growing on her as she ate.

Ardalon handed her a cup of water that she washed it down with before dipping a spoon into the stew, scooping up a heaping portion. Upon chewing it, she found that the meat was just as stringy as it looked, but it tasted vaguely like chicken, and the soft vegetables were easy enough to chew and eat. She ate a second, even heartier bite, humming around the spoon in her mouth as she licked it clean.

"The captain kept his own food stores for making better meals than he fed his crew," Ardalon said as he watched her with smiling eyes while she ate with obvious relish.

"Some things are just universal, I guess," she sighed as she scooped up something that looked like an alien potato.

The spices in the stew were unfamiliar and it could have used a bit more salt, but it was a million times better than the rabbit food or protein bars she'd eaten recently so she wasn't about to complain. Barely pausing to taste everything, she cleaned her plate, then used the dark purple bread to scrape up the rest of the sauce before downing her cup of water and working on the fruit again.

Her portions had looked small at first, but after all that time in the cage her stomach had shrunk and she was glad that Ardalon hadn't brought her more food. She'd have eaten all of it and then probably gotten sick. As it was, she already felt full, and her fatigue came roaring back, reminding her that she could use a bit more sleep.

The nanos took a lot of energy to heal her. She slumped against the pillows, sighing.

"We have a meeting to go to, and then you'll be able to rest more," he told her.

A meeting?

"With who?" she asked, glancing up at him.

He looked away, his posture stiff. "My superior, the chancellor, as well as representatives from each government within the United Council."

She popped the last fuzzy blue raspberry into her mouth and chewed on it while thinking, enjoying the way that the bright citrus flavor cleared the spices of the stew from her mouth. Truth be told, a meeting was the last thing that she wanted to be doing right now. She was clean from her shower and full. Fatigue weighed on her. She'd have loved nothing more than some good, solid sleep. Preferably at least twelve hours of it.

"They're trying to figure out what to do with me," she muttered.

He flicked his left hand in a gesture that she didn't understand. Nudging the food tray back from the edge of her pillow nest, she hauled herself up on the rim. His gaze trailed down her body.

"Is that one of the captain's shirts?" he asked. Ardalon's eyes widened, and his oval pupils broadened as he looked her up and down while she gracelessly pulled herself up to a sitting position on the ledge next to him.

She glanced down at the ruffled shirt that hit her at midthigh, the neck of it exposing a V of cleavage where it gaped on her smaller torso. She'd belted off the excess fabric at her waist. It wasn't haute couture, but it was clean and it covered her goods well enough to be called decent. It was going to look really weird with her boots, though.

You couldn't pay her enough to put her ripped flight suit back on. She'd washed the blood and dirt and funk out of it as best as she could in the bath with some soap, but it was still soaking wet and slightly grimy. Handwashing it in a bathtub with soap wasn't the same as actually laundering it with enzymatic chemical cleaners.

"I think it looks better on me than it probably ever did on him." She was thankful that she wasn't so large-chested that she couldn't manage without some bust support for a bit. She'd sacrificed another of the alien shirts to make herself some makeshift panties that she tied at the hip like a bikini bottom and a halter top.

If there was any chance she might be running for her life again, she didn't want to risk going commando anymore.

His eyes tripped up on her exposed legs and arms and cleavage as if he didn't know where to look, his large, triangular ears flicking.

The urge to reach out and touch them was difficult to ignore. Were they soft? Stiff? Was his velvety-looking fur coarse? She wanted to rub those ears and find out.

"Undoubtedly," he agreed, his voice low and rumbly. "But I'll find you something more... more appropriate for the meeting."

Oh, ho ho! Mister let me gawk at you while you're bathing in a waterfall doesn't have a problem with cuddling me al fresco in a cave, but suddenly my shirtdress isn't cool for anyone else to look at?

"What do you mean? This looks good to me," she teased him, leaning back on her arms. Kicking her legs back and forth, she knocked all of the pillows away from the edge of the bed depression. They tumbled down, sliding into the lowest point of the bed in the center until they were a riotous mish mash of different colors and fabrics.

Ardalon's eyes trailed down her bare legs and then there was a low, stuttering purring sound coming from his chest. He seemed to catch himself a moment later because he cleared his throat.

"Yes, you look fetching. However, the heads of foreign affairs will all be in one room together. Let's find you something a little less... eye-catching."

Her nipples hardened into twin peaks as his hungry gaze slid its way up her body to her face. "What if I want to catch someone's eye?" she asked him in a low voice. "A particular someone, I mean. Theoretically, of course."

What am I doing? I'm flirting with an alien... a hot alien, though. This is insane.

Bright gold eyes with green flecks around their oval pupils met hers. "They'd be a lucky male, hypothetically speaking."

Maybe not so insane then, if the gleam in his eye was interest. Perhaps his morning erection back in the cave hadn't been just a normal physiological reaction. It certainly explained all of the licking and nuzzling in the shuttle ride back to the ship. Perhaps this male was flirting back.

Quicker than she could track the individual movements, Ardalon stood and offered her a helping hand. Despite the lack of quality sleep, the shower and power nap and filling meal had helped restore her to some semblance of a human being again.

He pulled her to her feet, his hand warm as it wrapped around hers, the pads callused and rough against her skin.

CHAPTER TEN

SASHA

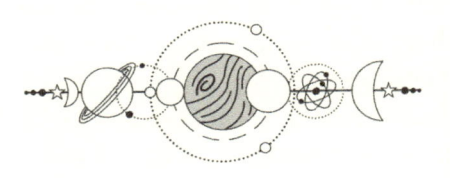

Hologram projections of the council members flickered over chairs around an otherwise empty table. They were the only two who were physically present. Everyone else had chosen to come to the meeting remotely.

She tried to pay attention to all of the bickering and political sniping, but the meeting just wouldn't end as it continued to drag on and on. They were going nowhere fast.

The Diggi delegate insisted that since their people had found her and made first contact, then their tribe had dibs. When Sasha had interrupted the tense conversation to point out that the Diggi's response to first contact had been kidnapping, torture, and enslavement, the room had erupted into barely constrained yelling as everyone spoke over one another.

The Raxion supreme general countered by saying that since Sasha had broken several laws during her 'unapproved arrival' to El'bazahara, that she needed to be taken into custody immediately for questioning.

Her alleged crimes included infiltration of their protected airspace, smuggling in unregistered weapons, destruction of public land, endangerment of a protected species, and failure to pass through customs and immigration. The last offense seemed like adding insult to injury in an effort to see what they could get to legally stick.

She didn't like the sound of their claim at all. It felt like they were hiding their motives with legalities, and she got the feeling that their desire to get their hands on her had more to do with their lizard doctor's medical report and less to do with them actually caring about her invading their airspace.

Yeah... no thanks.

The Diggi wanted her for pride or to soothe their embarrassment, and the Raxions wanted her to either punish her or make her into some sort of science experiment.

She wanted nothing to do with either of them. Both of their species viewed her as little more than an oddity or a thing to possess, and she didn't trust either of them.

Ardalon's eyes slanted toward her as she leaned over and bumped his shoulder with hers to get his attention. "What do your people want?" she asked him point blank. She didn't see how tiptoeing around the issue was going to get her anywhere. Things were better when everyone was upfront and honest as far as she was concerned. "Your chancellor guy hasn't said much."

Ardalon's ears flicked in her direction as he side-eyed her without turning. "I was on a secret mission. However, I can't get into the details right now," he answered her with a subtle nod toward the other United Council members.

The hologram of the Diggi tribal elder showed a puffed-up white and yellow bird lady in a hot pink and purple ruffled dress. The older avian alien was currently ripping into the bored-looking Raxxian general. Neither seem to be paying much attention to anyone else in the room.

"Okay," she prompted, watching him closely with narrowed eyes. "And?"

His ears flattened toward his skull, and he seemed to hesitate for a moment before he spoke. "There is a chance that you could help us with something important."

Well, that's not vague and ominous at all.

Glancing once more at the arguing Diggi and Raxion delegates, she sighed and turned her attention to the Kursh chancellor. Unlike Ardalon and the other policemen lions that she had seen recently, the chancellor was a pale shade of fading golden brown.

A long scar bisected his left eye, leaving it opaque and—she assumed—blind. His hair was grayed with age, and he was the first Kursh that she'd seen with a grown-out beard.

If she had to choose an alien race to trust, her gut told her to go with the lions. "Okay," she whispered, knowing that he'd hear her with those ears of his.

Those ears flicked rapidly, and she watched as he blinked at her for a moment like he was surprised. "You don't even know what the job is. It's potentially dangerous."

She smirked and fiddled with the ruffles on the dress that Ardalon had dug up for her to wear out of some crate he'd found in the Diggis' cargo bay. They still needed to find her some shoes, so the outfit was still a work in progress, but she had to admit that the ruffled wrap dress was pretty.

I haven't felt pretty and feminine and soft in a long time. It's been jumpsuits and social isolation for way too long.

"You'll be a part of it?" she asked as she glanced around the room to be certain that they weren't getting too much attention from the others.

Maybe she should have been more worried. The argument between the Diggi and Raxion emissaries was still raging, although the Kursh chancellor was only glancing at them from the corner of his good eye from time to time.

"The whole time," he said in a reassuring tone.

"Okay. Fine, I'll do it. I have conditions, though. One of

those is that you get me out of the rest of this meeting right now." She couldn't take much more of listening to these two aliens argue about her like she was an object to be owned.

I'm not a thing to be bartered over.

If anyone was going to be doing the bartering here, then it would be her.

Ardalon fiddled with the wrist watch thing that he always wore. Even when he'd gotten naked in the cave to keep her warm and alive, he'd kept it on. Her second condition was going to be getting one of those watch things of her own.

I need the alien version of the internet. What if Kurshes have really weird penises?

Not that it had felt weird when it rubbed against her butt. Still, a girl had to be sure. A moment later, the chancellor's hologram projection rose from his chair which finally got the other two's attention.

"Esteemed colleagues," the chancellor started in a dry, rumbly voice, "I have received information that concerns Mistress Sasha and a matter of Kursh national security. Per article thirteen subsection four of the United Council agreement, the Kursh people are granting her emergency citizenship and all of its protections. Your requests and complaints may be directed to my secretary."

The Diggi elder squawked her protests while the Raxion supreme general looked actually interested for the first time.

The chancellor turned to regard Ardalon and her for a moment. "I trust that Agent Bavara will handle the details," he hinted.

She knew when she was being dismissed, and she didn't need to be told twice. Glancing at Ardalon, who had already risen from his chair and was beckoning her to follow him, she rose too. It was a relief to be done with the boring meeting and all of the rude staring and even ruder attitudes.

Nothing could be worse than having to sit through two more hours of listening to that Diggi female squawk.

It was so much worse than she could have ever imagined.

The skimpy, glittery, barely there outfit that someone had scrounged up from... somewhere could fit into a teacup. Glitter, it turned out, was literally universal. The outfit they'd handed her was basically underwear, and even that was a generous comparison.

"Yeah... that's gonna be a hard no," she said matter-of-factly.

Davi looked confused as he glanced between her nonplussed face and the balled up pleasure district underwear in her clenched fist.

"But this is standard attire for bed warmers," Davi explained for the fourth time.

She practically forced him to take the skimpy bikini from her as she headed over to the collection of silky, sheer, and bedazzled clothes that they'd pulled out of another crate. "There's no way my boobs won't fall out of this. Also, there's a huge hole in the back. My ass is going to completely hang out if I wear that."

Davi held up the offending panties with the aforementioned giant hole in the butt area. "It's for your tail."

She snorted as she threw skimpy garments left and right out of the crate of sex work clothes. "Yeah, I don't know if you've noticed, buddy, but I don't have a tail. And I get that you need me to pretend to be a sex slave for this honeypot scheme of yours, but I'm not showing my ass to a room full of horny perverts who think they get to buy me if they have enough credits."

This might work.

Pulling a sheer red bit of gold-edged fabric from the crate, she shook the stray bits of glitter off of it and turned to show it to Davi. He was staring at her ass.

"Yeah... you don't. Weird," he mumbled, his brow furrowed and his ears flat against his blonde, fluffy mane.

She could feel the tips of her ears getting hot as he seemed to snap to attention and drag his face up her body. "You guys don't have a tail either," she grumbled. She'd stared at Ardalon's butt enough to know that she'd have noticed it if he did. She wasn't sure why, but she was a little bit offended.

His eyes widened until she could see just the tiniest rim of white around his enormous irises. "What?" he sputtered, "I'm not a tailless."

"What? Dude, you guys totally don't have tails!"

She'd know, considering that she and Ardalon had gotten all naked and cuddly in the cave. It *was* dark... but she'd have noticed a fracking tail.

Davi's chest rumbled with a barely audible purr and suddenly he seemed to be leaning a little closer to her than he was a second ago. She held the pretty red fabric to her chest like a shield and took a half-step back.

"Are you saying that you want to see my tail, kitten?" he purred. His ears twitched, and she swore that she could see his curly blond hair get even fluffier as he stared at her. Eyes gleaming, his face sharpened as he stared down at her.

"Nope. I'm good. Thanks for the offer though," she protested, her face blushing with embarrassment until her ears felt hot with it.

"Davi," Ardalon barked from the open doorway. They both turned and glanced his way. His broad shoulders and arms were tense. "Go clean out the cages, and don't forget to feed our good friend Asa," Ardalon ordered.

Davi backed away from her and the crate, edging around

Ardalon, who didn't budge at all to let the guy through. Their broad shoulders rubbed, and they stared at one another for a moment before Davi glanced back at her with one of his fangs showing in a crooked grin.

"The offer stands, kitten," Davi said, and then he winked and he was gone.

Hoo, boy. When did it get so dang hot in here?

Ardalon's irritated look softened as he glanced between the garments in her hands and her face. He prowled over to her with the slinky, liquid walk of a natural predator, her body going tingly in response to it.

"So, was... was Davi hitting on me?" It had sure seemed like it. She was still struggling to come to terms with this tail thing, and Davi had really caught her by surprise.

Ardalon paused. "He struck you?" His posture changed, going rigid.

"What? Oh, no. The translator messed that one up, I think. I meant... was that flirting? Showing, umm, sexual interest?"

She could feel his body heat from how close he was standing. Her fingers itched to reach out and touch him. His fur was softer than it had any right to be, but the body under it was all hard muscle and male. Very, very male. Her ass still had the impression of his rock hard penis embedded in it from their survival cuddling in that cave.

"If you have to ask, then he must not have been doing it correctly," Ardalon rumbled as he trailed a featherlight touch down her shoulder and bicep, cupping her elbow.

"Hmm," she hummed, "I don't know, there's bound to be cultural hiccups. Maybe you should show me. So that I know what to expect, of course, since we're different species and all. You know... for scientific research purposes."

The barely-there touch firmed, and then she felt the barest hint of claws. Her skin broke out in goosebumps as the fine hairs on her arms raised up. His hand slid up, curving around to her back, moving up again. Her breath hitched. The gentle prick of his nails on the back of her neck as he carded his fingers through the hair at the nape of her neck made her body thrum.

"Anything for science," he growled, leaning down and speaking right into her ear as he pressed the side of his face against hers.

He rubbed their skin together, and she could feel his warm breath on her ear. It made her shiver as he kept playing with her hair, gently raking those claws through her strands. The idea of those sharp-as-knives nails on the back of her vulnerable neck made her wet between the thighs.

"Yup. For science. Science is so good. Like… so, so good. I love science," she blathered on as he rubbed his cheek against hers, the natural musky smell of him filling the air between them.

Ardalon's chuffs turned into a deep, rumbling purr. The hand on her neck held her still as he rubbed his other cheek against her face and her breath hitched for a second when she thought he was going to kiss her as he switched sides. Instead, he teased her. Leaning down, crowding her, he slid his other hand around the small of her waist. She groaned, soft and low in the back of her throat, tipping her head back now that he had her caged within his arms.

How long has it been since someone held me like I was precious?

Her hands tangled in his shirt. It was an absolutely ridiculous garment, and she'd noticed that none of the other lions wore them. They wore streamlined suits with colorful patches on the shoulders instead, but she didn't mind the odd clothing he wore, especially not when it exposed such a magnificent chest.

The V-shaped split down the front of his shirt was loosely laced, making it easy for her hand to slip between the open space and stroke the divot between his pectorals. His rough tongue licked a stripe down the side of her neck, and then her earlobe was in his mouth and he was sucking on it.

"Fuck yes," she moaned, leaning into him until they were pressed together.

Her nipples were so hard that she swore they could have cut shield glass, and then his hand at her waist trailed lower, cupping her ass as he gave it a little squeeze.

She'd never felt more grateful in her life before to be wearing a dress because all they'd have to do was shimmy it up. Her makeshift panties were going to be soaked straight through at this rate. Ardalon nibbled on her ear while he purred as she tugged at the laces of his shirt so she could slide her hand in deeper, feeling more of him.

"Sasha," he groaned into her ear after he released her earlobe from his teeth. She loved how deep and husky his voice was. How full of need he was for her. She liked hearing him come undone. It made her want to press on, to see just how much she could push it.

Trailing her fingers down his chest and abs in gentle caresses down his front, she worked her way down until she found the growing bulge within his skintight leather pants. He twitched at her touch, hardening further, the size of him overflowing her hand.

How'd a girl get so lucky?

It was her turn to torture him now. She enjoyed listening to the sounds he made as she palmed him through his pants, tracing her fingers over the length of his growing erection. It had to be uncomfortable for him. Those pants were pretty form-fitting.

"Stop teasing me, kitten, unless you want to get involved in some… scientific… experimentation," he panted.

His claws pricked her through her dress as he kneaded her backside and dipped his other hand down to join the first on the globes of her ass. His thumbs rubbed over the spot just below the base of her spine. It was where a tail would be, she guessed, were she a lioness. She wondered if he was interested in their alien differences as much as she was.

What will he feel like inside of me?

She wanted to find out.

I'll volunteer as tribute for science.

His muzzle slid against her cheek until his lips were hovering just above her. He still hadn't kissed her yet, and she could feel the radiating heat from him as his face hovered right over hers. Her fingers found the bulbous tip of his cock through his leather pants, and she traced the length of him to see how big he really was.

"Sir, has the female finished dressing yet? The photographer is here," a lion she'd never seen before said from the doorway.

The grip on her ass flew away from her body like she was molten hot and he'd been burned. She jumped, her hands springing off of Ardalon's goods like she was a guilty kid who'd just gotten caught with her hand in the cookie jar. Both of them turned to the doorway where a Kursh officer stood hesitant with a confused expression.

His nostrils flared, and then he took a couple of loud sniffs before taking a big step back out into the hallway.

"I'll just, uh, go wait with the photographer. They're setting everything up in the captain's suite," the officer stammered out an apology, then hightailed it out of the room like his tail was on fire.

Ardalon closed his eyes tight and sighed as he took a half-step back from her and it was all she could do not to scream in frustration.

So close.

He opened his eyes and bent down, picking up the forgotten bit of fabric that she must have dropped at some point during their flirting. With a sigh, she took it from him. Time to go play dress-up and help catch an evil crook.

"Science must wait," Ardalon mumbled as he adjusted his clothes to try, and fail, to hide his rather impressive erection.

"Raincheck?" she asked him with a side-eye as she ran the silky fabric through her fingers.

He blinked, and his ears swiveled. "What does a bill of sale have to do with the weather?" he asked.

Frowning, she thought about it. "Huh. I have no idea, actually. It's just something we say. It means that something is to be continued later."

"An idiom. We have our own strange sayings too, I suppose," he said. "I had better go so you can get dressed."

His eyes tracked her movements as she held her slave girl costume to her chest and cocked her head at him. "What, all of a sudden you respect a woman's right to privacy when she's undressed?" she asked him, thinking about how he'd stared at her when she was naked in that water.

Ears flattening to his skull, his eyes rounded. "I owe you an apology. That was... I... There is no excuse," he stammered, blinking rapidly.

Quirking a brow at him, she shifted on her feet and fisted a hand on her hip. "Uh huh. So your people *do* have rules about modesty and privacy."

He bowed at the waist, his head hanging until his brown locks fell forward, obscuring his face. The little silver beads that were woven into them clinked as they moved against one another. "You have my neck."

She blinked at him. "Umm thanks, I think? Sorry, but what does that mean?"

He straightened, a hand raking through his locks as he scratched his head. "It is our sincerest apology. We will speak later. There's much for us to discuss, actually, but now isn't the time. Dress, and then I will take you to the captain's rooms. I'll wait outside for you while you ready yourself."

She nodded and watched as he left, the door closing behind him.

It took her a solid half an hour to wiggle into the modified slave girl costume that she'd finagled. It took two bandeau tops tied together so that they crossed, twisting at the breast bone, for her to actually be what she'd consider dressed. It covered a lot more boob this way, and the back still fastened. The tail hole panties kind of fit her, even though they were a bit snug at the hip. She ended up having to hike them up a little so they weren't cutting into her thighs.

The scarf thing, which had maybe been meant to cover up her hair or something, got ripped in half and tied around her hips.

She tucked the frayed ends into the panty, hiding it. The effect was like a loincloth, and while the fabric was sheer, she was still grateful to have another barrier between her butt and the world. She wasn't a prude, but being in little more than a bikini and walking into a lounge club full of pervy aliens with questionable morals was enough to give any girl the heebie-jeebies.

There weren't any cosmetics, so she had to make do with just a clean face and finger-combed hair. She'd left it down to curl around her shoulders like her own sort of lion's mane. Once she was ready, she palmed the door open. Ardalon's eyes lingered over her as he looked her up and down, his head cocked as if to say follow. She did. He led her through the ship without a word, his countenance shifted from amorous to all business.

The look on the photographer's face as she stepped into the captain's rooms told her that she'd done things right. Ardalon shifted from foot to foot behind her as he looked at everything in the room but her. The photographer stared at her for a moment before fiddling with something in his hands.

It was a silver and black orb. When he slid his hand over a glowing stripe, it popped open like a flower and began to hover in the air. He motioned for her to step further into the room.

"Is that your camera?" she asked as he made an adjustment to it by pulling a light up from a divot. The light extended upward like a vine and curved forward toward her. Another vine of lights extended outward on the other side as well. Mentally, she added that awesome camera thingy to her list of guilt gifts that she was going to demand from the Kursh for agreeing to play along with this charade.

"Perhaps... position yourself on the pillows?" the photographer suggested in a hesitant manner, his eyes flicking toward the captain's bed depression and its massive amount of pillows.

He appeared to be as uncomfortable with this as she was. His eyes barely settled on her before they were looking away again. It made her less nervous that he wasn't straight up staring at her or, worse, ogling.

"Umm... okay," she agreed, climbing down into the pit as carefully as she could, still barefoot. She still hadn't gotten those shoes. The crawl through pillow mountain in the giant beanbag bed was difficult and she almost fell on her face twice. Eventually, she managed to get to the middle of the bed where she settled in a half reclined pose that she hoped appeared languorous and flattering.

The camera made a faint electronic noise, and the light vines occasionally dimmed and brightened, also changing hues as needed. The camera moved about the room in what looked like an independent manner until she saw that the photographer was controlling it with his wrist device. The same kind of device that Ardalon wore.

Definitely need to get me one of those.

Shifting from reclining to sitting to kneeling, she struck a variety of poses and hoped they didn't make her look like an idiot.

Ardalon stepped further inside of the room, his arms crossing over his chest. The photographer audibly swallowed, and then the camera packed itself up as the male caught it out of midair, turning it off.

"I'll just go... umm... p-process these," the photographer mumbled. He backed out of the room without turning his back to them, each step looking awkward. When the door slid shut with the photographer on the other side of it, she sat on her haunches and glanced over to Ardalon.

Ardalon's gaze wasn't heated, though. The guy who had licked her neck until her thighs trembled was gone, and in his stead was Mr. Cool, the professional cop.

"Let's go over it again," he demanded.

She rolled her eyes and sighed. "We've gone over the plan like a dozen times already. I won't forget."

He made a low noise of irritation in his throat. "Once more."

"You're going to take me to a place that has a black market in the back, and you'll be with me the entire time," she started. Adjusting the strap of her bikini top where it was starting to slide and dig into her armpit, she continued. "There will be undercover agents planted in the room. Ones I've never seen before so I don't accidentally give them away." She placed her hands in loose fists on her knees as she settled her back against the mountain of pillows. "You're going to offer to sell me to some rich guy, and then when he pays for me, you'll arrest him."

He crossed his arms over his muscular chest, and she looked up at him, appreciating the view from her spot down in the bed pit.

What I wouldn't give to have that camera thing right about now.

Ardalon looked like an imperious overlord. His face was serious and his posture stiff as he squared his broad shoulders.

Maybe I can keep the slave outfit when this is over? Roleplay is fun.

"And?" he hinted.

"If we get separated, don't panic. My fake slave collar has a tracking device embedded in it, and you'll come and find me," she finished.

His probing eyes softened. "Are you worried?"

He took a few steps forward until he was at the edge of the nest, sitting in one smooth movement.

She shrugged. "Not really. You're the only one here who I trust."

And she realized that she did trust him. Yes, he was getting something that he wanted from her, but she was getting something too. Protection, companionship... maybe feelings? That was early, though, and something to worry about later when she was out of survival mode.

They hadn't known each other long enough to have more than some physical infatuation and hormone spikes. All she knew was that he seemed kind, protective, and sincere. She'd had exes that only had one of those traits, and that was being generous.

"I won't let anything happen to you," he told her.

Nodding, she settled her legs at her side and sprawled out on the pillows. She was doing her best to give him bedroom eyes. "I believe you. But you could protect me a lot better from over here." She patted one of the little decorative pillows next to her.

Ardalon breathed a heavy sigh, but he didn't crawl into the bed with her. "I will take one of your weather receipts, kitten. There are still details and preparations to sort out. And I have been unsubtly reminded that you cannot be brought to market smelling like anyone... intimately."

The room felt stuffy, and Ardalon groaned. "Your skin is changing colors again."

Having attention called to her blushing had always made it worse. Her face felt beet red and the tops of her ears were hot. "Okay... umm... good to know your sense of smell is *that* good."

Ardalon stood in one lithe stretch and made his way over to the door. "Get some sleep. Shower, eat, and rest. Someone will bring you a food tray. I'll come fetch you myself when it's time to leave."

Sasha nodded, too distracted from her embarrassed internal ramblings to pay him too much attention as he palmed the door open and stepped into the hallway.

"Okay, yeah, cool," she groaned, rubbing her forehead.

Throwing herself backward on the pillows, she kicked her heels against the bean bag bed and covered her eyes, groaning.

CHAPTER ELEVEN

ARDALON

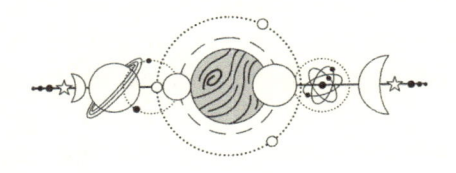

His balls felt swollen and close to rupturing as he focused on clicking Sasha's fake slave collar into place around her throat without ogling the bare skin that was on display. Her bright, kohl-rimmed eyes bored into him. The lock clicked, and he finished securing it into place with his com. The chip in her collar was paired with his device.

There was only room for his smallest finger underneath the edge of the lightweight metal. Rumion was a lightweight conductive metal, but it was also nearly indestructible. It would take a plasma cutter to get it off of her without his biosignature key to undo the locking mechanism.

"There. Now, let's test it," he said as he pulled out the fake training remote. He set it to its lowest setting and pressed the button. "Feel that?"

She squinted her eyes at him until a line grew between them, then shook her head from side to side. Slowly, he turned the dial up. Her mouth parted into a round shape, and then she snorted. It was a quick inhalation of air.

"Tickles," she said, her fingers coming up to lightly touch and explore the collar on her throat.

Turning the dial up to medium, he watched her reaction. The furrow between her eyes grew deeper, but she didn't cry out in pain or fall down to the ground.

"Oof," she exhaled as her nostrils flared.

He turned the dial back down to the lowest setting. "Too much?" The goal was not to actually harm her, just to give her a cue to act as if she was being punished with an electric shock.

She laughed. "I'm fine. Maybe we should establish a safe word, though."

Ears pricking forward to listen for the slightest signal of something wrong, he twisted the dial up to the maximum setting and pressed the delivery button. Her nostrils flared, but she seemed unharmed. The tech guys who'd modified the controls appeared to have successfully dialed down the intensity of the shocks until they were just an irritating nuisance.

"If you feel the tickling or this last setting, you should cower and pretend to be in great pain. It's a punishment stimulus for training and control purposes."

Lifting his finger off the button, he slipped the device back into an interior pocket within his clothing. Something nagged at him, a wariness that Senator Brodyn had fallen for their bait too quickly. They'd barely sent him the encrypted file of photos and video clips before the senator had replied with his bid and an invitation to meet in person.

What Ardalon had expected to take many hours had taken less than two.

Brodyn must be very eager for an exotic pet, indeed.

The thought left a sour taste in his mouth, and his nerves were stretched taut. Perhaps the chancellor was right and he was just nervous now that the plan he'd spent over five months perfecting was finally coming to an end.

The chance to catch Senator Brodyn breaking important

council laws was worth the risk, otherwise they wouldn't be where they were after such a long operation.

"Dog collar, got it," she said. "Woof."

"Stay close to me," he warned her, motioning for her to follow him. Together, they headed into the loading bay where they board a cruiser with Asa, who was sitting there in the pilot's seat, waiting for them. The Diggi gave them a disgruntled look before settling his feathers.

"I'm just happy to finally have shoes," she sighed, looking down at the soft-soled slippers that Davi had resourced from somewhere for her.

"We won't be in the seediest parts of El'bazahara, but we still need to be cautious," Ardalon told her. "It'll be filled with criminals. Slavery is illegal, even all the way out here on the fringes, but... the settled galaxy is large and the Peacekeepers are spread thin enough as it is."

Sasha settled into her chair and buckled her lap belt. Asa glowered at them from his seat but thankfully remained silent.

They'd bought his cooperation with an immunity deal, but neither of them were very happy with one another. He'd have liked to see the pirate rot on a prison moon for his crimes, but he'd let this one small mouse go in order to catch bigger prey.

With a smooth launching sequence, the cruiser was sailing toward El'bazahara's grittiest port.

Once they were within hailing range, the port authority pinged their system. It was Asa's border agent contact, who'd already been arranged well in advance before Ardalon's intervention in the pirates' plans.

Senator Brodyn had thought he was going to be buying an extremely rare and critically endangered Vizula. He'd been offered a one-of-a-kind bed slave instead. Thankfully for them, he'd proven amenable to the switch.

His corruption was deeper than they'd ever hoped to prove.

If we land him for this…

The bribed border control agent flashed them a sly grin, sparing Sasha just one puzzled frown before he'd given them the landing coordinates for their docking spot within the crowded port. As their coms disconnected, Asa landed them in the port with precision and experience.

He might have been a filthy pirate and a poacher, but the Diggi had spent his lifetime in the stars and it showed in his handling of the vessel.

When Asa reached over to disengage his safety belt, Ardalon took the opportunity to lean down and slap a beam shackle to the male's foot. The Diggi squawked and tried to dodge, but he was faster. Once Asa was chained to his chair, Ardalon unbuckled his safety belt, reached up high, and flipped the ship's console into stasis mode.

The life support would stay on with the core generator, but nobody would be able to use the commutations relay or engage the engine.

"What's the meaning of this? We had a deal! Back-shooting Kursh scum, I knew you couldn't be trusted," Asa spat as he glared arrows at Ardalon.

"I don't need you sabotaging this. You'll stay here until this is over," he commanded.

Ignoring the pirate's scathing protests, he turned to Sasha. She tucked herself close to him, two of her fingers worrying at her collar. A hint of fear crept into her scent, the smell of her turning sour, as they approached the door.

Good. Fear will keep her close and cautious.

The door slid open, and the noises and smells of port assaulted them. The scent here was the same as any other port. No matter what planet you were on, they all smelled the same. A mixture of fuel exhaust, rotting garbage, piss, and burning metal. His nostrils pressed shut in disgust, blocking the majority of the scent from his sensitive nose, until he adjusted to it.

There weren't any footsteps behind him as he descended the metal stairs.

Turning to look behind him, he saw that Sasha was standing in the open doorway with a strange look on her face. Her lips were parted, eyes were wide and unblinking.

Turning to glance at the filthy view, he tried to imagine seeing it for the first time with brand new eyes. Tall buildings in a bizarre mashup of different styles, dimensions, and materials, each one taller than the next as they all tried to outdo their neighbor. Everyone wanted to be housed in the tallest apartment in El'bazahara. It was the only way to get the sunlight that the Raxions craved.

Dark shadows stretched across the crowded walkways, casting the streets of the city in a perpetual twilight even though it was still a few hours 'til sunset.

Neon signs and holographic displays blinked, flashing into the dim recesses as they attempted to lure patrons into the bars, restaurants, shops, and brothels. Street vendors and prostitutes called out their wares, the noise of the crowd drowning them out as they competed with one another to be the loudest.

Scaled aliens in all manner of dress walked by. Raxions were the most common here on this planet, although there were enough Diggis and Kurshes woven into the throng that they wouldn't stand out too much.

Well, I won't stand out.

His ridiculous clothing had been chosen to make him look like a ruffian, but not one who was too dangerous. He wasn't meant to attract too much attention, either good or bad. Sasha, however, was a shining beacon of smooth, soft skin and alien otherness. She was going to stand out no matter where she went, regardless of the oversized cloak that was covering as much of her body and face from view as possible.

"Keep your hair covered and your face angled down to cast it in shadows. Walk behind me on my left," he reminded her.

She snapped out of her silent musings and nodded, then tipped her chin down in a submissive gesture as she moved into place behind him.

It was all he could do to keep his instincts in check. The sight of her coming to heel at his back made his cock pulse, wanting to swell. The bite marks in his shoulder, faint as they were, sent heat through his blood.

Lightball... Cardenas' game winning seven to four during the last inning of the final season... gods damn it... Tiyana, Matiyah, and the rest of cubs... there.

His forming erection shrank, and then he could walk again.

Get ahold of yourself, idiot.

With his body wrestled back under control, he led her down the ship's ramp and they made their way through the port.

The ship closed up tight behind them, and they weaved their way down the boardwalk, merging right into the thick of it. A few well placed elbows and snarls carved them a path through the people, although his peripheral senses were in overdrive as he focused not only on their surroundings, but also on making sure that Sasha stayed behind him, safe and unmolested.

A few strangers gave her more than a cursory glance, but with the cowl of her cloak pulled down over her hair and forehead, they could only see the point of her chin and her lush pink mouth. The rest of her face was covered in shadows and fabric.

The grunge-filled dockside with its cheap wares and working-class residents waned, and then they were in a slightly less shabby—but no less seedy—part of town. Vendors here had their wares laid out on tables for buyers to browse instead of keeping them safely locked away.

Food stalls changed from readymade takeaway foods to made-to-order, dine-in meals. The prostitutes standing on the corners under their blinking neon signs looked less blissed out on drugs.

One of them, a Raxion prostitute in a metallic strap dress that was more straps than dress, made a point of angling herself toward him as she traced one painted claw down the gently curving line of her body. Sasha pressed herself closer into his side until she was nearly walking on top of him.

Jealous?

His chest swelled with satisfaction. He grinned, pleased that she seemed territorial, and shook his head, declining the silent invitation. The prostitute merely shrugged, shifting her attention to the next potential customer walking down the street.

Sasha sniffed the air as they passed a cluster of restaurants, and he wanted to pause and ask her what smelled good to her, figure out what she might like, but then the curious double-take of a passing Diggi reminded him that they weren't sightseeing and they didn't have time to dawdle.

They absolutely couldn't afford to draw attention to themselves. He reached back and grabbed her by the elbow, his chest filled with the deep rumbling of a warning growl as the Diggis fled, melting back into the crowd.

He hurried their pace along, and then they were through the worst of it. Three turns down side streets later, they were threading their way between dumpsters and discarded refuse at the back of a nude lounge. He checked the pin on his com to confirm that they were at the right place. He banged a fist on the hollow doors and tried to ignore the feeling of Sasha brushing against his back, her soft body pressed into his side.

A moment later, the door opened a crack and a disgruntled employee leaned out of it.

"This is the kitchen," the male told them in a bored voice.

"You gotta go around." He swirled two fingers in a lazy circle and moved to shut the door in their faces.

He slammed an arm into the closing door, keeping it from clicking shut. "I'm here for the auction."

The worker's eyes narrowed in distrust, but the male was no longer trying to close the door on them. "Look, I don't know you. Beat it. I don't know what you think—"

Ardalon pulled the hood off of Sashas head, the neon lights playing over the contours of her face and smooth, alien skin. "I'm gonna be a rich male by the end of the night. Open the viruking door."

The staff member blinked at them in stunned confusion for a moment before glancing over his shoulder and craning his head back out into the alley so he could look up and down both sides of the street.

"Get in before someone walks by," the male said.

The door opened and he reached back, pulling Sasha through it with him as they passed the worker. The male leaned down to sniff the top of her head, and Ardalon growled a warning at him.

"Unless you've got credits to spend, don't you viruking touch my property. She's not for the likes of you. You keep your dirty claws off of her."

The kitchen door shut behind them, and the guy bolted the row of locks on the door one by one.

"Hey, sheathe your claws. There's no harm in sniffing. The party's downstairs. Now get the viruk out of this kitchen before I regret letting your ass in here," the guy snapped, angling his head toward one corner to show them the way.

Ardalon looked at each lock, letting his implant record each one, before he looked over the faces of everyone in the club's kitchen, then mapped their route through it as they threaded their way between cooks and waitstaff until they found the nondescript door that led them down into the basement. Despite its bland appearance, this door was made from solid, heavy metal and a few laser marks decorated it, barely scratching the surface.

The guard outside of the impenetrable door was huge, muscled, ugly, and mean-looking.

"What?" the guard barked out in a deep voice. The Raxion's front brow ridges were calloused and cracked like he had taken a lot of fists to the face in his time.

"I'm here to sell," Ardalon growled back.

Sasha stared at the scaled door guard with wide eyes. Ardalon pressed a hand to the small of her back in what he hoped was a reassuring gesture hidden as a display of ownership and possessiveness.

The thug at the door grunted, and Ardalon wondered if the male was only capable of one-sided conversations. The bouncer scanned his wrist at the door and it buzzed, then opened for them.

Inside the hidden underground chamber was another lounge. One with darker, sometimes forbidden tastes. Prostitutes and scantily-clad entertainers wandered freely between patrons as slaves sat on the floor by their owners. All sorts of illegal things happened here in these illicit places. Blood sports, slave auctions, weapons deals, and drug sales.

This group of buyers and sellers was the absolute worst of both criminals and the privileged elite who bankrolled them.

There were shrieks of laughter, pain, and pleasure amongst the general drinking, gambling, and carousing. He scanned the lounge and let his eyes skip over the senator, pretending not to notice him.

Senator Brodyn was flanked by two guards, and he was currently engaged in conversation with one of the minor princes of the southernmost Diggi tribe. He tried to place the male in his memory of their line to the throne, but their Empress had over a hundred offspring and he didn't remember this one in particular.

A Kursh prostitute passed, staring at him with hungry eyes before glancing at Sasha and seeming to change her mind. Her tail twitched in an angry arc before she veered off to the other side of the room, perching herself on the lap of a Raxion.

Pressing Sasha forward, he found an empty spot at the crowded bar for them to wait in. Approaching the senator directly—especially while he was speaking with a noble lordling—would be a mistake. It was better if he saw them from the corner of his eye, summoning them to him instead. He focused on staying alert while appearing to be at total ease.

"What can I do for you?" the bartender asked as he collected an empty drinking glass from another customer, spiriting it away below the bartop.

"Two swallows of fire water, on ice," he told the male as he pulled a scrubbed credit stick from within one of his many hidden pockets.

He tapped it to the reader and watched as the bartender turned, grabbing a clean glass and a bottle of maroon-colored liquor from the bottom shelf. The bartender poured a healthy measure into the glass then plopped two perfect spheres of ice inside, sliding it forward, before turning and facing his next customer.

Dismissed, Ardalon took a small sip of his drink and swirled it so that he could survey the room with one elbow slung over the bartop casually, Sasha curved into the hollow of his body as she looked around, her eyes moving from person to person.

A round table of five gamblers erupted into threats of cheating, and someone pulled a small blaster from its holster. They were waving it about, spouting all sorts of threats and hostilities. He kept an eye on them from the corner of his view as he continued to scan the room with all of his senses, taking small sips from his drink.

He recognized a Raxian officer in plain clothes. The male

was flirting with a dancer. A Kursh enforcer was throwing dice at a gaming table.

Sasha fidgeted, playing nervously with a strand of her hair. It was difficult to pretend to ignore her, but he did. With his focus on no particular spot in the club, he could tell the exact moment that the senator finally noticed them. Guards peeled away as the princeling rose, headed into some deeper back room of the club.

The senator's bodyguards glided through the rowdy crowd. "Come with us," one beckoned, leaving no room for either refusal or negotiation. The other curved around behind them as if he planned to herd them forward should they attempt to disobey.

Obliging, they followed. He knew that Sasha was just a step behind him, but it was difficult to resist the temptation to reach out and hold her hand. A protective gesture because the crowd was rough and dangerous, and a claiming one too, as his mark demanded.

Ignoring his baser instincts, Ardalon did neither. He took small sips from his drink instead and pretended to be enjoying the rough burn of the bottom shelf liquor as it carved a path to his stomach.

The senator was dressed expensively in a well-cut suit of black silky fabric. A hint of frill at his sleeve was the only allowance that the serious male made for foppery among this den of criminals and lowlifes. His slicked back, pale gold mane was twisted into a knot of braids at the back of his nape. He stood and smiled, a flash of white fang, as his lackeys brought them forward. The guards moved to stand at attention on either side of their private sitting area.

"Have a seat, please, and I shall order us some refreshments," Senator Brodyn said, an order hidden under the guise of a polite demand. He waved them over to an empty chair. He sat, glanced at her, then at the floor, and after a moment's hesitation she sat at his feet and leaned her weight against his leg. Letting his body slouch into the chair, he held his drink up until the spheres of ice clinked against the crystal glass.

"I'm set, but thanks," he deflected, taking a measured sip. The way that the Senator's eyes roamed Sasha made Ardalon feel hopeful for his plan yet conflicted and repulsed all at once.

An odd feeling, to be sure.

The senator's lip curled upward exposing one gleaming, white fang. "I insist," he drawled. "Have you ever had a glass of Perussia Blue? It's exquisite. It'll be a once-in-a-lifetime treat for you, I'm sure. The fruit is grown high in the mountains here. It can only be harvested under very specific circumstances. There's a great deal of science to it, I'm told. Something about soil pH and the acidity levels of the rain. The real trick to it, though, is aging it in charred barrels made from Ratlata wood."

The senator turned his attention to one of his bodyguards and flicked his fingers at him in an imperious gesture that showed the male was used to being obeyed. "Two drinks of Perussia Blue, and something sweet for the... lady."

Ardalon faked a smile of gratitude as the bodyguard went off to fetch their drinks. "So you like her? If not, then we'll hit the auctions. She should fetch enough for us all to retire on, I think."

The senator cupped his chin in his claws and made a show of perusing as much of Sasha as he could see through her cloak. "Interesting, to be certain. Very interesting. The photographs did not do her justice, although I can hardly see her through all of this fabric."

Palming his drink, Ardalon found the edge of Sasha's cloak and tugged the hood back, flipping one edge of the cloak up over her shoulder to reveal her scantily clad body. "That's all you'll get to see of her before I have a credit stick in my hand."

The senator sighed in appreciation and leaned back in his chair. "Such impossibly smooth skin. No claws or fangs or spinal ridges. In truth, I have never seen such a creature. She looks soft and pliable. Docile too. Are there more where she came from? We could make a fortune selling them. You would source them while I handled distribution using my connections. I'm sure that we can discuss pay cuts and the specifics with the captain. Where is he, by the way? I'd expected him to be present, as usual. A very strange deviation…"

Ardalon scoffed and let a look of disdain cross his face. "Captain's busy whoring. We've been out of port for so long fetching goods from all over, I'm sure you know how it is. She's a one of a kind, as promised. Not even the emperor has one like her in his harem. Nor will he. Not unless you decide to make her into a gift for him."

The senator's eyes gleamed dangerously with interest at that statement. "My dear cousin… he *would* be furious if he learned that I had such a pretty treasure within my grasp that was not for him. He never did like to share his toys, not even when we were cubs."

Feeling dangerously alive with the rush of anticipation, Ardalon managed to keep his facial expressions under control.

The senator was within his grasp, and he could practically feel the claws of justice closing around the arrogant male.

"What color is her cunt?" the senator asked, glancing at her.

Sasha made a choking noise, then coughed as if she was trying to mask it. Her face turned pink as she covered her mouth and coughed into her hand, clearing her throat.

"You know, I never checked," he told him. "The captain made sure that none of the crew touched her that way. Said he'd space us if any were stupid enough to try it."

The bodyguard returned with a tray of drinks which he distributed amongst them. Ardalon took his crystal glass of smoky blue liquor as Sasha was handed a glass of some blended pink and orange concoction that had a twist of citrus peel and a little yellow flower delicately perched on the rim.

She sniffed it first, then took a cautious sip followed by a second longer gulp, and finally made a breathy little sigh of pleasure.

The senator smiled at her, drinking from his own glass of chilled blue liquor, and the bodyguard returned to his post.

"I find it unnerving," the senator began, "when my contact changes at the last moment. One can never be too careful these days. So I hope you understand when I say that a small act of good faith is in order here. Tell her to suck your cock."

His glass nearly slipped from his fingers, and Sasha choked on her drink, sputtering and coughing for real. "Excuse me?"

The twisted Senator set his glass down and smiled, that same damned fang peeking out where it touched his lower lip. "Open your fly, pull out your cock if you have one, and tell her to suck it. Really, the concept is not complicated."

Surprise faded, leaving tension behind.

He knows. He has to know. Brodyn doesn't share. He's infamous for it after he cut off the hand of the last male who dared to touch one of his females at a party.

"Well, if you can't get it up, then I'm sure that one of my guards would be happy to take your place. Vigo, pull out your cock," the senator ordered.

The bodyguard's hand went to the buttons on his coat, flicking it open before sliding down to his pants.

Sasha pressed her body even tighter against his legs, but as he glanced down at her he saw that she wasn't clutching at him in fear. Her eyelids were heavy and her body struggled to remain upright and conscious as she slumped against him. The pink cocktail dropped from her loose grip, hitting the floor where it broke, splattering its contents across the cut stone.

He moved to press his panic button from a hidden pocket only to find that his body was sluggish and failing to respond. Even blinking and swallowing took a conscious effort. His heart was pounding a rapid staccato in his chest as his panic swelled.

We're dead. I've doomed us in my arrogance. Oh, Sasha. I'm sorry for dragging you into this.

The senator grinned, his face triumphant. "Oh dear, the neurotoxin took effect rather quickly. I suppose it is a good thing that you only took a sip or two. If you'd drunk the whole thing, it might have killed you. Poisoning isn't really my forte so I can't be blamed, really. Ergo, you were a bit heavy handed, I think. Vigo, for the gods' sake put your cock away. I wasn't serious."

"Sorry, sir," the bodyguard who'd delivered the drinks apologized, the other shoving himself back into his pants and putting his clothes back into order without a word despite his straining bulge.

Senator Brodyn stood and came toward them. He crouched and brushed a strand of hair away from Sasha's slack face. A possessive growl built in his throat as Brodyn's claw traced the contours of her plush lips and tapped her on the nose. He tried to lunge forward to throw the senator away from her, but his body only managed to slide down in his seat. He was locked in. Betrayed by his own body, his control taken away from him by whatever foul concoction was slipped into his drink.

"A noble effort to save her, I'm sure," the senator mocked.

"Don't struggle. The more you struggle, the more the poison will circulate, and the longer its effects will take to wear off. It's ingenious, really, and terribly ironic that the male who invented it also died from it. Too little has absolutely no effect. Too much freezes the lungs, and one suffocates while still fully conscious."

"I usually prefer a more direct means of dealing with my problems, but I've been advised that killing you would likely cause me too many problems for me down the road. Did you know that I have loyal males on my payroll within your ranks? No? So naive," he said.

"We met once, you know. At a state assembly several years ago. I have an excellent memory for faces. You were just gaining a reputation, moving up in the ranks. The shining star who everyone spoke about. A tailless. Can you believe it? You were a diversity hire, but then you had the audacity to be good at your job. Consider this a warning to slow down. All careers have to end somewhere... for people like you."

A claw at one of the ties on her top cut through the fabric like butter, the fabric flopping over to reveal one breast. The senator's eyes dropped, watching his nail trace over her skin until her nipple pebbled underneath the touch.

"Pink," the senator gloated, his smile widening until both fangs gleamed against his lower lip. "How lovely and strange."

Despite the warning, Ardalon struggled, demanding his body to move. A finger, a toe, anything at all. Despite his efforts, nothing so much as twitched. All he could manage was a withering glare that promised pain and suffering upon the senator when he was recovered. If the senator received that message, then he didn't betray any hint of concern on his punchable, smug face.

The male smiled, his eyes glittering as he slid a claw down Sasha's body, nudging the edge of her cloak off her shoulder. "Your people are also incapacitated. I would tell you to look around and see that for yourself, but, hmm, I suppose you can't." The senator grinned.

"I'm taking the female as payment for my supreme mercy. I could have disemboweled you right here and now with my claws. I think I'll retire to my summer home while the dust settles. Goodbye, Agent Bavara. You've lost, true, but don't let that get your spirits down too much. Greater males than you have tried and failed to ruin me. Don't take it to heart."

A bodyguard bent down to hoist Sasha up on a shoulder as Ardalon struggled against the poison's hold. The veins in his forearms and neck bulged as he strained to make his godsdamned body move. His thumb twitched, his head feeling like it was about to explode as he concentrated and redoubled his efforts.

The senator's mouth pursed as he looked at Ardalon with disdain. "Vigo, take care of the fool before he kills himself. I don't need a royal hand slap from my cousin."

Ardalon's face exploded with fire, his body hurtling over the side of a chair as a fist crashed into his head and knocked him clear over the armrest of his chair until he was sprawled on the floor. Drool and blood leaking from where he'd cut his lip on his teeth, it dripped onto the cold stone floor. His left arm was pinned beneath his body, and the room faded to black around the edges as if he was entering a tunnel.

All he could hear was roaring and ringing in his ears before he heard nothing at all.

Sasha

She had a wicked hangover and her mouth tasted like cotton. Sasha wanted nothing more than to roll over and go back to sleep, but the urge to pee wouldn't let her rest. She blinked grit from her dry eyes and sat up, surveying the room. Where was she? Ardalon and she were at the club… meeting with the… senator. She definitely remembered walking in. The rest of it was a hazy blur of half-formed memories that slipped away even as she tried to remember them.

The harder she focused, the less distinct they were.

The room she woke up in was well lit and mostly bare of furniture. Disentangling herself from the sheets, she rose from the bed, grateful to see that at least she was still dressed. Her top shifted as she rose, and she saw that the flimsy fabric had ripped apart. Fingering the edge of the material, she frowned.

Not ripped. Cut.

Her blood ran cold in her veins, her heart dropping into her stomach. Rubbing her hands up and down her body, she didn't sense anything wrong with her other than the dry mouth and the urgent need to pee.

Scanning the barren white walls of this strange new room, she spotted a familiar glowing sigil that she'd come to recognize as their bathroom marking. She made a beeline for the room. The tile floor was cold under her bare feet, and for a brief moment she mourned the loss of her shoes. She'd just gotten them, and already they were gone.

The bathroom was just as utilitarian as the bedroom had been. Whoever had decorated these rooms didn't love color or knick knacks nearly as much as the Diggi. They were functional, if boring. At least the toilet was easy enough for her to find and use.

As she shucked her makeshift panties down, she sat and peed, sighing in relief before cleansing herself. She washed her hands, then brought cupped handfuls of water to her mouth, drinking right from the tap.

She felt more like a human being with two of her needs satisfied. Now, she just had to figure out what the frack was going on. There was nothing in the bathing room other than a wall dispenser filled with lightly scented cleansers and a shelf filled with towels. There were zero personal effects or decorations, and that fact only made her curiosity deepen.

Leaving the white bathroom that could have belonged in a

hospital, she moved onto the bedroom and inspected that next. It was more of the same.

White walls, cold tile floor, spartan furniture with little more than bedsheets and a spare set of blankets in a drawer, but there was a closet filled to the brim with women's clothes. They hung from pegs or lay folded on metal racks. It was all a mixture of smooth black leather, gemstone or sparkle-covered fabric, and sheer flowy things that were meant to drape and tease. There was something there in every color of the rainbow, and the clothes range from princess to stripclub to dominatrix.

The door slid open, the senator walking in, flanked by the two bodyguards she'd seen with him at the club.

Shit.

He smiled a crooked, fang-filled grin at her. She hated him, viscerally and immediately. She'd known men like him before. Guys that took everything and wanted more, then left you empty.

"Oh, you're already awake. Very good. I find it's best to get the first time over with quickly. The longer I let things wait, the worse you females tend to build it up in your head."

His words translated in her mind, his lips not matching what her brain registered as he spoke. She'd gotten used to it with Ardalon, and familiar with it with Davi. Seeing another—seeing someone who looked like both of those males but who had none of the warmth or kindness in him—was startling.

She frowned at him. "Excuse me?"

"Oh, of course, the sleeping draught tends to make one confused for a time. Shall I explain? Take off your clothes and get on the bed. I'm going to viruk you," he said matter of factly.

Her eyes widened as she stared at him in shock, and then her head fell back and she laughed, her breath wheezing out between snickers as she tried to regain control of herself and speak.

"That's... that's a... good one. Thanks, but no thanks, mister."

He narrowed his eyes at her, his ears twitching backward as he tilted his head. "Hmm... right. The hard way it is, then. Strip her."

The bodyguards surged forward, grabbing her. She tried to back away from them, but there was nowhere to go and nothing to aid her. The room was small, and aside from large, heavy furniture and clothing there wasn't much in there, nothing that she could throw at him or turn into a weapon.

Is this asshole seriously going to try to rape me?

One of the guards grabbed her arm during her distraction, and then they had her pinned into a corner. The harem girl outfit was ripped from her body. Their sharp nails tore through the filmy material like it was made of tissue paper. She elbowed them and screamed at them and writhed in their grasp, trying to catch them in their eyes or sensitive noses with her nails.

The guards didn't seem intent on hurting her, but they weren't too careful not to damage her either.

Their nails caught her incidentally, cutting into her. Once she was naked, her outfit a puddle of shredded fabric at her feet, they let go of her.

Shaking with stunted rage, she fought the urge to huddle in the corner like a scared animal. The metal collar around her neck was the only thing still on her. Her hands twitched with the urge to cover her breasts and shield her body from their view, but she also didn't want to give them the satisfaction of seeing her afraid or cowed.

They could take her clothes away, but she would be damned if she let them take her dignity from her too. She glared at the senator as his bodyguards stepped away from her and went to guard the door.

His hands moved to the line of buttons that connected his

black jacket. "You're pleasing enough to look at, that's good. It helps. Not that I wouldn't have screwed you anyway, but I'm glad nonetheless."

"I'm so glad I please you," she said in scathing tones as her hands clenched into fists at her sides.

Her eyes darted from the disrobing senator to his two guards. Both of them had one of those laser guns on their hips, secured in a holster. If they wore more weapons than that, then she couldn't see them.

She needed to get them out of here. Three against one was more than even she could handle, especially when she wasn't armed but her enemy was.

The Senator smiled, tossing his skirted jacket aside, and began to work on the buttons of his trousers. The top of his pants slid down on his hips, and she could see that yes, the Kursh really did have tails, but for some reason they kept them hidden underneath their clothes. His tail unwrapped from his waist, curling behind him. It was distracting her, and she forced her gaze up his body to find him watching her.

"Sarcasm," he said, "is the defense of a simpleton, as my nanny always said before she struck me for it."

She narrowed her eyes at him. "Maybe she didn't hit you hard enough. Your manners are shit."

His thumbs dragged his pants down his legs, his half-hard cock bobbing free.

I will not look at it. I won't…

She glanced down his lean body.

Holy shit.

Her eyes snapped back up, taking in the smug look on his obnoxious face. He looked so much like Ardalon, except that he looked nothing like him at all.

It was… weird. Familiar. Horrifying.

The senator kicked his feet free from his shoes and pants

while he shucked his lacy black shirt off next, throwing it aside. Her back hit the wall as he stalked forward, closing the distance between them and leaning into her space to sniff exaggeratedly at her neck and chest.

"You're spiced with anger... not soured with fear. How *interesting*. I look forward to breaking you. Let's make a game of it, my pet."

Before she could stop him, he'd threaded his hands through her hair, tightening his fist into her nape, and pulling her head to the side. Her scalp stung and burned as he pulled her forward toward the bed, leading her by the fist locked at her nape. She hissed at him through gritted teeth as the backs of her legs hit the side of the bed.

"Get on the bed and spread your legs for me and I'll even let you cum," he drawled in a purr of rolling vowels. "If you beg."

Her response was a swift kick backward toward his dick.

She would have headbutted him too if it wouldn't have probably scalped her in the process with his claws. He dodged her kick, using his free hand to slap her for her efforts. The crack of his open palm against the side of her head was blinding while he still had her by the hair. His nails scratched through her scalp, and she felt hot, sticky blood trickling through her hair. The side of her face felt like it was on fire, and her vision blurred for a moment.

He sighed, a drawn out and suffering sound. "I commend your heroic efforts to protect your fragile femininity. However, if you try to strike me again I will have the offending appendage removed. Without anesthetic. Understand?"

The backs of her knees hit the bed, his body pushing her forward with no chance for escape from him. His erection pressed against the soft part of her belly, a drop of pre-cum smearing across her skin. "You don't need your limbs to get viruked, pet."

"You're mine now," he said. "The life you had before me and this room is dead. We can do this the easy way, where you open your cunt for me and I reward you with food and entertainment and baubles, or we can do this the easier way, where I bind you, take you anyway, and beat you until you stop fighting. Which would you prefer? I can go either way, really. Tears and screams neither excite, nor disgust me. Ladies' choice," he growled.

The Senator released his grip on her hair, pressing his palm flat to her breastbone, then shoved her back so she fell, sprawled out, onto the bed. He loomed above her, one hand stroking his intimidating length as he fisted his barbed, studded penis from root to top until another pearlescent drop of pre-cum beaded on his tip. The base of him swelled, getting bigger. He fisted his cock and stroked, growing his penis even larger.

Getting herself back under control, she tried to think, her mind racing.

Scent. He can smell my moods just like Ardalon and the other Kursh.

She did her best to think of anything that might make her afraid instead of angry. It wasn't difficult. Of course she was angry, but there was fear there too hiding underneath the bridled rage.

She was probably never going to see home or her brother and his new wife again. If they ever earned a family license, she'd never meet her niece or nephew. She was alone in an unfriendly world that seemed to be constantly trying to sell, cage, eat, rape, maim, or kill her.

Ardalon, the only one who had been decent and nice to her, might be dead. She had no friends here... no allies... not even people of her own kind. The only person who might come and save her was likely dead. This asshole didn't seem like the kind to leave witnesses behind.

Nobody will mourn me if I die, alone and frightened in this sterile white coffin of a room.

His lips curved in a farce of a smile, his top teeth and their wickedly sharp double incisors showing. Suddenly, she understood why Ardalon had always gotten creeped out whenever she'd tried to smile at him. His smile wasn't friendly at all. Terror settled in her gut, fighting for room against her anger.

"Well?" he prompted her.

"Make them leave.... please," she whispered. "I... I don't want them to watch," she pleaded.

The senator cocked his head, then looked over his shoulder at his guards and made a shooing motion at them.

"Sir, perhaps—"

"If I desire your opinion, then I will ask for it," he snapped at them, his hand still stroking his cock. "What harm could she even do to me? She's weak. No claws, no fangs. Get out."

With downcast eyes, the two bodyguards pressed a palm to an unmarked spot on the wall and left the room, letting the door slide closed behind them.

Her fear settled, leaving her feeling cold and calculating.

Sliding her body up the bed, she leaned herself back on her elbows and tilted her pelvis, bending her knees. He needed to come closer for this next part, and she needed to avoid his claws as much as she could.

His hungry gaze slid along the line of her thigh, and he seemed mesmerized by what he saw when he glanced between her legs.

"Pink," he smirked. "Delightful."

Just a little closer.

The senator squeezed himself, pumping harder, stroking his cock and smearing the glistening bead of fluid down his shaft. The barbs along his length slid with the skin as he moved his fingers over them.

Her heart raced in her chest, her breath coming in fast pants as he took the final half-step forward to position him at the juncture between her thighs. His knees hit the bed. His body was warm against her cold skin in the chilled, empty room, and his fur was as soft as velvet. Her stomach churned with revulsion. Bending her leg, she lifted it up over his shoulder, draping it there to pull him into the cradle of her hips.

"You like it deep, huh?" he asked as he looked down at her where she was spread open before him.

She pretended to be confused. "This isn't how your people do it?"

He shrugged.

Wait. Don't waste it.

She could feel the tip of him brush against her entrance, and it made her want to vomit.

The thought of him invading her, taking her, was torture. Gold eyes that were the wrong shape and color stared down at her with triumph in them as he stroked a hand down her tense and trembling thigh. He rubbed himself up and down along her slit.

Not yet. Wait for it.

Another question was forming on his lips when he leaned his face closer, tilting his balance forward.

She sprang into action, swinging her other leg up.

Wrapping one leg around the other, she locked her ankles and squeezed her thighs, clenching them tight and secure around his neck.

He exhaled with the surprise of it.

It was a mistake she'd take full advantage of.

More force, more pressure, more twisting as he struggled to break the hold she had on him with her legs. She twisted her torso, using the bed as a fulcrum to drag him onto the bed with her. His hand that had been stroking her thigh raked at her, his claws digging into her skin as he made a strangled noise.

She choked him.

The senator tried to buck free of her, but her weight was supported by the bed, and he was half-standing, half-lying down, off balance and struggling for air. She squeezed his neck harder, clenching her teeth and hissing as she ignored the claws that raked through her flesh, rending it open.

Sasha ground her teeth, struggling to keep her advantage, the muscles of her thighs burning with the effort to keep her hold on him as he tried to break free.

Pain and heat licked across her legs and belly. He struggled to find purchase, his claws ripping at every inch of her that he could find. She squeezed harder, doubling over to protect her soft belly.

His tawny face darkened around his lips and eyes, his wide, flat nostrils flaring desperately for the air that she wouldn't let him breathe. A strangled moan slipped from his throat. His weight began to topple forward, and the claws sunken into her hips and thighs loosened, his movements slowing. Both of them were covered in the crimson stain of her blood. The sheets were a ruined disaster.

The senator croaked, and then went limp, his body collapsing on top of hers.

She squeezed harder.

If this was a ruse, then she wasn't going to fall for it. Instead, she counted to one hundred, then counted back to zero. Her panting breaths sounded overly loud to her, echoing in the small room despite the roaring of blood in her ears.

He'd cut her body into ribbons of agony and pain.

"You should have listened to your guards, asshole," she whispered, afraid that if she spoke too loud, the guards might hear her from the other side of the door.

After an eternity of silence passed, she gathered one of his limp arms in her hand, checking him for a pulse. No matter where she pressed along his wrist, she couldn't find one. Even if, by some miracle, he wasn't dead, he'd at least be unconscious by now.

Unhooking her feet, she grimaced, letting her ravaged thighs fall open. The senator collapsed, going completely limp and heavy, his dead weight landing on top of her. Ignoring the pain that made her want to scream, she reached forward and checked him for signs of breathing. Sticking her fingers under his nostrils, she waited.

He wasn't breathing.

She'd killed him.

When she shifted, his head flopped down onto her shredded abdomen and she almost cried out from the torment of it, biting her lip to stifle the sounds at the last second. She put a knuckle between her teeth and bit, internally screaming.

All of the movement had reopened the shallower wounds that were trying to knit themselves back together, and she let out a hiss through her teeth, then flinched, turning her head to check on the door. It remained shut.

A thought occurred to her. The guards were used to the senator's antics. No doubt they had certain expectations.

Aware that they'd been mostly silent for a long time, she let out the moan that she'd been holding back as she unstuck herself from the bed.

The door remained undisturbed, and she allowed herself the luxury of taking a few moments to focus on her breathing as she inched the senator's weight off of her. Either the guards couldn't hear her through the walls or they were used to pain-filled moans and odd noises coming from this room.

Sasha slid herself out from under his corpse, inch by agonizing inch. Her blood had made a slippery, sticky mess of the both of them, but her nanos were already working to repair the damage. One particularly large gash on her hip showed a sliver-wide view of pale yellow bone before it sealed closed right before her eyes. Assisting the healing process, she pressed the wider lacerations together until they knitted enough for her to take a deep breath. The less scar tissue her body had to make, the quicker she would mend.

I still have the guards to deal with.

Ragged breaths and whimpers escaped her as she lay still against the bed and waited for the worst of her wounds to close. Once she was able to move without excruciating pain ripping through her or her deeper wounds reopening, she slid her legs under her and knelt over the dead senator's body.

His passive gaze was locked straight ahead and there was a slackness to his features. For as long as she lived, she'd never be able to forget his face right now in that moment.

Careful not to disturb his body too much, she slid off the bed, hissing when first her feet and then her knees hit the floor. Her tender muscles tensed, threatening to give out from under her as she struggled.

Taking a deep, shaky breath, she grabbed the senator's clothes and dug through his pockets. There had to be something useful there. In the waistband at the back of his pants, where she assumed his tail was kept out of sight, was a pocket hidden in the lining of the fabric.

It contained a small black disc which she thought was like the one that Ardalon had used to pay for their drinks at the bar. Other than that, his pockets were frustratingly empty. Of course the pampered, rich senator didn't carry a weapon on him. She took the payment device and palmed it anyway.

All right, time to get creative.

Waiting for the bodyguards to rush in was a terrible idea, but her options were slim to almost none.

The closet and the bathroom were her only hiding options, but they were obvious. The bed rested on an elevated platform.

She glanced at it again. Perhaps she didn't need coverage. Just a moment of surprise. An idea came to her, half-formed and shoddy, but it was the best that she could come up with under the circumstances.

Her legs protested when she stood and put weight on them. Her abdomen tensed, but none of her healing wounds reopened. She had to hurry before the guards got curious. Grabbing the dead senator by a wrist, she dragged him through the room and into the bathroom. He flopped like a two-hundred-pound ragdoll into the cleansing stall, and she did her best to prop him up in the corner.

Making two trips from the bed to the bathroom, she smeared a trail of blood along the way as if he'd dragged himself off to die.

Cutting his hand off with his own claw was more difficult than she'd thought it would be.

His fingers required a constant pressure on his large knuckles to extend the razor sharp claws. Blood oozed from the messy wound as she sawed through the layers of skin and fat and tendon. Once she got to the wrist bones where his hand connected to his arm, she had to hang his hand over the trim of the shower's base and use her heel and body weight as leverage to break the bone.

It took two well placed stomps to wrest the appendage from his body.

"Who's getting pieces cut off of them now, huh, you son of a bitch?" she spat at his corpse.

The vengeance upon his body felt cathartic, although the waning of her adrenaline left her shaky. She needed to eat soon. Healing this many wounds so soon had depleted a lot of her energy.

The bodyguards had to die first, though. Or be incapacitated. She wasn't picky.

Satisfied that her half-assed plan was as in-place as she could get it, she made her way back to the bedroom, cautious to not disturb her painted blood trail.

Wedging herself underneath the bed's platform, she lay there and waited, the senator's disarticulated hand grasped in hers. Her stomach revolted at the feeling of his dead hand pressed in hers, holding her back even as she cradled it to her body for fear of dropping it and losing it in the dark underneath this bed.

She waited, taking advantage of the opportunity to rest, heal and recover until she had to fight and most likely kill again. Surviving was what was important. Her conscience could wait.

Regret was a luxury for the living.

Time passed, but without a clock she couldn't say how long it was before there was a timid knock on the door. Her heart leaped into her chest, pounding a rapid staccato that had her holding her breath. She double-checked her position under the bed and got her impromptu weapon ready.

They knocked again, this time a little more forcefully, and then they paused for a moment before they called out.

"Sir?" one of the guards said through the door.

"If you don't answer then, we're coming in, sir," the other added.

They paused, but then the door slid open. She couldn't hear the mechanism, but from her unobstructed view of the floor she could see their legs as they entered, spotted the massacre that was the blood-splattered room, and hesitated.

"Sir!"

"Shit."

They fanned out. One followed the blood trail to the bathroom and disappeared from view. The other paced the length of the room and looked about. The rustle of clothing was probably them pulling out their weapons.

There was a startled shout from the bathroom, and then the

other guard moved close enough to the bed where she was hiding.

Pressing her thumb into the largest knuckle on the senator's hand, she lashed out, dragging it as hard as she could across the back of the guard's ankle, slicing deep. He stumbled to his knees and hit the floor with a shout, dropping his weapon in the process.

Blood splattered across the tile.

She thought it was a universal goon rule that you wore combat boots, not loafers. Flat dress shoes left your ankles open and unprotected. All those tendons that make walking possible were so easy to target if you knew exactly where to stab and cut.

Taking advantage of his confusion, she grabbed him by the leg and pulled him down and toward her. He was too big to fit completely under the bed, so he only slid halfway under it before getting jammed. The guard tried to kick her with his uninjured leg, but he couldn't see her.

She laid her weight across his knee and pinned him down, then set her borrowed claws to the unprotected juncture of his thigh and stabbed again and again. The talon caught on something hard—his pelvis, maybe—and it took a jerk to rip it free.

He screamed and growled and tried to fight her off of him as she cut and stabbed and ripped.

Hot, salty blood sprayed in arcs as she hit an artery, splashing her and the underside of the bed indiscriminately. It didn't take humans long to bleed out from a femoral artery injury. The Kursh appeared to be made approximately the same as her.

Each kick aimed at her head drained him faster and faster until he went still and quiet.

She didn't waste time checking this one for a pulse. Instead, she dropped the Senator's hand and crawled through the growing puddle of slippery blood and wrapped her hand around the handle of his pistol, wresting it free from the holster on his waistband.

The other guard came out of the bathroom with his gun drawn and aimed widely. He went still when he spotted her, squatting on the floor, covered head to toe in the blood of his boss and coworker. She aimed her stolen pistol at his head and flicked off the safety. Her finger was slippery on the trigger, but her arm didn't shake despite her fatigue.

"Do you want to die today?" she asked the guard. "Is defending your dead boss's honor worth your life?"

He hesitated to pull the trigger, his eyes skittering between her blood drenched form and his fellow guard, who laid there slack-faced and pale-lipped from blood loss. The Kursh bodyguard was still wedged halfway underneath the bed, the puddle of his blood seeping up his back and staining his tawny velvet skin.

"Not particularly," the guard answered.

The muzzle of his gun wavered, drifting to the side in a gentle arc as he surrendered to her. His unoccupied hand rose to show that it was empty. "I'm just going to set this down and kick it over to you," he added with wide, white-rimmed eyes.

"Smart male," she encouraged him, watching for any hint of deception.

True to his word, he bent down and set down his laser gun, kicking it over to her. It stopped short of her, so she kept her gun trained on him with no hint of hesitation in her practiced stance. She could hold this pose for hours. The military had trained them for endurance as well as accuracy.

Blinking clumping drops of blood from her eyelashes, she cleared her vision, staring him down without bothering to rise up off the floor. "Where am I?"

"The senator's ship," he answered, his hands held up, palms forward and fingers spread in the universal sign of surrender.

She resisted the urge to roll her eyes at him. "I figured that much from the look of the room. Are we docked? Flying?"

He twitched. "Flying. We were headed h-home."

Nodding, she prompted him to continue with a wave of her borrowed gun.

The guard slowly lowered his hands toward his legs, but his weight shifted. One leg moved forward and the other back. His face looked even and calm, but she knew a defensive gesture when she saw one.

"Is there anyone else on board?" she asked him. "If you say no and you're lying, then they're dead, so think carefully before you answer."

His shoulders tensed, and he spread his fingers wide again at his sides. Cupping her grip in her other palm, she steadied her aim, giving him a stern look.

"No," he said. "It's just us. The ship's on autopilot."

She squeezed the trigger and shot him in the head, the blast hitting its mark right between his eyes. He collapsed onto the floor, and she stayed where she was to see if he got back up again. The gun was on its lowest setting, so she hoped it had only stunned him, but she also had no idea what a direct stun to the face from one of these things did to a person.

She'd never gotten the chance to ask the Diggi how her shots felt after she'd escaped from their captivity.

It'd be really great if aliens stopped trying to abduct me.

The guard's chest rose and fell, although he didn't look comfortable with how he was laying on the floor in a crumpled pile of bent limbs.

Good. Fracker was going to let that dude rape me. He's lucky I don't chuck his unconscious body out of the nearest airlock and let him die out in the vacuum of space.

With the second guard incapacitated, she ransacked the clothes and found a collection of sturdy belts that looked and felt like some sort of leather. It was difficult to roll the unconscious guard over, but she managed it while she pulled his arms behind his back and bound them together from wrist to elbow. She bound his knees and ankles together with two belts as well for good measure, then stuck a wad of ripped-up cloth in his mouth and kept it there with one of the skinny belts.

Now that she'd gotten firsthand experience with their claws and fangs, she'd decided that the Kursh were a lot more dangerous than she'd thought.

With the second guard trussed up safe and sound, she picked up the senator's oh-so-useful hand and set the palm to the unmarked door, opening it.

The door slid open, and she made her way methodically through the hallway with the gun raised and set to kill. Slowly, she explored the ship, checking every room one by one and clearing them all before she let her arms drop, her muscles aching and sore.

Using the senator's hand to open the locked door, she saw that the guard hadn't been lying. The ship looked like a private puddle jumper, and the control panel was flying it for them.

An AI came online, asking her if she required any assistance when she approached the cockpit. It looked rarely used.

This was a small ship, the rich alien asshole version of a luxury space yacht. It was probably what he used to planet hop.

Checking the navigation pane, she saw a whole lot of black and stars out front, with just the odd bit of satellite or meteor or space debris floating about. From what she could read of their mapping system, it looked like she had a little time before they got close to their pre-programmed destination.

Good, because I need a shower, some food, clothes, and a nap, and I'm not too particular about the order.

CHAPTER TWELVE

SASHA

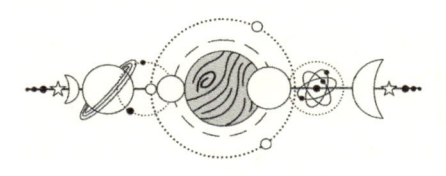

Once she was showered and clean, she sorted through the closet of debauchery and found the least offensive thing that existed in it.

It wasn't an easy feat.

Underwear was impossible to find unless someone thought that string was underwear, which she did not. At least there were bras, although they were more of a tight band that barely covered her chest. It was indecent at best, and completely impractical at worst.

Abandoning the fruitless search for appropriate undergarments, she settled on a short leather skirt, a lace camisole, and a silky wrap top that at least covered her arms even though it was sheer. Taking the last remaining belt, a silver studded black one, she wrapped it around her hips, and stuck her pilfered gun in it at her back.

At least there were boots in a variety of sizes and shapes to choose from. She picked the one with the least cutouts and the shortest heel and they were only slightly too wide in the toes for her feet.

Rustling sounds from the bedroom pulled her attention away

from her task. Shutting the walk-in closet door behind her, she turned and looked at the last remaining guard, who was glancing about the room with a dazed expression. Concussions were disorienting, but it looked like he would be fine. Probably.

He mumbled something from behind his gag and looked at her with a pointed glance to the corner of the room where she'd dragged the two dead bodies and piled them together.

The senator had already started to go into rigor, and she'd needed his corpse out of the shower so she could bathe. "I don't give two shits about you, do you understand? You're lucky that I don't just kill you right here, right now, for what you've helped him do."

He grimaced and wiggled where he lay on the floor, bound and immobilized.

Walking over to him and crouching so she was closer to his eye level, she stared at him, prolonging the eye contact to the point of discomfort.

"Your boss kidnapped and tried to rape me, and you and your buddy there helped him do it. If enslaving innocent women is your idea of a good job, then I guess it's a great thing that you're going to be looking for a new one because your boss is dead. Consider this a golden fracking opportunity to better yourself. Just don't mistake my empathy for softness. After I shut this door, I swear to God, if I ever see your face again, I'm shooting it. And the setting won't be on stun. I will paint the walls with your brains."

His golden eyes were piercing as he stared at her. She rose, mindful of her short skirt, and turned on her heel, walking away from him before she did something rash like commit pre-meditated murder.

She looked over her shoulder, catching his eye. "I'm no one's property."

Holding the senator's hand up to the reader, she opened the

door, ready to head back to the piloting console to watch the ship as it readied itself to land. Having to carry around a disarticulated hand made her feel like a deranged psychopath, but she was practical down to her core. A survivor.

I'll do whatever it takes to survive… anything.

After raiding the ship's tiny kitchen, her belly was deliciously full, she was napping in the padded captain's chair when the AI blasted a proximity alert over the intercom.

"I'm up, I'm up," she mumbled out loud as she sat upright and rubbed the sleep from her eyes. A planet loomed before her on the display. It was large. Green and blue, with white clouds that swirled across its surface, obscuring the brown mountainous peaks and the lit-up swaths that were cities. She damn near cried at the sight of it.

Silently she prayed for a planet without jungles filled with dinosaurs. She wasn't going to be avoiding cities and crashing onto the ledges of canyons anymore.

Strapping herself into the pilot's harness system she started playing around with the ship's landing mechanisms. It was similar enough to the Diggi's ship that she thought she'd already gotten it mostly figured out.

"Senator, shall I land the ship at Port Jervaissa as usual?" the AI asked her politely from a hidden speaker located somewhere overhead in the white metal ceiling.

"Uh… yeah. Sounds good," she answered.

"Of course, Captain. Retinal scan commencing… Scan failed. Please reposition for retinal scanning to engage the landing mechanisms," it intoned, its forward momentum slowing.

Sighing, she shut her eyes and cursed.

I need to go borrow an eye.

SASHA WALKED AWAY FROM THE SENATOR'S SHIP, ANXIOUS TO put distance between it and her without jostling the crowd too much. It was midday from her estimate based on the location of the sun overhead. The senator's ship had closed up tight behind her. She felt reasonably sure that someone would come check on it and it's occupants.

Not my problem.

A few people glanced at her as she passed them, but nobody yelled, "Stop, seize her!" so she guessed that it was okay for now. After that disaster with the alien dinosaurs, she had no desire to be anywhere away from people… even if those people weren't human.

Lion aliens surrounded her with only a few of the lizards and birds to break up the crowd. From the corner of her eye, she would catch sight of a male who had a build similar to Ardalon, and her heart would start racing. None of them were him. Her stomach twisted, but she forced herself to focus on the here and now.

Regrets were for the living, and she needed to get as far away from the senator's ship and the soon-to-be rotting corpses inside as she could get.

Man, these boots suck for walking in.

It was too bad the senator only liked really impractical shoes on his women. Still, they covered her up to mid-calf and they kept her feet off the hot pavement, so it could have been worse.

The aliens who were rushing or milling about were as curious about her as she was about them. These were the first lionesses that she'd been able to stare at and study. Plus, the children.

Holy crap, the kids are stinkin' cute.

She'd actually squealed a little too loudly when she saw the first one, making too many people look at her, so she ducked down a side street and began to head in another direction, wandering aimlessly. The further that she got from the port and what she assumed was the downtown area, the nicer the buildings got and the more elaborately dressed the people were.

Both sexes wore some sort of tunic and pants combination, except for the elderly females who wore a suffocatingly long, elaborate-looking dress trimmed with contrasting embroidery. As businesses gave way to what she thought were residences, she began to get a few derisive looking glances as people looked her up and down and shook their heads.

Clothes. I need better clothes. Gotta blend in.

It took her a while to find a side street with open air vendors selling tables full of their wares. The few shops she'd tried to enter had quickly kicked her out. As she elbowed her way through the crowd, she'd taken note of all the goods for sale and the people who were buying and selling them.

The deeper back she got, the crappier and more worn-out looking the goods got until she'd hit what looked like the secondhand resale area.

In the very back of the stalls, she spotted an elderly Kursh male sitting on a blanket with bundles of patched, faded clothes spread out and separated by color. He was whittling a small piece of wood with a tiny pen knife as he looked her up and down, doing a double-take when he spotted her eyeing his wares.

"Do you have something that will fit me?" she asked him.

His deep brown eyes scanned her from head to toe, and he hesitated for a moment before nodding and picking out a green and gold set of clothes from his pile.

"This will flatter the color of your hair," he said as he handed it to her.

She took the clothes from him and pulled out her stolen credit stick. "Can I pay you with this?"

He looked around, so she did too, but nobody was paying them any attention as the crowd chatted and haggled, going about their business. He nodded, holding out his wrist, and she saw that underneath his long sleeve he had one of those wrist communication devices. He pressed something on the side, and it beeped and lit up orange before fading back to black.

Holding up her new garments, she gave him smile eyes, tucking the credit chip back inside her cleavage where it was safe from potential pickpockets. "Thank you."

He nodded and returned to his carving.

She turned to leave, then stopped and spun back around to face him. He was the first alien she'd met since landing who hadn't looked at her exposed thighs and glared at her. "I haven't seen any shoes yet. Do you know where I could buy some?"

"Down that aisle," he pointed with his pen knife.

Looking in the direction he was pointing, she gave him smile eyes again and bowed at the waist like she'd seen Ardalon do once. "Thank you."

The used shoe seller was a dozen stalls down from where she'd bought her clothes. The seller was hesitant to even talk to her before she'd flashed her credit stick at him, and then suddenly he was all business, polite and friendly. He ushered her away right after she bought a pair of lace-up leather ankle boots.

They were sturdy-looking, if a bit worn, but more importantly they didn't scream "sex worker."

I'd love to find a vendor that sells undergarments.

With new clothes and shoes acquired, she weaved through the back alleys until she found an empty one, and then she changed quickly. The pants had to be hiked up to just under her boobs because the average Kursh female was taller than her, and the tunic hung all the way down to her knees instead of mid-thigh like it did on the other ladies, but she was grateful to be dressed in something decent.

The boots were a good enough fit, although they rubbed a bit and made her feet blister since she didn't have any socks.

Throwing the senator's clothes into what she thought was a trash can, she ditched the alley.

Now that she was properly dressed for their city she was getting fewer stares from the people around her. She followed her nose until she found something that smelled so delicious it made her stomach rumble.

The side street emptied out into a main thoroughfare, which butted up with another at a five-point town square where a cafe was roasting something on a spit. The food smelled amazing, but the people eating there were dressed in nicer clothes than hers and she didn't want to attract a lot of attention by going to what might be some sort of fancy restaurant where she'd stick out and attract too many looks.

Turning away from the cafe was difficult, but eventually she wandered far enough that she found what looked like a hole-in-the-wall noodle stand.

Faded, peeling pictures of food lined the window, and the name and prices were written right there on the posters with chipping paint. The people inside were eating quickly, and many of them were there alone. Nobody was particularly well-dressed or ragged, but somewhere in between. Satisfied that this restaurant was acceptable, she joined the line.

Patrons were served in a fast, no-nonsense manner. People who hadn't already decided what they wanted to eat by the time they got to the counter were berated and sent to the back of the line. By the time it was her turn, she was ready.

"I want that, two of those, and do you have beer?" she ordered as she pointed to her selections.

The Kursh server leaned forward, sniffing at her before snorting and shaking his head. He scooped her mountain of food onto a plate and passed it down the line without a word. The cashier popped the top off a dark bottle and handed it to her. She juggled everything while she paid, then sat and started to stuff her face.

Oh, man, it's good.

Humming while she ate, shoveling food into her mouth as fast as she could chew it, she washed it all down with a sip of cold beer. Far sooner than she'd have liked, her plate was empty and she leaned back in her chair, placing a hand over her stomach.

Now that one need had been settled, another grew. She was getting tired. It had been an exhausting last couple of days.

Do they even have hotels here? I don't have any sort of identification to check in.

A rented room was probably out of the question, even if her stolen credit stick probably had enough funds on it to rent a penthouse suite.

She was going to be sleeping rough, which was fine with her at this point, but she hadn't seen much in the way of public parks and benches and she wasn't thrilled at the idea of sleeping out in the open without a knife. Her stolen pistol was going to run out of juice at some point. Thinking back to the wares being sold at the marketplace, she tried to remember if she'd seen anyone selling weapons.

Exhaustion pulled at her, and she slumped down into her chair. The spoon clinked when she discarded it into her empty bowl.

"Sasha," someone said behind her, the voice familiar.

She whipped her head around, her chair almost toppling over

and taking her with it. Ardalon was standing behind her. Without even thinking about it, she jumped up and flung herself into his arms, the chair crashing to the floor behind her.

The proprietor of the restaurant yelled at them, but the only thing that mattered was Ardalon's arms tightening around her and the way that he buried his face into her hair, snuffling loudly as he smelled her. His breath puffed against her forehead, tears pricking hot and scratchy against her eyes where they threatened to spill over and fall.

Relief washed over her as they hugged one another.

He found me! I don't have to be alone anymore.

The uncertainty of everything faded into the background, and she knew that no matter what happened, she wasn't going to have to face it alone.

"You f-found me," she sobbed, her throat tight with emotion.

He squeezed her even harder, the pricks of his claws kneading into her back as he pulled her closer and held her tighter. The soft, downy fur of his face brushed against her cheek as he pulled back and studied her.

His eyes were warm and soft with something that looked a bit like affection, and her heart beat fast and wild in her chest.

The chef yelled obscenities at them, ordering them to leave before he dragged them out himself.

Ardalon cupped her elbow in his large hand, steering her away from the onlookers in the crowded noodle shop. "I'm very glad to find you safe and sound," he said, his voice thick and husky.

The sun had set while she was eating, and the sky was a dusky shade of deep blue, brilliant purple, and burning orange as the last of its rays sank beyond the horizon. Stars twinkled faintly with their brilliant lights wherever they weren't obscured by tall buildings and trees. A few people walked by, oblivious to them.

His eyes were large and luminous as he stared down at her like she might disappear if he took them off of him for more than a second. She felt the same way. Like he wasn't really there and if she blinked he'd be gone. She'd hoped he would come for her. She'd worried that the tracker in her collar might have been turned off or malfunctioned. That the senator had done something nefarious to it while she was drugged and sleeping.

Her stomach fluttered as they stood there, together, on the sidewalk in front of the restaurant's glowing amber lights.

"I'm glad to see you too, big guy," she told him.

His hand smoothed up her arm until he was cupping the back of her head, his fingers entangled within her hair. She leaned toward him, caught in the gravitational pull of his hypnotic, golden eyes. They glimmered in the darkness, the shining eyes of a predator who had his eyes set on his prey.

She was glad to be caught, as long as it was him.

Only him.

Ardalon raised his other hand until he was cupping her face. As he leaned down, she tipped her head up, aware of the height difference between them as he loomed over her. His beaded locks fell over his shoulders, brushing against her neck. Warm breath fanned her face. She smelled him—spiced, musky, male—and the smell of it wrapped around her as he tugged her closer until they were pressed flush against one another. He felt like home.

When did that happen?

She didn't care how or when it had happened. It didn't matter how long they'd known each other. Sometimes your heart just knew.

Lips parting to open for him, she let her eyes drift shut as he leaned down to kiss her. His soft, forward-pointing nose wasn't made to fit against hers, and their faces bumped together because of the awkward angle. They both laughed, his a soft chuffing sound and hers a faint wheeze.

Ardalon tilted his head more to the side as she surged up into his arms, pressing her mouth to his. Their lips met, and they were both so eager for it that they devoured each other. His tongue darted out to swipe across her lower lip. The hand in her hair tightened, tilting her head back and forcing her up on the tips of her toes as he pulled her deeper into their kiss.

She moaned, opening for him, their tongues tangling together as they explored one another, careful of his fangs.

Wrapping her arms around his neck, she pulled him down to her, rocking against him as they stood there in the street and kissed.

She should have been alarmed by how much this he'd come to mean to her, but she couldn't summon any fear or doubt. Not when he kissed her like she was a warm, crackling fire and he was trying to get out of the cold. Like she was his salvation.

He wrapped himself around her, hard and soft and warm. The embrace sent a shiver down her spine as he pressed her back until she bumped into the wall, his body fitting against her until he was settled into all of her hollow places. Entangled, meshed together, her body burned for him as a dormant part of her stirred to waking with every stroke of his tongue.

He kissed her until she burned for him, hot and bright.

Hands sliding down his strong, lightly furred shoulders, she squeezed the muscles there, enjoying the feel of him beneath her hands. Her core throbbed, empty and hungry, demanding more than a kiss. She wanted to sink her claws into him and never let him go.

Ardalon pulled back from the kiss, his lips leaving hers, and tipped his head down so his forehead thunked against hers. He purred.

"I thought I'd lost you," he confessed.

Her eyes opened, and she smiled, enjoying the way that he was still holding her like he was scared to let go. "Worried about me? I can take care of myself."

Not that she wanted him to ever stop worrying about her, though. She could be on her own. She had been on her own for a very long time. She was used to watching her own back and make the hard choices. Sometimes, though, she thought that it would be nice to have someone watch out for her, someone to come home to after a long day, someone to wake up next to.

Someone like him. Strong, but kind.

He laughed. "I never doubted that."

He pulled back, looking at her without letting her go. One hand roamed her hair, her back, her arms, her fingers. He traced all of her divots and sloping curves, touching her like he was afraid she'd disappear if he severed their connection. The pads of his fingers were rough against her skin. Her nipples hardened at the rough sensation, enjoying how alive it made her feel.

"Are you all right?" he asked. "Did he... hurt you?"

Her thoughts flashed back to the ship. To the horrible things that happened there. The threats the senator had made and the things she'd had to do.

Her smile faded, her expression growing tight. "I'll be fine."

"S-Sasha," he said, hesitant. His mouth closed and he blinked, then started again. "We're going to find him. His chip has gone dark. I don't know how he did it, but we'll find him. He'll pay for... for whatever he did. I promise."

He brushed a wayward lock of hair behind her ear.

Ardalon looked down at her, his face tense. She wasn't used to someone trying to take care of her. She'd always been the one doing the work and taking care of others.

"That's not... ugh... okay... it's, umm, bad," she told him, her heart spasming for different reasons now as guilt ate at her with its sharp edges.

Ardalon's eyes squinted and his ears flattened toward his skull. "What do you mean? We found his ship. It will take us a little while to overcome its security feature and force it open, but he's not getting away with it this time. He can't sweep kidnapping and... and more out the door like sand. Not with all of the evidence we have. He'll pay for his sins, for once."

"Umm... okay," she hedged, "so about that..."

CHAPTER THIRTEEN

ARDALON

Senator Brodyn was dead. Very, very dead. Not only was he dead, but he'd also been partially dismembered.

Ardalon could smell the stench of decay even before they'd stepped inside of the ship. Once Yeevar had gotten the ship cracked open with his computer overrides, the scent of stinking gasses and clotted blood swirled deep into his sinuses.

His face scrunched as he tried his best to block it all out and ignore it. It wasn't the first time he'd smelled a corpse, and it probably wouldn't be the last either, but it was something that you never quite got used to.

Sasha grunted behind him, one hand pressed against her nose and mouth. It made sense now, why she hadn't smelled like fear, and why she'd smelled faintly like blood when he'd found her. He'd just thought that she'd been injured and healed. He never would have guessed this.

"Okay, so I understand that he was attacking you and now he's dead… but the hand?" he asked, disturbed.

She shifted behind her, her feet shuffling on the floor. "I needed his, uh, claws, and then the palm to, uh, open the doors."

He looked away from the corpse to glance at the surviving

bodyguard who Davi was busy arresting. Sasha had left the male restrained and tied up on the sticky floor of the bedroom. He didn't envy the male. Being locked up for hours in a small room with that stink… ugh.

This scent is going to be stuck in my sinuses for days.

Considering that the virukin had helped drug him and kidnap Sasha, holding her hostage, Ardalon didn't actually feel all that sorry for him. Davi tightened the beam cuffs on the bodyguard until the male roared.

"And the, uh, eye?"

"The ship uses retinal scans," she answered.

Looking back at the complication dropped on his head, Ardalon sighed. "Right. Okay… I have to call the chancellor," he added with a grimace. He rubbed his forehead and the growing ache within it as he used his implant to ring the chancellor on a secure connection.

The chancellor answered the ping, his usual gruff greeting cut short when the video link connected, transmitting the very dead senator lying partially dismembered on the bathroom floor of the ship.

"Shit," the chancellor cursed directly into Ardalon's brain. Months of planning, maneuvering, and research, thousands of hours of work… and the viruker was as dead as a rodent in a svenii den.

"I am arranging to have his remains transported to the palace for funeral rites. His ship is being cataloged for evidence and is currently being locked down. I'll have two guards on the door at all times until it can be brought back to Kreshalla," Ardalon said.

The chancellor sighed. "Good. I am pulling you off of active duty for the time being. Let me see what sort of damage control I need to spin. Take some time off and lie low while we sort this out."

"And for Sasha?"

Silence stretched in his mind as Ardalon waited until the chancellor came to a decision. "She must be contained until we know what the emperor wishes to do. I can make some calls, speak to—"

"Sir," Ardalon interrupted, "I will take full responsibility for her."

It was my fault she had to resort to such violence. My fault she was taken in the first place. My arrogance in thinking that he'd be able to outsmart such an evil male.

The chancellor chuffed out a, "Fine, just keep her concealed and contained," and then the connection cut out without any further ceremony.

Sasha stared at him with large, worried eyes as if she was waiting for his judgement to be passed. His judgement was not the one that she should fear, however. This was bad. There was no telling how the emperor would react to the news of his cousin's death, even if the senator wasn't a favored family member or well liked by the court, they were still blood.

She bit her lower lip, worrying it, and he glanced at her blunted canine.

She wasn't intimidating to look at. Short, softly curved, with large, round eyes and no fangs, or claws, or spikes. No venom. Her skin was soft and smooth.

And yet, she was a survivor. Capable. Strong. Tenacious. He shuddered to think of what a warrior of her kind would be like. If she was capable of killing two of her three captors, sparing the third by choice…

He thought back to her cunning when she'd escaped her cage and loosed the stolen animals to serve as her distraction while she ran. Cunning. Not to mention the rapid healing of her people's advanced technology.

Her species must be extremely fierce to have survived,

becoming their planet's apex predator without any obvious physical adaptations for such a thing.

"I got you in trouble. Us in trouble," she said, her tone flat and her scent sour. Her mouth was a thin, flat line.

He made a move to smooth down a wayward strand of her soft hair, but he stopped himself. This room was a crime scene. Corpses laid at their feet. It smelled like death, and they weren't alone. This was neither the time nor the place for any sort of affection.

"He was a monster. You got me a well earned and long overdue vacation. Come, I'm done here, and if we hurry we can make the first shuttle out," he told her.

Her eyes widened slightly, the whites showing more around her round iris. "Where are we going?"

Davi led the cuffed bodyguard away, another officer coming in to photograph the crime scene, taking scans and recordings. The officer placed holo markers over splatters and blood drops, numbering the points of interest in the scene. Ardalon nodded at the male as he worked around them with diligent precision.

"Home. I'm taking you home with me," he answered, looking back at her and holding her gaze.

The landing process at Omenus, the largest hub on Kreshalla, took longer than the actual shuttle ride between the two jump points. They were scanned, screened, and sprayed with decontamination gasses. Sasha coughed, and he was irritated with himself for forgetting to warn her to hold her breath. It escaped him sometimes that she knew nothing of his culture or their ways.

"Are you well?" he asked her.

Sasha wiped tears from her eyes and bobbed her head.

Grabbing her elbow and stopping their progress, much to the annoyed shouts of the line of travelers behind them, he stooped down to peer into her face. It was pinker than usual, but otherwise she looked like herself. If there was some change in her for the worse then it was too subtle for him to tell.

"Sasha?"

"Yeah," she croaked between coughs. "I'm fine, but that stuff tastes like ass."

He grimaced, pulling her toward the gangway where a bored security officer checked everyone's identification. They waited their turn, and he watched Sasha as she watched everything around them. He tried to imagine what her own home was like. What was familiar, and what was strange.

"Is it strange? The city, I mean." He wanted her to like it. This place, his home. Somehow, it had become important to him that she could be comfortable here.

She looked around, her gaze skipping over everything, moving over the floating hologram screens that advertised everything from vacation packages to socks in a bag for travelers who had forgotten to pack their own. A mother with her cubs passed by a clutch of Raxion tourists. There was an elderly Diggi couple looking at sightseeing ads on their old, outdated handheld.

"It's weird. A lot of it's the same, just... different. That doesn't really make sense, does it?" she asked as she glanced up at him, stepping closer into his side when the crowd surged behind them.

He curled an arm around her shoulder in reflex, tugging her into his side, and she smiled up at him with soft eyes. Her body settled into the crook of his. Something brushed against his back, and he realized it was her hand. She was holding him back.

Her fingers flattened along his spine, and he could feel the heat of her smooth skin through the thin fabric of his shirt. He liked it. Nobody, other than his mother when he was just a small cub, had ever touched him so intimately and tenderly.

His com vibrated against his wrist, and he looked down, reading the text. "My brother-in-law is nearly here. He's working his way through traffic at the terminal."

She tensed, her gaze moving away from the vending machine she'd been looking at to glance at him. "Your brother-in-law... I have a brother. Had. I don't have him anymore, I guess... I'll probably never see him again."

Her face shuttered, her expression smoothing into something hard to read.

His stomach clenched, not liking it.

What could he say? Her assumption was correct. Even if they knew where she came from and how she'd gotten here, the empire wasn't likely to just let her go.

If one of her kind, a small female, could take down two fit and healthy Kursh males at the height of their prime, then his people would be right to be wary of encouraging any sort of open communication or movement with her species. Their alliance with the Raxions and Diggi was strained enough without adding in some unknown entity with more advanced technology than theirs.

Shifting his hand down to thread their fingers together, palms meeting, he took her by the hand and walked her through the terminal.

People stared at them, doing double-takes and talking to one another as they passed, but Ardalon ignored it. Following his lead, Sasha did too. She fell into step behind him as he maneuvered them through the crowd and moved them closer to where his brother-in-law would be waiting. A hawker shoved a holo ad feed right in his face, and Ardalon snarled, swiping his claws through the mist until it cleared.

"That's so cool," Sasha said under her breath as she twisted around to look behind them, watching the man's ad machine spit out more displays as he threw them out into the crowd.

"Ignore them. Speaking to them and looking at them only encourages them to be even more of a nuisance," he warned her.

Once they were clear of the worst of the crowd, he led her onto the conveyor, catching her against him when she lost her balance as it started moving them at a rapid pace.

"Apologies. I should have warned you. I didn't think about it," he said.

She laughed, looking down at their feet where the disc of flooring zipped them along its magnetic route. "This is so cool."

"You're cold?" he asked, tucking her back into his side again to share his heat with her.

He would need to get her warmer clothing, to make up for her lack of fur. The traditional kaftana she was wearing hung loose on her small frame, the sleeves swallowing up her hands unless she kept them rolled up. Still, the material was thin and worn, suited more for summer than spring.

A breeze from the speed of their journey rustled her long hair, whipping it behind her. The thin, fine strands seemed to float on the breeze, not like his own coarse hair at all.

She buried her face in his chest. "I'm fine. You worry too much."

His thoughts flashed back to the senator's blood splattered ship, the image appearing in his mind's eye before he could stop it. She wasn't helpless, no matter how small and soft she looked. He needed to remember that.

Her fingers grabbed a fold in his shirt and twisted, playing with it. "Is it because, umm," she hesitated, "you like me?"

His thoughts shifted gears again, remembering the way she'd kissed him back when he'd forgotten himself and kissed her. Her lips and tongue were even softer than her skin and hair. It made him wonder how soft her warm, wet cunt would feel.

"You're purring again," she murmured, her hand stroking his rumbling chest.

"You seem to have that effect on me," he admitted. It wasn't just because of the bite bond, no matter how thin and fragile that tenuous tether was between them. He felt it, anemic but there, whenever he focused on her. He did like her. He'd liked her even before she'd marked him.

Still need to talk to her about that.

She looked up at him, her chin pressed to his chest. The view from this angle made her eyes look wide and innocent. Sasha's mouth was crooked as her eyes squinted up at him in a smile. "I like you too."

Before he could second guess himself, he reached down and cupped her chin, tugging her up on the tips of her toes as he bent down and kissed her again. Soft and sweet, her mouth relaxed underneath his as she kissed him back. Her lips parted, that little tongue of hers darting out to trace the seam of his lips. He opened for her, letting her deepen the kiss, and met her with his own.

Sliding a hand down her back, he fisted one round globe of her ass and squeezed, enjoying the way that it gave underneath the pads of his fingers. She moaned into their kiss, the sound traveling right down to his cock. He kneaded her backside, his other hand sliding down her chin to cup her by her throat.

Ardalon pulled her more firmly against him and trapped her there, his tongue tangling with hers as he squeezed her rump and settled his thumb over the pulsepoint in her throat, enjoying how he could feel her heartbeat speed up even as he smelled the sweetness of her growing arousal.

She gasped, a tiny hitch of noise coming from her throat, and he felt her swallow despite his grip, yet her scent never soured with fear. If anything, it bloomed harder, wrapping him in pheromones, dragging him down into a haze of lust like he'd never felt before.

Viruk, she makes the best noises.

His cock twitched, thickening and pressing painfully against the front seam of his tight leather pants. They were both so enraptured with one another that they didn't notice the conveyor coming to a slow and gentle stop, or the Kursh male standing there, staring at them with a horrified look on his face.

"I did not *ever* need to see *that*," his brother-in-law complained.

Hands falling away from Sasha, he looked at the male who was standing there rubbing his closed eyelids like he could erase the mental picture from his mind if he just pressed hard enough.

"I recall having to put up with much worse when you were freshly bonded," Ardalon snarked back.

Ferand gave Sasha a slow once-over, his expression confused and surprised. "What is that?"

Ardalon growled a warning, his look serious. "*She* is not a 'that', or a 'thing.' This is Sasha and she is... " He sighed, his sentence trailing off half-formed, his mind shorting out. A complication. An alien. His sort-of bond mate.

The best thing that had ever happened to him.

"Hello. I'm Sasha, and I'm a human," she said as she took a half-step away from him and turned to face his brother-in-law, her hand moving back and forth in the air in some sort of foreign greeting he'd never seen her make before.

Ferand fisted his hands on his hips and looked down at Sasha, his ears flat against his golden hair. "It talks."

He cut his eyes at his brother-in-law, not happy that his family was embarrassing him by being rude and xenophobic. "Call her an 'it' or a 'thing' or a 'that' again and I will show you why and how I was the premier of my class."

Rolling his shoulders, Ferand looked between them. "Always

so serious, brother. You can't blame me for being curious. I have never seen a 'hyoomen' before. Where is your luggage? This is the convi I rented to pick you up."

Ardalon set his hand to Sasha's back and propelled her toward their borrowed transportation. "We have no luggage. I brought nothing on this mission except these clothes, and Sasha has... well, she has nothing with her as well."

He grimaced, remembering that her suit and boots were somewhere back on the Diggi pirate ship. Hopefully they hadn't been catalogued as evidence or she might never get them back, and that was also based on the assumption that the xeno specialists hadn't already snagged them for study and dismantling.

Ferand looked him up and down. "That is the stupidest outfit I have ever seen. What are you supposed to be?"

Ardalon stepped off the conveyor and gave his sister's mate a shove toward the convi. "Just get in and drive. I do not require your opinion on my appearance."

Grinning to show off one fang, Ferand hit a button on his com which opened the convi's door wide enough for them to all get in.

"Is this our ride?" she asked, her face lighting up as the side dissolved open, showing the seating arrangements inside. The four seats were positioned around a small center table.

It was a comfortable-looking mid-tier model and had probably cost his family a pretty credit to rent. Ardalon flicked one ear at his brother-in-law, who shrugged in response to the unspoken question.

"What? I thought you would have luggage," Ferand justified the unnecessary expense.

Sasha poked her head into the convi and looked around, then climbed right in as if she'd done this before.

"Nobody brings luggage on an undercover mission, Fer. I

was at work, not on a pleasure voyage," Ardalon muttered as he climbed in too, settling on the chair next to hers.

She was busy stroking the synthetic material of her chair.

Ferand made a show of giving Sasha a very thorough once-over. "Seems like you brought back a souvenir." He climbed in next, tapping his com again to shut the door behind them. The side of the convi closed, encapsulating them as it came to life, its electronic controls lighting up as it prepared its engine.

Ardalon reached out and flicked Ferand's ear, satisfied with his brother-in-law's flinch.

"Oww! That was uncalled for," Ferand complained, setting his com to the table where the controls for the convi flickered to life. He booted it up and watched it go through it's automatic checks as he typed in their home address.

"Can I drive it?" Sasha asked, her voice breathy with excitement. Her eyes were wide and gleaming as she stared at the controls and leaned over the table, the glow reflected in her round, glossy eyes.

"No!" Ardalon said, louder, quicker, and more forceful than he'd intended.

Ferand glanced between them, the convi peeling away from the curb as it began to move on its pre-plotted course. It weaved into traffic, slowing for pedestrians and speeding up once it hit the long-haul part of the roads. The city zipped by them outside the transparent window as they gained speed, heading home.

Sasha glared at him with narrow eyes, her bottom lip distended and her mouth flat. "It was *not* my fault the pod crashed."

Ferand choked out a sputtering laugh. "What? You were in a crash landing? Wait... *it* was flying a—"

Ardalon growled, his gaze swinging back to his brother-in-law who was one completed sentence away from getting a fist to the face instead of a flick to the ear.

Ferand flinched, holding his hands up in surrender. "Sorry! That one was an accident, I swear. I meant to say 'she' was in a spaceship crash? I need to hear this story. In excruciating detail, please. Leave nothing out."

His brother-in-law's gaze swung back to Sasha, his head tilted as if he was trying to figure her out.

"That is classified," Ardalon deflected, leaning back in his chair, his hand on Sasha's thigh underneath the table.

He gave her soft skin a squeeze, enjoying the way that it gave underneath his fingers. She was muscled like a fighter, but with a soft layer of padding over top of it that was driving him crazy. He wished they hadn't been interrupted.

Her legs parted just enough to give him access to the rest of her thigh. He let his hand settle just above her knee. A fresh waft of her pheromones tortured him as she shifted in her seat.

A hand lifted to cover his nose, Ferand grimaced and fiddled with his com. The windows of the convi cracked, letting fresh air in.

Sasha leaned into the window closest to her seat and watched the scenery pass by. The city limits were fading as they made their way out to the residential plain. The buildings grew shorter, spaced further apart until there was more land to see than businesses. They were going to hit the tunnels soon, and he wondered what she'd think of them. He'd heard they were a bit off-putting for those who weren't used to them.

"Whatever," she grumbled in a low voice. "I'd have landed it just fine if they hadn't shot me down."

Ardalon shifted his attention back to his brother-in-law and raised a solitary claw in warning. "Do not ask questions, and do not repeat what she just said to anyone."

CHAPTER FOURTEEN

SASHA

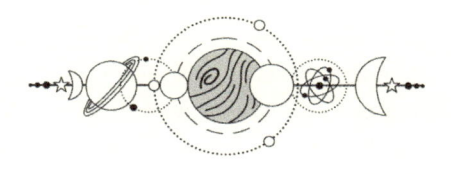

Seeing Ardalon's familial banter with his brother-in-law made her heart ache for her own. She tried to push the feelings of loss from her mind, choosing to focus on the alien world around her instead. His touch on her leg was grounding, a comfort in her loneliness.

Once they left the city behind them, the road curved, heading down into the ground. They passed into a system of tunnels that were lit with blue and amber lights. The automated car zipped through it so quickly that the lights blurred together.

It looked like the old movies and what humans had once imagined flying at warp speed would look like. The reality was a lot less exciting.

She must have made a sound because they were both looking at her with expectant expressions on their leonine faces.

"What?" she asked.

"Are you... uncomfortable?" Ardalon asked, his hand squeezing her leg under the table.

She shook her head. "No, I'm fine. I just had a funny thought. My people used to think that those lights zipping by like that," she pointed out the window to the lights, "is what faster than lightspeed travel looks like," she finished with a laugh.

"But it's... not..." Ferand added, looking at her with a weird expression.

She glanced between them, wondering if they were joking and she just didn't get it due to cultural differences and mistranslations.

"Of course not," she answered, glancing between them. They were still staring at her. "What?"

They looked at one another for a beat, the silence stretching between them as their car traveled through the exceptionally long tunnel. There was no end to it in sight and she wondered how far it went.

"Your people's ships can travel faster than the speed of light," Ardalon summarized, his voice strange.

"Of course. Well, only some of them. The big ones. Not all ships can do it. It takes a special kind of engine," she told him.

His brother-in-law cocked his head, his ears twitching where they poked up through his light amber colored hair. "How does that work?"

"FTL travel doesn't look like anything," she told them. "Space gets bubbled, and that pulls you from point A to B... unless you get the math wrong, and then you're just dead. Crashed into a giant, frozen asteroid and obliterated in an instant, or materialized inside of a moon and crushed."

They stared at her like she'd grown a second head.

"H-How do they make space bubble?" Ferand asked.

She blinked at them and set her hand on Ardalon's threading their fingers together on her thigh and shrugging her shoulders. "I have no idea. I'm just an aerospace communications engineer, not a physicist."

Ferand reached up and rubbed the ear that Ardalon had flicked earlier. "I failed to understand most of that. Her words are not translating properly. Do you know what she's talking about? What is an enjuneer?"

"Oh," she stumbled, trying to figure out how to explain her boring ass job to an alien. "Umm, it means I work with machines launched into space, things used to talk for long distances or relay information across the solar system. I fix the broken ones."

Ferand glanced between her and Ardalon, then settled back into his chair, his arms crossed over his chest as he stared at his brother-in-law. "Ah, well that explains things."

Ardalon's hand on her thigh tensed, his claws pricking her through the thin fabric of her pants and tunic. "Do not try to confuse her with doublespeak. She won't understand the nuances of our language or speech, and it's rude."

Chastised, Ferand dropped his eyes, his ears flattening to his head. "My apologies. My mouth opens before I think sometimes."

She looked between them, squeezing Ardalon's hand on her thigh in a comforting gesture. "What is he talking about?"

Ardalon's ears dropped too, laying flat in his brown locks. Golden eyes locked with hers as he shifted in his seat to face her as much as the bucket chairs would allow. "He is referring to my status among my people as an ashima."

She frowned, not following what he was saying. "I don't get it, sorry."

Nodding, Ardalon's hand untensed, his claws retreating. She looked down to see if her clothes had any pinholes in them. Not that it truly mattered. She wasn't attached to them beyond their usefulness. His gaze dropped, settling on her chin.

"The ashima are those who carry undesirable genetic traits, thus they are not allowed to breed, lest they pass those traits on to their cubs. Their tails are docked at birth so a future mate will know their status before bonding," Ardalon explained.

"You've seen that my coloring is darker than the others?" he asked.

She nodded. She had noticed that, but it hadn't been much more than a solitary thought before she dismissed it. People dyed their hair all the time. Hell, when she was a teen she had sunset colored hair once with a shaved undercut and a handful of facial piercings. She'd just assumed that his coloring was darker than the others.

"A rare recessive trait, harmless in and of itself, except that this phenotype frequently occurs along with the Kinjef gene, a heart disorder that few cubs survive past puberty," he finished. "I carry a single copy of that gene."

Her jaw dropped open, anger choking her. "You... I'm sorry... what? Having brown hair means they cut your tail off so you can't get married and have babies? That's barbaric!"

His eyes rose, meeting hers, and there was some emotion hidden in his face that she couldn't discern. It was the first time in a while that she wished his kind did more than squint their eyes and flick their ears to show how they felt.

"That disorder is truly gruesome," Ardalon justified. "It is a horrible way for a cub to die," he whispered.

"The pack needs strength to survive," Ferand added as if reciting some pledge by memory.

She glared at his brother-in-law, willing him to shut up with her mind. Sasha reminded herself that she was going to be a guest in his family's home, and the last thing she needed to do was be rude to them. They were being kind enough to host her while Ardalon's boss figured out what the government wanted to do with her since she'd killed the emperor's rapist cousin.

Crossing her arms over her chest, she slid down into her seat and stared at the ceiling of the car, her lip sucked between her teeth so she didn't open her mouth and start yelling.

"Sasha?" Ardalon asked, his tone worried.

"I'mfineI'mjustmad," she mumbled, slurring the words together. She bit her lip again so she didn't say something she was going to regret. Her foot bounced against the floor as she struggled to take that unspent energy and funnel it into something else that wouldn't get her in trouble.

The thought of someone holding down a baby version of Ardalon while they cut off his tail with shears—just because he was born with brown hair and might possibly have a kid one day with that gene—made her want to rampage.

The two of them, having picked up on the change in her mood, let her exist in silence for the rest of the trip. Tipping her head to the side, she watched the lights in the tunnel fly.

Ardalon's hand began to lift off her thigh, but Sasha unclenched her arms so she could put it back, threading her fingers with his so that they held hands as he rested his arm there. The point of contact between them made her feel more solid.

Anchored.

I hate everything about this fracking place, except him.

Ardalon's family home was located mostly underground, and it reminded her so much of growing up on Alpha Centauri that it made her homesick.

More people than she'd thought could possibly live together were waiting for them at the front door when their car exited its tunnel. The car opened, letting them out, and then his brother-in-law tapped a long string of things on his com and she watched as it closed up and zipped off without them.

A lioness holding a swaddled cub in her arms stood there with two other young lion children around her feet. As soon as Ardalon stepped out of the car, they jumped forward, mobbing him, tugging on his shirt, all of them yelling over one another to be noticed first.

Sasha looked around, her eyes bouncing between Kursh males, females, and children as she watched their exchanges. Ferand peeled himself from their small group and made his way over to the lioness holding the tiny cub.

He greeted her with a cheek nuzzle. A few of the adults were also crowded around Ardalon, touching him on the arms and back occasionally as he spoke with them.

Awkward and alone, she stood there and watched, hands clasped in front of her.

"Who's the weird bald lady?"

She looked down. A cub was staring up at her, his tail swishing behind him in a tense arc. At least she thought it was a boy. She wasn't really sure how to tell their sexes apart when they were this young.

The cub's pale gold mane stuck up in every direction, two tan ears poking through them. His tail swished behind him underneath the hem of his shirtdress. She glanced at his bare feet and saw that they were very similar to a human's, just like their hands.

"Hello, I'm Sasha," she said.

The mother holding the tiny cub in her arms came forward to drag the boy back into the crowd of Ardalon's family. She looked at Sasha with the same cautious wariness in her body language that people had looked at her with, back when she'd left the senator's ship.

Guess it wasn't just the slutty clothes they all hated.

"Sasha, is it?" A tall, thin lioness came through the crowd. She was older than the rest. The short fur on her face had turned silver with age around her eyes and muzzle. "My son told me that he was bringing a guest home with him, although he was sparse with the details. I can see that he left much out of our conversation."

Ardalon set down the two cubs that he'd been holding up off the ground with just his raised arms. "Matta, there are things that can't be said over unsecure lines."

The older lioness raised her hand, two fingers held up as if to silence any further interruptions. They stared at one another in silence. Sasha squared her shoulders and met the woman's gaze without flinching. She had the feeling that there was more subtext to this conversation than she knew how to decipher. Some animal instinct deep within knew that you never looked away from or backed down from a predator.

His mother was older and thin, the muscle mass of her youth faded, but there was a wiry look to her. As if she was used to being underestimated and had overcome it. Sasha held her head high as she met the female's gaze.

Ardalon stepped toward them, the cubs falling back to let him through their numbers. "I gave my word to the state that I would keep her safe until the emperor has made—"

"The emperor may rule our people, but I am the matriarch of this den, and my word will be respected and obeyed," his mother interrupted him, leaving zero room for arguing.

Ardalon's steps paused, his posture stiff.

Sasha tipped her head down slightly. "I can go, if I'm not welcome here."

She wasn't sure what she would do if his mother didn't agree to let her stay, but the thought of coming between Ardalon and his family was unbearable. Nothing was more important than family. She'd wrecked his life enough already, and he'd been nothing but kind to her. He'd saved her life more than once.

She owed him.

She cared about him.

His mother's ears flicked. "Where will you go?"

Sasha shrugged, all of her breath escaping her in one long sigh. "I have no idea. I have nowhere to go."

The matriarch's eyes dropped, roving over her, looking her up and down, inspecting her. Sasha wasn't sure what the female was looking for, but her instincts said that if the female didn't find it, then things weren't going to go well for her.

"You may rest your weary head and tired feet with us," she said, finally, then turned and left, heading back inside their home.

Only the door of the house and a few high windows were visible. The rest of it had been buried into the ground, the size of it hidden by the earth that covered the house's gently sloping roof. The grass that grew on the roof of the house had been manicured to a short length so it blended into the greenery around them.

The house and the tunnel that the car had come out of were the only signs of modernization that she could see. There weren't even any artificial outdoor lights.

The kids ran off to play with a ball that hovered and glowed, their excitement for their uncle's return diminished in light of finding their lost toy among the grass.

Ardalon approached her, his hand on her elbow, as he deflected the rest of his family's curious questions and led her through the house's open front door.

"Well, that was intense," she said as she climbed down the stairs and looked around his home.

It was beautiful.

Whitewashed walls with wooden beams made up an enormous dome. Archways intersected it with tunnels and rooms leading off of the main room. A sitting room was sunken into the center of it, couches and chairs and ottomans interspersed throughout the room along with tables of varying sizes. Artwork and plants adorned the walls, leaving no inch of bare wall space.

Skylights lit the room brighter than she'd thought was capable until she really looked at them and realized that the windows were angled. Larger on the inside, they let in as much light as possible while exposing very little of the house outside.

After spending so many months cooped up in her tiny ship, and years in her cramped singles apartment, she found his family's house bafflingly strange. Beautiful, but huge and strange.

What do they do with all this space?

She remembered the sheer number of people she'd just seen outside. His family was large. She hadn't even known that families could be that big.

Do they all live here? Together?

Suddenly, the huge house with its offshoots of rooms made sense. They'd need places to gather, and spaces for solitude.

"She is particularly protective of me," he said, his hand coming up to curl behind her back as he nudged her toward a tunnel on the left and led her deeper into his home.

Sasha had to bite her tongue. She wanted to say that a mother who'd let her baby's tail get docked at birth wasn't a good mother. She didn't understand it at all.

They're so strange.

"Are you hungry?" he asked.

Focusing on the hand at her back and the warmth of his body in the chilly tunnel, she shook her head. "I'm still full, just tired." Bone-weary and exhausted was more like it.

Locked in a cage, running for her life, crash landing, running for her life again, getting kidnapped... her mind skipped over the rest of the details of her time on the senator's ship, not wanting to revisit it. She needed rest. Nanos and adrenaline could only keep her going for so long before she stopped functioning on fumes and her body started to shut down, forcing her to rest and recuperate.

He led her down a dim hallway. "I will show you where you

can sleep," he said as he urged her along. "It is, uh, that is to say... we do not keep a guest chamber here."

She stifled a yawn, covering her mouth as her blinking got slower. "I could probably sleep on the floor right now—that's how tired I am."

The short burst of energy she'd gotten when they'd landed in his city had faded, leaving her fatigued. He stopped her, his hand tight on her back as he pushed her up against the wall and caged her against it with his body, his leg wedged between one of hers. She blinked up at him, processing the abrupt change in him a little too slowly. A shiver licked down her spine, her body pulsing with interest once things registered.

"That is not... I am trying to say that the bed you will be sleeping in is mine. You don't have to share it if you'd prefer to sleep alone. To not share it with *me*," he growled, stressing the last word.

Spreading her hands on his chest, she felt the broad, hard planes of his muscles as he towered over her. She searched his face, one brow crooked in disbelief.

"The guy who cuddled me naked in a cave with his dick wedged between my asscheeks is suddenly concerned with respecting personal space?" she teased him.

He blinked down at her, his entire body tense. His chest filled as he took a deep breath and let it go, the movement shifting the baby hairs that framed her face. "Survival is different. You know this. We needed to share body heat."

She grinned before she could stop herself, knowing that his people didn't like it when someone bared their teeth because they took it as an act of aggression. Letting her hands slide down his chest, she explored the lines of his abdomen, feeling the dips and curves of each and every muscle.

His frilly shirts hid how muscular he really was, but she remembered how he looked from the few glances she'd gotten of him. She knew that his adonis belt was a deeply carved vee that led to an impressive package, even if she hadn't gotten a very good look at it.

Her mind flashed to the naked, aroused senator before she pumped the brakes on that train of thought, shoving those memories back into the depths of her mind for unpacking later.

This was Ardalon, and she was safe with him.

Hooking her thumbs in the waistband of his leather pants, she pulled him even closer. His thigh wedged between hers, hitting the core of her. She was too tired for sex, but her ladyparts hadn't gotten that memo. She throbbed for him.

"I remember waking up with you holding onto my boob like it owed you money," she teased him.

His eyes dipped down to her chest, even though the tunic she wore was loose and modest. "They're very soft," he groaned.

She nodded, twitching her hips against his thigh, rubbing herself along his leg because she was a horny masochist. "They are. I'm very soft in general," she replied, thinking of how the military had always given her a hard time about having to tailor her uniforms to fit her properly once she rotated out of active duty.

She wasn't infantry anymore. The busted satellites didn't care if she had a little padding on her.

He groaned, the sound doing dirty things to her, making her wet for him.

"You are," he agreed. "Deliciously soft. Sasha, will you share my bed with me?"

"Yes."

The word was barely out of her mouth before he'd scooped her up and lifted her, his arms locked underneath her butt and her cleavage mashed against his chest.

He kissed her, his lips finding hers in an impatient frenzy. She didn't know how he managed to carry her down the corridor without tripping over something. All she knew was that he was kissing her and she was safe and they were definitely going to fuck... right after she got some sleep.

Something beeped at her back, and then they were in a room but she saw absolutely none of it because Ardalon was too busy kissing the breath out of her.

The door shut itself, the lights responding to their movements as they entered his room. He carried her to the bed and set her on it, leaning forward to maintain their constant contact as he covered her with his body and followed her down.

Breaking their kiss, she leaned back into the bed to look up at him. "I want to sleep first, but I also want to see you. Watch you masturbate. Is that," she chewed her lip, hesitating, "is that okay?"

Face serious, as if she'd just given him some great task to do, he nodded. Ardalon withdrew, his hands trailing over her body for one last touch until he stood and backed away from the bed.

He started with his boots, unlacing and kicking them off. His socks were next. The leather pants unlaced instead of having a zipper, and she wondered how impractical that was—until he pulled his white shirt over his head and tossed it aside, and then she wasn't thinking about laces at all.

Leaning up on her elbows, she watched him undress. He made a show of sliding his leather pants down slowly, his fingers moving over his abdomen as he undid them. The fur on his belly was lighter than the rest of him, except for a dark line that trailed from his navel downward until it disappeared into his pants.

God, I love a happy trail.

Inch by inch he slid his pants down, moving with a languid grace as he peeled them off, stepping out of them. One cock and two balls, but that was where the similarities ended. His penis was a velvet-furred sheath with a growing, pink organ that was extending out of it as he swelled and grew.

She watched, enraptured, as he stroked it, his penis filling out to an impossible size. He was textured. Small bumps the same color of his skin decorated the length of him in orderly lines. The tip of his penis was sloped and hooked instead of the familiar domed mushroom shape she was used to.

Palming himself, Ardalong stroked, and she watched how he used his sheath to masturbate himself with every tug. A bead of clear fluid gathered at his tip. She licked her lips and wondered how it tasted.

"I usually lie down," he said, his voice deep, half-growl. His breathing was fast and hard as he stroked himself.

She nodded and rubbed her feet together, trying to kick her ankle boots off, but they stuck.

Ardalon stopped, kneeling down next to the bed as he unhooked the laces of her shoes and took them off, setting them on the floor beside the bed more carefully than she would have. He leaned down and pressed a kiss to her ankle where the hem of her pants had ridden up.

Shifting backward, Sasha made room on the bed for him, lying down on her side as he crawled in beside her, his hand going back to his cock as he fisted it again and tugged. She cuddled into his side, fitting them together, and pressed her cheek to his chest so she could watch him better.

He grunted, his hips twitching as he started tugging faster.

The wet pink end of his engorged shaft filled his entire hand as he stroked himself.

She wanted to touch him, to see if it was as soft as it looked. Feeling bold and curious, she slid her hand down his front until she hit his velvety sheath, stroking a finger over it and the balls that hung underneath.

His hips bucked and he cursed, something that didn't have meaning to her translators.

Heart pounding in her chest, she brushed her fingers over his hand, feeling him. He was soft, the feel of his skin smooth, yet textured too. To her surprise, the bumps were underneath his skin and they moved if she pressed on them with force. His momentum stopped, his hand releasing his dick as he paused and let her explore him.

Ardalon pressed his muzzle into her hair while she touched him, her fingertips barely touching as she gripped his cock and gave him an experimental tug.

Groaning, his hips bucked.

A drop of his arousal dripped down her knuckles.

She stroked him again, firming her grip and working on sliding that soft skin over the hardness underneath it until she was mimicking his movements. More pre-cum gathered at his tip, dripping down and sliding over her fingers as she worked her hand up from his base all the way to his sloped head and the tiny hook that curled it under.

He pulsed in her hand, his breathing coming faster as she worked him. She slid his velvety soft skin over that hardness and swirled her fingers around his sticky, dripping tip.

"S-Sasha, I—" he stuttered, his hips thrusting with her tugs, fucking her hand while she pumped him.

She pulled harder, her fingers tighter, and worked her hand faster. She wanted to see him spill his seed, to be the one to make him cum, so she hurried her pace. A hand on her backside palmed one cheek of her butt and squeezed.

Tight tugs on the shaft followed by a loose rolling movement over his weeping head, she smeared his fluids down her fingers and used the lubrication to pump harder. Faster. Firmer. His hips rose off the bed, nails pricked her ass as he squeezed, and he growled as he came.

Ardalon's hips bucked through his orgasm, the muscles on his lower abdomen contracting with each jet of cum that ran down her hand. His cock twitched, his balls pulled up tight against his body.

Cum spilled from his tip, spraying lines of seed up his belly and over her fingers. It was thin and messy, dribbling and pooling.

She worked him through his orgasm, pulling more and more cum from his body with each tug of his pulsing cock. It twitched in her hand, one last bead of release leaking from his softening member as he began to shrink again.

She raised her cum-covered hand to her face and smelled it. Musky. Male. Not very different than she'd expected. She licked a finger clean and considered it.

"V-Viruk, Sasha, that was... seven hells."

He purred, his chest rumbling underneath her cheek. She wiped her slippery fingers off on his abdomen and closed her eyes. Fingers carded through her hair as he lay there, panting as his breathing slowed.

Sasha smiled, enjoying the pleasure of it. She'd always loved it when her hair was played with. "I like being woken up with sex," she told him, her body already on the verge of falling asleep out of its sheer exhaustion.

The fingers in her hair stopped, and she made an irritated whine. He jostled her as he got up off the bed and stood, using his discarded pirate shirt to wipe the cum off his stomach. She cracked one eye open to glance at him to see if he'd heard her. He was staring at her with those golden cat eyes of his that seemed to see everything. His pupils expanded and contracted as he met her gaze and held it.

"You want me to wake you up with..." he hesitated.

Sleepy, she nodded, her eyes sliding shut again.

She was nearly asleep already when she felt a blanket being tucked up under her chin, the soft mattress dipping as he got into bed with her.

Sensations that didn't quite match her current predicament eased her from her current dream, turning it erotic. Transported from the half-memory, half-dream of her time at the academy, her consciousness shifted, following the ghostlike sensations. She rolled with it, diving into this newer, more pleasant thing.

A slow caress of her arm, a faint touch down her ribs that halfway tickled, she turned into it. He slid his hand down her body, running it over the soft skin of her thigh, creeping inward.

The blankets shifted as she stretched, eyes closed and mind fuzzy, her tunic riding up to expose the waistband of her pants. They were in a state of disarray, which wasn't unusual. She'd always been an active sleeper.

That roaming hand found her waistband and slipped inside, tracing a light and teasing path down her abdomen.

He found her juncture, a finger sliding along the seam of her lips, exploring. She shivered, her body clenching, empty and aching. Eyes still closed, she pushed her head back into the bed and raised her hips, leaning into that gentle, teasing touch.

Ardalon purred as he explored her, touching every inch of the outside of her body. Her nipples pebbled, aching to be pinched and rolled between two fingers. Moaning, she twitched her hips as she tried to rub herself harder on his hand. He'd yet to spread her open, content to play with her outer labia and hair. Moisture crept, her body throbbing in invitation, more than ready for him.

He seemed to be enjoying this agonizingly slow exploration of her body.

Sadist.

Cracking her eyes open, grateful for the low amber glow of

his dimmed wall lamps, she arched her back and tugged her rucked up tunic over her head. The rush of cold air on her breasts made her nipples so hard they ached.

He seemed to take this as some sort of signal. He withdrew, hooking her pants by the waistband and dragging them down her legs. She helped him, lifting her butt off the bed so he could work them down, then bent her knees so he could pull them off her and cast them aside.

Sasha watched his face as he looked at her, naked, exposed and aroused for him. He'd seen her nude before, but this time was different. She let her bent knees fall open, enjoying the way that his breath hitched and his eyes fell to her center, like he was caught in her gravitational pull.

Biting her lip, she watched him stare, nerves fluttering in her belly as she wondered if she looked weird to him.

He reached out, his fingers spreading her, touching her like she was made of glass.

"I won't break," she reminded him, urging him on.

Gold cat eyes flicked up, meeting hers and holding her gaze as he firmed his touch, his fingers sliding through her folds and spreading her arousal. He grazed her clit. Lifting her hands to play with her breasts, rolling her nipples in rough circles and squeezing, she bucked against his hand and moaned.

"You're beautiful," he told her, leaning over her to capture her mouth with his.

He kissed her, his tongue tracing the seam of her lips, the fine-grit sandpaper texture of it making her shiver, and then his hand began to move. He found her clit again and circled it, his touch light until she moaned into their kiss.

Heat rushed to her core, her pussy throbbing as he teased her, spread her wide, and used her moisture to rub slick circles around her clit until she was breathing heavy, her tongue rubbing against his as Ardalon devoured her mouth.

Hips twitching, she fought the urge to writhe underneath him as pleasure built, a tight sensation winding, tighter and tighter with every movement of his hand.

A finger slid down and pressed against her entrance, then dipped inside as his thumb kept up its constant motion. Her body pulled him in, clenching around his probing finger, eager to be filled.

Still, it wasn't enough. She needed more from him, wanted everything.

Breaking their kiss, she gasped, throwing her head back when his finger sank all the way inside of her.

"A-Ardalon," she gasped, her clit throbbing and her center clenching around him, trying to suck him in deeper, trying to wring more from him. The desperate urge to cum was all that mattered. "P-Please," she begged, riding his hand, wishing he'd add a second finger inside of her so he could fill her up.

She was too empty, having not been touched for way too long. Couldn't he see how much she needed him?

"Cum for me, kitten," he purred, his thumb continuing its rubbing against her clit.

"I need you," she whined, not too proud to beg if that's what it came down to. His cock had been a little scary at first. Different and intimidating. But now, with his hand buried in her cunt and his thumb damn near vibrating on her clit, she craved it. Wanted him to sink himself inside of her, fill her up to her cervix, and fuck her so hard she couldn't sit down after until her nanos patched her up.

The finger inside of her moved, exploring her from the inside. "You're too small, kitten. We won't fit together."

Sasha blinked at him, confused, not wanting to focus on anything but the pinnacle that she was straddling.

"W-What?"

Her body spasmed, confused until she caught that wave of pleasure again as his thumb re-centered on her clit. She panted.

"I'll stretch," she asserted, wishing he'd add a second finger and start pumping them.

His hand withdrew from her completely, and she nearly cried out, just barely stopping herself from groaning in frustration as her building orgasm faded. Ardalon sat back on his knees and peered down at her vagina, his ears flat as he assessed it.

Exploring her channel, he inserted a finger inside of her again, then withdrew and added a second. Her wetness eased his entrance, her swollen flesh giving way to the insistence of his fingers as he pushed them into her and pumped.

Her eyes fluttered, her clit pulsing in pleasure. She was engorged. Swollen and needy, she wanted to cum.

"Ardalon, I swear to God, if you don't fuck me right now, I'm going to flip us and then I'll be the one on top," she growled, her hips moving with a mind of her own as she tried to work herself with his hand.

His ears dropped flat, his eyes narrowing. The fingers inside of her withdrew and then pressed in again, a third one stretching her wide with a delicious burn. She bit her lip, biting back a grunt while her body worked to accommodate him.

She was dripping, her cunt slippery from her near-orgasm before. It eased his thrusting as he buried three fingers into her channel and pumped. The movement rubbed against something wonderful inside of her.

Hips shifting, finding a new momentum that worked, she met his thrusts, grinding her clit onto the pad of his thumb as he hooked his fingers inside of her and pumped.

"Viruk, the noises you make," he groaned, rising to his knees between her thighs.

When his hand withdrew from her pussy, she gave into her urge to groan at the loss of him until she saw that he was readying himself, stroking his sheath until his textured pink cock fully emerged. He was already swollen, a vein on the top pulsing as a bead of pre-cum dripped from his tip and landed somewhere on the sheets between them.

Fully erect, Ardalon grabbed her by the hips and tugged her down, leaning his body into the cradle of her hips as he spread her wider and fit himself to her entrance. The tip of his penis sank into her.

The way he was shaped, tapered at the tip and then wider toward his sheath, made his entry easy until she hit the broadest part of him. Nostrils flaring, she exhaled, forcing herself to relax. To open for him. The final stretch burned until her body gave way to him and he was fully seated in her.

Filled to the brim and stretched wider than she'd ever been, he moved with a cautious thrust to start with. Ardalon pulled back, his eyes locked down at where they were joined together.

The soft bumps that decorated his cock massaged her from the inside out, rippling over her sensitive places with each withdrawal.

"F-Fuck, oh my God," she exhaled, her body clenching around him.

He surged forward and stuffed her full of alien cock until the soft, hooked tip of his penis hit her cervix, demanding she yield to him, take all of him. She squeezed her eyes shut and fisted her hands in the sheets, arching her back as he moved again, thrusting faster.

He was holding her by the hips, keeping her body in place and still as he built up his momentum, each insistent press forward rocking her up the bed while he tugged her back down and ground them together.

Her breaths came out in rapid pants, heart hammering in her chest, the pulse between her thighs matching its tempo as she clenched around his cock. He bottomed out inside of her with every thrust, the velvet of his skin rubbing against her swollen lower lips and butt, yet another reminder that she was being fucked by an alien.

"So... so good," she panted, her neck straining as she arched, her focus narrowed down to the point where they connected.

His pre-cum eased the passage of his massive penis as he took her, stretching her wide. She cracked her eyes open and looked down her body until she saw where they were connected. The sight of his studded pink cock pistoning in and out of her swollen pussy drove her wild.

She undulated her hips, meeting his thrusts, grinding herself on him as he worked himself inside of her.

Ardalon growled, the sound of it making the hairs on her arms stand up and her nipples tighten. It was the sound of a predator, and it activated some primordial instinct buried deep within her mind. She went completely still, freezing in place.

The hands on her hips tightened, and then her world spun as he flipped her over onto her belly. Her hands slapped against the bed, the air knocked out of her in surprise.

His cock tugged free of her, and she whined, hating the loss of him when she was already halfway back to her orgasm. Hands on her legs grabbed her, nails pricking at her soft skin as he bent and pulled her, forcing her into the position that he wanted. He tugged her hips up, a hand between her shoulders pressing her torso flat against the bed.

She wiggled up onto her knees and spread them wide, sinking back into it as she pressed her face to the bed and tilted her pelvis so that her body opened for him.

Waiting for him, impatient that he'd stalled her pleasure again, she loved this new side to him. Pushy, and a little feral. She'd always enjoyed it when her partners got a bit aggressive in bed.

"You don't move," he ordered, his voice a deep half-growl.

Something probed at her entrance, and then he thrust, seating himself inside of her in one short move. If she hadn't been this wet and half-fucked already, it would have hurt.

She gasped and fisted her hands in the bed as he withdrew until his cock nearly left her, then thrust all of the way inside, the soft hook on his penis hitting her cervix.

"F-Fuck, Ardalon," she whimpered.

The hands on her hips held her into place underneath him as he took his pleasure, plowed her cunt and spread her wide. The combination of their fluids and arousal eased his brutal thrusts as he claimed her. Forced her into compliance and fucked her breathless.

Those bumps on his cock rippled inside of her with every thrust and tug, her pleasure building once again until she was a panting, trembling mess, her pussy throbbing.

"Please," she begged.

She wanted to cum, *needed* to cum, had to have that release more than she'd ever needed anything else in her life.

Her body was a coiled spring, pulled taut and thrumming, waiting. Her thighs tensed with the force of its build, a terrifying and beautiful thing that threatened to destroy her once it hit.

"I... want to... bite... you," he growled between thrusts, the bed hitting the wall with each pump of his hips.

Her gentle, timid lover was gone, and she loved it.

A hand grabbed one of hers and bent it back, and then the other, until he had them both. With her arms pinned against the small of her back, she wasn't able to stop herself from moving with each and every thrust.

He stripped all control from her as he fucked her.

Her toes curled, her body spasming around his dick, a preview to the orgasm that was coming. His thrusts were coming faster, harder, and deeper. He seemed to have swollen even more. Wetness spread down her inner thighs as he fucked her into the bed, his hands clenched tight on her to hold her in place underneath him.

"Y-Yes," she panted, not caring if he bit or scratched her in the process as long as he didn't stop again. "Do it."

Her pleasure had built to an impossible height. Denied twice, it towered in front of her, waiting to obliterate her once it hit. A hurricane with her caught in the middle, in the eye of the storm, waiting for it to move and wreck her from the sheer force of its wind and waves.

He fucked her faster until she was a moaning mess underneath him, the bumps on his cock massaging her from the inside, his slanted tip battering her cervix and the force of his thrusts tugging on her folds and clit.

She held her breath when that spring wound down, the world falling away from her for those two seconds, and then she came. Her cunt spasmed around him, milking him, as she cried out with her release.

Waves of pleasure rippled through her, her pussy throbbing with every contraction.

He released his hold on her wrists, his hand sliding up her spine, moving to her neck, until he'd threaded into the hair at her nape. He grabbed a fistful of hair and squeezed, pulling her up off the bed until she was kneeling, impaled on his cock and trembling with the force of her fading orgasm

Ardalon forced her to arch, pulling her head back.

He leaned down, curled over her, his panting breath warm against her throat as his thrusts changed to slow, grinding ones that tugged at her swollen entrance and folds. He wrapped his other arm around her, a hand splayed possessively over her belly as he pulled her back onto his thighs, penetrating deeper, and locked her into place.

Overly sensitive now, aftershocks still pulsing through her, she shivered.

Her walls were still fluttering in the aftermath of her release when he set his teeth to the skin at the juncture of her neck and shoulder and bit.

She sucked in a hissing breath between her teeth as his incisors broke through skin.

With his jaws locked on her, he pumped, grunting as he came. Deep thrusts buried his cock inside of her as he growled while biting her. She could feel him twitching inside of her body, pumping her full of cum.

Growls switched over to purrs as his jaws released her, lapping at her skin where he'd broken through in the four places underneath his canines. Still buried inside of her, he emptied himself until there was nothing left, his thrusts stuttering to a stop after he'd pumped himself dry.

His jaws relaxed as he let her go. "Are you all right?" he asked between swipes of his tongue as he licked her shoulder clean.

A trembling sigh rattled from her throat. "I'm perfect," she moaned, letting her head loll back onto his shoulder as she slumped against him, feeling boneless.

He shifted, his softening penis pulling out of her.

The mess they'd made was immediately apparent. His seed, thinner and more copious than she was used to, ran down her inner thigh. It was going to make a mess of their sheets. She tried to squeeze her legs closed, to stop its smearing, but he was still holding her in place and laving her neck and his bite marks with his sandpapery tongue. Her lips twitched with a smile.

"How are *you*?" she asked, settling her hands on the arm that was splayed across her belly, holding her in place as she half-kneeled, half-straddled his lap.

His chest rumbled with a purr, the vibration transferring through to her where they pressed together.

"You turn pink when you cum. Your throat and breasts," he answered, his purr deepening. "I like it."

She stifled a giggle.

Ardalon nudged her to lie down onto the bed and settled down with her until they were curled up on their sides, spooning. His tongue still worried over the bite mark he'd made between her neck and shoulder. The arm on her belly shifted higher, grabbing one breast and holding it just like he'd done in the cave.

"It'll heal, I promise," she told him, hoping he'd let her go so she could roll over and start kissing him, maybe work him back up for a round two if his refractory period could handle it.

His purr stuttered, then stopped, his tongue withdrawing from her skin. Ardalon pulled away from her, levering up onto his elbow, his attention rapt on her punctured skin as he watched it closely.

It felt hot, her nanos already working to repair it. She craned her head around to look at him and saw that his ears were flat, like they moved whenever he was irritated or angry.

"What's wrong?" she asked, confused.

He sighed. "Your bite will heal. Our mating link will likely always be one-sided."

Knocking his hand off her breast as she turned over in the bed, burying the already healing bite mark into the pillows so he'd stop focusing on it and look at her instead. She raised one hand up to cup his face, stroking it softly.

"I don't understand what that means," she told him. "Talk to me."

His gaze flashed to hers before he shut them. After a long pause, he opened them again. "On the ship, in the medical bay when you were scared... you bit me."

Sasha nodded.

"You initiated the bond. A weak one, which I suspect is

because your teeth are mostly flat and didn't penetrate deeply… but still, I can feel it there," he explained.

She frowned, trying to follow along but not really understanding the significance of it. The translators in her brain couldn't account for species and societal differences, just the meaning of the words themselves.

He must have seen her confusion, because he continued. "You bonded me to you. As your mate."

Her mind was mulling it over, working overtime to put the pieces together. "The bite… mated us," she summarized, her stomach sinking and filling her with dread. "And for your people, mating is…"

"For life."

She was going to be sick.

"Did we just… get married?" she asked, pulling away from him so she could sit up.

This was not the typical post-coital pillow talk she normally engaged in after mind-blowing sex, and she needed a second. Needed a whole damn lot of seconds.

His ears twitched within his locks. "If that is what your people call mating, then yes. Does your species not pair up for life? To cohabitate? Raise cubs together?" They went flat again.

Sasha grabbed the rumpled blanket and tugged it up over her nakedness, needing to feel less exposed. Less vulnerable. "They do—I mean, some of them do."

She frowned. "Some people get married and it doesn't always work out, so then they split up. Some people never want to get married and they're happy to be on their own. Others date a lot of people and don't want to be tied down to just one person… or some of them even have multiple partners they're committed to."

The way that he was staring at her made her feel self-conscious.

"That sounds... chaotic," he mumbled.

Eyebrows rising and eyes slowly blinking, she shrugged, the movement pulling at her shoulder, the bite marks pinching. "Yeah... it is, I guess."

"Are you... did you already have a mate?" he asked. "Before you came here?"

She shook her head. "No. I dated a few people over the years, but it just never worked out. My brother is married, though, and blissfully happy with his wife. They were together for five years before they got their marriage license, and now they're working on earning their family license so they can have kids."

His ears went flat again. "The translator is not working. What does a certificate have to do with mating and having progeny?"

"Umm... okay, so when two people decide they want to get married they fill out paperwork and pay the government a fee and then usually they have a wedding... a ceremony for their friends and family to celebrate with them. They need another license later to get their birth control implants shut off so they can have kids."

He rolled onto his back, a hand splayed across his belly, his soft penis flopping against his leg. He didn't appear to be self-conscious about his nudity at all.

"I find that very strange. What business does your government have with mating if two adults know in their hearts or minds that they should bond?" he asked.

She thought about it from his point of view for a moment before she agreed. "Yeah, I guess it's kind of weird. I think it has to do with money. The government makes money off of people getting mated and having kids. Our planet got way too overpopulated for a long time before we eventually spread out to colonies and terraformed a bunch of planets and moons. The mandatory birth control makes sure that only the people who are serious about having children can do so."

Shifting into a seated position, she got comfortable, the sheet tucked up under her armpits.

"I can understand why your people would want to control their breeding if they don't typically mate for life, but I wouldn't want my friends and family to watch my mating," he added in a disgusted voice.

Eyes wide, she shook her head, letting out a bark of surprised laughter. "No! Oh my God, no. They don't watch *that*. It's a ceremony. You exchange rings and hold hands and an officiant reads from a book or recites something, and then you're married. Everyone eats and drinks, and dances after."

He leveled her with a probing gaze. "If you require jewelry for your mating, I can buy a ring. I like the idea of it. If your body will not wear my bite marks, then a ring will be a physical reminder, at least. Even if only you and I know its significance. Others won't recognize it... I could speak to my matta about having a party."

Her mouth ran dry. "Okay... swinging back around to the whole 'I mated you' thing..." she hesitated.

Ardalon laid a hand on her sheet draped thigh, his attention back to focusing on her. "If you are worried that I regret it, then the answer is no. I thought that you were interesting the first time I laid eyes on you. When I saw you overcome and outsmart the Diggi at every turn in your escape, I was intrigued. When we shared our body heat in the cave, I knew that I wanted you, kitten."

The hand on her thigh squeezed it in a gesture of reassurance.

Her breath hitched, the fear subsiding a little. She hadn't intended to mate him. Wouldn't have done so if she'd known the significance of her little act of rebellious aggression.

She was startled to realize, however, that she didn't regret it. Not a single bit of her. She regretted that she'd done something so important out of ignorance, and the knowledge that she had an entirely new culture to learn about scared her, but... Ardalon didn't. He never had.

You can't marry an alien, something whispered from deep within her psyche.

She shoved the intrusive thought away. *Already did, I guess.*

It was scary. Not in the 'near death experience' sort of way, but more in the 'diving off a twenty foot tall diving board' sort of way. Her pulse slowed as her panic subsided. "So how does this... work? What do your people do to get marr... to be mated."

Reaching down, she grabbed his hand and threaded her fingers through with his. He squeezed her hand, and her heart melted, a smile tugging at her face.

"When a courting couple feels the desire to mate, she will mark him, signaling her acceptance of the match, then he will mark her back. Or if they desire a traditional mating, she will bite bond him and run instead."

She frowned, confused, wondering if she'd heard him wrong or if they were still having translator issues. "I'm sorry... She runs away from him?"

Ardalon nodded. "Yes. She will run, and he will chase her. Run her down, force her to her knees, rut her, then seal the bond with his bite. It's an old tradition that's falling out of favor."

Her tired, battered core throbbed. A bead of their combined fluids leaked down her inner thigh as her body pulsed at the thought of Ardalon chasing her through the tall grass outside of his home and...

He groaned, nostrils flaring, his cock twitching where it laid on his thigh. "Sasha, if you keep smelling like that," he warned her, his voice pitching low again.

She shivered, her pussy clenching again, sending more of his seed and her arousal down her thighs and buttocks until she was a slippery mess. It couldn't be helped. She liked him like this, all dominant and possessive.

It made her feel small and feminine and, most of all, desired in a way that no guy had ever made her feel before.

Ardalon chasing me, catching me, taking me down, fucking me like he'd die if he didn't sink his cock into my pussy...

He pulled her down onto the bed and curled her into his side, then spanked her. His hand came down on her ass with one sharp smack that was more surprising than painful. She flinched even though it didn't hurt.

It wasn't like she didn't enjoy being spanked and roughhoused a bit during sex.

"Pay attention, kitten, or your wandering thoughts will distract us both. This conversation is important.."

Her core pulsed, another line of fluid dripping down her body. He kneaded her ass, massaging out the faint sting he'd just slapped into her.

His hand wandered over her backside, paying particularly close attention to the cleft between her buttocks. Where a tail would be, she realized, if humans still had tails after evolution got rid of them forever ago.

He seemed obsessed with it, an unconscious preoccupation that likely stemmed from his own lack of a tail. The one that had been docked from him at birth. A coldness settled in her belly, cooling her arousal.

She was still angry on his behalf about that.

"Do you regret mating me?" he asked. "I know you didn't realize the significance of what you'd done, otherwise you might not have done it."

Spreading her hand through the fur of his chest, she played with the hair, scratching through it down to the skin with her short nails. She tucked the top of her head under his chin, enjoying the faint rumble in his chest.

Would she not have done it if she'd known?

She didn't have an answer for that question. No, she didn't regret mating him. She might have even chosen to do it under different circumstances... but she didn't want it to be undone.

Cupping his face, she pulled his mouth down to hers and kissed him, pouring her heart and soul into the meeting of their lips. This was her answer. Tangible proof that she accepted him and chose him above any other. After a moment of hesitation, he matched it, kissing her back.

Slow and sweet, she pulled him in tighter and kissed him until they were both breathless and his penis hardened, pressing against her belly and leaving a smear of cold dampness on her bare skin as it twitched. She worked an arm down between them and stroked him back to life.

Hitching her leg over his, she guided him into her.

Wrapping her arms around his neck, she showed him the difference between sex and making love.

CHAPTER FIFTEEN

SASHA

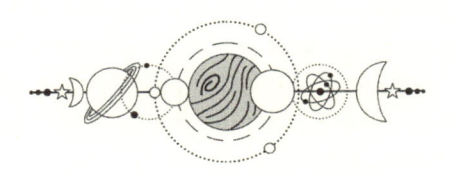

Sasha was watching Ardalon's sister Enaiya prepare dinner while the lioness' children played with their light ball toy in the kitchen.

"This is a pompot," Enaiya told her, raising up a dark red piece of produce that she explained was a starchy vegetable they frequently used with a variety of their meat dishes, curries, and stews. "You eat meat, yes?"

Sasha nodded. "Humans eat pretty much anything. We're omnivores, and I've always liked trying different cuisines. My brother always hated when it was my turn to pick the takeout menu. He doesn't like anything that isn't pasta or synth steak."

Flashing the lioness smile eyes, she took a vegetable from the sack and picked up a knife from their knife rack and got to work on cutting it.

"Thinner pieces," Enaiya said, showing her how to julienne it properly. "Or it doesn't cook all the way through."

It reminded her of a potato… if potatoes bled red juice when you cut them.

Ignoring the red juice that was staining her fingernails pink, Sasha worked on cutting it just right, hoping that if she helped make dinner and the food was good that Ardalon's mother might start warming up to her.

Already pissing off the in-laws.

The knife slipped in the red juice and nicked the side of her finger, cutting it open. "Ouch, damn it."

Enaiya glanced over and saw Sasha's bleeding finger. "Clean it, then put pressure on that. I'll fetch you a bandage."

Distracted with trying not to bleed all over the alien potatoes she'd already cut, Sasha didn't stop Ardalon's sister before she'd left the room.

Her cut began to burn, the juice from the pompot stinging in her fresh cut. Setting the knife down on the cutting block, she tried to fiddle with the faucet that she'd seen the female get fresh water from. She needed to wash the irritant out before her wound closed on its own, trapping the caustic juice inside until her body finished neutralizing it.

She waved a hand over the sink's black sensor. Nothing happened. She stuck her hand under the end of the faucet. Still nothing. She looked around for a handle or button, but didn't find one.

How the hell do they work this thing?

With their mother out of the room, the children came closer, staring at her with an intensity that would have been frightening if they weren't so small and fluffy.

"You smell like matta after she fights with patta," the female cub announced.

The male cub at her side wrinkled his nose, his nostrils flaring like he agreed with his sister. They both had white spots on their fur, and Sasha wondered if that was a marking unique to them or if it was something that changed with age as they grew up.

They were pretty stinkin' adorable.

"You stink," the male cub agreed.

Not that cute.

Sasha blushed, looking away from them. "Do you know how this thing works?" she asked, nodding toward the sink.

The male cub chuffed. "Of course! We're not babies like Matiyah," he added with a glance toward the youngest cub who was still playing with their glowing light ball on the floor.

The little one, Matiyah, looked up at the mention of her name. "Hey! I am *not* a baby!"

"Okay... well, I don't know how to use it. Do you think you could show me?" Sasha asked, watching the blood drip down her finger, the cut still burning.

"I know how to use it too!" Matiyah yelled, pulling herself up off the floor and toddling over, her tail swiping the air behind her as she crossed the kitchen.

"Awesome, any day now," Sasha muttered under her breath while she focused on keeping the small wound open so it didn't heal yet.

Matiyah walked up to the counter and raised her arms, gripping the edge of it as if she intended to climb up on it so she could show Sasha how to use the sink.

Sasha's eyes flicked to the counter where the little girl was actively climbing on, and saw the cutting board with the cut up burgundy space potatoes and her abandoned knife on it.

"Oh, frack."

She moved before she even had a conscious thought of moving. Matiyah's fingers hit the edge of the cutting board. It slipped forward and she fell back, the knife falling with her.

Sasha reached out and caught it before it could land on the little girl. Unfortunately, she caught it with her palm, and not her grip. The knife sank inches into her hand, running her straight through with its wickedly sharp blade. Gnashing her teeth to keep from shouting more expletives, she closed her eyes and breathed through the pain. Matiyah was sprawled out on the floor and crying, and the older cubs were screaming.

"What the seven hells is... oh my gods and goddesses," Enaiya said, returning to the kitchen with a handful of first aid supplies.

"I didn't know how to turn on the sink," Sasha explained, her hand on fire from the juices that coated the blade.

"Matta, we didn't do it!" the older kids insisted, stepping back from the scene that was unfolding. "Matiyah was climbing again, even though you told her not to!"

Enaiya rushed forward, dropping her supplies on the counter before bending down to pick up her crying cub, holding the little girl to her chest as the child cried. "I will... ugh... oh, gods, I'm going to fetch my brother."

The lioness left the kitchen, one child in her arms and the others following on her heels, leaving Sasha alone. She sighed. "I still don't know how to turn on the sink."

Resting her knifed hand on the counter, careful not to drive it in deeper, Sasha went back to the sink, trying to figure out how the fracking thing turned on. After what felt like five minutes to her, and an eternity to her burning hand, she gave up, her good hand strumming her fingertips on the counter as she grew resigned to wait until someone showed up.

"Sasha?" Ardalon called from the doorway. "My sister told me there was an accident."

Swiveling to the doorway, she raised her injured hand and pointed at it.

His ears flicked flat to his head before returning to normal. Looking around the room, he glanced at her, the burgundy alien potato chunks and their juices splattered all over the floor, and her standing there, impaled through the hand with her kitchen knife.

"Should I even ask?" He seemed exasperated.

"It was either my hand, or your niece's face," she answered. "I can't figure this stupid thing out," she said, waving her good hand at the sink. "I need to rinse the alien potato juice out of my hand before I let it close or else it's going to be burning me for hours."

He strode forward, crossing the kitchen. "Poeh-tay-toe? Ah, that's a pompot. Caustic when raw, delicious when thoroughly cooked. You turn the sink faucet on with two quick taps here on the spigot."

She watched as he tapped the faucet, turning it on.

Fracking finally.

"What can I do to help?" he asked.

She stuck her impaled hand under the water and kept it there until the external burning stopped and the knife was cleaned of acidic alien potato juice. The water ran pink with the mixture of pompot juice and her blood.

"After you take the knife out, I need you to pry the wound open so I can wash it out before it closes. If I try to do it, I'm not going to get it all," she told him. "You'll have to be quick. My body is already trying to heal."

Stepping up behind her, Ardalon reached around and pulled out the knife. After the initial tug, flesh sticking to the metal because of her body's attempt to heal around the knife, he tugged harder until it pulled free. He grabbed the sides of her wound and ignored the hiss she made between clenched teeth as she stuck her hand under the running water and flushed it.

The bleeding worsened, the water washing away the nanos that were trying to heal her. After a minute or two of cleaning it out, the burning stopped. "It's good now."

He let her palm go and she pulled her hand out from under the faucet so that she could finally clot. Ardalon tapped the faucet off, then opened a paper package and handed her a soft piece of white cloth. She pressed it to the biggest part of the wound and held the edges of her skin closed while her nanos worked.

Her hair shifted, and, looking up through her eyebrows, she realized that he was pressing a kiss to the top of her head.

He straightened up. "Thank you. My nieces and nephews are like my own cubs to me, since I'm unable to have any of my own."

Her belly fluttered.

"It was my fault anyway. I left the knife on the counter and she was climbing up to show me how to use the sink," she told him, not wanting him to feel grateful when it was just her fixing another mess she'd made.

He blinked at her. "Enaiya left her young cubs in the kitchen where there's many dangers, and Matiyah climbed onto the counter. The blame is shared, and it was an accident. How is your hand?"

Peeling the cloth off her palm, she showed him that it was already halfway healed. Only the deepest portion in the center remained. Dried bits of blood flaked off the shallow ends of the wound when she brushed them off. She didn't even need to hold the edges of the wound closed anymore. "I'm fine."

He patted her on the hip. "Good. I think that's enough cooking for you today. Let Enaiya finish up. She enjoys the task. Besides, I want to show you something."

She followed him out of the kitchen, then through the empty common spaces before walking behind him down the hallway that led to his chambers. While he busied himself with tapping buttons on a small silver ball, she flopped onto his bed and got comfortable. Color exploded around the room as the ball began projecting images on the walls and ceiling.

He cycled through some sort of menu filled with alien writing she couldn't read, and then the program he selected began to play.

Ardalon crawled into the bed beside her and tugged her into his side. Together, they curled up as they watched what he'd wanted to show her. It was some sort of alien movie involving a Kursh couple who were pretending not to like each other, a stolen statue that was apparently a very big deal, and a team of Raxion bad guys who were trying to get the statue back and kill the couple.

"Is he spitting acid?" she asked, bewildered when the big bad Raxion guy had the Kursh heartthrob cornered in the grand finale fight scene. The rock he'd spat on, where the hero had just been standing, began to dissolve. "That's wild. He just destroyed a rock with acid venom."

Ardalon chuffed. "They can actually do that."

"What…" Sasha trailed off, her eyes wide. She remembered all the times the Raxions she'd met had turned bright yellow, their skin lighting up whenever they got angry. That was them making acid venom?

His chuffing deepened, turning into a full-blown rumbling laugh at her surprise.

She slapped his stomach, enjoying the way that the air whooshed out of him, and enjoying the feel of his abdominals even more. Tracing her fingers down the middle of him, she went lower, exploring his body. His chuffing stalled, turning into a purr.

Her attention shifted away from the movie. Tugging his shirt out of the waistband of his pants, she slipped her hand down until she hit his sheath. The hand that had been on her lower back moved lower, cupping the round globe of her butt. He squeezed it, his penis twitching in her hand.

Exploring his body, tracing the edge of his lightly furred sheath, she coaxed his penis to life, feeling victorious when he swelled, his tip extruding into her waiting palm. It was slick and soft, the texture barely noticeable until he became fully engorged and popped out.

His heavy breathing tickled her hair as he kneaded and massaged her ass, playing with her while she played with him.

She felt like a teenager again, making out with her boyfriend and giving him a handjob while they both hoped his parents didn't hear them doing it. Licking her lips, she decided to give him the full teenage rebellion experience.

Unlacing his pants, she opened them just enough for his swollen cock to bob free, and then she shimmied down the bed. He let her go, his hand sliding up her back as she worked her way down him until his penis was level with her face.

"What are you—"

She fisted him by the base and licked him.

His hips bucked up. "Holy seven hells, Sasha."

Laughing, she then enveloped him with her mouth. His hips twitched, his cock driving to the back of her throat. She breathed through it, sucking on him, tasting the musky maleness of his pre-cum as he coated her tongue. The texture of his penis developed, and he swelled to the point where he filled her mouth completely, her jaw aching as she struggled to contain him.

Sucking as she worked his cock in and out of her mouth, she dragged her tongue up the underside of him, licking each and every ridge and bump she found.

He brushed her hair out of her face, holding it to the side as she sucked on his cock, one hand fisted around his enormous base as she took all of him that she could and swallowed him down to the back of her throat. She looked at him, enjoying the shocked expression on his face. The fingers in her hair fisted tight, and his hips thrust.

She gagged on him, fighting through it as she re-adjusted her grip on him and sped up her pace.

"S-Sasha, hng," he moaned.

A stroke of her tongue on his underside, a squeeze of her hand and then a tug, she bobbed on his penis, swirling her tongue around his leaking tip, then playing with that small hooked bit that protruded. He groaned, cursing under his breath, his head thrown back as his fingers tightened in her hair until they pulled, her scalp burning a little with a delicious, naughty sort of pain.

Cursing, he groaned. "Viruk, kitten."

She liked seeing him undone. Liked watching him lose himself in pleasure.

Sasha fucked him with her mouth, drank that thin, alien seed down as he spilled it, her hand massaging and tugging on his base as she jerked him off. He was close, if his panting was any indication of his pending orgasm. She watched him struggling to breathe, his muscles tight and tense as he lay there.

His breathing was tense, half-growl and half-exhale.

Fisting both hands around his base to stroke him faster, Sasha focused on his tip, exploring it with her tongue, licking into the divot of his slanted tip and flicking that tiny, protruding end of it.

She didn't know what its purpose was, but he moaned whenever she played with it, so she did it again. And again. And again.

The hand in her hair tightened. Ardalon's hips surged up, and his grip on her urged her down. She opened her throat and took him all the way back, swallowing. He bucked, his hips moving of their own accord as he came. Seed poured down her throat, filling her mouth. It would have leaked around the edges of her lips if her mouth weren't stuffed absolutely full of him.

Sasha swallowed, her grip on his base tight.

She milked him, her thumb and fingers locked into a tight ring, drinking every last drop of cum until he started to soften and shrink. Letting him go, he plopped out of her mouth with a soft pop.

She smiled, licking her lips, then wiping the rest of their mess off her face. His head was thrown back and his eyes were closed.

"That's a blowjob," she told him, going back to stroking his abdominals and the Adonis belt that led to his impressive package.

"I enjoyed it," he exhaled, his breathing slowing.

Chuckling, she buried her face in his side and smiled. "Most guys do."

He growled, the hand on her hair dropping to her shoulder. Ardalon hauled her back up the bed like she weighed nothing. Surprised, she stared at him, and saw that his ears were flat, hiding in his hair, and his wide bridged nose was wrinkled, his eyes squinted.

"I will not share you, Sasha. I am not one of your human males, content to take many mates or discard the one who is marked as mine. Your bite marks may have faded, but your soul is marked. You're still mine, just as I'm yours," he snarled.

Blinking, she was stunned at his abrupt change in mood.

Her body enjoyed it. It liked the burn in her scalp, and the way he lost control and hauled her around, forcing her where he wanted her.

"You will never again speak of mating other males when we are in bed like this."

He rolled them until he was on top of her, pinning her to the bed. A thigh worked its way between her legs, spreading her open until he'd hooked it into her juncture and settled it there.

Her body thrummed, her pussy throbbing where his knee was jammed up into it. His hand moved to the base of her throat, his fingers spanning the distance and settling on where he'd bitten her the day before.

Ardalon groaned. "See how you respond to me? Want me? Never forget that. You are mine, and I will never share my mate."

Wiggling against his hold, she rubbed herself on his knee, her eyelids fluttering. She'd gotten aroused from blowing him, but this bout of possessiveness from him was tipping her over the edge to full blown horny. Her body pulsed, dew sliding through her folds as she rubbed herself on his knee, seeking stimulation. Wanting more.

His nostrils flared as he smelled her, scented how excited and wet she got when he acted like this. She liked seeing him unhinged. Reduced to a primal state of being and driven mad with lust for her.

"Ardalon," she said in a breathy pant. "Hurry up and fuck me."

He growled again, his grip on her throat firming.

His eyes narrowed. "Say it first."

She stared at him, confused in the blaze of lust that was driving her mad. "I want you to fuck me... now? Please?"

He shook his head, his knee pressing harder on her cunt. She groaned, needing friction but finding none of it. Pinned to the bed as she was, there was little she could do about it.

"Say that you're mine," he ordered.

"I'm yours," she answered, pleased but also disappointed when he let her go.

He was undoing the buttons on her borrowed shirt and shoving the fabric aside, his hand shifting to grab her breast and squeeze. The knee in her juncture was grinding, rubbing her through her pants. Her nipples hardened, aching to be touched. Ardalon obliged. He pinched her nipple between two fingers and tugged, playing with them the way he'd seen her play with them earlier.

"I'm... hng... God, yes... I won't take any other lovers, but I swear... you need to fuck me right now, or..." she said between panting breaths.

Each pinch and flick of her nipple sent a pulse down to her pussy. She was swelling, aching and needy, and terribly empty.

Ardalon bent his head down to her breast, taking the small rosy nub into his mouth, alternating between biting and licking it. He reached down, shoving his hands into her pants until he found her folds, which were already wet for him. Stroking through them to find her clit, he growled around his mouthful of breast when she jerked in response.

And then he was gone and off the bed, standing in front of her, his pants still unlaced and his half-hard cock bobbing free.

He hooked her baggy pants by the waistband and yanked them down her legs.

She clenched around air, eager and ready. "Oh, fuck yes."

She wasn't prepared for him to grab her by the ankles and tug her down the bed, bending her in half and pressing her knees to her chest. He opened her wide, his eyes stuck on her sex. Flushed pink with arousal and glistening, she needed him.

"This cunt is mine now," he demanded.

She held her breath as he bent down, kneeling on the floor in front of the bed, and set his mouth to her.

"Oh, fuck," she breathed out when his tongue lathed her from bottom to top in a single swipe. His tongue was broader than a human's, touching all of her at once. It was also very, very rough.

She yelped, shifting away from him.

"What's wrong?" he asked. "Do you not like this?"

Sasha looked down between her legs at him. "I do, but... your tongue feels like sandpaper and I'm very sensitive down there."

Ardalon frowned, his attention rapt on her exposed pussy as he looked at her and thought. Sasha grabbed her legs and held them open wider so she could see him better. "You liked it when I touched you before," he said as his hand went to her sex, found her clit, and circled it as if proving a point. He rubbed her until her breathing hitched, his finger smearing her honey through her folds as he played with her, teasing her.

"I... hmm... do... that's... very good."

"I want to try something," he said, bending his head back down between her thighs.

He rubbed her clit, finding the rhythm and movement that she enjoyed until her core was clenching, and then something wet and warm nudged at her hole. His tongue thrust inside of her, curling in on itself so it penetrated instead of licking.

Bucking against him, trying to work that tongue deeper, she threw her head back and moaned.

His tongue speared her, unfurling all of the way inside of her, filling her up as his thumb rubbed circles around her clit, working her toward an orgasm.

"Oh, that's good... very good... oh, God, *that*... do that again," she told him, adjusting her grip on her legs. They'd started to close on their own during her distraction.

Ardalon did it again, his tongue pushing deeper.

Panting, forgetting to keep her legs up, she let them go. Her thighs settled on his shoulder, trapping him there as he ate her out, his tongue fucking her while he strummed her clit with expert precision.

Fast and intense, her pleasure swelled, her body already tensing.

She reached a hand down to his hair to drag him in deeper and keep him there. Threading her fingers through his locks, she found one of his ears and played with it, enjoying the texture of the coarser fur that covered it.

He purred, his tongue vibrating inside of her as he fucked her with it.

"F-Fuck," she moaned, her breath coming faster and faster as that familiar wave swelled and built. She squeezed her legs around his head and writhed, pulling him in deeper and keeping him there. "Oh, God."

Playing with his ear, she rubbed its point and stroked the buttery soft inside of it. Seeking more of that rumbling as he purred, she tried to rub herself against his face. The vibrations travelled all the way up inside of her through his tongue.

She spasmed, her core clenching. The wave built higher, and higher.

He rubbed her clit faster, rolling her small nub in circles, purring the entire time. The wave crested, and then she came with a cry, spasming around his tongue as waves of release rippled through her, her body tensing before falling limp.

Withdrawing, he nipped her inner thigh, his canines pressing on the sensitive skin there. She nearly slid off the bed, her reactions slow as she basked in the afterglow of her orgasm.

Ardalon caught her, picked her boneless form up, and tossed her into the middle of the bed, then climbed in beside her, settling the blankets around them. She curled into him again, enjoying the way that he curved himself around her. He was warm, his body heat working better than any heated blanket she'd ever owned. His family's house was chilly, as was common with subterranean and partially buried homes.

Alpha Centauri had been like that too.

"Mmm," she moaned, slinging her arm around his neck and threading her fingers into his locked hair. She found one of the beads he'd woven into it and played with the charm, twirling it around the lock it decorated.

"Nobody else wears their hair like this," she said, the thought popping into her head. "I like it."

"Do you?" He seemed surprised. "It was for my assignment. To make me look the part of an outcast, and blend in better among the Diggi crew. Their race is fond of frills and beads and shiny things."

She remembered the frilly shirts that the birds had worn, as well as Ardalon's outfit. She sort of missed the pirate look he'd sported. Now that he had access to his normal wardrobe, he'd started wearing other things. The pants were similar—they still laced instead of snapping or zipping—but his shirts were slick and trim, fitted in a way that showed off his lean and muscled form, covering him down to the elbow without any embellishment.

She wrapped a lock around her finger, rolling it and feeling the texture of it. "Humans wear their hair like this sometimes. It's familiar to me, I guess."

"Do you miss your home?"

Absently playing with his hair, she thought about it. About her shitty little apartment underneath Alpha Centauri. Her crappy job. The appeal of a military career had worn off quickly. She'd never gotten on with the jarheads or the rank chasers. It was a job that paid well, and some of the benefits were nice once people stopped shooting at you.

Getting sucked into a wormhole because they'd sent her out alone to the far reaches of space with faulty tech and bad intel wasn't one of the things she'd miss about her career.

Or, worse... they'd sent her to that quadrant on purpose to see what happened to her if she got sucked in.

She wasn't sure which option was better. Criminal negligence, or playing God at the risk of innocent lives.

Can you even track a locator chip through a wormhole?

She didn't think they could. Likely, they assumed she was dead. It was probably for the best. Humanity had a nasty habit of invading places they didn't belong and either stripping the planet or moon of its natural resources before moving on, or conquering wherever they'd landed if they liked it.

"I'll miss my brother... I'm never gonna get to see him and his wife have kids and be the crazy, cool aunt who spoils them rotten, then hands them back hyped up on sugar with a new toy that makes a complete racket. I'll definitely miss chocolate... and movies, and reading." She sighed. "I'm going to have to learn how to read all over again."

Worse, she was going to have to learn *everything* again. Social cues, societal norms, body language, money, food... almost all of it was different. Similar, yet not the same.

He squeezed her to him. "You're an aunt now with plenty of cubs to spoil. We have movies, and I'll teach you how to read our language. What's chocolate?"

She buried her smile into his chest and tugged on the lock she'd been playing with, teasing him. "It's a sweet dessert that melts in your mouth. I... don't know how to describe the flavor to someone who hasn't tasted it."

He chuffed with laughter. "Females of all species love sweets, it seems. I will buy you sweets, as well as a ring. Is there anything else you require to be happy here... with me?"

"No," she told him, letting the lock go and setting her hand on his chest, her bent leg threaded between his as they laid there entwined together.

Truth be told, she didn't even need the sweets or the ring. As long as she was with Ardalon, she knew she'd be happy.

She was falling in love with him.

He leaned down and captured her mouth with his, pulling her into a kiss.

CHAPTER SIXTEEN

ARDALON

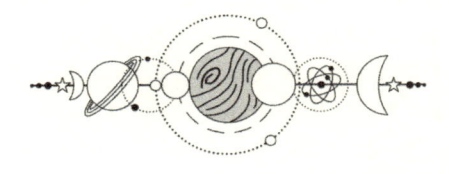

After their nap, they were called to join the rest of the family for dinner. Taking enough time to grab a quick shower, Sasha stood under the dryer with him until the blast started.

She yelped, then darted out from under its heat, her skin pink just like when she flushed with embarrassment or pleasure. He flexed his arms over his head, letting the heated air blast the water out of his hair and fur.

"I'm just going to dry off with a towel," she told him as she pulled a drying cloth out of the open linen closet and rubbed herself down with it, starting with her dripping hair.

He got a full view of her plump ass when she bent over to wipe the droplets of water off her legs.

There was a sliver of space between her full thighs as she bent over, and the seam of her sex peeked through that tiny gap as she rubbed the cloth over her feet. Clenching his teeth and turning around to let the heated air blades dry his back, he closed his eyes and concentrated on getting his body under control.

Over his formative years, he'd heard males talking about the insatiability of a newly formed bond. When she'd bitten him in the medical bay, he'd thought that the urges and needs had bypassed him. Maybe because she was a different species, or perhaps it was because her blunt teeth hadn't penetrated deep enough. The need to protect her, to keep her near, had been there, but not the lust-drunk need to possess her like he'd been warned to expect.

But now that they'd lain together...

He understood it now. It felt like something within him had shifted and come alive after lying dormant within his genetic coding.

His cock twitched in its sheath, the tip protruding, and he reached down, pushing it back in as he focused on drying off. Even though his back was turned to her, he still felt her through the bond.

Rubbing the mark on his neck, he waited until she was done to turn back around. He pressed a kiss to her cheek and slipped around her, heading into the bedroom and going right to the box that he'd dug out of the basement earlier.

"I borrowed these from storage," he told her as he opened it and handed her a stack of clothes. "From when my sisters were younger and shorter."

Looking through the items he'd spread out on his bed, she picked out a set of green and blue pants with a matching tunic decorated with a gold trim. The clothes were smaller than the ones she'd bought from the street vendor, which meant they'd fit her better. She wouldn't have to roll the waistband or sleeves up to keep them out of her way.

The quality of the material was better too, and he smiled when he saw her stroking the soft fabric with the pads of her fingers.

The feeling of meeting one of his mate's needs, providing for her, bloomed through him. Satisfaction.

"These are perfect, thank you... Hey, do you know where my

flight suit is?" she asked him as she dropped her drying cloth and dressed.

Her breasts jiggled when she worked the pants up her rounded backside until the waistband sat at her navel. She was curvier than the intended wearer of her borrowed clothes, the fabric stretching taut as she pulled the garment on.

He looked away before his cock could attempt to rise again. "Most likely they are in evidence. I will put in a work notice requesting their return once they're done processing and documenting it."

If they haven't already handed it over to the scientists to pick it apart so they can study its alien tech.

Grimacing, he went to his closet and pulled out a simple outfit, dressing and shoving his unruly cock down into place, lacing it in before it could get any further ideas. If he gave into temptation, they were never going to leave the bed.

Not a bad idea.

Shaking his head to clear it, he tugged a shirt on and tucked the hem of it into his waistband.

"I hope you're hungry. Enaiya has been cooking all day," he told her.

"Absolutely starving," she answered, tugging the embroidered tunic into place over her bust.

He looked her up and down, enjoying the sight of her in his people's clothing. She looked good in it. In the future, she'd need tailored clothing, but these would do for now until he could get to the city to take her shopping.

When everything has settled. We don't even know what the emperor plans to...

Shoving the intrusive thought from his head, he palmed his door open and led them down the hallway toward the common rooms and the dining room. They were the last ones there, everyone else already seated and eating.

Pointedly staring at his younger brother until Vani scooted down the bench to make room for them, Ardalon pointed to where Sasha should sit, then sat down next to her.

Cutlery clacked, and the cubs were babbling at their end of the table, the youngest one making quite the mess as Ferand fed her while she spat out nearly as much food as she consumed. Ardalon grabbed dishes from the center of the table, filling both of their plates as he leaned down and explained to her what each one was.

Sasha took a tentative bite of the roasted chivoo, humming with pleasure around her fork as she chewed it and swallowed, then stabbed it, pulling off another serving. He twitched at the sound, discretely adjusting his pants under the table as he grabbed the pitcher of water and poured them their drinks.

"It's so good," she told him, moving her fork from dish to dish as she tasted a little bit of everything.

"We're very lucky. Enaiya used to be the head chef of a restaurant in the capital until she met her mate, Ferand, and decided to take time off from work while they raise their young cubs," he explained, nodding to Matiyah and the cub that his brother-in-law was attempting to feed. "You already met Matiyah earlier. She is the little one you saved. Their youngest, the infant there, is Loni."

Sasha licked her fork clean and set it down, taking a gulp of her water. "You have a big family."

Ardalon scanned down the table, noticing his younger brothers' curious glances at Sasha, his sister's preoccupation with cleaning Matiyah's sticky muzzle, and his matta and patta who sat at the head and foot of the long table.

"For now," he agreed. "Until my brothers are mated and they head off to their mates' households."

She looked around the table, the skin between her brows creased. "That's strange to me."

Stabbing his fork into the food on his plate, he took a little bit of everything so he could taste it all in one bite, ignoring Enaiya's withering stare as he desecrated her cooking with his unusual habit. "How do your people live?"

Sasha moved the food about on her plate with her fork. "Adults live on their own until they meet their mate, and then they live together. Some have kids. Others don't, either because they don't want them or they physically can't, or they can't get a family license for whatever reason."

He frowned. "That sounds lonely. How do you raise cubs without the help of your entire family? Cubs are a lot of work. Rewarding, but exhausting too."

She jerked her shoulders up and down in a quick gesture, trying a bite of the roasted pompots that she'd helped cut up earlier. "I don't know. It's hard, I guess. Unless you're rich and you have live-in help, your kids end up in daycare while you both work."

"Dae kaeer?" he said, sounding out the foreign word. "This word isn't translating."

"You pay someone to watch your kids while you work. They watch a lot of them at once, until the kids are old enough that they can go to school," she added.

He blinked, looking at his nieces and nephew. "That sounds... horrible." The thought of his nieces and nephews going off to be raised by strangers didn't sit right with him at all.

Her lips twitched, and then she smiled with her eyes and grabbed a roll off the basket in front of them. "I suppose it is. Maybe your way is better."

His youngest brother Mahmed, who'd been stealing glances at his mate and eavesdropping the entire meal, leaned down. "Are you really a science experiment that escaped some secret government lab?"

Sasha's spoon dropped to her plate mid-scoop, a bit of mashed rubi sliding off it. "What?"

Ardalon reached around her, his thumb and middle finger pressed together in a ring as he aimed it toward his insufferable little brother's ear to flick it, but Mahmed dropped his ear before Ardalon could make contact.

Vani turned on the bench, butting his way into the conversation until they were flanked on both sides. "I read that there was some huge cover-up of an alien crash landing. A bunch of people in El'bazahara saw a strange spaceship fall out of the sky. There's recordings of it. They keep getting taken down as soon as they're put up. They can't make mirrors of the videos fast enough."

"So?" Mahmed prompted, leaning into her space on the bench.

Sasha looked at him with wide eyes. Ardalon growled low in his throat, a soft warning for his brother to back off. Mahmed frowned at him, confused, before sitting up straight.

"Ardalon!" his matta scolded them from her end of the table.

All three of them, him and his brothers, turned their heads at once to look at her. She was shaking her head and pinching the bridge of her nose. "Back for one day and already fighting with your littermates," she sighed.

He bowed his head out of respect but felt his spine stiffen all the same. Base urges to flex his hands and let his claws extend swirled inside of him. He fought it back, keeping his hands flat on the table so that wouldn't happen.

"My apologies, matta. The mating instincts are... difficult to adjust to."

The table went dead silent.

Everyone stopped eating and talking, even the children, as all eyes turned on the both of them. He felt Sasha stiffen against his side as the entirety of his family narrowed their focus on them.

Their mating bond, weak as it was, sent a faint pulse of her unease through to him. It was a pale shadow to the terror, pain, and anger he'd felt her endure during her brief capture with the Senator, but it set him on edge nonetheless.

"You are mated," his matta repeated, the words slow and precise as she spoke carefully. "To this... this... I don't even know what species this female is."

Realizing that he'd virucked up and they now had to have this conversation like this, he took a deep breath and focused on the exhale. "Yes."

His matta leaned forward, her palms resting on the table as she stared them both down with her sharp green eyes. He'd always hated it when she pinned him with her gaze like that. It made him feel like a cub again.

"You will explain," she ordered, her eyes flicking between him and Sasha.

"You know that I'm duty bound to keep certain information confidential," Ardalon reminded her.

His matta narrowed her eyes, her gaze swinging to his side, to Sasha. "You, then. Speak for yourself and explain, since my son will not. His loyalty to his profession and our Emperor is impeccable, but this is my den and I won't be kept ignorant of the goings on within it, no matter what oaths my son has sworn."

Sasha fidgeted, the bench squeaking as she shifted her weight. "Uh... all right. That's totally fair. I'm not sure how much astrophysics I can explain with the translators, but I'll try. I'm a human from a planet we colonized called Alpha Centauri."

She paused, taking a deep breath before continuing. "I work in the engineering department for a military branch called Starfleet. I was out in a deep pocket of our solar system to repair a broken satellite when I got sucked into an Einstein-Rosen bridge. I'm not sure if it was a genuine surprise and the scanners just didn't pick it up, or if they sent me out there to test the wormhole and see if I died or not. Went through it, wrecked my ship I'm guessing... I don't know about that part, I was unconscious, and then I woke up in a cage."

Sasha made an up and down movement with her shoulders.

"You think your people might have sent you through it on purpose?" Ardalon asked, stunned. He couldn't imagine such a thing. His job was dangerous at times, but his superiors would never purposely send him out into danger unprepared like living collateral.

Sasha grunted and leveled him with a neutral look. "I certainly wouldn't put it past them."

Trying to pick the strange idiom apart, he grew distracted as Sasha finished relaying what had happened. Her time in the cages with the Diggis, her escape, the crash on El'bazahara, and then his rescue of her from the 'dine'sors,' as she called them.

She inhaled, continuing. "I thought they were moving onto science experiments and he was holding me down... so I bit him," she added. "At the time, I didn't know anything about your species or your mating bonds."

Underneath the table, her hand found his knee and rested on it, the gesture offering a sense of comfort even though he could still feel a hint of her anxiety through the bond. She seemed calm on the outside, but it was clearly a mask.

If he focused on it, he could feel a little of how she felt. The feelings he got from her were less wispy now that they had lain together and he'd filled her with seed, soaking up the essence of her fluid in return.

His matta stood, her chair scraping against the stone-tiled floor.

Hands flat on the table, she leaned on it, her voice dropping into a low growl. "You have bonded my son to you without my family's blessing, without a proper courtship, and with no thought for your future. Where will you live? How will you provide for one another if you have no kin? No home?"

The pang of immense sadness that he felt through the bond made his heart sink into his stomach. Pulling his hand off the table he grabbed hers, tugging it into his lap and stroking the back of it with his thumb.

She gripped him back, her hand tense.

"Enough," his patta said, standing and startling everyone, including his matta.

Ardalon swiveled in his seat to stare. His patta wasn't a male who openly disagreed with his mate. For him to speak up, it meant that he felt strongly about the subject matter.

"Enough," the older male continued. "This is not how we would have wanted it to go, but it has happened, and there is no undoing it now. They will live here while we figure this mating out together. As a family. Besides, our son is hardly the first Kursh to mate with a different species. And with his status..." he sighed. "He was never going to lead a conventional life, as we both knew."

His patta turned to face him and nodded, a sharp jerk of his chin. "I wish you happiness, my son," he added, and then he sat.

Ardalon felt acceptance in a way that hadn't happened since he'd proved his peers wrong and gotten admitted into the academy. The day he'd brought home his letter, his matta and patta had been so proud of him.

The room was silent and still until his matta sank into her chair, her expression softened from anger to grief.

The others took their cue, ignoring the uncomfortable tension and returning to their meals. The clink of cutlery filled the silent room until low murmurs of conversation started up again.

Sasha exhaled, the tension leaving her muscles as she slowly relaxed in her seat next to him.

They finished their evening meal in silence until dinner was done and they could once again escape back into his rooms. His littermates had been pestering him nonstop about what had happened, who this female was, *what* this female was, but Ardalon didn't feel ready to share her with them just yet.

If his instincts had their way, they'd den up in his rooms and not leave it again for an entire month while he seeded her daily and sank his fangs into her neck until she finally scarred one day.

Grabbing two rolls of bread out of the basket that was handed to them, he set one on each of their plates. She was going to need her energy for what he had in store for her.

CHAPTER SEVENTEEN

SASHA

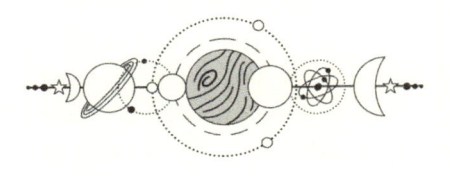

She was full of delicious food, which made her tired. Her body demanded she find somewhere to nap. They excused themselves from the dining room, dodging his younger brother's endless litany of questions, and made their way back to Ardalon's room.

"Well, that was intense," she said once they were alone again.

He palmed his door open and she followed him in, throwing herself onto her side on the bed as she toed her borrowed slippers off and tugged one of the pillows into place in the crook of her neck. She watched him as he undressed, careful and methodical as he got ready to put his clothes away into their respective storage.

"My matta means well..." he answered, his voice soft. "She just needs time to adjust. It's a big change, and it's not one that she thought I would ever go through."

The muscles in his back bunched when he tugged his skin-tight shirt over his head. He turned as he worked his long locks through the neck hole, so she watched the movement of his abdominals instead.

Her core clenched just looking at him.

With one need satisfied, another rose to take its place. After nearly half a year of forced celibacy, her body was demanding. When he pulled the laces of his pants apart and started sliding them down, she throbbed. He turned again, giving her a full view of his glorious ass. It was round and tight, with just a hint of a bump where his tail might have been before they'd removed it when he was born.

"She will adjust," he repeated, the pants going lower, exposing the breadth of his thighs and the curve of his calves. "They will come to accept you."

"Uh-huh," Sasha answered, not paying attention anymore.

He stepped out of his pants and folded them, adding them to his pile, then gathered up his clothes and put them away.

Shamelessly, she watched him every step of the way as he walked toward the bed. He'd been beautiful from behind, but he was stunning from the front.

He frowned. "You're clothed."

She blinked and looked up, tearing her eyes away from his sculpted Adonis belt. "Hmm?"

Ardalon slinked forward, reached out and encircled her ankle, and tugged until he'd rolled her onto her back. Knees on the bed, he crawled on top until he loomed over her. She met his gaze as he leaned down, their noses almost touching.

Lips parted, ready for a kiss, she blinked when he set a hand to her throat and tipped her jaw to one side, his fingers firm.

Hot breath washed over her ear as he leaned down until his muzzle brushed against her. His hips were fitted into hers as his weight settled just enough to remind her that he had the upper hand. That she was pinned underneath him.

"You will never wear clothes in this bed again unless you'd like them shredded off you," he growled.

A shiver ran down her spine, the hairs on her arms rising

with goosebumps. Her core clenched, a reminder that she was empty and her body wanted to be filled. He licked the side of her neck, his tongue dragging up the pulse point there just under the surface with his sandpaper tongue.

The feeling of it, rough and abrasive and surprising in its suddenness, made her gasp and twitch.

His hips pressed her down, pinning her harder into the bed with his bodyweight. He was thickening, and she could feel him through the tight, thin material of her borrowed clothing.

Her body reacted on instinct as her nipples tightened and moisture grew.

Ardalon sniffed, the sound of it loud with his face hovering right over her ear. "My mate likes this idea," he chuckled, then licked her ear again and rocked his swelling cock against her center.

It made her wish that she was already naked so she could hook her leg over his hip and let him find his way inside of her as they rocked. "It definitely... has... its appeal," she panted between licks of his tongue as he sucked on her earlobe, his fang grazing her every once in a while.

She was already wet, arousal creeping between her folds as Ardalon thrust against her through her clothing while he nibbled on her ear and neck, his fingers on her throat and chin keeping her head turned, and his body keeping the rest of her from moving at all.

The only freedom that she had was with her hands, but she knew that if she touched him when he was like this, all dominant and possessive, that he'd just restrain her in response.

Not a bad idea, actually.

Just as she was contemplating wiggling underneath him to provoke him, he turned her face toward his and crashed his mouth down onto hers. It startled the breath out of her. She gasped, and he took advantage of that. His tongue pressed between her parted lips and invaded her mouth, stroking hers as she rushed to kiss him back.

He devoured her mouth. There was no other word for it. She didn't even notice that he'd dragged a hand down her body until he found one of her nipples through the tunic and pinched.

She arched underneath him, her hips trying to rise off the bed, but he didn't budge. His erection, nestled against the apex of her thighs and rubbed against her as his tongue twined with hers.

Nipples tightening to the point of pain, she moaned into their kiss, her clit throbbing, begging to be touched. She needed him. Wanted him inside of her, and not just with his tongue. Fighting against him, she tried to rise up off the bed so she could strip.

Ardalon denied her.

He pinned her down, his hand leaving her nipple to find her wrist and pin that arm to the bed.

Rising just enough to break the kiss, he rubbed his cock against her over and over again until she thought she would die if he didn't fuck her right then.

"Well?" he asked, his mouth brushing against hers as he spoke.

She tried to capture him in a kiss again, but he evaded her, his hips rubbing harder and the hand on her wrist tightening. "W-What?"

"You will not wear clothing in this bed again, kitten. Say it," he ordered. "I want access to your sweet cunt at any moment whenever we lie together in this bed."

She flushed, heat rising to her cheeks and throat. Her pussy throbbed and more arousal grew between her lips until she felt slickness spreading every time he dragged his hard cock over her slit.

"I... I won't—oh, God—w-won't wear clothes to bed again," she promised.

He pressed a quick kiss at the corner of her mouth. "Good girl."

Her clit throbbed in response, but all he did was grind that cock against her until she was panting, her body begging for release.

"Please," she begged, feeling like she was on the brink with need.

Chuckling, Ardalon kissed her again, then pulled away. She groaned at his withdrawal, her body still drunk with desire. He peeled himself off of her, his hand going right to his cock as he palmed it and squeezed, throwing his head back with a look of agonized bliss on his face as he grunted.

Looking down her body, she saw him. He was dripping a steady drizzle of pre-cum, the fluid trickling over his knuckles as he fisted his penis and stroked himself while he stood there at the side of the bed. She watched him touch himself, his cock swollen larger than she'd ever seen it before. It nearly filled his entire hand.

She watched the textured pink part of him slide in and out of his tawny brown sheath as he stroked himself.

He stopped, his fist tight as he gripped his base and squeezed, then angled his head as he peered down at her. "If you don't undress right now, kitten, then I was serious about disrobing you with my claws, and you have few clothes you can spare until I can take you shopping," he reminded her.

The mental image of Ardalon hooking his claws into her clothes and tugging until they shredded off of her distracted her for a moment before she rushed into action, tugging the tight tunic top over her head and shimmying out of the slim-fitted pants. She tossed both items to the floor.

The next moment, he was on her. Legs yanked open and bent, he crawled between her thighs and lined them up. His cock rubbed up and down her slit, spreading his pre-cum and her honey around until, with a shallow thrust, he spread her folds apart and found her entrance.

She wrapped her legs around his hips and tried to pull him in, to make him hurry. Her pelvis rocked, trying to spear herself onto him, but he only buried to the tip.

Ardalon chuckled, grabbed her legs, and bent her in half, putting her knees up on his shoulder. Hips lifted off the bed as he kneeled, his angle pinned her into place until she couldn't move. She gripped the sheets, twisting the fabric, needing something to hold onto.

The tip of his cocked nudged at her entrance again. A teasing presence. He rubbed them together again, his penis gliding through her labia, spreading their fluids up and down until she felt like a slippery mess.

"You are not in charge right now, kitten," he told her, his cock continuing that slow, languid rocking motion.

She grunted, a little angry that he wasn't already fucking her after all that teasing. "What's taking so long?" she whined.

He turned his head and bit her thigh, his fangs applying enough pressure to pinch without cutting the skin. Sasha gasped, not expecting it. His hips thrust, and then his cock pushed a little bit deeper, but it wasn't enough.

She wanted him to fill her, to stretch her and stuff her full, then fuck her until she couldn't remember her own name.

Sandpaper tongue lapping at the faint mark on her thigh that was already healing, he continued his slow torment of penetrating her without actually fucking her. The head of his cock teased her entrance, sliding in and out in shallow thrusts as he bent over her, folding her in half, the angle changing to something even worse. A tease.

It was the opposite of what she wanted, of what her body craved.

She growled at him, her hands leaving the bed to grasp him

by his sides. Her fingers settled into the shallow depressions between his ribs as Ardalon rocked them together, his cock barely penetrating her.

"Give in, Sasha," he told her, his pelvis brushing against her swollen clit. "You are mine, and I will only viruck you once you've fully surrendered to me. To us."

Nails digging into his velvety skin, she tensed, her thighs squeezing tighter around his neck. She enjoyed the facade of being bossed around, but she'd never actually given anyone that sort of power over her before.

Surrender?

A twinge of fear flashed through her. One last barricade to true intimacy. Something she'd never had with any of her exes. She balked, her thighs pressing closer as if she could close them even though that was impossible with their positioning.

He stroked her body, fingers gliding over the sides of her thighs and hips and the outer edges of her breasts. "Shh," he shushed her, his hands still stroking. "My kitten is safe. Give in to me, let me take care of you. I will be so good to you, kitten. So good," he promised, his cock sliding through her labia, stroking her clit with every swipe.

"My beautiful, ferocious mate," he praised her.

A part of her wanted to pivot and throw him off of her. To straddle him and take what she wanted on her own terms.

She'd never let someone in all the way, never let them become too important to survive without once, inevitably, they decided to leave. Her job was too demanding. She was too emotionally distant. They didn't like that she was messy with her things. She didn't make enough time for them. Forgot important dates.

The impulse to shut him out and stop this thing that felt dangerous and frightening was there, as it always was.

But this was Ardalon, and she trusted him, even if the

thought of that scared her just as much as it thrilled her. He'd come for her to rescue her. Twice.

When was the last time someone had gone out of their way to help her? To try to save her?

A rational person would have walked away when she'd crashed among the dinosaurs instead of risking their neck. Instead, he'd carried her when she'd been crippled with a primordial type of fear.

Eyes scrunched shut tight so she didn't have to face his expression, she forced her body to relax.

Bit by bit, her legs went slack, and then her hands were the next part of her to soften as she let them drift back down to the bed. The way he touched her was nice. Soft and sweet, the pads of his fingers rubbing circles in her skin until she tingled. Each swirl of his thumbs on her thighs softened her, pushing that unease away.

Ardalon won't hurt me.

He purred, his hands massaging her hip as he stayed there, barely seated inside of her as he caressed her sides. Sasha's jaw unclenched and then, as if a damn had burst, she mellowed.

Her body went limp underneath him, the tension melting out of her.

"Shh, so good, kitten. I'll take such good care of you," he said. His angle changed, and then the tip of his cock was back at her core.

His thrusts were shallow, teasing and patient. Leaning forward so that she was truly bent in half, he set his hands on either side of her head and caged her in, trapping her under him.

Hard and pulsing, his penis pressed deeper. He rolled his hips and buried it to the hilt, bottoming out in one smooth, slow push. She sighed when he hit her cervix, stretched her, filling her completely.

"Say it. Tell me you're mine," he demanded.

The withdrawal was just as smooth and slow, his tip pausing at her entrance for an agonizing amount of time as he waited. She opened her eyes and looked at him. His face was close enough to kiss if she strained and lifted her head.

"I'm yours," she answered, shuddering with the rightness of the words.

He was an alien, a stranger she hadn't known two weeks ago, yet none of that mattered. Her body and heart had known what her mind had struggled to accept.

Bright amber eyes with green flecks around the oval pupils stared at her with an intensity she'd never seen in them before. Hips pressing forward, he surged into her again. Her body gave into him first, and then her mind followed. It felt like she was sinking into the bed as a calmness settled her nerves.

Canting forward, faster with every stroke, he kept his word. Pleasure stoked within her with each thrust, the angle of his entry hitting her front wall until her breathing grew ragged.

Everytime she tensed, chasing that glorious sensation to the end, the muscles in her legs and belly tightening, he slowed his pace and brought her back to the starting point. Whenever she made an irritated whimper, he kissed her. He rewarded each moan that he wrung from her tired and sensitive body with a deeper thrust.

Pleasure swelled again, spreading through her body in pulsing rings that started at her center and made her vision swim.

He thrust harder, deeper, then let out a low growl as he unhooked her thighs from his shoulders and sat back on his knees. Her butt slid down his lap as he jostled her, but his hands on her hips stopped her from disconnecting with him.

Ardalon tugged her back into place, and then began to move. He was pushing her back into that wave of pleasure, his cock stroking her from g spot to cervix as he thrust, his hips snapping forward to fuck her harder with his hands on her hips to keep her from sliding off his lap from the force of it.

The textured bumps of his shaft pulled sensation after sensation out of her, coaxing her back to that precipice with every stroke. Another wave of pleasure rippled through her.

She arched, throwing her head back and letting her eyes close.

"Mine," he grunted, the end of his slanted cock and its soft, hooked tip hitting her cervix and battering against it, forcing her body to give in, to surrender to him and adjust.

Clenching around him in response, she came. It moved through her body with a warmth that started from the top of her head before flowing down to her toes as her pussy fluttered around his cock.

Moaning through her body's rhythmic squeezing and pulsing, she focused on the little aftershocks. Some part of her that wasn't buried in pleasure from her release enjoyed the grunting sounds he made as her clenching pussy milked his pumping cock.

His breath hissed with an inhale of air, and then his fingers dug into her hips, the tips of his claws noticeable. She looked at him, drinking in the sight of him as he lost control of his body.

Hips snapping forward now that her orgasm had finished, he fucked her until his pace faltered, his eyes intense as he stared her down.

Ardalon dropped his head forward, his nostrils flaring as he tugged her body down onto his dick with every thrust. He groaned, and then he came, cock buried as deep inside of her as he could get as he pumped her full of cum, slow thrusts working her tired and spent body as he emptied himself, filling her.

Finished and satisfied, he leaned down and pressed his mouth to hers in another kiss. A chaste and gentle meeting of lips instead of the consuming intensity of before.

Sasha reached up and wrapped her arms around his neck, weaving her way underneath his mane of locks as she tugged him down on top of her, needing to feel the grounding weight of his body on her.

"I'm too heavy," he protested, falling to the side instead, grabbing a handful of her ass to keep them connected as they adjusted their position on the bed.

She brushed a beaded lock out of his face and gave him a faint smile without any teeth. "I can take it."

Ardalon did the same, taking a wayward section of her hair and tucking it behind her ear. "Just because you can take it doesn't mean that you should have to. Even the strongest of us must heal from their battle wounds."

Her heart twinged, tears pricking unexpectedly at her eyes. Not wanting him to see what effect his words had on her, she leaned into him, burying her face in his chest as she let out a shaky exhale and beat the tears back with willpower.

She felt raw and exposed in a way that she couldn't fully understand, let alone begin to explain.

Arms wrapped around her hips, and he held her as she curled up into him. His softening cock popped free, unlocking them with a rush of warmth that trickled down her body as their fluids dripped down her inner thigh and buttocks. Her hair shifted as he pressed a kiss to the top of her head and slid his fingers to the crack of her butt where they liked to rest.

Churning thoughts plagued her as she considered what had just passed between them.

Ardalon purred, the vibrations traveling from his body to hers through their points of connection. His hand left her backside to stroke her shoulders, then pet her hair. Little by little, she relaxed again.

"I love you," she whispered, too timid to say it any louder, but needing to say it before the moment passed. To put the words out there into the universe.

Fingers carded through her hair, massaging her scalp as they passed. "My heart is yours," he answered.

A happiness infused her entire being from the top of her head to her toes. It bubbled up through her until she felt like she was so light she could float away. They might have met in the most bizarre of circumstances, and he was an alien, but she couldn't regret the way the universe had brought them together.

Smiling, listening to his rumbling purr and feeling the vibrations through her cheek, she closed her eyes and slept.

CHAPTER EIGHTEEN

SASHA

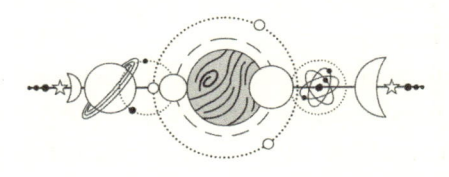

Lifting her pastry high above waist level to avoid having it taken out by a flicking tail, Sasha scooted back on the couch, protecting her snack from the cubs who were busy running amuck in the living room. She glanced toward the doorway that led to the kitchens.

Ever since the knife incident she'd been banned from setting foot inside of it. Since she'd always loathed cooking, she wasn't too torn up about it. Ardalon was still busy fetching their breakfast.

"Not fair! You had it all morning," Tiyana whined, stomping her foot as she scowled at her brother.

Cardenas made a face at his sister, tucking the light ball under his arm when the little girl made a move to grab it and take it from him. "It was my toy first, I only let you borrow it because I got bored."

Sasha took another huge bite of the buttery, nut-filled pastry and licked her lips clean of flakes as she watched the drama unfold.

Tiyana growled, the sound high-pitched and comical, and then she dove. The cubs crashed to the ground, the light ball slipping from their grasp, forgotten. Eyebrows raised in surprise, Sasha watched the two of them wrestle on the floor.

The little girl was smaller and not as strong as her brother, but she seemed ruthless and good at pinching. Small hands worked their way into difficult-to-reach places, grabbing soft areas and squeezing. Cardenas yelped and flipped them on the ground.

"Oww!"

The two cubs rolled around, hitting the light ball in the tussle. The toy lit up as it careened across the room, zipping about in a random pattern as it activated right before it crashed into an ottoman and broke.

Hearing the sound of their coveted toy being destroyed, the cubs stopped their fight, looking up with twin horrified expressions.

"Look at what you did!"

"It's not my fault! You made me fall on it!"

Sasha chuckled and shoved the last of her pastry into her mouth, chewing as she got up off the couch and wandering over to the busted toy. The shell had split in half, and tiny gears and wires spilled out onto the floor as the light ball's glow flickered and dimmed before cutting out completely.

"It's ruined!"

Tiyana began to sniffle while her brother hit the floor with his fist and made a low growl in the back of his throat.

"I can probably fix it," Sasha muttered, looking the pieces over to see if any of the scattered parts looked irreparably damaged.

The little girl stopped crying, both cubs rising up off the floor.

Licking the food residue off her fingers, Sasha scooped up the broken pieces and brought them over to the coffee table. Laying everything out, she peeled the two halves fully apart, making a mental note of what wires were attached where and studying how the gears fit together.

"Y-You can?" Cardenas asked, stepping closer.

Engrossed in studying the alien machinery, she looked up, surprised to see that the cubs were still there and they were staring at her. "Uh... yeah. But I'll need tools."

Cardenas flicked his tail, then turned to run off. "I'll get them!"

"Wait! Not fair! I know where the tools are too!" Tiyana shouted, running after him.

Sasha laughed as she watched them take off, then turned her attention back to the broken toy in front of her. If she understood it, then she knew which part was the power source and she had a good idea of how to fit it all back together. Whether the cracked casing would hold was another matter. She didn't know what tools they kept in their house.

Ardalon came out of the kitchens carrying two loaded plates as she was laying the bits and pieces out on the table.

"What happened here?" he asked as he set their food down on the table, careful not to cover up any of the toy's many scattered pieces.

"They had a fight and broke their toy," she answered, pulling the larger half of the shell into her lap and turning it over in her hands.

He sat on the sofa next to her and watched her turn it over in her hands as he grabbed a piece of fruit off his plate and popped it into his mouth. The next piece that he took, he gave to her, holding it near her face until she leaned over and opened her mouth, letting him feed it to her.

Sweetness and the tang of citrus burst in her mouth as she chewed it.

"Do you think it can be fixed?" Ardalon asked, turning his attention back to his plate.

She shrugged, squinting as she played with the pieces that could be coaxed back into place with her pinky. "Maybe. It doesn't look like anything's cracked but it's going to take me a bit of playing with it to figure it out. It's... different."

Ardalon fed her three more pieces of fruit off his plate while she worked. She tucked a wire back into its channel with her nail, then lined a few gears back up. They fell again, dropping into a deep part of the casing. Cursing under her breath, she tipped it upside down and shook them out. Something that had held them in place was gone.

If she looked closely, she could see that a piece of casing had broken off inside.

The noise of something scraping against the floor announced the cubs' return before they emerged from the tunnel that led to their family's suite. "Ugh, so heavy," they complained as the two of them dragged a giant box between them.

"We didn't know what tools you needed," Cardenas said.

"So we brought all of them," Tiyana finished.

Her lips twitched with the urge to smile, but Sasha stifled it, careful not to flash her teeth at the cubs. "Good. I think I've figured out how to fix it," she told them as they hauled the tool box across the room and let it fall at her feet with a heavy *thunk*.

Sitting back to eat, Ardalon worked his way through his plate while Sasha opened up the tool box and started rifling through it. Some of the items inside were familiar-looking enough that she could hazard out what they did. Others were completely foreign to her.

"What's this?" she asked, holding up an object that looked like a fat pen, but was clear all of the way through except for a blue liquid core that sloshed when she tipped it.

Ardalon twitched his ears, chomping on a bit of roasted meat that crunched under his teeth. "I have no idea. Ferand is the handy one."

Tossing it back into its drawer, she rummaged around until she found a tube of what she thought was glue as well as a tiny alien screwdriver. Their screws used a crescent moon shape to fit the driver to the screw, which intrigued her.

The cubs watched her as she fixed it.

Using a dot of glue to repair the piece that held parent gear in place, she waited for it to harden, then worked on connecting the other pieces together. A few times she had to take things back apart as she figured out what order to connect things in, but then she had everything put back into its proper place.

Wedging the loose wires back into place, she stuffed everything inside as she fit the two pieces of casing together, pushing on it from all directions with her fingers until something gave and it clicked.

Shouting came from another end of the house, echoing down one of the hallways. Everyone looked up as Enaiya barreled into the living room, her ears flat to her head and her fingertips ending in claws.

"You cannot be serious!" Enaiya yelled.

"It wasn't my fault!" and "It's fixed now!" the cubs shouted over one another, rising from where they'd been sitting on the floor, watching Sasha fix their toy.

Enaiya turned her attention to Ardalon, her mouth split into a grin that wasn't pleasant at all. Teeth gleamed, her canines fully visible as Enaiya flashed her teeth while she yelled at them.

"You have brought a murderer into this home," Enaiya seethed, one claw pointed at Sasha as the lioness' attention swiveled to hers. "My cubs live here. What were you thinking?" Stepping forward, Enaiya grabbed her cubs by the collars of their shirts, tugging them up off the floor and into her legs. She held them pressed to her body as she leveled Sasha with a glare.

Sasha's heart dropped into her stomach, her body filling with dread.

Ardalon stood, angling his body so that Enaiya's line of sight on her was interrupted. "Sister, please, I would have never brought her here if I thought that she would ever harm—"

Enaiya gasped, taking a half step back, dragging her shocked cubs with her. "It's really true. I hoped that Mahmed and Vani were making some of it up. Elaborating, to make the story better. I saw the footage and photos, but still... Ardalon, how could you?"

His younger brothers edged their way into the room, their eyes moving over everyone as if they didn't know where to look first. Sasha glanced at them, more hurt than she thought she had any right to feel when they wouldn't look her in the eyes.

Gripping the repaired toy so tight that her knuckles turned white, Sasha sat on the couch, silent, while Ardalon fought with his family.

"These are matters I can't speak on," he reminded them, his voice gruff and only one notch lower than a yell.

Enaiya picked her daughter up, popping her on a hip while she wrapped an arm around her son, pulling him behind her. "There are leaked recordings of the carnage that happened in that ship, and reports from hundreds of witnesses who saw a strange, furless female wandering the markets smelling like blood."

Ardalon put his hands up in the air, spreading them wide as if he could block the words if he made himself larger. "It's more complicated than that."

"What is complicated?" Ardalon's matta said from her own hallway. "So much shouting. What happened?"

Sasha turned her head in time to see Ardalon's parents come into the living room before she dropped her head, keeping her eyes focused on the toy in her lap. Her heart was hammering in her chest, her palms sweaty with fear and adrenaline. The urge to jump up and flee was there.

"That *thing* he brought here is a killer! They're saying that Senator Brodyn is dead," Enaiya shouted.

Everyone began to talk over one another, their voices jumbling as Enaiya shouted, the cubs began to whimper, and Ardalon's parents tried to get the household back under control.

I'm never going to belong here.

Closing her eyes, she focused on her breathing, working to steady it while trying to stop the tears that pricked at her eyes. She felt sick, her breakfast sour in her stomach. Dread suffocated her.

Should have stayed with the dinosaurs.

Nervous laughter threatened to erupt from her throat. She must have made a sound because everyone paused to look at her. Ardalon's expression was grim, his ears flat and the muscles in his back taut, visible through his tight shirt.

I should have known this wasn't going to end well.

Ardalon was fighting with his sister while his younger brothers grabbed the cubs and edged them out of the room. Aware that she still had their toy in her hands, her numb mind stuck on returning it to them, she double tapped the on button and watched it power up.

Light danced over her hands, the arguing stopping abruptly as she tapped it off and stood, stepping around Ardalon. He looked at her and tried to block her with a hand on her elbow. "Sasha…"

Sasha shook her head at him and walked up to his sister, holding the toy out to the female.

Enaiya glanced between her and the toy, her chest heaving and her eyes angry.

"I'm not going to feel sorry about or apologize for killing the male who was trying to rape me," Sasha told the lioness.

His sister stared back at her, her expression wavering between confusion and outrage.

She waited for the female's translator to finish, then handed the toy over. Sasha waited to speak again until the female had taken it, clawed fingers curling around it protectively.

The room was quiet with a heavy silence that filled the air. "He told me that if I tried to hit him off me again, he'd cut that hand off because I didn't need limbs for what he wanted to do to me. So... yes, I killed him. It was him or me, and I chose myself."

Sasha turned, looking over her shoulder at Ardalon. "I'll wait outside. I'm going to go get some fresh air."

He tried to reach out for her as she brushed past him, but Sasha dodged his grasping hand. She didn't want to be touched right now. Didn't want to break down in front of a room of strangers who hated or feared her. Her throat felt tight as she dug her nails into her hands, fighting back the tears.

The memory of that male's hands on her body made her skin crawl. She wanted to stand under a boiling hot shower and scald his touch off her skin. Strip away every cell of her body that he'd touched. Contaminated.

They started arguing again, but she was too focused on her own pain to pick apart their voices, and her two translators struggled when multiple people spoke over one another, their voices layering in a confusing jumble.

Slapping her palm to the sensor pad, Sasha was hit with a blast of fresh air as the front door opened and she stepped outside. Sunlight glinted off the dewdrop-coated blades of grass. Moisture dampened the hem of her borrowed pants and feet. She was barefoot, her slippers left in his room and too far away to retrieve now. It would have meant walking past them.

Birds chirped from their hiding posts in the trees, and a faint breeze rustled the grass and leaves on the few trees that decorated the grassland.

Arms crossed, she headed toward one of them for lack of

anything better to do. A tear rolled down her cheek, and then another.

She was sobbing by the time she reached the tree. The bark was rough under her hand as she sank onto the ground and leaned against it, but she didn't care. There was no amount of physical pain that could overshadow how she felt. Dirty. Tarnished. A walking disaster that left nothing but chaos and ash in her wake.

He's only putting up with me because I alien-married him by accident.

She hadn't given him a choice. She hadn't known what she was doing at the time, but she'd still done it. Bitten him... mated him to her. What she'd done had taken away his decision. Was she any better than a predator like the senator?

Crying into her hands, sobbing so hard that her entire body shook, Sasha mourned. Between sobs, she breathed in ragged pants as she tried to calm herself. Rubbing the heels of her hands into her puffy face, she scrubbed the tears out of her eyes.

A twig snapped behind her, her body going completely still on instinct. It took her a moment to remember that she was in the alien version of a backyard, not in the wild.

Looking over her shoulder, she watched as Ardalon's father approached her, his steps measured and slow as he picked his way over the uneven terrain. She felt more tired than she had in ages, her mind just as exhausted as her body had been before the rest and recuperation she'd gotten in the last two days.

"I thought that someone should keep you company," he said, coming closer. "Do you mind if I sit with you?"

She wanted to be alone, but she also didn't want to be rude to the male who'd stood up for his son just the other day. Shaking her head, she watched as he sat down on a tuft of grass near her. His knees creaked as he sat, and he grimaced as if that embarrassed him.

Clearing her throat, she looked away, finding a long blade of grass and twirling it around a finger. "Are they still fighting?"

He sighed. "Ardalon is explaining what happened, finally, and Enaiya is doing more arguing than listening. She's always been that way, even when she was a cub."

Sasha swallowed and snapped the blade of grass off, twisting it around her finger like a ring and tucking the ends in. "She's protecting her children. I can't blame her for that."

If someone had protected her and her brother like that when they were young and needed it...

The silence stretched between them as Sasha got lost on that train of thought, her mind wandering to old hurts. She worried the blade of grass wrapped around her finger until it snapped, falling apart. Glancing down at her lap, she brushed away the broken strands.

"My son cares for you. To be honest, I never thought that I would see him mated and settled."

She sighed, ripping off another blade of grass and starting over. "Because he's a... I don't remember your word for it."

"One of the ashima, yes."

Sasha cringed at the word and its context, ripping up grass and scattering it on the dirt.

"Just two or three generations ago, he would have been killed at birth, not just docked," he told her.

She flinched, her whole body twitching at the idea of it. Anger replaced fear and sadness, calming her. She was used to being angry. Comfortable with it in a way that she'd never been comfortable with being vulnerable.

"There are some remote, more traditional towns where that is still the case. Although if asked about it directly, they would deny it. It's something we don't speak of when it happens. The cub was weak and never took a breath, they'd say. And no one wants to ask questions. It's a deeply painful subject."

The thought of Ardalon being killed as an infant simply because people thought he might pass on a bad gene if he had a child with the wrong person made her blood boil. She'd thought the tail docking had been bad enough, but this was worse.

"I can see that you care for him, just as he cares for you. I'm glad to see him mated and happy, and my mate is too, although she may not always show it. It's all she's ever wanted for him. For all of our cubs."

Sasha grimaced, guilt replacing the anger and cooling her urge to hit things. "He didn't have a choice, though. He feels that way because of the bond."

He cocked his head, the movement catching the sun's rays on his golden mane and pulling her attention back to him. "Doesn't he? Ah... I see. My son hasn't explained things thoroughly, I gather," he added with a chuckle.

Flicking her eyes up to look at him, Sasha met his gaze.

"He never expected to be mated either, and likely didn't pay as much attention to his studies on that matter, as he should have, when he was taught about it as a youth. What do you know about the bond?"

Dropping her eyes, she threaded her hand through the patch of grass at her feet and gathered up the dew drops on her skin. "That it's permanent. A once in a lifetime thing, and it makes him feel things. Like... he said he can feel me through it, and it makes him want to be near me. An empathic connection... but ours is one-sided. Either because I'm human or because of the way I heal."

His father folded his hands in his lap and flicked his ears once. "I see. Well... yes and no. Yes, the mating bond is permanent and he will have a vague sense of how you are feeling through it, but it doesn't control us. It can amplify our feelings, but it can't create an emotion that doesn't already exist. If you hate your mate, the bond won't force you to love them."

She looked up at him again, studying him.

He was graying around the muzzle too just like his mate, but his eyes were the same as Ardalon's, the same mix of gold and green.

She hoped that he was right, that she hadn't accidentally forced her mate into caring about her because of two seconds of impulse control and a bad temper. A little of her guilt and insecurity faded.

A noise in the distance drew their attention away from their conversation. Sasha looked up at the patch of shorn grass that surrounded the tunnel they'd driven through when they arrived. A convi exited the tunnel, turning off into the makeshift parking space and idling.

"Strange. We're not expecting any visitors," he said, turning to stare too as the convi parked.

Her heart sank, dread once again swallowing her whole.

They were out of time.

A part of her had known that this was coming. That their happiness wouldn't last. *Couldn't*. Not after everything that had happened. Sasha wasn't a happily ever after sort of person. Good things didn't happen to her.

Whispering, she asked Ardalon's father the question that she'd been wanting to ask someone, but hadn't had the courage to voice until now. "What happens when one of the mates in a pair dies?"

He was silent for what felt like forever. "It varies, but if the bond is true, the one who is left behind sometimes stops eating and drinking until they also perish shortly after."

The convi door opened and a Kursh male in a dark uniform stepped out and started heading down the long stretch of dirt road that led toward the front door of the den.

Sasha stood, her body acting on instinct before she'd

consciously made a decision. The officer glanced their way and paused mid-step before recovering, heading over to them.

"I should fetch my son," his father said, standing and hurrying toward the den.

As the officer got closer, Sasha could make out more details and she saw that it was Davi, Ardalon's subordinate from the pirate ship. With long strides, Davi closed the distance between them, wading through the tall grass.

"Good morning, Sasha," he greeted her.

She cocked her head and stared at him. "Is it? Is it going to be a good morning for me? You're here with a formal pardon from your emperor, then?"

His ears dropped flat, pinned to his head and hidden within the fluff of his golden mane. "Ah... we should... maybe," he stammered, looking between her and the den.

Sasha looked at Ardalon's home and committed it to memory. Mentally, she was saying goodbye to it and the fantasy that it had represented in her mind. Cooking together and then eating the meals they'd prepared, playing with his nieces and nephew, watching movies together, learning how to read again, talking for hours, making love all night... it had been a nice fantasy while it had lasted, but she'd known that it wasn't going to be a long one.

That this didn't end nicely for her. Not after everything that had happened.

Not after what she'd done.

She remembered how the senator's eyes had turned red, the blood vessels popping as she'd squeezed his neck with her thighs until he suffocated and died. Sasha tried to summon up an ounce of remorse, but couldn't. Her only regret was hurting Ardalon in the process. That hadn't been her intention.

Especially not now, when she knew that she cared for him. Loved him, even. As crazy as that seemed. She hadn't known him two weeks ago, and now she couldn't begin to imagine a life without him in it.

"We can do this right here. I speak for myself," she reminded Davi, tapping her neck and reminding him that she'd been implanted with one of their translators.

Davi straightened. "I have a warrant for your arrest and questioning. I'm supposed to bring you straight to the palace and put you directly into the custody of the palace guards. They didn't even want me to come and fetch you myself, but the chancellor insisted on that one courtesy. It was the only leniency that he could get you."

Nodding, Sasha stood and brushed stray bits of grass off her pants. A few pieces clung to the wet parts on her hem. "All right. Let's go." Coldness settled over her, blanketing everything and leaving her emotionally numb in its wake.

He cleared his throat and reached into a pocket on his belt, pulling out a pair of faintly glowing circles. "I hate to... I'm sorry, but it's policy. You've been flagged as extremely dangerous. If I don't..."

She glanced down at them and nodded again. "Handcuffs? Sure. Do you want my hands in the front, or the back?"

"The, uh, the front is fine," he said as he reached forward and placed one of the cuffs on her extended wrist.

Instead of opening and shutting it with a mechanism, the light passed through her skin, and then once the other wrist was enclosed, he pressed them together and they locked into place, the color brightening. They were lightweight, but secure. She wouldn't have known she was wearing them if she couldn't see them.

She wondered how they worked until reality settled again and she realized that it didn't matter. None of it mattered anymore. She'd been living off borrowed time ever since she'd gotten sucked through that wormhole.

"Let's go," she said, heading toward the convi.

Davi hesitated for a moment, then chased after her.

The front door banged open and Ardalon was running through it, yelling for them to stop while he rushed to catch up to them. Screwing up her resolve, Sasha took her emotions and buried them until only a sterile calmness remained. She wiped all expression off her face, then turned around to face him once she got to the convi door.

"Sasha," he panted, his eyes wild as he looked between her and Davi. "My patta said... Davi? What is the meaning of this... Why is she cuffed?"

Davi winced, his ears flattening again. "She's being arrested. I'm sorry, sir. The orders came right from the top."

Ardalon shouldered his way past Davi and cupped her shoulders with his hands. "Sasha, I will—"

"Don't bother. You've outlived your usefulness," she cut him off, her voice flat.

He reeled back like she'd hit him, his ears flattening. "W-What?"

"It was fun while it lasted and the sex was good, but it looks like you're not as important as you thought you were," she told him. "Bye."

"What are you... Why are you saying this?" Ardalon asked, his eyes searching hers.

She shrugged, doing her best to look like she didn't care about what was happening. He needed to distance himself from her, politically and personally. She knew that he wouldn't do what he needed to do in order to survive this without a push in the right direction.

Ardalon saw the bad in the world and wanted to fix it.

She, on the other hand, was a realist.

She understood that the bad was there to stay no matter what anyone tried to do about it. It was just how the universe worked.

A gear didn't just decide not to turn while the other ones kept spinning.

"Look," she sighed, "it had its moments, okay? You got more attached than you should have. It happens, but you've outlived your usefulness and I'm not really all that interested in you anymore. To be honest, I'm kind of relieved that this charade is over. It was getting tedious."

It killed her to say it. To see the flash or hurt and pain in his eyes as she spoke.

A necessary evil, to spare him a lifetime of hurt. Or worse.

Ardalon shook his head as if he could shake her awful words out of the air. "This isn't... I don't believe you."

She smirked, letting her lips part to show off her teeth as she gave him a slow up and down with her eyes. "You're not even a whole person. Why do you think you'd have been able to keep my interest long-term? Sorry that you believed me, I guess. You really must have been desperate to believe it. That's... kind of pathetic. Goodbye, Ardalon."

Sasha turned away from him, ignoring his pleas and shaking off the hand he laid on her shoulder. Double tapping one of her cuffed hands on the door's handle, she waited for it to open, then hopped inside and settled herself on one of the chairs.

"No!" Ardalon shouted, his attention turned to Davi as the two males argued before their voices pitched too low for her to hear.

She ignored them, staring out the opposite windows and watching the stretch of grass rippling with the wind. The sunlight glinted off it in rolling waves making it look like a large body of water, not land.

There was scuffling, followed by more arguing, and then Davi got into the car and shut the door.

The seals latched, silence descending on them. Davi brought the navigation table to life, then started typing as he routed their course and started the vehicle. The engine hummed, the sound of it nearly drowning out Ardalon's screams and the bangs of his fists as he beat on the convi until it pulled away from its parking spot.

He drove them into the tunnel that led to their thruways, and she was glad when the darkness of it dimmed the car.

Tears rolled down her cheeks, her eyes hot and itchy and her lower lip trembling as she silently wept, struggling to maintain that cold indifference. How did their psychic empathy of the bond work? Was it range-based? Did it depend on eyeline? She should have asked more questions while she'd had the chance.

"That was—" Davi started.

"Shut up, Davi," she interrupted him, the words coming out wobbly because her throat felt choked with tears.

Davi shut up.

Closing her eyes, she dropped her handcuffed hands into her lap and focused on her breathing, working to wrangle her emotions and keep the sadness and pangs of loss underneath the bitterness of her anger and despair.

If she was being walked to her execution, then she was damned well going to go on her own two feet.

Sasha was just glad that the convi was dim inside of the dark tunnel, the bright streaks of passing lights outside as she sat there, crying, regretting the horrible things she'd just said to the male she loved.

He'll be fine... He has to be.

CHAPTER NINETEEN

SASHA

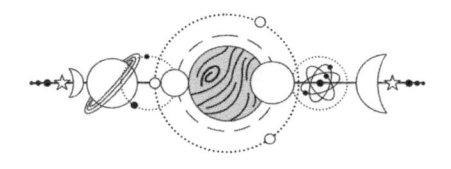

Davi didn't hand her over to the palace guards so much as they hauled her out of the convi the minute they arrived at the palace. Sasha didn't even have time to really look at it. She was tugged off balance, nearly stumbling from the force they used as they hooked her by her elbow and pulled her out of her chair.

They surrounded her. Her hair was lifted, and then something was snapped around her neck. It vibrated for three seconds, and then a zap of electricity shocked her. Crying out from the surprise and pain as the impulse traveled down her body, she reeled back only to be caught by her arms and shoved forward.

"Fracking hell, okay," she grumbled, twisting her head to the side to see if she could get the collar to loosen.

It was tight enough that she couldn't forget its presence without being so restrictive that it was difficult to breathe. When Ardalon had collared her with that fake slave collar, he hadn't made it this tight.

Guards in burgundy uniforms edged in gold brocade marched her through a gate and past the guards who stood there with sharp tipped staves in their hands, and forced her down a cobblestone path. The slim road twisted through some sort of garden, winding through shrubbery and scattered trees and the occasional bed of flowers.

"I can walk," she insisted.

In return, they were silent.

Her foot skidded on a loose rock and her ankle nearly gave out, but the palace guards ignored her sharp inhale. Fingers dug into the soft skin of her arm to keep her from falling as they hurried her along.

She barely had a second to look around and take in her surroundings. The palace was a pale stone building inside of a carefully tended garden, surrounded with a ten foot tall metal fence and an army of armed guards. The sun caught off the blades of their staves, reflecting the light with a wicked gleam.

They turned, leaving the gardens and heading up a stone staircase, as they headed into the palace itself.

People who were walking in the covered outdoor walkway scattered as they passed. When they entered the building itself, the temperature dropped until her skin felt chilled despite the warm and pleasant day outside.

Lights overhead and on the walls kept the palace from looking gloomy, but their artificial flames didn't give off any heat. As they brought her through the hallway and in various doors that led to other areas, turning a different direction each time, she gave up on trying to keep track of the way they'd come.

There was no getting out of this. No grand escape. No rescue party.

Feeling defeated, she shifted her focus to the beauty of the palace instead. The stone they'd made into building blocks was nearly pure white with lines of shimmery webbing that shot through it. Occasionally, the stone columns that supported the arches and roof were carved with an intricate relief. She tried to look at the pattern, but they rushed her by it too fast for her to do more than catch a glimpse.

The ceilings were painted with murals of nature scenes and hiding, snarling animals, and there was gilding nearly everywhere. She'd never seen such wasteful frivolity before. It must have cost an absolute fortune to build.

It's pretty, though. A beautiful waste of precious resources.

The next door they came to was closed. The door itself was enormous, the top of its rounded frame nearly twice as tall as her. Giant gold door handles hung from it at chest height.

The two guards stationed outside of it didn't spare her or her manhandling guards a second glance. They stared straight ahead, their staves raised at attention. Only the way that they clenched their hands around their weapons showed that they'd noticed her arrival.

"So we're... uh, going in *there*, I assume," she whispered, hating the way her voice echoed down the empty corridor. There were a few rugs on the stone floor and tapestries on the stone walls but they did little to absorb the bouncing sounds.

None of the guards acknowledged her or her statement.

Her heart was racing in her chest despite her cool outward demeanor. She didn't want the guards to know that she was rattled. Smoothing her expression out, she stood there and waited.

Time passed as they stood there, waiting, until a smaller door set within the larger one opened. She blinked, wondering where that seam had been in the wood. On some unspoken command, her guards pulled her through the small opening and then the hidden door was shut behind them.

The room beyond the giant door was enormous with wooden benches lining the wall. Aliens, mostly Kursh but a few Diggi and Raxions scattered throughout the crowd, all stared at her from their places. An ornate carved chair at the end of the room towered over her from its raised dais.

Sasha glanced at the male sitting there, then looked away when she saw that his attention was centered on the small group of people surrounding him. The guards forced her to the center of the room, then stopped.

"Supplicate," one ordered, his voice low and gruff.

She frowned, confused. "What?"

A boot to the back of her knees sent her down to the floor, her legs buckling as their grip changed to her shoulders, shoving her down onto the floor until she was kneeling.

Biting back a yelp, Sasha sat on her heels and put her handcuffed hands on her thighs.

"Kneel, got it... Could have just said so," she muttered under her breath.

A hand grabbed her by the back of the head, shoving it forward so that her chin was tucked to her chest. Biting her lip to avoid saying anything else, Sasha kneeled there on the floor while the people in the room talked among themselves.

They left her like that until her knees began to ache.

She recognized the intimidation tactics they were using. Large doors and high, arched ceilings, raised platforms, enormous rooms sparsely decorated with oversized furniture, and the silent armed guards in their matching, stark uniforms and weapons.

Everything was designed to make the person on the other side of that dais feel small and powerless. Disadvantaged. Cowed.

Studying the marbling of the stone they'd made the floor out of and noticing how ridiculously clean it was, she wondered how many people it took to keep it this clean. Sasha waited until she was addressed.

"So, this is the creature," a male said.

The conversation in the room stopped. She felt them staring at her, their eyes boring into her back and sides. Deciding that it was okay to lift her head now that she'd been addressed, Sasha raised her chin.

The male on the throne stared down at her, his chin propped in his palm as if he was bored. His coloring was bright and golden like the others of his species, but his clothes were more ornate and small jewels had been woven into his hair in various places, setting him apart from them. The wall behind him was covered in windows fitted with colored panes of glass that cast their colors over the white stone walls as the light shone through them.

Giving him a slow once-over, she turned her attention to the people who surrounded him.

A female Raxion in one of their plain brown suits and a Diggi in a whirlwind of brightly colored clothing and scarves were among the many Kursh standing there in their embroidered kaftanas at the emperor's elbows.

"Is its mind slow?" the emperor asked, turning to direct the question to the male on his left.

Sasha flicked her eyes back to the male on the throne, giving him her full attention once more. "My brother would say yes to that question," she answered.

The crowd alternated between gasping and tittering, but the emperor's attention sharpened as he turned back around, looking down at her. He blinked, slow and lazy, as he stared, and then he shifted in his seat, sitting back and strumming his fingers on the arm of his chair.

Don't provoke him, idiot, she cursed herself.

This was the male who was likely going to decide whether she lived or died, or rotted in some prison or work camp for the rest of her miserable life.

"So... it's not a dumb beast after all. The real question now is if it's intelligent," the emperor drawled.

The people surrounding him tittered, whispers flying as they laughed and gossiped.

He glanced at the Raxion male on his left and flicked his ears. "It's difficult to imagine how such a small, weak thing got the better of my late cousin."

The Raxion bent at the waist and leaned down. "True, your most graciousness, although it's said that the females of many species are the most vicious."

Sasha gritted her teeth at the insult, locking her jaw before she said something stupid that got her hanged. She met his gaze, doing her best to keep any sign of challenge out of her face, as she kneeled there and waited. The room went silent again, a hush settling over the crowd as everyone looked between her and the emperor, waiting for his signal.

"Indeed." His fingers flicked, a lazy ripple of digits that fluttered over the rounded end of his throne's armrest, and that was it.

The guards grabbed her by her arms and hauled her up on numb feet, and then they were dragging her back the way they'd come. Back down the enormous throne room and through the small cut out of the enormous door. The throne room erupted into chaos behind her, and Sasha wondered what had just happened and what sort of decision was made and communicated with finger wiggling.

They took her through the palace until the hallways narrowed and the furnishings became less ornate until eventually they became plain and utilitarian. Even the stone was darker here. A grate-covered stairwell was opened, and she was nudged inside.

One guard peeled away to lock it behind her as the other

grabbed her by the handcuffs that bound her wrists together and pulled her down the spiral stairs.

If she thought the palace had been chilled, underneath the palace was even colder.

It was a dungeon, she realized. The gray, rough cut stone was poorly lit with sconces that did little to chase away the shadows. They went down until her head was dizzy from turning in circles, and then the staircase ended.

Rows of nearly transparent glowing cells lined the walls of the castle's basement. Only about half of them were occupied. Some of the prisoners looked up at her from their cot as she passed, while others sat with their backs to the sheer, electrified walls that kept them in place.

A few came closer, their fingers resting on the false walls as they leaned forward and sniffed.

The guard pulled her to an empty corner of the room, then shoved her forward. Stumbling before she caught herself, Sasha spun to look at him before he could walk away and leave her there.

He turned as if he planned to do just that.

"Hey!" she shouted, making him look at her. Lifting her tethered hands up, she shook her handcuffs at him. "These can come off now, right?"

His ears flicked, and his lip curled like he wanted to snarl, but he came back over, reaching over the scorched line in the stone that marked where the walls would be once the force field that kept the prisoners locked away was activated. He set his thumb to a flat part on the middle of the cuffs. The mechanism that kept the cuffs lit up and solid flickered, and then went dark. He undid them by pulling them straight through her skin.

The sensation was tingling and unpleasant, like the charge of static electricity that gathered on the skin just before contact with a piece of metal that shocked.

"Thank you," she told him, figuring that rudeness would get her nowhere, but maybe they'd treat her less unpleasantly if she was polite. There was a hum, and then the forcefield that activated her prison's walls turned on. They flickered to life just like the cuffs had. Touching the surface with the tip of one finger, she felt its solidness with a hand. The prison walls might be transparent, but that didn't make them any less real.

The guard left, his steps silent. But that wasn't right. It wasn't just his heavy boots that she couldn't hear. Sasha couldn't hear anything but the sound of her own breathing.

Looking down the row of glowing cells, she saw prisoners in varying states within them. Some were sleeping or sitting, a few were pacing or exercising, one was clawing at his glowing walls as he watched the palace guard leave, and another was staring at her while he masturbated.

Eww, gross.

She ignored that one, giving him a sneer that let him know exactly what she thought of him and his decision to pleasure himself while ogling her, before she turned away.

The cells were quiet, the thing that powered the walls also making them soundproof. A necessity, she imagined, if you lived on top of your own prison. That way you didn't have to hear the bellows of rage or mad barks of laughter or angry screams while you tried to enjoy your in-between snack of tea and cakes.

Looking around, she was thankful that she had her own toilet, and a tiny sink mounted above it, although she regretted the fact that there was zero privacy. The masturbator was going to get an eyeful of her ass whenever she needed to pee. Still, at least she had a real toilet this time and not just a waste hole and dried leaves.

"Back in a cage," she sighed as she dropped down on the cot and hung her head.

The tears welled, obscuring her vision and rolling down her

cheeks. They were never more than a moment away ever since she'd gotten into Davi's convi. Not since she'd left Ardalon.

The thought of him made her heart curl up with grief, her last memories of him and his look of shock and betrayal as she said what she'd said. To protect him, save him from his own optimistic blindness.

The world was ugly and cruel, filled with people looking out for themselves no matter who got hurt in the process. The poachers, the slavers, the males who bought those slaves... people were people, no matter how alien they looked on the outside, and most of them were horrible. Selfish and ambivalent.

Her lip wobbled, and, since she was alone for the first time since she'd forced herself to walk away from him, she let the feelings flood her. She was grateful that her cell was soundproof so that nobody would hear her weep.

Falling onto the cot and rolling so that her face was pressed into the musty blankets and she couldn't see her fellow prisoners, she fisted her hands in the thin, scratchy sheets and cried until her entire body heaved with the force of her sobs.

He was going to hate her.

He'd think that she'd never loved him, cared for him, and that she never could have because she'd called him defective. A male who was less than others. Not that it was true, not to her.

Ardalon was the only one who'd shown her an ounce of kindness and compassion since she'd gotten sucked into that wormhole and spat out on the other side of the universe. The knowledge that she'd protected him was the only sliver of hope that kept her from sinking into complete and utter despair.

I hope he loathes me. At least then he'll be alive.

Hate could keep a person alive just for the spite of it for decades. Her mind knew that this was for the best, even if her heart was shattered into a million pieces. Either she was going to rot in this prison until her mind snapped and she went mad, or they were going to execute her. At this moment, she wasn't sure which option was worse.

A small part of her wished she'd just died in the crash. The little taste of happiness and normalcy that she'd had with Ardalon had given her too much hope and she should have known better. That wasn't how the world worked.

This—a prison filled with mad murderers and unhinged criminals rotting away underneath a wastefully elaborate palace stocked with imported sweets and gilded filigree—was how the world worked. Even on an alien planet, it seemed.

Those who had the power took more of it, crushing everyone underneath them in their continued rise.

Not the senator, though. Not anymore. Her thoughts flashed to the senator and the smug, confident way he'd told her exactly what he did to females like her. How many had he done it to? Dozens? Hundreds? He would never do it again.

Grinning, with tears running down the curve of her cheek until a droplet rolled down her lip and spread a salty tang inside her mouth, she laughed between sobs. At least she'd taken one of the bastards with her. That rapist would never hurt another female again.

She just wished that she hadn't lost everything in the return.

CHAPTER TWENTY

ARDALON

Ardalon sat on his bed with his head in his hands as he replayed what had just happened over and over again in his mind.

The curl of her top lip and the way she'd bared her teeth at him and the skin above her nose had wrinkled, the hard edge to her voice and how she'd looked at him as if he disgusted her. Like everything that had happened between them had been false, some act to manipulate him.

He couldn't make sense of it. He knew it was a lie. It *had* to be. But he'd felt her through their bond, felt her anger and irritation, and it bothered him how he hadn't felt any hint of fear or sadness.

She'd seemed... repulsed.

"You got more attached than you should have."

Her caustic words replayed in a tormenting loop of pain until it was all that was left.

The distance between them had dulled their already faint connection through the bond mark on his shoulder. Reaching out to it mentally, he tried to chase the sensation, but felt an aching absence instead. It was still there, but it was stretched gossamer thin. Too shallow and one-sided with far too much distance between them.

"I'm kind of relieved that this charade is over. It was getting tedious."

His ears dropped, and the urge to bury his face into the pillow and scream until he was hoarse rose. She was gone. He'd barely had her, and already she was gone. He'd been a fool. A stupid fool who'd seen what he'd wanted to see. Gotten attached to the first female who'd let him even so much as look at her.

"Why do you think you'd have been able to keep my interest long-term?"

Why would any female want him? She was right. He was defective, and he'd been deluding himself by thinking that she could look past their differences and his status.

Ardalon collapsed onto his bed, curling his hand into a fist and thumping it, angry with himself for being so gullible. She'd just wanted her freedom, and he respected that. He wished that he had freedom too. Instead, he was trapped within the confines of his genetics.

He'd always prided himself on being a good judge of character, listening to his gut instincts. It baffled him to think he'd been so wrong. She *was* an alien... but still, he wasn't used to misjudging people.

His sheets smelled like her.

Nose twitching, he reared up off the bed and ripped them off the mattress, throwing them onto the floor behind them as he stripped it bare. A cloud of smells were thrown into the air, assaulting him. The smell of her skin that the musk neutralizers in the cleanser couldn't mask combined with the scent of her arousal.

He needed to air the room out, couldn't think when it smelled like... like her lying under him, her arms wrapped around his neck and her cunt fluttering around his cock as she moaned his name into his ear and shivered with her release.

How had she... She hadn't faked that. He'd seen the look in her eye when he tamed her. How she'd relaxed and gone soft and pliant underneath him. Trusting. He'd felt the moment she stopped fighting and chose to let go. Let her hard edges soften so their bodies could connect on a level that was deeper than their minds, something more instinctual than consciousness alone.

Ardalon replayed their interactions in his head, looking for inconsistencies.

Hints of a duplicitous nature, or manipulative tendencies. He remembered how excited she'd been to inherit passed down clothing. How she'd taken the hit from the knife to protect a cub that wasn't hers, or kin. The way she'd protected his back when they'd been on El'bazahara.

He recalled that moment on the poacher's ship just before her disastrous escape, when she'd gotten into the cruiser and he'd tried to stop her from making a horrible choice that he thought meant certain death for her, infiltrating Raxion controlled airspace in an escape pod she didn't really know how to control.

He snorted, shaking his head and blinking hard at the thought. He almost laughed at the memory of the look she leveled Asa with as she started the flight sequence, the gesture she'd made with her middle finger and the comical expression she'd twisted her face into.

Stubborn. She really doesn't trust anyone, huh?

His heart twisted at the thought. "Viruking seven hells," he muttered, raking his hands through his hair.

She doesn't truly trust anyone but herself. Not even me. Not even after everything...

He sat, his weight falling onto the bare mattress as he leaned his elbows on his thighs and dropped his head. Anger replaced grief, filling him with purpose. She'd said those things to push him away and drive a wedge between them, he was certain of it now.

It was the only thing that made sense. Sasha was acting under the delusion that she was making the right decision. It was the poacher's stolen pod all over again. She'd thrown a metaphorical cage open and run.

Rising with a growl, he padded over to his wardrobe and tugged the door open, searching for the nicest thing he owned. He was going to need it.

He had a meeting with the emperor to arrange.

And when he got his mate back, he was going to tear her backside up so hard with the flat of his hand until she learned her lesson and stopped making decisions alone—because she wasn't alone anymore.

She was his, the one he loved.

CHAPTER TWENTY-ONE

SASHA

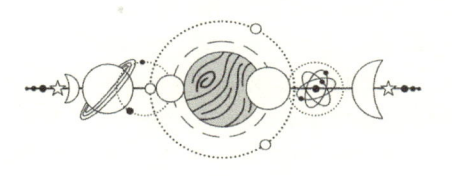

THE FORCEFIELD THAT MADE UP HER PRISON FELL AND SOUND rushed in, waking her from an exhausted sleep. Blinking her bleary eyes open, she popped her head out of the bunched up blanket and looked to see what had woken her.

A guard and a lioness stood at the boundary of her cell, staring down at her. The female took a step forward until the guard's arm shot out, blocking her from coming closer.

"Careful. Only the guilty ones sleep," he growled, leveling her with a glare, his ears flat and a slight curl pulling up his upper lip.

The female nodded, her attention turning back to Sasha now that she'd been warned. "You are summoned. Come with me. Obey, or you will be cuffed and dragged."

Sighing, Sasha pulled back the thin, scratchy blanket and rose, her skin chilled from the cold air of the sunken prison now that she was out of her makeshift cocoon of warmth and privacy. Everything sounded too loud, her body having gotten used to the deafening silence of her own breathing and pulse. She wasn't sure how long they'd left her there, whether it had been an hour or ten, but it wasn't enough.

Her body felt sluggish and slow to respond as she followed the female out of her cell and through the prison.

She must not have been walking fast enough for the guard's tastes because a hand in the small of her back shoved her forward so roughly that she stumbled over an uneven edge in the stone floor and nearly fell.

"Move faster," he snarled at her back.

Sasha regained her balance and bit the tip of her tongue to avoid turning around and giving the guard a piece of her mind. The heavy collar around her neck was a constant reminder that she was just one button-push away from being a puddle of writhing agony on the floor. Inhaling, she sucked cold air in through her nose and held it before letting it back out.

"There is little time to ready you, but you stink and I can't have you at his table looking like this," the lioness grumbled.

They corralled her up the spiral staircase, the guard behind her was a constant reminder for her to behave as the lioness led her through the maze of a palace. They stuck to what she assumed were the servants' areas where the hallways were smaller, the staircases steeper, and the decorations less elaborate.

The room they brought her to was ridiculous in its frippery. The ceilings were tall and painted, and every inch of decor was covered in either a painting or gilding. Small trinkets lined tabletops, not a single speck of dust to mar their shiny surfaces. It made her wonder how many hours and people it took to keep this place so clean.

Inside of the room, there was a tub set into the middle of the tile floor. Gold colored taps extended up from the floor, a spigot angled down so that it would fill the tub with water when activated.

All of this space just for bathing?

The ridiculousness of it was both amazing and horrifying.

Two finger taps on the head of the faucet had it filling with a rapid flow. "Strip," the lioness ordered, turning around to face her once the door shut behind them. "So you can be bathed."

Sasha glanced behind her and saw that the guard had stationed himself at the door, his eyes looking straight ahead at the opposite wall as he ignored them. "Yeah... that's not gonna happen. I can bathe myself."

"If that were true, then you wouldn't smell like whatever male rutted between your legs this morning." The lioness flicked her ears. "You will strip, or you will *be* stripped." With one hand raised, the female flexed her hand, extending her claws.

Phantom feelings of Kursh claws ripping through her thighs and hips made her pelvis ache despite how cleanly her wounds from the senator had healed. Gritting her teeth, Sasha grabbed the hem of her tunic and pulled it up over her head. The guard's lack of interest in seeing her exposed body gave her little comfort.

The lioness watched her undress, eyes sharp, missing nothing.

Sasha toed her way out of her slippers and worked the tight pants off next, holding the clothing and feeling awkward about not knowing what to do with it. The lioness had no qualms about manhandling a naked woman into the bath.

The water was hot, which made her yelp as it stung at her chilled flesh, but then she thawed, the feeling coming back into her numb fingers and toes. It started with sharp stabbing pains until it mellowed and she could relax and enjoy it. She hadn't realized how cold she'd been.

The torrent of hot water that cascaded over her head still shocked her.

Gasping, then sputtering as she inhaled droplets, Sasha gripped the gilded rim of the tub. Hands went into her hair as the lioness covered her with cleanser and worked it into a lather. Screwing her eyes shut so the suds didn't work their way into them, Sasha submitted to the thorough washing. Her hair was rinsed, and then more of their cleanser was worked over every inch of her body with a rag that scratched her delicate skin.

The lioness was exceedingly thorough.

Sasha's face heated, embarrassment coursing through her as the female soaped up a rag and plunged it under the water's surface down between her legs.

"I can do that part myself," Sasha protested, pulling away from the servant and causing the water in the over-full tub to slosh over its rim.

Her collar buzzed, the faint pulse of an electric warning against her throat causing her to go ramrod still.

What would happen if he shocked her while she was submerged in water? She didn't want to find out.

The lioness gasped, looking down at the front of her dress where water had splashed her and soaked through the fabric. "Do you honestly believe that I wish to touch a foul creature like you? I will do my job, as I have been instructed by my betters. If I sent you to him smelling like that, like some other male and sweat and stink, I would be punished. Hold still and let me do my job, or I'll have the guard over there hold you down."

Sasha glared at the servant, her hands so tight on the rim of the tub that her knuckles were white. With fresh cleanser on her rag, the lioness finished cleaning her, paying no more attention to her genitals than the female had to armpits or toes.

Once Sasha was cleansed enough for the female's satisfaction, the tub was drained and she was rinsed off and told to stand, then positioned over a marked spot on the floor.

A blast of dry heat enveloped her, scraping down her body and burning her to the point of pain as the water evaporated from her hair and skin, leaving her skin pink and irritated until it stopped.

There was a knock at the door and the guard stepped aside,

pulling it open as he moved. Another lioness came in with an armful of clothing in her hands. Sasha didn't even care what they'd brought for her to wear; she just wanted clothing. Something to cover her vulnerability and stop them from looking at her like she was malformed.

Eyes staring forward on the painted wall in front of her, Sasha let them dress her.

The fabric was heavy, yet soft, but she resisted the urge to run her hands over it to really feel it. After that manhandling, they didn't deserve to know that she liked what they'd brought her to wear. She feigned indifference. Her feet were guided into slippers and her garments were adjusted, and then they moved onto her hair. A brush was yanked through it, detangling any knots they found with brutal precision while the other lioness looked at her nails, pushing on the knuckle of one finger as if testing whether or not they extended.

The female seemed confused as she tucked a nail file back into a pocket in her tunic.

"There," the lioness she'd soaked with bathwater announced. "That is as good as it gets, I think."

Resisting the urge to cut the female with an irritated glare, Sasha's attention turned to the guard who'd stepped away from his post at the door.

"You will follow," he ordered, leaving the silent threat unsaid.

With a sigh, she fell into line behind him, knowing that if she tried to resist or run it wouldn't end well for her. Not with a palace full of guards and a shock collar around her throat. Still, the knowledge that she was completely at another's mercy was unsettling, and it chafed at her nature.

He led her through the palace, up a flight of stairs that emptied out into a much fancier corridor. Crystal statues and white, painted vases decorated every corner. They met others in the hallway, curious onlookers who stopped what they were doing to stare and watch as she passed them, silent and obedient, behind her guard. Males in austere uniforms and shining weapons flanked doors and archways in a show of power and a subtle threat for all who visited.

Not caring to keep track of the twists and turns and paths they took, Sasha stared back at the aliens they passed as she followed the guard to wherever he was leading her. The courtiers were mostly Kursh, but a few Diggi and Raxions were thrown into the mix. All of them stared.

When the guard paused at a door, Sasha nearly walked straight into his back. The males at the door opened it, and she was ushered inside, alone, the door slamming shut behind her.

It was some sort of dining room, although she'd never seen a table so large before. Everything in the palace was built to an enormous scale, built for these aliens who were taller than her. Even the chairs were slightly too high for her, and she had to lift herself up on the armrest to get her backside into the seat.

There were only two places set at the long, grand table. Sasha took the chair that was less ornate, its carvings simpler. With her nails she traced the designs cut into the wood while she waited.

A door hidden in the painted walls opened, startling her. She watched as servants came in, one by one, carrying gleaming dome-covered trays and containers of food. Her stomach rumbled once she smelled it, a reminder that she hadn't eaten since breakfast when Ardalon had fed her pieces of fruit by hand while she fixed the cubs' toy. Her heart ached at the thought before she shoved that emotion away, boxing it up and shoving it into the back of her mind.

She didn't have time to break down again right now.

Without a word or a glance her way, the servants dropped off the trays and dishes and bowls of covered food, then disappeared back through their hidden door. It closed, and she stared at the painted mural trying to determine if she could see the seam, wondering just how many hidden doors she'd passed without noticing.

Fingers tapping on the armrest of her chair, figuring that if she lifted a domed cover and helped herself to food she'd be punished, Sasha waited.

The door behind her opened, and she craned her head to watch as the emperor entered flanked by two males, one dressed in finery like the many courtiers who filled the palace and the other in a more severe cut of cloth that was dark, edged only in a dark trim that nearly blended in with the sharp lines and seams of his plain kaftana.

"The Raxion delegate has reported back. Shall I leave the documents with you now, or send them to your secretary?" the severe male asked.

"Leave it," the emperor answered without looking at the male as he sat, sliding his lace-edged sleeves up his forearms. "I will look it over now."

The documents in question were pulled out from a hidden pocket and Sasha was startled to see that they were pieces of folded paper.

Who still writes on paper?

A servant she hadn't noticed joining them stepped forward with an empty tray which the papers were set on so they could be delivered to the emperor without being handed over directly, hand to hand. The emperor took the letters off the tray and made a shooing motion at both males.

Without another word, they bowed their heads and left the room.

Sasha watched them leave and waited until the door clicked shut behind them before she glanced at the emperor. His attention was on the folded sheets of paper that he'd picked up from the tray. He pressed a thumb to a red disc that covered a ribbon that was wrapped around them.

The ribbon fell off, and he brushed it aside, unfolding the slim packet while he read what was written there.

Sasha glanced at the food trays and flattened her lips, realizing that he didn't intend to eat anytime soon. She went back to studying the room's frescos. They depicted a jungle scene, but hidden among the leaves and bushes were small animals that stared at the viewer from their secret places among the shadows. She was so busy picking the complicated painting apart that she didn't notice his gaze on her right away.

"The Raxion government wants to buy you. Tell me, what interest do they have in a murderer? What makes you worth this price to them?" he asked her, his chin cupped in the palm of one hand as he leaned on the arm of his chair and stared at her.

She glanced down at the scattered papers and the foreign glyphs she couldn't read. Affecting a bored countenance, she shrugged and turned her attention back to the mural. "Maybe they just like my soft pink skin."

The weight of his gaze pulled at her, but she refused to look at him as he chewed on her words.

He shifted in his chair, his clothes rustling as he leaned back. She watched him in her periphery, her gaze locked straight ahead. "Unlikely. They're a serious people, and they don't partake in the slaving business often, at least not with soft females. Strong males, prisoners who can build or fight, yes. Bed slaves? No."

She cut her eyes at him and tilted her head. "I guess that's more of your people's thing, then."

His ears twitched. Not a full flick, like she was used to seeing, just a small twitch that she wouldn't have noticed if she didn't know to look for it.

"Is that why you killed my cousin? Because he tried to bed you, strange little thing that you are?"

The urge to dig her nails into the wood of her chair was there, and she struggled to stay calm, to not rise to the bait he was laying in this verbal trap for her. "Sex and rape are different. Also, he threatened to cut off my hands. Self-defense isn't murder."

He blinked at her, letting the silence stretch between them. His eyes were green with no hint of brown or gold in them to add any hint of warmth. They were rimmed with a dark outline, and she wondered if that was cosmetics or just his natural coloring. The effect was striking.

"I am aware that you were offered temporary citizenship by my chancellor, yet I think that you are unaware of our laws. Ignorance of them does not excuse you for your actions, however. Your killing of my late cousin has created quite the legal and moral dilemma among my justices. They argue in a constant circle amongst themselves. It's enough to make my head ache from their endless debates."

Arching a brow, she stared back at him. "It would have been better to let him rape me?"

"Politically? Yes."

"That's disgusting," she answered before she could stop herself.

He lifted a filled glass to his lips and sipped at the liquid inside. "My cousin needed to be checked. He'd grown too bold. But dead... no, that's not what we wanted. Your actions have placed the peaceful rule of my nation into jeopardy. The first discovery of life outside of our solar system... and it's killed the fourth heir in line to rule."

"With the leaked footage of you, and now the Raxion military's interest in you, this is not something that will be easily forgotten. Our three races are at an uneasy alliance, the result of an arms race that left us all poised for mass destruction until a treaty was enacted before we destroyed ourselves. Any disturbance in that balanced scale could tip it to one side, resulting in a war we have been avoiding for seven generations now. I will not lead my people into death and destruction for the benefit of one."

Letting her anger and irritation out with a sigh, Sasha forced herself to relax into her seat, turning her attention back to the mural with its hidden animals and painted landscape. "I don't understand why you've brought me up here just to tell me that you haven't decided what to do with me yet."

"I wanted to see what my cousin thought was worth the trouble of getting caught slaving. His proclivities for buying exotic pets was always just that—pets. Animals, not sentients. It made me curious."

She snorted, shaking her head, then leveled him with a flat look. "I wasn't the first female he bought. He told me so himself. Right before he told me what he liked to do to them if they fought back. You didn't know your cousin as well as you thought you did."

He brushed a nail over the seam of his flat lips as he stared back at her. "That allegation will be looked into, and if I find that you are lying… well, it's no matter. We'll know soon enough if your words are true. My cousin's ship was filled with cameras. The recordings are being decrypted as we speak. I will know the truth, then, of how and *why* you killed my cousin."

She remembered the feeling of a neck between her thighs and the panicked way he'd gurgled as he'd died between her legs. He'd suffered less than he deserved, although she wasn't stupid enough to say those thoughts out loud. Instead, she met his gaze and held it in silence. She had nothing to hide from him.

"You're not scared of me," he murmured, looking thoughtful.

Standing from his chair, he sauntered over to her side of the table, leaning back against it and invading her personal space. "Not intimidated or enraptured. It's... refreshing. I see why he was drawn to you now. It's not your softness or how strange you are. Your one-of-a-kind status, lost from wherever it was you've come from. It's how you look through a person's affectations and see the truth within them."

Frowning, Sasha leaned back in her chair, trying to put a little distance between them as much as her chair and the table would allow. He reached a hand out and she held her breath as he rubbed a knuckle down her cheek and twined his finger around a section of her hair, rubbing it as if he was exploring the texture.

"What is it with you males?" she exhaled, annoyed.

The finger wrapped in her hair tugged, pulling her head back to expose the line of her throat and the shock collar clamped around it. The Emperor leaned closer, sniffing. She held her breath when his nose pressed against the side of her throat, then he leaned back, cocking his head as he looked down at her. "You smell ripe. It's intoxicating."

She frowned again. "One of your servants bathed me. Thoroughly, I might add. I should smell fine now."

He chuckled, a low purr that reminded her so much of Ardalon that her heart hurt at the sound of it. "No," he laughed. "You smell fecund, not noxious."

At her blank expression, he continued. "Fertile, female. You smell like one of our females when she is fertile. It's a subtle smell that most won't even know they're parsing out as they sniff it."

Davi hitting on her on the poachers' ship, Ardalon's erection in the cave, the way that strange males had sniffed her in the port and the females had glared at her. She reframed all of these interactions she'd had with this new information. "That doesn't make any sense. We're different species, and I don't ovulate with my birth control implant."

The emperor chuckled again, easing the pressure he put on her scalp as he leaned back again. "Nobody knows all of the secrets of our mysterious universe. Your presence here should be proof enough of that. Join me in my bed, and I will pardon you, kitten. You will live here in my palace. Service me, and I will shelter you."

Not caring if it yanked her hair out of her scalp, she pulled away from him, plastering her back against the carved back of her chair. Her heart was racing, her hands damp with sweat.

Not again.

"No, thanks."

He let her go, his hand withdrawing from its tangle in her hair. Putting both palms on the table he stared down at her, the picture of bored privilege as he looked down his nose at her. "I'm not a male who drags the unwilling into my bed. Perhaps after a few more days spent down below, your answer will change." He glanced behind her, then raised one hand and rolled his fingers in that same dismissive gesture he'd made before.

"What, no dinner?" Sasha asked with a pointed glance at the elaborate place settings and trays of covered food on the middle of the table. A guard peeled away from his station at the door and came over to them.

Lifting the lid off the nearest dish, the emperor glanced down at it and smirked, revealing one glinting white fang. The smell that arose from the unveiled plate made her stomach rumble audibly. "A few days of hunger and boredom might make you more pliant."

The guard reached for her shoulder, but she stood before he could touch her. The emperor was taller than her by nearly a foot, but that didn't stop her from lifting her chin at him as she stood, careful not to brush against the too-close male. Her chair scraped against the floor behind her. "I wouldn't count on that."

His fang-filled smile widened, his eyes sharpening with interest as he stared down at her and set the cover down on an empty stretch of table. "Tell me why the Raxions want to pay a small fortune for you alive... or warm my bed. That's the price of your freedom, kitten. I'm a patient male. I can wait for you to break."

"You'll be waiting a very long time," she warned him, not bothering anymore to keep her dislike of him from her face.

He gave her smile eyes in return, his ears perked forward through the bright golden fluff of his jewel-encrusted hair. "I look forward to the day you give in and give me what I want. And, kitten," he hesitated, tapping her nose with a finger, "I always get what I want."

Looking behind her, he folded his hands together and glanced at the guard who stood watch at the door she'd come in through. "Take her back down to her cell. Bring her back to me in two... no, three days. We'll see if she's more cooperative once the hunger's fully settled in. No meals."

Her chair was pulled away from her, and then the guard had grabbed her by the arm and marched her back out into the hallway. Sasha kept her eyes forward, her jaw clenched tight in irritation. She refused to let them all see how distraught he'd made her.

Whatever they threw at her, she'd survive. No matter what.

Or she'd go down swinging. Either way worked for her.

CHAPTER TWENTY-TWO

SASHA

Her cell was cold and silent. The guards put her back in, but let her keep her new clothing. It was warmer than what she'd been wearing before, so she was thankful for that, although she'd have never admitted it.

After filling her empty, cramping belly with handfuls of cold water from the tiny sink above her toilet, she'd collapsed back into bed, tugging the thin blanket over her head to conserve body heat and shield herself from the cellmate three rows down who liked to masturbate while staring at her.

Time passed with agonizing slowness. With no windows or timed receiving of food rations, she had no way of telling how many hours she spent huddled on her cot, knees to her chest and arms wrapped around her legs.

She drank, she paced, she pissed, she slept, and then she whispered to herself just to hear something other than the sound of her own breathing or the pounding of her pulse in her ears.

When the walls of her cell dropped again days later, she covered her ears to shield them from the noise. Curled up under her blanket, she didn't have the energy to even poke her head out this time to look. Light hit her eyelids, making her squint them shut even harder.

It was too much.

Everything was too loud, too bright, too caustic.

Had it only been three days like he'd said? She couldn't tell. It might have been a week for all she knew. It certainly would explain how frayed she felt. Unraveled at her edges.

She'd known that torture was a possibility, but she hadn't expected it to nearly break her this fast.

"What's wrong with it?" a female asked as the blankets were stripped off her. "Is it sick?"

She was pulled off the cot, her brain sloshing around inside of her head with the movement. Dizziness kept her from struggling as a guard and a servant brought her upstairs, half-pushing and half-pulling to get her up the steps.

"Weak after just a few days without food," he growled. "What a pathetic species."

Sasha didn't have the energy to correct him. It wasn't the fasting. God knows she'd endured worse than a few days without food during her training with Starfleet. It was the silence. Not solitude, but complete silence.

On her ship, she'd had plenty of ship noises to stimulate her mind, and holovids when she wasn't working. When that hadn't been enough, she'd talked or sung to herself or to her animatronic plant clock Joana.

Humans weren't meant to be stuck alone in a soundproof box and forgotten about for days.

Mind dulled from sensory deprivation, she was maneuvered through the castle and brought to the bathing chamber. She didn't fight the females' hands this time as they stripped her and nudged her into the bath.

They scrubbed her with cleanser, rubbing feeling back into

her numb fingers and toes, her skin scraped deliciously raw from the rough rag they wiped her down with. Chin tucked, she didn't even care about the hot water they poured over her to clean her hair and work it into a lather.

She barely remembered to close her eyes when they rinsed out the suds.

The females chatted while they worked. After the body dryer finished blasting the top layer of her skin off, she began to feel a little more like a person.

Her detached mind tethered itself back into her body, thread by thread.

The females dressed her, muttering under their breath as they twisted her into clean clothing and untangled her matted hair. They were gentler as they worked a comb through the tougher sections until they could get a brush through the locks. She ignored their questioning eyes, staring straight ahead, soaking in all the sounds she could hear before they stuck her back in that coffin.

She never thought she'd miss the poachers' cage. At least she'd just been cramped and dirty, not half-insane from silent isolation. Their questions went unanswered as Sasha ignored the females who readied her and the guard who stood watch at the door.

Feet slipped inside of shoes, she was put back into the care of the guard who took her by the arm and brought her through the hallway when she failed to follow him, ignoring even the faint warning buzz of her collar.

The hallway hurt.

Everything was loud and overwhelming, the colors too bright and the people too loud.

Closing her eyes, she tried to shut out what she could before it completely drowned her, dragging her under the waves of noise. She was brought back to that same dining room and pushed down into a chair by her guard when she made no move to seat herself.

"What's wrong with her?" a male asked from her side.

She knew that voice. Spurred into movement, her control over her body poor from her time in a tiny cell that was precisely forty steps in all four directions if she walked heel to toe from one electrified wall to the next, she looked up.

Horror washed over her.

Ardalon looked down at her, his ears flattening to his head with every second that she stared at him in stunned silence. Panic clawed up through her veins, chilling her from the inside out, making her twitchy with the urge to act. To move. To do something before they hurt him, or threatened to hurt him in order to get her to do whatever it was they wanted her to do.

It would take her four seconds to get to the emperor if she could make her body jump and go over the top of the table.

There were knives all around her, set out next to the plates and their weird little three pronged forks. Failing that, crystal glasses could be broken and turned into a jagged weapon.

The perfect thing to slit a royal throat.

Careless.

She could probably take the emperor hostage before anyone realized what was happening. They always underestimated her. Smaller and shorter than them, no claws or fangs. They thought she was without a weapon. They didn't realize that Starfleet had made her body into the weapon.

She didn't need a gun to feel safe when she'd been conditioned to improvise, her body able to heal anything short of complete exsanguination or beheading.

"She doesn't seem very pleased to see you," the emperor drawled from his seat at the head of the table.

"I've never seen her this terrified before, not even when we faced down a pack of diplocus on El'bazahara," Ardalon answered.

Glancing around the room, she saw that it was far less empty than it had been before. The chancellor sat to the emperor's left, with the stern male in the chair on his other side. Ardalon took the seat she'd been in previously, putting her two chairs down from the emperor who sat at the head of the long table.

The stern male pulled out a com, its clicking sounds making her eye twitch as he tapped on it. "It looks like her cell was set to maximum filtration."

"Was she screaming?" the chancellor asked.

"How long was she in complete seclusion?" Ardalon demanded, his voice angry, the sound of it making her wince.

Her heart was hammering in her chest, the muscles in her legs and shoulders tight with the urge to spring. She needed to wait. Wait and listen for the right moment. Everyone looked at the emperor. Sasha took their distraction as an opportunity to inventory every item in the room, cataloging which ones could be made into weapons or shields if she needed them.

She was not going back in that cage. Death was kinder, if it came to that.

"Five days. The talks dragged on," the emperor answered.

The chancellor steepled his fingers on the table in front of him. "That constitutes a violation of the Sentient Species Protection Act. There will need to be an investigation to ensure that this is not happening routinely."

A hand on her wrist made her flinch, feeling angry that she hadn't seen it reaching toward her, until she realized that it was Ardalon. He set his hand over hers, the weight and warmth of his velvet skin comforting. "I'm here," he whispered just loud enough for her to hear it.

She knew that. That was the problem. He was here, in this nightmare of a palace, instead of at home where he was safe. These people were animals, and she hated them.

"Find out which guards were involved," the emperor said to the stern male, who nodded, his head still bent over his com. "Those responsible will be handled. Now, let's finalize everything and move forward, shall we?"

With the wave of his fingers, the emperor signaled for the servants to uncover the food set before them. The smell of it turned her stomach, flooding her mouth with saliva that felt too thick when she tried to swallow it back. She was ravenous and repulsed at the same time, her stomach threatening to purge its bile even as the rest of her demanded sustenance.

Her plate was loaded for her, but she couldn't bear to look at it. Closing her eyes, she breathed through the nausea until she felt like she had her body back under her control. Ardalon wasn't eating either. She glanced at him, eyes going back and forth between him and the rest of the table, anxious to make sure that he was okay. That he hadn't been taken prisoner too.

The others ate, following the emperor's lead, and she watched, her eyes constantly moving. Her hand was squeezed in a comforting gesture, but she was too anxious for it to soothe her. The sound of the door opening tugged at her attention.

A Kursh female dressed in a plain gray kaftana that lacked any embellishment, even embroidery, entered the room and nodded at the occupants in greeting. She pushed an empty place setting aside, setting a black bag on the table at the far end.

Ardalon's grip on her wrist tightened as her mind struggled to understand what was happening and what this change signified. When the female flicked her bag open and began to pull out a needle-tipped syringe, Sasha knew.

"No," she whispered, "n-no, no, no."

Shaking his grip off her, ignoring the sting of his claws as they raked over her wrist, she struggled against him. She stood, ready to fight. When he grabbed her by the back of her tunic and pulled her back down into her seat, she elbowed him in the gut and tried to land the next blow in his face.

"No! You promised!" she shrieked, bucking against his hold and sliding along the seat, slouching forward. If she sacrificed the tunic top, she could slide right out of his grip and go under the table, escaping that way.

He growled, knocking his chair over as he stood and pulled her up out of her chair as if he knew what she was planning. Nostrils flaring and a wrangled scream ripped from her throat, she stomped on his boot with her slippered foot and aimed her elbow at his throat. Ardalon let go of her shirt to grip her by her hair, his fingers threading into the hair at her nape and squeezing, yanking her head back.

The collar buzzed a faint warning at her throat, but she was too pissed off to care.

Let them tase me into unconsciousness. At least then I won't have to be awake for this violation.

"You promised me," she hissed. "You said it would be my choice, and I said no."

Ardalon lifted her off balance until she was standing on the balls of her feet, his hand fisted at the nape of her neck the only thing keeping her from stumbling. She swatted at his hand, not caring that every hit she landed on him hurt her just as much as it hurt him while they were connected like this.

"I did. I promised you that, and now I'm breaking it. I'm sorry, but I will not let my mate hurt herself for some misguided notion that she can sacrifice herself," he told her as he dragged her into his chest and released his hold on her hair, clamping her flush against him in a bear hug instead.

Mentally, she fought him, her body stiff as he held onto her and kept her still. He was lucky that, mad as she was, she didn't actually want to stab him with the knife from her place setting.

"I'll just, uh, collect the sample, now, yes?" the doctor asked, hesitant to approach them.

Ardalon worked one of her arms out from where he'd caged her in with his body. Sasha buried her face in his chest, tears of frustration pricking at her hot eyes.

A tourniquet was wrapped around her bicep until the feeling in her hand grew muffled. The prick of a needle told her that the doctor was collecting blood. Blood and nanos.

She could see it now. Kursh supersoldiers lined up in rows in an invincible army.

How long would it take them to cut through anyone who defied them with their claws, and fangs, and blasters? How many more could they kill if they could heal as fast as they could wound?

Exhausted and realizing that it was pointless to keep fighting them because they were going to take what they wanted from her no matter what she had to say about it, she gave in and sagged against him, letting him take the burden of her weight.

The needle was pulled out of her skin and a bandage was stuck on top.

A pointless gesture.

The tiny hole was already healing.

"You've just started a war," she told them, shivering.

She knew the horrors of war intimately.

Ardalon dropped his chin on top of her head, his purr rumbling through her where they were pressed together. The soothing gesture did little to calm her. She was tired, exhausted from the aftermath of being flooded with so much adrenaline and starved for five days while being tortured.

"The Raxions were aware of the tech, and it was only a matter of time before the Diggi found out too," the chancellor interrupted in that authoritative voice of his. "They would have come for you. Now, you will be protected by the crown with all of your needs provided for, including security. We have already intercepted two foreign attempts to gather information on your whereabouts."

From prisoner to protected asset in the span of one blood draw. She needed to sit. Legs buckling, she didn't protest when Ardalon scooped her up into his arms and held her to him.

"My recommendation is for her to eat something soon," the doctor butted in, "and drink more fluids. I believe she is dehydrated, although I would need to see the Raxion doctor's scans to make a better educated guess."

He turned them so they could both see the occupants of the table. The doctor was putting her equipment away, tucking everything back inside of her bag after spraying it down with something that smelled like a disinfectant.

"I would like to take her home now," Ardalon said, adjusting his hold on her. Sasha threw her arms around his neck to take some of the burden off him.

The emperor held the test tube of her stolen blood up to the light, looking through it as if he could see the nanos without a microscope if he looked hard enough. "Take her. I have everything I need from her, and I know where to find her if my scientists need more."

Glaring at the smug bastard, Sasha stared at him until the emperor stopped ogling her blood and returned her gaze. "If I ever see your face again, one of us is dying," she told him in a flat voice devoid of emotion. It wasn't a threat, but a promise. She stared him straight in the eyes until it fully registered, his lips curling in a fangy grin in response as the male laughed.

The chancellor sighed, pinching the bridge of his nose and

wincing. "Agent Bavara, please educate your mate on our laws before she commits more treason."

The stern one gave her a silent, assessing gaze as Ardalon carried her from the room. Shutting her eyes, she ignored everything around them as he brought her through the palace, down through the gardens, and bundled her into an idling convi.

CHAPTER TWENTY-THREE

SASHA

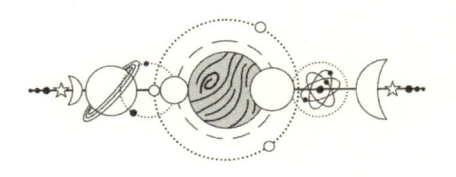

He set her in her own bucket chair, then hopped in beside her and shut the door behind him. She watched out the window to avoid looking at him, but she wasn't really seeing the capital as the convi drove them through it, navigating down cobblestone streets, and then paved ones, weaving through pedestrians and traffic until they hit the tunnel system that branched out and lead to the smaller cities and towns.

The blue and amber lights that lined the tunnel flashed past as they picked up speed.

"I know you're mad at me," Ardalon said, finally, breaking their tense silence.

Sasha sighed, pressing her forehead against the smooth, cool glass-like material that made up the transparent window. Was she mad at him? Of course there was anger there. Betrayal and sadness too. Mostly, she was tired.

"And I don't care if you're mad at me," he added, his voice sharpening, "because I'm mad at you too."

She turned to face him, eyes narrowed and ready to fight now that they were alone. She couldn't believe that after betraying her wishes and putting himself in danger, he had the audacity to be angry with her.

"You could have died. What if I'd believed those foul things you said? Left you there? Do you honestly believe that they wouldn't have figured it out? The chancellor explained everything to me when I called him. The Raxions petitioned to have you, through financial or legal means, but it wouldn't have been long before they got impatient. They've uncovered at least two illegal plots to obtain you through whatever means necessary. There was no other option, Sasha. No other choice that kept you safe and out of that prison. Kept you from being kidnapped, killed, or made into a political pawn."

Hands clenched in the fabric of her pants, she glared at him. "It wasn't your choice to make! It was mine!"

He growled, his upper lip peeling back in anger as his ears flattened. "Everything that concerns you, concerns me. You're my mate! If you force me to choose between your safety and your wishes I will choose your safety every single time! I will burn it all down for you, don't you understand that? I would kill to protect you."

His chest heaved as he yelled at her, his hands gripping the lit navigation table. "Do you truly not want to be with me? The emperor would grant you accommodations in any city of your choice, if you'd prefer. I c-could put in the transfer request."

She reeled back from him like he'd hit her and blinking. "N-No, I..."

"You're not in your world anymore, Sasha. There are things about my world, my culture and its politics, that you don't understand yet. You need to trust me. I will never betray that trust unless you are doing something stupid that will get you hurt, and then you'd better viruking believe that I will do whatever it takes to keep you safe, no matter how mad it makes you, because I love you. You carry my heart."

She wanted to fight with him, to argue that he didn't know what she needed more than she did, but a small part of her worried that he was right. That she was so far out of her depth she was drowning.

It felt like she'd been so focused on surviving that she hadn't had a moment to think. And the time she'd spent with Ardalon at his home had been borrowed time. She'd pushed everything away to the back of her mind because she'd known, deep down, that the peace wouldn't last. Avoiding unpleasant problems that couldn't be solved with punching or running had always worked out for her in the past.

The things the emperor had said to her rose to the surface of her muddled thoughts. One last straw to grasp onto. "You only want me because I smell fertile to you guys, or whatever, and I bit you. It's not even really your choice. You don't want *me*."

His eyes flashed in the light, the only warning that she had before he grabbed her by the elbow and hauled her out of her chair, pulling her into his lap.

He stroked a hand through her hair. "I love my mate, even when she is so infuriating that it makes me want to shake her. I will never stop chasing you, no matter how far you try to run from me."

Fat tears swelled, rolling down her face before she could stop them. She sniffled, then hiccuped. He rubbed her back with soothing circles as she threw her arms around his neck and nestled her face into his throat while she cried.

"I-I'm sorry," she gasped between sobs, her throat tight with choked back tears. "I-I didn't mean those things I said."

"I know," he told her, "I spoke with my patta after I was done moping. He told me what you asked him, and I realized that you thought you were sacrificing yourself. Foolish but noble, even though it was misguided. The information about your blood was out there. Too many people learned about it for the secret to be contained forever. If I have to choose between my emperor taking a few test tubes and another race kidnapping you and draining you dry, I will choose my people."

Wiping the tears off her cheeks, she leaned back and looked him in the eye. "I meant it, Ardalon. This will lead to war. When the Raxions figure out what you have…"

He shrugged, the human gesture looking so strange on him that it made her smile before that tiny burst of happiness faded, swallowed back up by misery.

"Our treaties have been strained for decades, each race stepping closer to that fine line without crossing it, seeing how far they can push. War is inevitable, whether it is this conflict, or another doesn't matter in the end. It has been coming since before I was born. And we may not even see it in our lifetime. You may not have a good opinion of our emperor, but he is much more level-headed and moderate than his matta was before she died and passed the dynasty to him. Under his matta's rule, I would have been killed at birth. Her son is progressive."

Closing her eyes, she shuddered, thinking that he still didn't quite get it.

He was a cop, but she'd been a soldier before she'd been taken off active duty and stuck over in engineering because she was smart and good with her hands.

War was… There wasn't a solitary word that could encapsulate the horrors it brought with it. All she could imagine was the cities she'd seen, bombed out and reduced to burning rubble. Children orphaned. The lawlessness and crime that surged afterward when survivors took advantage of the chaos, leaping at the chance to seize power.

He continued, ignorant of her thoughts. "Besides, the Raxions have most likely already retrieved any trace of you they could from where you crash landed on their planet, injured and bleeding. And we assume the Diggi have your ship, whatever is left of it from your trip through this space bridge of yours. Giving a sample of your nanos to my people may very well prevent the war you worry about."

Wanting to disagree with him, but knowing that it was pointless to argue, and even more of a waste of time to keep fighting with him because they already had her blood, she turned her face to the side and took in a deep breath, letting it back out slowly as she stared off into the distance, looking at nothing.

She couldn't stop them from doing whatever it was they wanted to do with it now that they had it.

How long will it take them to re-engineer my nanos?

He rubbed his hand up and down her spine until the tension faded from her body. "You aren't alone anymore, Sasha. We are bonded, and neither of us should make important decisions alone. Do you see how much it hurts when one of us makes a decision that affects the other, too?"

She nodded. It hurt her deeper than she'd ever let anyone hurt her ever since her parents had left her and her brother behind as teenagers to go be groundbreaking scientists on the new colony. There just hadn't been room for children, especially two who weren't brilliant or skilled in something useful for their terraforming project. "I'm sorry. I didn't mean what I said, I just…"

Didn't want you to follow me and get hurt.

"You're not damaged goods," she told him, pulling back so she could look him in the eye so that he'd know she meant it. "I just didn't want to… to drag you down with me."

Reaching up, he brushed a lock of hair behind her ear, his finger lingering over the rounded top of it. "You have protective instincts, but I'm not some young cub who needs to be shielded from a falling knife. I'm your mate. Let me protect you while you learn our ways." He slid his fingers down her throat, setting his thumb to the lock on her collar until it clicked open, slipping off. "I love you."

Reluctant to give someone that much power over her, but knowing he was right, she nodded. "I love you too."

She did. She loved him more than she'd ever loved anyone before. The thought that he was going to be there with her for the rest of her life was terrifying and thrilling at the same time. She clung to him, wrapping her fingers into his locks and twining them around her fingers.

She loved this bossy male who saw what she offered him and demanded more, wanting all of it, the good and the bad. He wasn't afraid to pin her down when she ached to run.

"Did they hurt you?" he asked, his face intent as he studied her. Not that her body would have betrayed any hint of crimes committed upon it. Short of amputation, she'd heal whatever wounds were inflicted on her.

"Not as much as they could have," she answered, knowing it wasn't what he'd want to hear but hesitant to lie to him again after they'd just talked everything out.

Before he could speak, she leaned down and kissed him, pressing her mouth to his to silence him. She was tired of talking. Her head hurt from it. She just wanted to feel something real, something good. Lazy and sweet, they kissed, arms wrapped around one another until the convi slowed, the navigation table chiming the alert that let them know they'd arrived.

The thought of getting up off his lap and walking back into that home filled with people who didn't want her there...

Anxiety shot through her. She looked out the window and cringed. Ardalon nudged her off his lap and reached for the door, sliding it open. He hopped out of the convi and turned, holding his hand out for her. Biting her lip, Sasha screwed up her courage and put her hand in his.

She'd just survived facing down a palace full of guards who

hated her, an alien prison, and a smug bastard of an emperor. So why was she so terrified that his sister and mother still hated her? Her stomach churned with bile, and she thought she was going to be sick until the feeling passed.

"Come," he nudged her, closing the convi door behind her. It inched its way back toward the tunnel, abandoning her. "I've sent a message in advance asking everyone for space and time. Let's get you fed, like the doctor said, and then we'll rest.

Nodding, she breathed a little easier knowing that they weren't about to be ambushed by his entire family all staring at her on their doorstep like they had the first time.

Sasha followed him in, knowing that she had a lifetime of new things to learn on this strange, new planet, terrified of everything she didn't know, but comforted knowing that Ardalon would be there at her side sharing all of the good and the bad with her.

He led her down the path cut through the tall grass, turning to look over his shoulder at her as he flashed smile eyes at her. "Welcome home."

One foot in front of the other, she took a step and then another, following him into their new life.

EPILOGUE
3 MONTHS LATER

"Now?" Sasha whined, trying to peek from under the bottom of her blindfold where her nose lifted the edges of it.

The fabric was mushed back down her face as Ardalon walked her forward and moved the covering back into place, his hands going back to her shoulders as he encouraged her to take a step, and then another.

Feet testing each step before she put her weight down, she walked forward at a glacial pace. She knew that he'd never lead her blindly into danger, but it was still nerve wracking to be walking around blind. They were outside, she knew that much. She'd nearly shrieked when she felt the first slap of cool, slick grass against her hand. He'd laughed at her until she elbowed him in the stomach.

"Almost there," he whispered, his mouth just inches from her face.

Nudging her forward one baby step at a time, they stopped and she tried to listen and hear where he'd taken her. Alien insects made their usual nighttime noise, but that didn't tell her anything she didn't already know.

"Now," he said, the fabric of her blindfold rustling as he untied it from around her head.

The blindfold slipped, and she blinked her eyes against the bright lights that shone through the darkness. Multicolored lanterns glowed all around them, decorating every surface and hanging from trees as well.

His family was there, as well as Davi and the chancellor and a few others who Ardalon had slowly introduced her to over the last three months since her return from the palace.

"W-What…" she mumbled, looking around at the gathered crowd. Was this some sort of Kursh festival or holy day? He hadn't told her that today was a special one.

Ardalon squeezed her shoulders, then stepped around her and took her by the hand. "It is our mating ceremony. Come."

She looked around again, noticing how everyone was dressed in their best garments. A small table had been brought outside, and food and drinks were laid out.

Her eyes misted with unshed tears. His father handed her a glass of punch and pressed his forehead to hers, purring, as he congratulated them on their mating. She took a sip, enjoying the burn of the chilled drink as it ran down her throat, thankful for its alcohol content. His mother was the next to come forward, take her by the hands, and congratulate them.

As if a barrier had been broken down, everyone came up, one by one, touching her and Ardalon on their elbows as they wished them a lifetime of happiness together. One by one, they peeled away, returning to their own small groupings as they talked among each other, eating and drinking.

"Here, eat this before you get as drunk as an oolin that broke into the aging barrels," Enaiya said, thrusting a loaded up plate into Sasha's empty hand.

"Uh, thanks," Sasha said, grabbing the plate and juggling to balance it along with her glass.

Enaiya patted Sasha on the shoulder, then walked away. That was likely all the fuss she'd get from that female. For Enaiya, food was her love language, so being fed by her was as much overt acceptance as Sasha was going to get.

It had taken weeks for his sister to trust Sasha around the cubs again, but once she saw that Sashsa didn't have anything nefarious planned, she mellowed. His mother had been more of a challenge, but seeing her son happy and settled made her come around as well.

His younger brothers came up next, all awkward and gangly as they hugged her, mindful of her loaded-up hands, and then they ran off again.

"Where are the cubs?" Sasha asked, turning to see that Ardalon had his own glass of alcohol that he was draining. Her lips twitched with a suppressed smile. It made her feel better to know that he was just as nervous about all of this attention as she was.

"Ferand took them down by the creek so they wouldn't make noise and give away the surprise. I can ping him and tell them to come back," Ardalon answered, draining his glass and tapping on his com. "Is it right? Is the celebration missing anything?"

Adjusting her hold on everything, Sasha tucked her empty glass between her body and arm. She slid into Ardalon's side and wrapped her freed up arm around him. Pressing her cheek against his chest, she looked at everyone enjoying themselves. "It's perfect." He pressed a kiss into her hair, making her smile.

High-pitched shouting interrupted the mood as the cubs came roaring up the small hill, their light ball zigzagging through the tall grass as it cycled through its random pattern of lights and obnoxious sounds.

Ardalon sighed. "Did you have to make it so loud? Enaiya won't stop chewing on my ear about the racket that thing makes now that you 'upgraded' it."

She laughed, watching the cubs chase their toy around as Ferand headed over to greet his mate and accept a plate of food from her. "It's better now. I improved it."

They ate and drank, then danced when someone set their com to broadcast, playing music. Ardalon spun her in circles, and she stepped on his boot-covered toes, hips swaying out of time to the beat.

"Bavara, I will see you again soon. Let me know when you've settled back into your desk," the chancellor said, nodding at them as he said his goodbyes and started walking back out to the road. Sasha watched the graying male leave.

"Are you sure you're all right with me going back to work in a few days?" Ardalon asked her for the hundredth time.

She turned to face him, grabbing his hand and squeezing it. "It's fine. School is keeping me busy anyway. I can read books meant for six-year-olds now," she bragged, wiggling her eyebrows at him.

He chuffed with laughter. "It will come together," he promised her. "You just have to be patient."

With the chancellor's departure, the others took their cue, leaving one by one. Ferrand carried two half-asleep cubs up to their den while Enaiya held the youngest one to her chest. The light ball was forgotten about among the grass as the party emptied out.

"Party's over," she said, glancing at Ardalon.

"Yes," he agreed, pulling a small bag out of his pocket. "I know that your human marriages are backward, the joining and then the celebrating after, but this seemed more prudent." Ardalon fiddled with the knotted drawstring, growing frustrated before he gave up, extending a claw to cut out the knot. He pulled out a ring and held it out to her.

Sasha looked at it, her breath hitching in her chest. The metal was white with a blue undertone, and it had been polished until it shone like a mirror, catching the moonlight and colored party lights, reflecting them back. Ardalon lifted her hand up and slid it onto her finger.

Etched lines carved into it flickered to life, a faint blue light glowing the second it made contact with her skin. It pulsed, the ring growing warmer as it soaked up her body heat while she stared at it.

"Is it right?" he asked, spinning the ring around her finger until she saw that there was a small stone set into the metal. Dark, flashing shades of purple, blue and black, it seemed to soak up whatever light shone on it.

"It's perfect," she sighed, spreading her fingers wide so she could marvel at it.

"We should use the table, I think," he said, turning to look at the small table that had been brought out to hold the food that Enaiya had made.

Arching a brow, Sasha grinned. "You want to viruk on the table?" she teased him, not hating the idea, just a bit surprised. Her mate had a hearty appetite, but he wasn't one to be adventurous outside of their rooms no matter how much she begged.

He leveled her with that look he gave her whenever he was counting how many spankings he was going to give her later whenever he got her alone. Sasha grinned harder, flashing him a canine in response. A cheeky challenge. Something he'd make her pay for later, when they were in bed and he did things that made her squirm and pant.

"You are much smaller," he said, patting her on the top of her head like one would a dog.

Sasha stared up at him, eyes narrowed. She fisted her hands on her hips.

"It's for the bite mark. I would like you to deepen it tonight," he told her, moving toward the table in question. "The table will even our heights and help you reach."

"Oh, right," she said, following him. He patted the top of the table until she hopped up on it. Hands on her knees spread her legs wide as he stepped into the cradle of her hips, his palms flat on the table behind her as he curved into her, their faces close.

Taking full advantage of the change in angle and his proximity, Sasha closed the gap between them and kissed him, enjoying the way his lips parted for her almost immediately.

She wrapped her arms around his neck, weaving them under the locks he'd kept for her because she liked them.

He kissed her back until she was panting, her nipples tight and dampness growing between her folds. Sinking the tips of her blunt nails into his shoulders, she pulled him in tighter and held him there, kissing him until her clit throbbed, begging to be touched.

He broke their kiss with a gasp and stared at her, his predator's eyes glowing soft and golden in the dark. "Now," he ordered, his voice deep and full of gravel. Unhinged.

She rolled her hips and rubbed her cleft against him, feeling how stiff he was in his pants. His erection strained, and she knew that he was already leaking for her, his tip glistening with beads of pre-cum, proof of how much he wanted her.

"Sasha," he groaned, his voice low and breathy. Strained.

Hands grabbed her ass, fingers digging into her soft skin as she kept tormenting him. Worked him up to the point where he normally got agitated, flipped her over, and took control back.

He rolled against her, his erection grinding against her core through their clothes until he grunted.

Smiling, she tugged his hair aside and moved him into place, pulling the edge of his shirt aside. There, barely visible in his fur-covered skin, she saw the tiny, pale marks she'd left behind when she'd bitten him back in the medical bay all those months ago.

Ardalon groaned when she set her teeth over the marks and

clamped down. The fingers cradling the globes of her ass tightened, his nails pricking at her as his knuckles flexed. She bit harder, scissoring her jaw until the first drop of blood hit her tongue. He purred, his hips twitching.

Ardalon slid his erection up and down the seam of her cloth covered slit.

Biting harder, she clamped her teeth down until her jaw ached and he cursed under his breath, the taste of him in her mouth as she marked him, driving their bond deeper into his skin until it hit the core of him. Changing him. Marking him as hers, forever.

"T-That's good," he moaned, putting his claws away.

Sasha released him, licking her lips clean and leaning back on her elbows on the table so she could look at him. He had a far away look in his eyes as he stared off into the distance, and then he glanced at her, putting a hand up to the bite mark at the base of his neck. "I can feel you better, deeper. It took," he told her.

"Good," Sasha nodded, then raised a leg between them, set her foot to his sternum, and kicked.

He fell back, exhaling as he sprawled out in the tall grass. She rolled, going up over the table and then off of it as his butt hit the ground. Landing on her feet and hands, she ignored the shock that ran up her legs at the impact, then jumped up into a sprint.

She ran.

He was behind her, only a few seconds slower due to her surprise attack. Grinning, she feinted left and dodged his reaching hands, going right, laughing when he slid in the tall, slick grass and went down. She added distance between them, racing over uneven, unfamiliar terrain.

She was headed down the hill, toward the same creek that the cubs had come from earlier. The sound of babbling water guided her, her body gaining momentum as she raced downhill.

Arms windmilling, she kept her balance through willpower and luck.

When she hit the pebbled, rocky bank, she took the risk of looking behind her. He was there, some distance behind her on the hill. Grinning, she splashed through the shallow creek, her slippers soaking through, and then she was on the other side and headed down the line of their property. There were more trees here to grant her cover. Ducking behind the biggest one, she dragged in gulps of air, straining to listen and see if she could hear him.

The world was silent, even the insects deathly quiet. Working to keep her breathing hushed, she put her hands on the rough bark and peered around the tree. Nothing moved, only the tall grass rippling with the wind. If he was lurking in them, crouched beneath their tops, then she couldn't spot him.

Steadying her breath, she waited. Her eyes scanned left and right, her ears straining to listen.

Arms grabbed her around her middle and she shrieked. He dragged her back against his chest and clamped her there, lifting her off the ground as he picked her up and walked them backward into the grass. Her arms were pinned, but her feet were free. Sasha kicked him.

He growled in her ear, the sound of it so menacing that it made the hairs on the back of her neck and arms stand up as her body broke out in goosebumps.

Teeth set on the base of her throat, pinching without biting as Ardalon growled again, the vibrations traveling through her.

Kneeling in the grass, he took her with him, his arms tugging her down until her body folded. He dropped her, shoving her forward so she had to brace on all fours or risk face planting into the ground. Hands moved down her body, the sound of ripping fabric following. She gasped when the chilly night air stroked her skin as he shredded her pants off her.

A cool breeze teased her arousal-damp folds as he exposed her, the material hanging off of her in ribbons as he bared her now that he'd caught her. She fidgeted.

"Don't," he warned her, a hand between her shoulder blades pushing her back down as she tried to rise.

She shivered, propping her cheek on the back of her folded hands as she sank into it, sticking her ass up in the air for him. Something blunt and firm nudged between her lower lips, sliding through them until he found her hole, pushing forward and slamming home into her with one insistent thrust.

Stretching, forced to take him without being widened first with fingers, she moaned.

He pulled back until he was nearly free of her, then sank himself to the hilt again, thrusting into her with such force that she rocked forward on her knees. Setting a brutal, unrelenting pace, he fucked her into the ground until her knees were scraped and raw. Walls clenching around him, Sasha grunted, taking it, her body begging him for more.

He fucked her hard and fast, the texture of his thick cock rubbing her with every thrust and pull. His sack slapped against her pussy, hitting her swollen lips and engorged clit.

She shuddered, her walls fluttering against him, pulling a ragged groan from him as he plowed her. His soft, hooked tip hit her cervix, pushing it aside as he sought more depth, cramming his dick into her as deep as it could get.

Fingers clawing into the soft, grassy earth, she took him, meeting each of his thrusts with a roll of her pelvis.

He leaned over her, taking one of her arms and pinning it behind her in the small of her back. Eyes opening, she glanced back at him, whimpering at the sight of him leaning over her, his fangs flashing in the moonlight and his beaded locks clicking together as he moved.

Ardalon's grip on her wrist tightened, and he shifted, his

momentum stuttering as he took her other hand and pulled it back as well, pinning them both behind her at the small of her back. Her cheek pressed against the grassy lawn, and he moved again, rocking her forward on her knees with every pounding movement.

Her clit pulsed, throbbing and swollen with desire and begging to be touched. Harder, faster, and deeper, he took her.

Claimed her until she was a panting, dew slicked mess.

Each tug pulled at her clit, and each thrust kept her panting, a lust drunk mess who desperately wanted and needed this release.

Her cunt fluttered around him, enjoying his snarls and growls and the way that he towered over her, speared on his cock and forced to take everything he gave her. Her mind wiped blank, her entire focus boiled down to them and their points of contact. She drank him in, loving the feel of his velveteen skin and the smell of his musk, enjoying the way he fucked her senseless in the dirt, like prey he'd caught with tooth and claw.

There was no dirty talk. No words meant to encourage, order, or punish. Just gasps, grunts, moans, and snarls as he took her in the dirt like a rutting, wild beast.

He came with a roar, his thrusting changing to something deep and slow, his cock pulsing and his balls drawn up tight as he flooded her body with his sperm. She felt the fullness within her, the building pressure that tugged at her throbbing clit as he emptied his sack inside of her, rivulets of seed already leaking around him as he rolled his hips, lazy thrusts milking the last of his fluid from him.

Ardalon tugged her up on her knees as he leaned her back, pulling her flush against his front. Letting go of her wrists, he hooked an arm around her front and held her to him with one arm wrapped around her middle. He set his teeth to her neck and bit, his hand sliding down her grass-stained front, pausing at her breasts long enough to tease one nipple through a rip in the fabric of her tunic as he inched his hand lower.

He slid it down her abdomen until he hit the curls between her thighs, spreading her sloppy folds open and making her shiver and moan when he touched her, finally.

Her pussy throbbed, squeezing his softening cock as he played with her, rolled her clit with his fingers until she was twitching against him. Bucking hips threatened to dislodge him as Ardalon fingered her, rolled her clit in rapid circles until she was clenching, her muscles taut and her breath hitching.

The orgasm washed over her, more of a tidal wave than a gentle swelling. Loud, she moaned with it, rocking against his hand as her pussy fluttered on his softening penis. He slipped from within her, a deluge of fluids seeping down her inner thighs with his withdrawal. His tongue lapped at the already healing skin at the base of her neck, the texture of his tongue making her groan and twitch.

"My mate," he growled, licking her neck and purring as she healed the bite marks.

Her lips twitched in a smile. "Did I do it right?"

Abandoning her already knitted together skin, he nuzzled his cheek against hers and slipped a finger between her folds, smearing their mess. He often liked to play with her after they had sex, taking pride from filling her up just to work it back out of her, enjoying the sight of her looking like a complete mess.

"It was perfect. Although I must admit, I was not expecting the kick."

Wresting her hands up to hold onto his trapping arm, she grinned. "I improvised."

Chuffing with laughter, he nuzzled her, rubbing his cheek along the side of her face, her neck, and shoulder. "My beautiful, vicious mate. I love you."

Twisting so she could kiss him, the stinging in her knees

fading as her wounds all healed, she pressed her lips against his. "I love you too. Is it done?" she asked.

He stared off into nothing again, his face blank and his eyes turned on something inward. "It's done. The bond is stronger. I can feel you more deeply within me now."

"Good," she nodded, knowing that it had bothered him how weak their bond was even though he seemed careful not to mention it too often.

Reaching for her hand, he held it up to the moonlight, and they both admired the way that her ring glowed with a soft blue light, pulsing.

"You have my heart with you too. With this ring, you'll know how I am even when we're parted," he explained.

Cocking her head, she squinted at the ring. "What do you mean?"

He turned it with one claw, forcing the gem back around so they could see it. "The ring is linked to my com's sensors. The glowing is my heartbeat. This way, even when I'm out on some mission and we can't speak, you'll know that I'm there with you in your heart, always."

"I love that. It's so perfect," she said, stroking his arm. "My mate is so thoughtful."

Standing, and bringing her with him, Ardalon tugged his tunic over his head and dropped it over her. The top was so long on her that it covered her to mid-thigh. He leaned down and pressed one last kiss to her lips. "I must be. Who else knows what sort of trouble my stubborn mate might get into while I'm busy undercover?"

Laughing and swatting at him, she took his hand in hers and they made their way back toward their den. Toward home.

Want to read the Bonus Epilogue?
Join the newsletter!

Want to see the art?
Subscribe to the Patreon!

Continue the series with book two
Doctoring Fate

AUTHOR'S NOTE

Thank you so much for reading Engineering Fate! I hope that you enjoyed reading it as much as I loved writing it. This book was a true labor of love for me. I started writing it years ago and picked it up and put it down repeatedly as I worked on other projects or didn't write at all. Continue the series with book two, Doctoring Fate, and follow Darcy through the wormhole.

If you have a moment, please consider leaving a review! Reviews are hugs for authors and help readers find the right book to add to their ever growing TBR pile. Hey... there are worse addictions out there.

For signed paperbacks and merch you can go to www.alexisbosborne.com and if you sign up for the newsletter you'll receive updates twice a month. For patron exclusive spicy art, ARCs, bonus scenes, polls, Q&As, and new release book boxes, join me on Patreon!

-Alexis

ALSO BY ALEXIS B. OSBORNE

Omegas of OAN Series

Omega Swipes Right

Omega Revealed

Omega For Rent

Omega Rescued

Omegas of OAN Boxset

Outer Limits Quadrant Series

Engineering Fate

Doctoring Fate

Sagittarius Quadrant Series

Ice Planet Prison

Mate for the Alien P*rn Star

ABOUT THE AUTHOR

Alexis lives in New York with her wife and step-son and a small horde of furry beings. She began her love affair with books at an early age, and began writing for fun in middle school. She fell in insta-love with the strange and unusual at an early age. When she's not reading or writing she can be found painting and making subversive cross-stitch. Her favorite fairy tale will always be Beauty and the Beast. Alexis loves all things fantastical, alien, and weird. She will never forget the gorgeous glory that was the late, great David Bowie. Sign up for the Newsletter to never miss a thing, or subscribe to the Patreon for ARCs, signed paperbacks, swag, and the good stuff (aka spicy art).

www.alexisbosborne.com

Made in the USA
Las Vegas, NV
25 March 2025